ANGELA DANDY

The Silver Sting

Gaia &
Fenrir

First published by Gaia & Fenrir Publishing 2022

First published in 2019 by SilverWood Books

Second edition

ISBN: 978-1-915208-10-1

www.GaiaandFenrirPublishing.co.uk

One

"For Pete's sake, Dot, will you come down from that ladder?"

"Shut up, Dennis. Someone's got to do it and I haven't noticed any of you men rushing into the shed and grabbing the loppers. I am up here now – just pass the bloody things up. If we don't get these last few branches cut back, we'll all be crawling on our hands and knees to get down the track. And I don't know about your knees, but mine aren't what they used to be. Just hold the ladder."

Gabby stopped short of the scene and watched anxiously. The ladder wobbled precariously as the elderly lady leaned forward, extended her arms, and chopped the overhanging branches away. Dennis ducked this way and that to avoid being brained by the falling branches while hanging on to the ladder for grim death.

There were moments when Gabby closed her eyes tight shut – she simply couldn't look for fearing the worst. It was an accident waiting to happen. Should she get out and offer to help? No, she decided – sit tight until the lady had finished and climbed down.

Gabby watched from the comfort of her little car. Holding on to the ladder with one gloved hand, the lady leaned back, admired her handiwork, shouted "Fore," and let the loppers fall to the ground, once more narrowly missing Dennis. Descending the ladder with the confidence of a steeplejack, she stood back with her hands on her hips and proclaimed a job well done. She had every right to be proud of herself; she was no youngster.

"Good job, wouldn't you say, Dennis? Know what they say – want a job done, ask a busy woman."

"Ace, old girl," Dennis replied, grinning. "But right now, I need a double whisky. One of these days you'll give me a heart attack with your antics. We'll clear that lot away tomorrow," he said, pointing at the pile of cut branches.

Dennis picked up the loppers while Dot shouldered the ladder. "Who's that, Dot?" he asked, nodding towards a young woman clambering out of a car.

"Search me. There's one way to find out." Dot started towards the car. "Can we help you, young lady?"

"I hope so. I didn't want to interrupt you earlier. That looked pretty tricky to me," Gabby said. "Actually, I'm looking for number nine."

"Max and Hetty, you mean? Hetty hasn't been well, you know – not at all well. Max has been so worried. And who would you be, young lady? Don't think I've seen you around these parts before." Dot asked sharply.

"They're my aunt and uncle. Uncle Max wrote to tell me that Aunt Hetty was ill. That's why I am here." Gabby coloured with embarrassment.

"Not very close then, are you? How long have they lived here? Let me see. It was 2003 when we all moved in and its now 2015. Almost thirteen years if I am not mistaken." Dot frowned, then muttered under her breath, "The trouble with young people these days is they just don't care about family."

"I am sorry. I do care about them, very much as it happens. It's a long story. Can you point me in the right direction, please?" Gabby asked, feeling the colour rush to her cheeks. She didn't need this woman to remind her of her shortcomings in that direction. She had done that for herself a hundred times or more during the drive from Chertsey to Stroud.

"Sorry, didn't mean to be quite so sharp. It's not my business anyway. No doubt they'll be glad to see you, whoever you are. By the way, I'm Dot and this is Dennis, my husband. You'll need to carry on up the track to the car park and leave your car there. Just watch the potholes on the way. They're lethal. The postman nearly disappeared down one last week, never to be seen again. Not that we'd miss him. He never brings good news these days."

Dot pointed in the direction of an open space in the distance and to the right of an old building. "You'll find Andy up there somewhere. He's meant to be mowing the meadow. Remember the old song 'Three men went to mow, went to mow the meadow…'? Not that that has anything to do with it. Just came to mind. The meadow – that's right. Andy, one of our fellow residents, is working on the meadow behind the car park. Rumour has it that it was once a croquet lawn, but the holes got filled in years ago. Andy had this idea that we should all spend the long summer days out on the lawn playing croquet and drinking Pimm's. Pigs might fly, but it's keeping him out of mischief. You probably think we're all bonkers – end of December and we're pruning trees and unearthing a croquet lawn. It does sound bonkers now I mention it. When you get to the car park ask Andy and he'll point you the way. Send Hetty our love and tell her that we'll

3

pop by later."

"Thanks. I will." Gabby smiled and got back in the car.

The track lived up to expectations. Gabby wove her way carefully around the potholes hoping that none were so deep that the little Fiat might disappear and be lost forever.

Andy stood back from the motor mower, pointed at it, muttered something at it, pulled the starting cord back as far as it would go and let it fly. The mower spluttered once and died.

"Bugger you!" he cried angrily, pointing his finger down at the mower, unaware that he was being watched. "You are bloody well going to work if it's the last thing you do. And I warn you, you're heading for the corporation refuse tip or the dump if you don't jolly well start behaving yourself. I hope you are taking me seriously."

"Hello, you must be Andy," Gabby called, as she opened the car door and climbed out. "Your friends down on the track said I would find you here. I'm looking for my Uncle Max and Aunt Hetty at number nine. Dennis and Dot said that you'd point me in the right direction."

"You know what, girl?" Andy replied, completely ignoring the question. "There's nothing that defeats me. I've been a handyman all my life and I've never been beaten yet! But this bloody thing – she's a real bitch. Typical woman, beg your pardon. What do you know about petrol mowers?"

"More than you might think," Gabby replied.

"If you can get this stubborn old girl to work then I will personally escort you to Max and Hetty's cottage, but I won't hold my breath." Andy stood legs apart, hands on hips and raised his eyebrows in Gabby's direction.

Pleased that she had worn trousers and flat sensible shoes,

Gabby rolled up her sleeves. "I think I used to own her twin sister, but it was a long time ago," she said with a grin. "She was a bitch too, but we eventually came to an understanding. What she needs is a lot of priming and then, with luck, she'll fire up."

Andy looked from Gabby to the mower and shrugged his shoulders. "Be my guest."

Gabby primed the pump, pursed her lips, narrowed her eyes and spat on her hands. "One, two, three," she counted, as she pulled the cord to its full length before letting go of it. The mower spluttered once and then again and reluctantly sprang into life.

"Well, well, well. Congratulations. You just proved me wrong. Better make hay while the sun shines and there'll be plenty of hay by the time I get through this lot," Andy said. "And in case you're wondering what a silly old codger like me is doing mowing a field, the answer is that I am digging for gold. Somewhere under this lot, there used to be a croquet lawn and I intend to find it."

"I know. Dot told me. Good luck," Gabby said, smiling.

"See the second cottage on the left of the big house? That's where Max and Hetty live. And by the way, thank you. What did you say your name was?" Andy shouted above the noise of the mower.

"I didn't, but it's Gabby. Is it okay if I leave my car here?"

"No one's going to steal it, that's for sure. We don't get too many visitors. They take one look when they see the Magnolia Court sign at the bottom of the drive and head in the opposite direction as fast as they can. Wise decision." Andy focused his attention back on the 'bitch'. "I'll come and find you if she plays up on me."

Gabby watched for a while as Andy set off in a straight line, muttering encouragement and unearned endearments to the lawn mower. Picking up her handbag, she locked the car and walked towards the cottage with mixed feelings. She couldn't remember the last time she had felt quite so scared – scared stiff of what she might find and scared stiff about the reception that she might get. However bad it was, it was no more than she deserved.

The gravel crunched under her feet as she walked from the car park and passed in front of what would once have been a very beautiful mansion, but which was now boarded up and in a sorry state of disrepair.

The second cottage on the left, she reminded herself as she passed the first, a small two-storey 'cottage' whose nameplate announced that whoever lived there had 'Dunroamin'. Gabby stood back and looked at her uncle and aunt's cottage with a heavy heart. Surely this could not be where they had lived for the past thirteen years? It was nothing short of a dump. Mould streaked down the once whitewashed brick walls from the low overhanging roof, paint peeled off the small leaded-window frames, the joints on the drainpipes had long since come apart and the double glazing was misted where window seals had shrunk in the sun.

Weeds grew through and around the short block-paved garden path and choked the shrubs on either side. This was all wrong. Aunt Hetty's garden had always been immaculate – weeds had never stood a chance. How long had it been like this?

For an instant, Gabby thought about turning tail and running back to the car and back to the safety of Chertsey. Not for one moment had she imagined that she would find anything like this. No one could live in this state; it was inconceivable.

Was it really eighteen years since she had last seen them? It must have been. The change of address card had arrived not long after she and Dave were married: *Peacock Cottage, No. 9 Magnolia Court.* Where in heaven had the years gone? How in hell had she let a slimy little man like Dave drive a wedge between her and the two people she had loved most in the world? They had been right about him; she had not – end of. Why hadn't she got over herself, swallowed her pride and simply admitted that she had made a mistake? Bugger Dave.

Two

Harry stood shoulder to shoulder with his father at the graveside and watched as his paternal grandfather's coffin was lowered into the ground. It was the second funeral of the day. The first had been his paternal grandmother's. Covering the funeral costs and giving them both a good send-off was the least he could do. Harry was a man of substance while his parents continued to live in the modest terrace house in which he had been born.

He had suggested to his father that a cremation would be more appropriate given the circumstances, but his father would hear none of it. Family members had always been laid to rest properly in a grave in the cemetery and not left in a jar on the mantelpiece. Harry didn't begrudge the cost of the coffins or the burial ground, but since his grandparents had already been cremated once he couldn't see the point in burying what little remained of them now. The fire had done a good job not only on his grandparents who were in Harry's view well past their sell-by date but also on one other tenant who had lived in the small block of flats.

Harry, the same five foot ten inches and build as his father, had offered to lend his father a suit, and buy his mother a dress for the occasion, but neither of them had taken him up on his offer. His father had a perfectly good black jacket and tie and his mother a 'classic' black dress that took her everywhere and had done so for the past thirty-five years that he could remember. To say that he was ashamed of their appearance was overstating the matter; he was simply relieved that none of his contemporaries from the golf club had been able to make it. Had they known about the funeral then many would have been present, but Harry had overlooked the delivery of the notices to them. Grandpa Trumper had been a popular cove in his time while Grandma Trumper was renowned for volunteering for anything from helping the homeless to knitting socks for orphans to hospital-visiting to fostering mistreated cats and dogs.

No one blamed him. Harry had all the necessary fire safety certificates for Waverley Court and all the electrics had been checked out just a few weeks before the fire – the certificate was dated 27 March 2001. The police had completed their investigations into the cause of the fire and concluded that it had been started accidentally by a candle left burning in one of the flats. The coroner's verdict was that of the accidental death of Harry's grandparents and a male tenant whom Harry was able to identify as a middle-aged man who went by the name of Sam Smith. He confessed that he knew little about the man other than he had been a tenant for a few weeks only, had paid the deposit on the flat in cash and had presented credible identification and references.

Fortunately, the other tenants had either been at work, away visiting family or down at the local at the time the fire broke out. The lives of one Asian couple, a family of four and a single female who 'worked nights' had been spared and all thought themselves to have been very lucky indeed. Harry rehoused them all in some of his other properties, all of which were vacant either because of their current state of disrepair or the less than salubrious areas in which they were located. Lucky to be alive, the tenants considered themselves highly fortunate to have a roof over their heads at all. Harry went up minimally in their opinions.

Harry sympathised with his father who bemoaned the fact that he had not been given the time or opportunity to say a proper goodbye to his parents. There were so many things that he would have liked to have said and so many things that he had intended to tell them 'one day', not least how much he appreciated all that they had done for him. In Harry's opinion, it didn't add up to much. If anything, his grandparents had been more generous to him than they had ever been to his father. People came and people went. They were old and it was their time. Move on.

* * *

Born Henry Trumper in March 1966, and renamed Harry within a matter of days, he was an only son and lived with his parents in a two-up two-down terrace house in the East End of London. It wasn't many years since the lavatory down the garden had been replaced by an indoor facility – a significant improvement over the hole cut in the wooden bench, bucket beneath, that had preceded it. Other than that one luxury, or necessity as some might consider it, everything at 9 Redlands Terrace remained much the same as the day the terrace had been built. Harry's parents were quite satisfied with their lot. There was enough money coming in from his father's market stall to put food on the table with sufficient left over to pay the rent, the gas bill and the coal merchant. The Trumpers were neither jealous of other people's possessions nor ambitious to achieve more in their lives. Neither were they ambitious for Harry. He had been born healthy with two legs, two arms, four fingers and two thumbs on each hand and five toes on each of his feet. It was a bonus that he had a fine head of wavy dark brown hair. Who could possibly ask for more? One day he would take over running the market stall and no doubt pass it on to his own son at some time in the future. That was the way it had always been.

The similarities between Harry and his father and grandfather stopped with their shared dislike of school and education. Harry did the least possible to avoid the headmaster's renowned skills with the cane and getting detention too often. To his utter dismay the teachers saw potential in him and worked tirelessly to persuade him that by not applying himself as he should, he was throwing away a wonderful future. Harry had no intention of throwing his life away like his father or his grandfather.

Harry excelled in maths; according to his teacher he could become a banker, a financier, a professor of mathematics, a scientist or an engineer – none of which appealed to him in the slightest. He didn't deny that figures fascinated him. He could add up a column of twenty or more numbers in his head in less time than it took for the teacher to tell them that they could "Start now."

Fascinated by his parents' weekly ritual of filling in the pools coupons and then demanding absolute silence when the Saturday afternoon football results came on the television, Harry took a leaf out of their book, drew up his own coupon, made up his own rules and sold lines to his classmates. On an average week he cleared two pounds and on a good week he pocketed four or more.

He didn't like bullies and made it his business to take care of those in his school who suffered at their hands. Of course, he was not a charity – all services had to be paid for. Protection en route to school and on the return home was charged out at one pound per month. Protection including morning, lunch and afternoon break carried an additional charge of fifty pence. Fortunately, Harry was well built and strong and knew how to use his fists if he had to.

By far the best of his moneymaking ventures was the acquisition and selling of examination papers. No one ever asked how he managed to acquire them nor did they argue with the price he asked for them. Harry was shrewd and set prices based on the level of desperation of his punters. He religiously observed the eleventh commandment – never get caught.

By the age of fifteen, he had accumulated the princely sum of three hundred pounds, which he kept in a shoebox under his bed until such time as he could open a bank account of his own.

When the time came to take GCEs, Harry failed to turn up. He didn't need bits of paper where he was going and he certainly didn't need A levels or a degree in anything. He had eyes and ears and a brain.

Alf, Harry's father, had a stall at the local rag market on Tuesdays, Wednesdays, Saturdays and Sundays selling an eclectic mix of ladies' fashion: crop tops, skin-tight Lycra pants, luminescent cropped trousers, striped jerseys, pink, purple, lime-green and yellow leg warmers, brightly coloured lacy bras and panties and pantyhose. It was all cheap and disposable. Each Friday he bought stock from his long-standing friend and supplier, Ali.

Alf was delighted when his son, having finished school, asked if he might work on the stall with him, although a little taken aback when he was presented with the terms and conditions. Harry wanted a fifty-fifty split of the profits. Alf thought about it for a few seconds and since it was his son's destiny to take the stall over from him in the years to come, readily agreed. Over the next two years, the stall changed beyond recognition.

Alf wasn't so sure that he liked the changes. Harry was ruthless. In no time at all Ali, his supplier of thirty years and friend for almost as many, no longer spoke to him. Harry had moved their business elsewhere. Alf couldn't fault his son's head for business – the range from the new supplier was a hit with customers and the price was right, but he didn't like his son's methods.

Within a year, Alf had been persuaded to open a bank account and keep accounts. The name on the chequebook was Harry Trumper. As his son patiently explained to him, it was the very least he could do to look after the business side of things; his father was not getting any younger.

Harry kept a sharp eye on those who bought from the stall and those who simply walked on by. "Madam," he called, as two late-middle-aged ladies walked by, "I've got a quality pair of trousers here which would look just right on you!" Harry held up a pair of skin-tight Lycra trousers.

"That would be me forty years ago, you monkey," one of the ladies replied, flicking her long greying hair over her shoulder. "But in case you haven't noticed, I would need four pairs of those to go around me backside! How do they get into those anyway – with a shoehorn?"

"We sell those as well," Harry replied in an instant.

"The colours are great, love. The style ain't quite me. All they seem to make for us older gals are loose-fitting clothes in grey, black, navy or beige. Time someone realised that fashion ain't just for the young."

Regular as clockwork the family took Sunday lunch with Harry's paternal grandparents who lived just a few streets away in a small semi-detached inherited from his great-grandfather. They were in their late seventies but still able to live a fairly independent life. Albert, his grandfather, played cribbage and dominoes at the local pub while Ada, his grandmother, as well as doing all her charitable deeds, knitted socks and sweaters for Christmas presents.

"Grandma, why do you always wear dull colours and clothes that hang off you?" Harry asked.

"You cheeky little devil. What a question to ask your old grandma. If you were sitting that much closer to me, I'd give you a clip around the ear. You're never too old for one."

"You'd be joining the queue," his father muttered under his breath while silently thinking that it was about time that somebody gave Harry a good clip around the ear. He was getting far too big for his boots.

"I didn't mean it the way it sounded, Grandma. It's just that I couldn't help noticing that lots of women your age, and quite a bit younger, don't seem to be interested in nice clothes. I mean, colourful clothes that fit really well," Harry added, trying to be more tactful.

Grandma sighed and got up to clear the dishes. "It's not that we're not interested, Harry, or that we don't like to look nice, but there just isn't anything for us. No one makes clothes for

14

the likes of us. No money in it, I guess. It's all about money these days."

Harry nodded. His grandmother was simply confirming what the two ladies had said just a few days ago. "So what's wrong with wearing clothes that are made for younger women?" he asked.

"Now where shall I start, young man? First, the shape. As you get a bit older your shape changes – things sag here and there, much as I hate to admit it, and the pounds go on every which way particularly where you don't want them to. So we don't fit your standard sizes. And because we sag in different places there are some parts of us that you don't want on show. See these?" Grandma rolled up her sleeves. "Batwings, bingo wings – that's what they're called. That's why you don't see many of us wearing sleeveless tops and dresses. Then there's the minor problem of getting things on and off. I can't remember the last time I was able to reach round to my back to do up a zip. And tiny buttons – my fingers aren't as agile as they once were. Ask me to wear that white frilly blouse of mine with the tiny pearl buttons down the front and come back next week to pick me up. That's how long it would take me to do them up. So bottom line, Harry, is we don't have many choices."

"Thanks, Grandma," Harry replied thoughtfully. "You've given me an idea."

It had been easier than he thought it would be. First, he sourced and bought on sale or return five reconditioned sewing machines, and then he employed five ladies to sew from home. His colourful and tailored 'couture range' for more mature ladies with batwings, pounds of flesh in all the wrong places and arthritic fingers, flew off the shelves.

Cleverly, Harry built a small, curtained cubicle at the back of the stall and installed a full-length free-standing mirror. Word soon got round and the business flourished. At the end of two years, Harry had amassed over four thousand pounds in his bank account.

Opening a bank account in his father's name, Harry transferred one thousand pounds into it and announced to his father that he had plans for his future in which a market stall had no place. He now had sufficient cash to put a deposit down on a property with enough in reserve to smarten it up before letting it out. Harry had his sights set on becoming a landlord – with not just one tenant, but many.

Dilapidated and unloved, Waverley Court was located just three streets away from Redland Terrace. From local gossip, Harry gleaned that the four flats that comprised Waverley Court had been empty for nearly five years, following the death of the owner. Now a For Sale sign had appeared nailed to the front wall of the property.

Harry opened the gate and walked the five short paces up to the front door. A series of doorbells, one per flat, had long since stopped working and a door knocker lay corroded and filthy on the step at his feet. Pushing aside the two-foot-high nettles and brambles that threatened to strangle the premises, he looked through the cracked window of one of the downstairs flats. Through the filth on the window Harry was able to make out a room that he presumed to be the sitting room and three doors leading off it – a kitchen, a bedroom and a bathroom, he imagined. What remained of the carpets had been torn up and heaped in a pile in a corner of the room. Several floorboards were missing and others were warped from the cold and damp. The wallpaper flopped lifelessly down the walls. He could imagine the smell inside. He didn't need to see any more; Waverley Court was just what he had been looking for.

The asking price was one hundred thousand pounds. Harry acquired the property for seventy thousand with a down payment of two thousand pounds. Fortunately the accounts that he had kept over the past two years, in combination with the fact that he intended to make one of the flats his main residence, stood him in good stead for a mortgage. Within three months the flats had been refurbished and were ready for their first tenants. He occupied one of the ground-floor flats and let the remaining three out. Harry had achieved his first goal, but there was no room for complacency. He had his sights firmly set on another property nearby.

A short stroll from Waverley Court, Harry never missed Sunday lunch with his grandparents, nor did he fail to notice that both his grandma and grandpa were ageing fast.

"Have you ever thought about moving somewhere so you wouldn't have to climb those stairs?" Harry asked, after helping to clear the dishes away into the kitchen.

"We couldn't leave this house," his grandma replied earnestly. "It's been in your grandpa's family since it was built. We're managing quite nicely so far, but I sometimes do wonder how we'll manage in a few years' time."

"It's just bricks and mortar, Grandma. There's no point in leaving it until you have to sleep on the sofa." Harry put his arms around his grandma and gave her a hug.

"You're a good lad, Harry – always thinking about other people. The world would be a better place if there were more like you," she replied lovingly.

"I might just have an idea – at least think about it. What

would you say to us swapping homes? You come and live in my ground-floor flat and I come and live in your house. We could do a straight swap to keep the paperwork simple. No more stairs to climb, less housework to do and grandpa would be within fifty yards of the pub. Best not to say anything to anyone until you've had time to think about it," Harry added, eager to prevent his mother or father having any say in the arrangement.

Within two months his grandparents had moved out of Porland Road and were safely ensconced in Waverley Court and Harry was the proud owner of a semi-detached house with a market value of sixty-five thousand pounds. With a loft conversion, Porland Road was easily converted into three flats.

Weathering the storm of the property crash of the early 1990s and capitalising on the surge in property prices in the late 1990s, fifteen years later Harry's portfolio topped three hundred properties of over two million pounds in value, with the price of property soaring by the day. Along the way he had taken no prisoners. He had made a lot of money but also many enemies. There were those who would happily see Harry Trumper clapped in irons and drowned in the Thames.

Three

Charles poured two fingers of Johnny Walker Black Label into a Speymore cut-crystal whisky glass. A few years ago it would have been Red Label into an Edinburgh crystal glass, and before that a pint of Young's bitter down at the local. Now he could afford the best and only the best would do – not that the whisky tasted any different at all. Topping the glass up with ice, he congratulated himself that at last he had educated the barman at the golf club in the art of pouring a good scotch: whisky first, ice last – never the other way round when he was serving a drink to Charles Fairbrother.

Standing well back from the window and shading his eyes from the setting sun, Charles gazed out at the view and contemplated his success. Maybe he had got a bit carried away with the Canary Wharf apartment which was way up in the sky with a thirty-foot wall-to-wall, ceiling-to-floor window, but he had bought it at a good price. Heights gave him the willies, but it was almost spring and he didn't mind admitting that he was feeling pretty smug with himself. Everything was coming together nicely, and it was almost time to launch himself on the world. At thirty-nine years of age he was healthy, wealthy and wise and a good catch for any woman. It was 2005 and time he settled down and had a family.

He felt good and he looked good – a lot of which was down to his personal trainer who had had him on the run, so to speak, for the past three months. If she had her way (which he only allowed her at night) he would be in the gym four days a week and other days would be filled with hours of yoga, complete with soothing music and chanting, Pilates and tai chi. Not for him. He had to admit that time spent working out on the punch bags in the gym had done him a power of good. The flab on his arms, legs and belly had melted away and been replaced by firm powerful muscles. For the first time in more years than he cared to remember he enjoyed admiring himself in the mirror. Danielle, his trainer, was a welcome distraction, but she had no place in his plans for the future.

Reclining in one of the cream leather armchairs recently imported from Italy, Charles rested his chinos-clad legs on the matching stool and flicked on the TV. He did not possess a pair of slippers and that was the way he intended it to remain until his dying day. If the rugs got grubby he would either get them cleaned or buy new ones. If the furniture got soiled or the wooden floor was scratched there was always someone who needed to earn some money who would sort it out. Life was too short.

A news presenter was relating the story of Prince Harry turning up at a fancy dress party dressed as Hitler. It hadn't gone down too well with the British public or his mum. Quietly Charles thought it hilarious, but then he wasn't a great royalist anyway. And then there was the eighteen-year-old who had secretly painted an eighteen-foot penis on the roof of his parents' one-million-pound Berkshire mansion. It had been there for a full year before anyone had noticed. The

TV camera zoomed in. It was perfect – the boy was a genius. Charles roared out loud, picturing in his mind's eye a bevy of aircraft circling slowly over Berkshire at the bequest of its passengers in order to get a bird's-eye view – the Bovingdon hold would never be the same again.

The last few years had been a bit of a roller coaster, but he had come through unscathed in the end. Indeed, he had emerged from them very well. With cash in the bank and a well-spread portfolio of investments that would provide him with a good income for life, he was able to enjoy the fruits of his labour. The problem of finding enough things to do to fill his time, following his retirement from business, was easily solved.

Charles had a passion for art, which had taken root just one year earlier and not too many minutes after he had walked into his first art gallery. At the time he had had no intention of either looking at the 'pictures', as he then called them, or of buying any. It had been bucketing with rain, and he was soaked to the skin. Every taxi in the King's Road was occupied and he needed to get into the dry. The art gallery provided the nearest shelter. There in front of him, the sole picture on a huge expanse of white wall was one that had clearly been painted by a six-year-old.

"May I help you, sir?" an assistant had asked.

"No," Charles had replied. "But what the hell is that on the wall?"

"That 'hell' is Lowry's own living hell. It is perhaps an apt way of describing it."

"Lowry?"

"Laurence Lowry, a painter of masterpieces just like this one. Born 1887 in Lancashire and lived most of his life in

Pendlebury. His works capture scenes of industrial England."

"Why didn't anyone teach him to draw?" Charles asked.

"That's his style – he's deliberately naïve. Let me tell you a little about the painting – that is, if you have time?"

The road outside was obscured by the rain cascading down the windows. Charles had the choice of either listening to the dealer droning on about a six-year-old painter or of getting soaked again. Charles chose the former option.

Emerging from the gallery two hours later, Charles was a wiser man and poorer by ten thousand pounds – although that was a mere drop in the ocean to him. He had bought a high-quality print, signed by Lowry, and he had got it for one thousand pounds less than the asking price. Most important of all, he had learned, it had been cared for and had not faded with time. It was to be the first of many Lowrys that Charles would acquire.

It was now a nightly ritual of his to wander around the apartment chatting with Lowry whom he was now able to find in each of the paintings, either with a suitcase in his hand or as a small sticklike figure standing remote from the crowds. Charles's more recent purchases from Lowry's well-known Horrible Head period gave him nightmares, and from time to time he wished he hadn't bought them.

Other painters interested him as well, and the walls of Charles's apartment were soon obscured by works of art.

* * *

Charles walked over to the cocktail cabinet and refilled his glass. He glanced up at the gold-framed photograph of Breeze, his latest acquisition, as he liked to think of her. In truth, he owned a share of her along with four other members of a syndicate. She was three years old, a chestnut and a thoroughbred, and in a few weeks' time she would be running in the Derby Stakes at Epsom. What Charles knew about racehorses and thoroughbreds could be written on the back of a postage stamp. Breeze, however, would be his ticket to the life he had planned for himself. His share had cost a small fortune by anyone's standards, but it would be worth every penny. As a part-owner in Breeze he would be entitled to entry to the members' and owners' marquee alongside all the other owners, officials and royalty that would be there on the day.

Breeze was running in the Epsom Derby on the fourth of June. Charles's Savile Row morning suit was ready and hanging in the wardrobe.

* * *

Charles lathered on a thick layer of shaving cream and extracted his very best shaving brush from the bathroom cabinet. Smooth as a baby's bottom, he thought, stroking his chin. Pulling a comb through his prematurely greyed hair, Charles put on his silver-rimmed glasses, stood back, and admired his reflection in the mirror. He hardly recognised himself.

Dressed and ready with half an hour to spare, he poured himself two fingers. It was far too early in the morning to imbibe, but he persuaded himself that a little Dutch courage would not go amiss, and besides it was the first day of his new life.

A voice on the intercom announced that his transport was

ready and waiting. The chauffeur-driven Rolls-Royce that he had hired for the day had arrived on the dot of nine. Charles removed his top hat and climbed into the back of the Rolls, reminding the chauffeur in no uncertain words that they were to arrive at Epsom at exactly eleven o'clock – not a minute before and not a minute later.

Charles climbed carefully out of the Rolls as a clock struck eleven and put his hat on. Consulting his mental map of the layout at Epsom, he turned left and strode confidently in the direction of the members' and owners' enclosure.

"Good morning, sir. The going is good. And there's an excellent race card. Enjoy your day," the steward remarked. Charles stopped and took a deep breath. The whole atmosphere was charged, electric and compulsive, and at the same time sedate, genteel and wholly understated. He felt very much at home. If he could have bottled the atmosphere he would have done so and probably made his second or third fortune. Lost in his own thoughts, he hardly noticed the light tap on his shoulder. She was a blond Cleopatra with shoulder-length straight hair and a full fringe that shone like silk. She was in her mid- to late twenties he guessed, and quite divine.

"I'm sorry. I didn't mean to startle you," she said, her long eyelashes fluttering over deep blue eyes. "It was just that you were looking a little lost, and I thought that maybe I could be of help." Charles recognised just a faint touch of Essex in the girl's speech.

Assuming that it was the correct thing to do, Charles removed his hat to greet her and then returned it to his head. "Good of you," he replied, pointedly looking at his gold Rolex watch. "I was just taking a little time out to soak up the atmosphere before heading to the champagne bar for a small glass before meeting some friends of mine. First time at Epsom– need to get my bearings. The name is Charles Fairbrother."

"Annabel," she replied. "Good to meet you, Charles." Annabel smiled to herself. If she wasn't mistaken, there was just a hint of an east end accent. She was pretty sure that she knew who he was even if he hadn't a clue about her.

"Like to join me?" Charles enquired. He glanced at her feet and her left hand. Five foot six without the four-inch heels, no rings on the left hand – promising.

"I am not sure that I should. I've already had two glasses with Daddy and his friends and he'll be wondering where I am," she replied coyly.

"Maybe next time?" Charles looked suitably deflated.

"How can I say no when you ask so nicely, Charles? And it would be good to get to know you," Annabel said, linking her arm in his and leading him off in what he assumed was the direction of the champagne bar.

Finding two high stools overlooking the course, Charles clicked his fingers at the waiter and ordered a bottle of Krug.

"I like your style and I just love these bubbles," Annabel teased, as she took her first sip of champagne. "Tell me about yourself, Charles. Where have you been hiding?"

For a split second, he was thrown off balance. "Hiding? I haven't been hiding anywhere," he replied rather more abruptly than either of them expected.

"I didn't mean anything. It's just an expression. Let's start again. Tell me about yourself." Annabel rested her elbow on the table and her head in her hand and looked into his eyes. "You fascinate me."

"Born Charles Edward Fairbrother in the suburbs of London. I have no siblings and my school days were nothing to write home about. Out of the blue, and when I was just eighteen, my father received a letter from an uncle in Australia. It invited my father, my mother and I to go and live with him in Australia. He simply wrote that we'd have a good life and prospects. That was enough for my father. As soon as the emigration papers were sorted, we hopped on a plane and left England behind. Am I boring you?"

"Not one little bit," Annabel replied, her eyes sparkling with interest.

"To cut a long story short my uncle died and left me his business. Some years later my mother and father died in a helicopter crash. I had nothing to keep me there. I sold up and came back to England. I am now retired." Charles drew breath and quietly congratulated himself on the story.

"Aren't you too young to retire?" she asked, feigning innocence.

"If you're asking how old I am, then the answer is thirty-nine. You can never be too young to retire, Annabel."

"So what exciting things are you doing in your retirement?" Annabel asked brightly.

"Well, I have a wife at home, two children, three mistresses and four dogs – Rottweilers all of them," Charles replied with a glint in his eye. "So not much time for anything else."

Annabel smiled knowingly. "I'm surprised that any of them let you out today without a leash. Or did you lock them all away in kennels before you left?"

Charles laughed. He liked her style, and she was nobody's fool. "A bit of an exaggeration perhaps. I have no wife, no children and no mistresses although my personal trainer would like to think she is, and I can't stand dogs that leave hair all over the place. For the record, I don't like cats either. Actually, I have a little personal investment in a horse which is what brings me here today. I play golf a couple of times a week, I exercise regularly at the gym and I have a passion for art."

"Now that sounds more like it." Annabel drained her glass and glanced at her watch. "I promised Daddy I wouldn't be long. Would you like to meet him?"

Charles raised his eyebrows; it was a bit soon to be meeting 'Daddy'. "I have to meet my partners I'm afraid, so another time, perhaps."

"Would one of those be a Mr Sinclair by any chance?" she asked, with a broad grin on her face.

"How could you possibly know that?" Charles frowned.

"That's Daddy. You see, I know all about you, Charles Fairbrother. You're the new shareholder in Breeze, aren't you?"

Charles nodded, hoping and praying that neither she nor her daddy knew too much about him.

With long odds, Breeze 'breezed in' in third place. No one was disappointed; they had all hedged their bets.

* * *

Charles and Annabel were married three months later at Chelsea Registry Office followed by a reception in a private room at the Ritz. No expense was spared. Even though Charles could have easily afforded it, he was delighted that he was not footing the bill. 'Daddy' was in his element and more than happy to give his daughter a good send-off – he looked upon it as an investment. Annabel was high maintenance and it was time somebody else footed her bills. He would give her a modest allowance, even generous in most people's eyes, but the major expenses would soon be Charles's responsibility. He couldn't have wished for a better son-in-law or outcome.

The champagne flowed from the moment the bride and groom arrived at the Ritz until well after they departed for their honeymoon. The seven-course luncheon was served to the one hundred guests by fifty waiters who stood by the ornately decorated walls in silence and waited patiently for a signal from the maître d' to clear or serve. The wine, carefully selected to complement each of the courses, was served by a separate army of wine waiters who looked to the head sommelier for their instructions.

Sid, one of the part-owners of Breeze, had readily agreed to be best man. He had made his fortune in the electrical wholesale business and never missed an opportunity to remind those he met that "There's money to be made in copper." Fortunately, he had taken a liking to Charles, whom he called Charlie most of the time, and described him as an "ace guy" and just right for his mate's beautiful daughter, Annabel. Confiding to Charles that he was "well jel", Sid had had his sights set on Annabel, but the feeling had not been reciprocated. There were no hard feelings.

No one outshone Annabel that day. Her ivory-coloured full-length satin dress was adorned with millions of seed pearls and the same seed pearls had been expertly woven into her hair and pinned to the top of her head. Around her neck she wore a Swarovski necklace that had been commissioned to complement her bridal outfit.

The five bridesmaids' dresses had been bought from Harrods but by the time they had been altered almost beyond recognition, the cost had well exceeded that of getting made-to-measure dresses in the first place. Together the bride, groom and bridesmaids looked stunning – at least good enough for a photograph in the society page of a county paper. Charles prayed that it would not happen. The very last thing he wanted was for his picture to appear in a newspaper.

The party continued long into the night as the guests retired to the Ritz casino. Charles and Annabel flew first class to Antigua to spend two weeks in a mini-mansion within a seven-star resort. Annabel was in seventh heaven. Charles was mightily pleased with his trophy wife and had no doubt that he would grow to love her.

Two years later their first born, Ethan, entered the world.

Four

Twenty-year-old Maria had arrived from Portugal three years previously. Ostensibly, Maria's role was to look after Ethan, now six, and Abby, five years of age – at least that was the story Annabel had told the agency. As it happened she was quite content and happy to look after her own children but a built-in babysitter and a live-in cleaner came in very handy.

Maria was more than happy to babysit – once, twice or seven times a week if that was what her employer wanted her to do. The kids were fun and, as kids went, easy-going and obedient. Maria ate like a horse and never put on a pound. She was everything that Annabel had herself once been, soft and kind, bubbly and playful, and apparently hadn't a care in the world. Irrationally, and in many ways, the girl annoyed her. She was just too good to be true. Everyone had their bad days but not Maria. It didn't help that the kids adored her.

After three years of being schooled by Annabel, Maria was an excellent cleaner. The Fairbrothers' house on The Hawthorns, a highly exclusive development of five houses, located just outside of Weybridge town centre, was Annabel's pride and joy. Charles, on the other hand, believed that a house was for living in, not for admiring. It was a constant source of irritation that he resolutely refused to take his outdoor shoes off in the house. Reluctantly, Annabel had had to extend the same concession to her father and stepmother who blatantly refused to visit the house if this were the case. Her father had accused her of being anal on one occasion. While she got the gist of his comment, she had insisted on him defining precisely what he meant by it. "Up your arse" was all he said. She had changed the conversation.

No dogs, no cats – Charles didn't like them either. Reluctantly she had agreed to the children being given two rabbits for Christmas, both of which lived in their own centrally heated 'mansion' in the garden and out of sight of the house. Maria had come close to being returned on the next fishing boat to Portugal when she had allowed the children to give their rabbits a guided tour of the house; the rabbits had left a tell-tale trail around the house. Maria had spent the next twenty-four hours on her hands and knees.

Maria was quite satisfied with her lot. She worked at cleaning seven hours a day, seven days a week. On average she stayed in to babysit three nights a week. It was a well-paid job that enabled her to send money back to her family at home.

Charles had a twinkle in his eye for Maria. He loved watching her as she dusted and cleaned the skirting boards in the house. Annabel had forbidden the use of long-poled dusters. Maria was to get down on her hands and knees and do a proper job with a proper duster. Thursdays were skirting-board days – one of the few days that Charles was at home and Annabel was at the gym. Maria had the most beautiful firm, small, round buttocks that he had ever clapped eyes on. She was thin but not bony and blessed with breasts that barely remained in her Lycra top when she was bending

31

down. Annabel had had words with her about her attire, but it had made no difference.

Annabel didn't miss much; she was realistic enough to know that all men desired those things that they could not have and probably didn't appreciate those things that they had as much as they should. For thirty-five, she knew she looked good, although sometimes she looked in the mirror and wondered where the old Annabel had gone. She had regular facials and the most expensive skincare regime that money could buy, but it didn't prevent her eyeing Maria with a certain amount of envy.

Charles lay back in the recliner with the *Telegraph* open in his hands and watched as Annabel lined up three small suitcases by the front door. He had not read one single word of the paper.

It was the school holidays and a ritual that the children spent three nights being spoilt rotten by their grandfather and grandmother who lived on the other side of Weybridge.

Annabel called at the top of her voice, "I'm off now, Charles. I'm staying overnight. I told you that Daddy has got those friends of his coming for dinner tonight. You know, the one that you can't stand the sight of and the same one who can't stand the sight of you either. I refused the invitation for you anyway. Don't I always think of you? We'll be having a few drinks and I don't want to drive. I'll be back tomorrow."

"No problem," Charles called in response. "And thanks for getting me out of it."

"Have a nice time, madam," Maria said sweetly, opening the door for her employer while planting a kiss on the children's heads.

Charles put the paper aside, took a deep breath and whistled silently. Boy, this was going to be the toughest assignment ever. "What's on your schedule today, Maria – that is, after dusting the skirting boards?" Charles asked.

"I'm just finishing up here, Mr Charles. Madam has asked me to change the sheets in the master bedroom next," Maria replied with a smile.

* * *

Charles poured himself two fingers, put his feet up again, savoured the moment and waited patiently. The master bedroom was directly above the lounge and he would hear her footsteps as soon as she started in there. Hearing the creak of floorboards above his head, he folded the paper and strolled slowly out to the hall and climbed the stairs.

"Maria, how about I help you with putting those fresh sheets on the bed? Why Annabel should need a seven-foot-wide bed I'll never know. Guess it could have something to do with my snoring although she's no innocent either, however much she denies it."

Maria felt, rather than heard, his presence before he spoke. She turned sharply to see her employer dressed only in his dressing gown, revealing a tanned muscular chest lightly brushed with dark hair. There was no doubt about his intentions. Her heart raced. She knew she should flee from the house, but she was rooted to the spot. Even in his mid-forties, her employer was gorgeous and this was the moment that she had dreamt about often, although never for one minute thought might happen.

Charles read her face and knew that she would not reject him and checked the time on his watch.

"I can change the sheets later if you like," she replied huskily, while slipping off her clothes. "So I guess there would be no harm done."

He had not planned to enjoy it as much as he did. It surprised him that she knew more tricks than he. He would have to be careful. He was on top of her, her legs spread wide. She cooed like a pigeon every time he thrust forcefully into her and pushed him away whenever she thought that he was on the point of losing control. She was a formidable lover and clearly one who was not going to be satisfied with a quick romp. Her pupils were dilated and he could see from her movements and the look on her face that she was on the point of a massive orgasm; he was desperate too. The world exploded as they both cried out and the door to the bedroom opened. A light flashed in their faces – once, twice and a third time. Annabel stood framed by the door, mobile phone in hand.

Annabel glanced across to the windows. They were all open to let some air in. July was hotter than usual and the air was completely still – noise carried a long way on days like this. The neighbours obviously had the same idea – windows were wide open in the houses to the left and right. This was one conversation that she was more than happy to share.

"Get out of my bed, get dressed, pack your clothes and get out of this house right now," Annabel screamed.

Maria knew better than to argue. They had been caught red-handed – and on camera.

Charles lay back on the bed exhausted and pulled the sheet up over his nakedness.

"And as for you, Charles Fairbrother, you disgust me." Annabel charged over to the bed, all guns blazing. "You didn't expect me back, did you? As it happens I forgot to take Ethan's medicine with me so I had to come back for it. And what do I find? I find you in bed with the au pair. You're going to pay for this, Charles Fairbrother," she yelled at the top of her voice. "Put some clothes on right now. I am going down to see that little hussy out of the door. You and I have some talking to do. Do not go away."

Taken aback, Charles looked up at his wife. He hadn't expected her to like it, but wasn't she getting things just a little out of proportion?

* * *

Annabel took the stairs two at a time and, in full view of the neighbours, helped Maria bodily out of the door. "Hope you have got your passport because there are going to be no references from me," she said, eyes drilling into the twenty-year-old who, suitcase in hand, took flight down the garden path.

"And now for you, Charles Fairbrother," she muttered under her breath.

"How could you? How could you go to bed with that slut of an au pair the moment my back is turned," she shouted at him. "What sort of a man are you? Just how long has this been going on? Ever since she arrived? Yes, I'd bet my bottom dollar on it."

"Annabel, take it easy, will you? We agreed, didn't we?" Charles replied quietly, taking a cautious step closer to her.

"Don't you dare come any closer. I never want you to touch me again. You are a dirty old man. Do you hear me? A dirty old man. How old are you? And how old is she, twenty? It's almost criminal. I have a good mind to report you to the authorities." Annabel was in her stride. She had no intentions of modifying her voice.

"Annabel, can you please keep it down a few octaves. The whole neighbourhood will hear. I don't think I need to explain, do I?" Charles put his hands together and took another cautionary step forward.

"Back off. If you think this is yelling then you wait until I really get steamed up. Anyway, why shouldn't all the neighbours know what a lying scumbag you really are? And it's my guess that you've been sniffing around that personal trainer of yours ever since we got married. Yes, I know about the two of you. But you've just broken the golden rule – you do not shit on your own doorstep. Get me? What does she smell like? Is that what I can smell when you get home? Do you need a bike to get fit or do you use her? I know where I'd put my money."

"Now you don't mean that, Annabel." Charles tried to keep his voice low and level. He wasn't quite sure what he had expected but it wasn't this. She was a firebrand. "Let's just talk this through, cool and calm, and see where we go from here."

"Talk it over? I have just seen you having it off with my au pair in my bed and, what's more, having a whale of a time. You never sound like that when we do it. What is it? Do I bore you now? Not excite you any longer? Well, let me tell you, Charles Fairbrother, that kids like Maria do it with old men like you for kicks but that's all they want."

He didn't see it coming. Annabel picked up a heavy bottle of Versace aftershave from the dressing table and aimed it at his head. He ducked in time to avoid injury but the half-opened

FOUR

window behind him shattered into a million pieces.

"Behave yourself, woman," he shouted.

"Me, behave myself? You're having a laugh, Charles Fairbrother. Well, try this one for size." Annabel yanked a bedside light out of its socket, threw back her arm and hurled it as far and fast as she could in the direction of her husband. Charles yelped and held his arm as a second window shattered.

"And while we are about it," she yelled, as she pointed at two suitcases, "these are yours and right now I am going to pack them for you and you can get the hell out of here." Annabel threw underpants, socks, shoes, shirts, and trousers into the first case and slammed the lid shut.

"You wouldn't dare." Charles stood with his arms folded and watched her in disbelief.

"There's number one," she said.

"Don't you dare," Charles threatened, but it was too late. By the time he grabbed her arm, she had reached the window and his case was dropping from her fingers. There was a loud crash as metal hit metal.

"My car!" he screamed. "That's ninety thousand pounds worth of car down there and you've just dropped a metal suitcase on her. I waited six months for that Ferrari to be delivered."

"Collateral damage," she replied with a smile of satisfaction on her face. She added quietly, "Enjoying it was not part of the deal."

"Enough," he screamed. "That's enough. You've done enough damage. I'm out of here before you kill me or I kill you." Charles almost slid down the staircase in his haste to put space between him and his wife. She had gone stark staring

37

bonkers. Was there something that he had missed when he had married her? Had they had the same conversation earlier that day? This was way beyond anything he had expected.

Charles grabbed the keys to his Range Rover, which seemed to have sustained less damage than the Ferrari, and raced out of the door, recovering his suitcases from the forecourt.

Annabel hung from the window and continued to throw projectiles at him. "Don't ring me, I'll ring you," she yelled. "Or should I say that you'll be hearing from my solicitor." Shards of glass cascaded to the ground as she slammed the window closed.

It briefly occurred to Charles that the only damage to the property so far was upstairs. He hoped and prayed that she would get over her tantrum before she went downstairs and found herself confronted by the Lowrys and the rest of his art collection. She had never liked any of them and even less so when he had told her that nearly all of them were copies.

Charles started the ignition, put the Range Rover in reverse and floored the accelerator. Doors opened and curtains parted as the neighbours watched him leave The Hawthorns.

* * *

The phones ran hot in The Hawthorns. Everyone wanted to know what juicy bits they had missed, if any. Most of them had got the gist of it and the men made a mental note that au pairs and personal trainers were definitely out of bounds from now on. All of them decided that it was best to keep their heads down for a while before offering their condolences to Annabel.

Within days it was common knowledge that Annabel had

met with her solicitor giving him irrefutable evidence of her husband's infidelity and was suing for a quick divorce.

Word had it that Charles had moved into a small cottage in Chertsey and, suffering great remorse, was planning to hand his worldly wealth, lock, stock and barrel, over to Annabel. Charles was the first to admit that he was the guilty party and as such he deserved to suffer for his misdemeanors. The men all thought he had lost his marbles.

Five

Gabby loved her small, south-facing two-bedroomed flat on the second floor of the six-unit seventies-built block. Set in its own small grounds with garages to the rear, should she ever have need of one, the block more familiarly known as Tudor Court was a hop, skip and jump away from the Thames. With a periscope on a long pole, it would have been possible to watch the small pleasure boats and the dinghies drifting up and down the Thames.

There were a few downsides she found to living in a block, not least attending quarterly residents' association meetings which would bore the pants off the most patient soul; and, living on the second floor, taking care to remove her hobnail boots before jumping up and down on the wooden floor. Getting furniture in and out of the flat was at times a challenge and carrying her weekly shop from the supermarket up three flights of steep stairs had seen her arms stretch from twenty inches to twenty-one inches at least. On the first day she had moved in she had received some excellent advice – never go upstairs or downstairs empty-handed. It had been a lifesaver.

The location could not have been bettered: ten minutes' walk to the railway station, a non-stop journey into London when there were no strikes or the 'wrong leaves on the line' or a signal failure at Clapham Junction, and finally a twenty-minute walk to the office in Fetter Lane. She had taken and passed her driving test 'just in case' but had never felt the need to buy a car or part with the arm and a leg it would have cost her to park it either at the station or in town.

Quite why she had chosen to settle in Surbiton, the TV home of *The Good Life*, she didn't know other than it enabled her to put a reasonable distance between herself and her ex-husband, Dave. Just thinking about the years she had wasted on him gave her cause to doubt her own sanity. Had she listened to her Aunt Hetty and Uncle Max so much might have been different, but in those days she knew it all.

Gabby loved her job. Words were in her blood. The flat was crammed full of paperbacks, hardbacks and magazines, all of which she resolutely refused to part with. With no qualifications to draw on after her divorce, she had started at the bottom of the pile as Girl Friday on a magazine. Simply being in the thick of it was enough for her, but she always knew that one day her turn would come and she would get a break.

It came in the most unexpected manner when the agony aunt on the magazine suffered her own agony and was unable to find the answer to her problems outside of a bottle. The magazine was due to go to press and no one had the time to read that week's readers' letters or dream up half-appropriate words of sympathy and advice. Gabby found herself sitting down at a desk with a stack of letters and emails in front of her. "Read those, pick the juiciest and most controversial ones and draft responses. There's a book of standard responses if you get stuck. And have the copy ready in one hour. Okay?"

She did, and the following week the magazine had a new

agony aunt who soon became the most sought after in magazine racks far and wide.

Since those humble beginnings she had worked on several women's magazines variously writing on the subjects of fashion, childcare, food, interiors, gardens and travel.

Of late she had started to take more interest in everyday things that affected people's lives, in particular, the social injustices that prevented people from achieving their aspirations. There were many. She no longer had to work a nine-to-five day in the office. Instead, she could choose to work from the office or home, provided that she turned in the agreed articles each week. The most daunting task of all was deciding which of the many social injustices that interested her should take priority over the others.

* * *

Gabby took the stairs two at a time – Saturday, all day and nothing to do. Was it a luxury or was it just sad? She enjoyed her own company, but there were times, especially weekends, when she would have given anything for some company in the flat.

Gabby picked up the pile of post, most of which were cruise brochures that she received on a daily basis. It was years since she had been on her one and only cruise – the last holiday that she had ever spent with Dave. It had been neither a memorable nor an enjoyable experience and not one that she wished to repeat. The brochures went in the recycle bin without as much as a second glance. To her joy, one of the envelopes contained a cheque for twenty-five pounds – God bless Aunt Hetty and Uncle Max who had given her premium bonds for her birthday ever since she was a child. There was one other envelope, postmarked Weybridge.

"Intriguing," she thought, turning the envelope this way and that while she thought about its origin. Sometimes it was much more fun to look at an envelope and guess its contents than to open it and find that it was no more than a begging letter dressed up to look like a personal letter.

She sniffed it and giggled; it was perfumed.

Gabby propped the letter up against the windowsill and made herself a cup of coffee. The celebrity on *Desert Island Discs* had just answered the sixty-four-thousand-dollar question – what book would she choose to take to a desert island apart from the complete works of William Shakespeare and the Bible? The answer was a book of sudoku. Gabby recognised a kindred spirit. She hoped the celebrity would also choose an unending supply of pencils and rubbers for her chosen luxury. She did.

Popping two slices of bread in the toaster, and making herself another cup of coffee, Gabby eyed the envelope. Best guess, she asked herself. Was it an invitation to a shop opening? Was it an invitation to join a new health club, which would be either too far away or far too expensive for her pocket? Could it be a letter that had been posted in Weybridge but originating from Kenya asking her if she could help some poor soul transfer his millions of pounds into England?

Gabby reached for a knife and carefully slit the envelope open and withdrew the gilt-edged card.

Dear Gabrielle,

I am organising a small school reunion drinks and

lunch party for all my girlfriends from Year 6, Burgess Comprehensive. I would be delighted if you are able to join us.

Date: 15 March 2014. Time: 11.30am.
Address: The Poplars, The Hawthorns, Weybridge, Surrey.
RSVP: Annabel Fairbrother née Sinclair.

Gabby screwed up her face. It was a long time ago, but she didn't remember anybody by the name of Annabel. At a stretch, she did remember Chloe, Jessica, Maria, Elizabeth, Theresa and Susannah, although she was quite sure that she would never recognise any of them if she passed them in the street. And then there was a girl called Belinda, and not forgetting Kate and Harriet, but Annabel? In her mind's eye, she could picture them all standing in a row in the Assembly Hall fiddling with their hair and filing their nails. There was someone missing from her memory – a girl slightly taller than all the rest of them with long blond hair, blue eyes and flawless skin. Bella – that was whom she had forgotten. How could she forget Bella? Bella, the bully, who made everyone else look drab. Her proper name was Annabel, but she always said, "Call me Bella." Bella from Essex who, it seemed, was now Mrs Annabel Fairbrother, a resident of Weybridge.

Gabby re-read the invitation. What a turn-up for the books. It was certainly addressed to her although for the life of her she could not imagine how Mrs Annabel Fairbrother had tracked her down. They had never been what you might call friends and indeed if she remembered correctly, they had literally come to blows on one occasion. It had all ended peaceably enough. Bella had thought better of reporting her to the Head and thereafter they kept their distance but treated each other with mutual respect.

The last time she had seen Bella must have been back in '95 so why on earth was she organising a reunion party almost twenty years later?

"'Curiouser and curiouser, cried Alice, who was so much surprised, that for the moment she quite forgot how to speak good English,'" Gabby quoted to herself. It was a most appropriate quotation.

Gabby finished her toast, leaving the crusts as she had always done as a child, and scraped the crumbs and leftover jam into the bin. Impulsively she put the invitation in the bin and dismissed it from her mind. "Now, Annabel Fairbrother, you've got jam all over your face – no more than you deserve," she said to the perfumed card in the bin.

The Poplars, The Hawthorns, Weybridge. Gabby tapped the address into Google maps and found the street view. There it was: a very smart property by anyone's standards. Set in a tree-lined close with five houses of equally enormous proportions, it was impressive. So this was where the beautiful Annabel passed her days. Not bad. Not bad at all.

Gabby eyed the bin, retrieved the invitation, scraped the jam off and grabbed her diary. It was no good – curiosity had definitely got the better of her and it so happened that there was nothing on her social calendar that day. One train to Weybridge, a fifteen-minute walk from the station – a no-brainer. Why not?

* * *

Annabel scuttled around the house checking that everything was just so. She couldn't wait to see their faces – Essex Bella made good. And, no man around the house to mess up the cushions and leave untidily folded newspapers about – men were both a blessing and a necessity, but now and again it was good to have a break; she could get used to it.

The caterers were in the throes of putting the final touches to the buffet display in the dining room. They had been given very specific instructions together with a photograph of how she expected the finished product to look. It was a rare occasion that she ever found anything vaguely informative or interesting in *Country Life* but last month had been an exception. There had been a double page spread of photographs taken of the deli counters in Harrods Food Hall. The caterers had raised their eyebrows when she had shown them the photographs and told them that this was precisely what she wanted for a small informal buffet party for her girlfriends. In moments they counted the profit they could make and readily agreed to prepare it.

Annabel's heart skipped a beat as she peered into the dining room. The presentation looked divine and was worth every penny she had paid for it, even if the average cost of one mouthful was nearing five pounds. But, she considered herself lucky. Charles could afford it or should she now say, she could afford it.

The drinks had been set up on an adjacent table covered in a pristine white linen tablecloth – nothing too ostentatious. She must not appear to be showing off. Bottles of Prosecco cooled in huge ice buckets and sat alongside jugs of freshly squeezed orange juice and chilled bottles of sparkling Evian water.

The doorbell rang just as Annabel checked her appearance in the hall mirror. Every hair on her head was in its right place. Too formal, too well groomed, she decided, as she ran her fingers through it and pushed a few strands behind her ears.

"Annabel, darling. You haven't changed one bit. I would know you anywhere. How long is it? But we all went our separate ways, didn't we? How you ever managed to find us all I'll never know. Although it's obvious really, isn't it – Internet and those sites where old school friends get reunited and Facebook. What would we do without Facebook? You know I must check my Facebook at least twenty times a day. I looked you up but couldn't find you so I did take just a little teeny-weeny peek at your house on Google maps. You have done well but we always knew you would – all of those men running around after you, you really couldn't fail, could you? And I gather that 'Daddy' did very well for himself later in life."

The woman on the doorstep drew breath. There was something familiar about her but for the life of her, Annabel couldn't put a name to the face.

"Henry, that's the chauffeur, dropped me off today. He'll park out of sight and then when I'm ready to leave, I'll give him a little tinkle. Roger – you remember Roger, don't you? Roger Dainton, the school athletics champion, my husband. Roger said that I must have the chauffeur today just in case I have a teeny-weeny bit too much fizz."

Roger – thank god for Roger. It had to be Chloe; the one and only Chloe who had suffered from verbal diarrhoea from the day she had been born.

"Chloe, well I never, you've hardly changed a bit. I am so

pleased you could come. There are only eight of us today, but that's not bad. It was pretty difficult finding everybody. So many people seem to have gone to live abroad."

Chloe hung her coat over the banister, made herself at home and helped herself to a glass of Prosecco. Chloe had never been one for hanging back.

"Ah, there's the door, Chloe. I wonder who has arrived this time," Annabel said, leaving her guest to help herself to yet more Prosecco.

Annabel jumped back in shock as a huge dog with black silky hair stuck its enormous head around the front door. Dogs had not been included in the invitation.

"You mustn't mind Alexander the Great, my dear. He's a Caucasian Shepherd dog, a rare breed and the sweetest in the world. We never go anywhere without each other. He's a good judge of character as well. In we go, Alex."

Annabel looked down desperately trying to hide her horror as Alexander the Great gave her toes the second clean of the day. "Elizabeth," she said taking in the visitor's clothes – black flowing garments, head to foot; it had to be Elizabeth. If she hadn't known better she might have believed that they were exactly the same clothes that she had worn as a teenager.

Alexander the Great padded through the door, sniffed the doormat, considered cocking his leg against one of the doorposts and then the banister, thought better of it, sniffed the floor and made a beeline towards the kitchen.

"The most intelligent friend I have ever had apart from Keith – my husband, you know – but you won't have met Keith. Lovely man. Barrister, you know." Elizabeth held up a carrier bag. "That dog can sniff a kitchen out from a distance of half a mile. He knows that's where he has his dinner and

48

he knows full well that his dinner is in this very carrier bag. Hot take-away from the doggy parlour. He loves them. Don't you worry, once he's woofed this little lot down, he'll be out for the count. We won't be disturbed until he's ready for his poop. And I always carry the necessary with me."

Elizabeth withdrew a small shovel from her pocket and a roll of black polythene bags and waved them at the horrified Annabel.

Jessica, Maria, Belinda, Harriet and Kate arrived shortly afterward. Everyone seemed to be in high spirits and chatted away together as if they were still teenagers. The most important guest, however, had yet to arrive – Gabby, the ugly duckling, whom she had uncovered living on her own in nearby Surbiton.

* * *

The morning had not started well – her hair looked as though she had been dragged through a hedge backward. "Gabby, my dear," she said to herself, "you look like a scarecrow but if they don't like me the way I am then tough luck." Five minutes later she relented and scuttled down to the hairdresser. Forty minutes later she emerged hardly recognising herself; the unruly mop had been transformed into a sleek copper bob. A young girl, arms adorned with gruesome tattoos, persuaded her that orange gel nails would complement her hair. Fortunately, she had planned to wear a cream trouser suit which would match both her hair and her nails. For a thirty-six year old, she didn't look that bad.

For once the train was on time, and travelling in the opposite direction to London, there had been plenty of seats.

The walk from the station had taken longer than she had thought but what did another ten minutes matter after twenty years?

The door to The Poplars swung open almost before she had touched the doorbell. Annabel had had one eye on her guests and the other on the front door.

"Gabby?" Annabel asked, trying hard to hide her dismay. Gabby was not the ugly duckling she once had been. Maybe she had miscalculated somewhere along the line, but it was too late for a change of plan now.

"Bella? Or should I call you Annabel now? Thank you so much for inviting me today. I was delighted to receive the invitation. I am so sorry that I am a little late. The train was on time but I didn't realise it was quite such a walk from the station."

"Gabby, you look so well. It's wonderful to see you. You haven't changed a bit. Let me take your coat," Annabel said, planting a smile on her face. "Come in and say hello to the others."

Much to her surprise, Gabby found that she was genuinely interested to find out what had happened to her 'friends' since school. Chloe was the same scatterbrain chatterbox that she had always been. Elizabeth proved to be by far the most interesting of the party, having graduated with a degree in the history of art and shortly afterward changed her allegiances to archaeology. What Elizabeth didn't know about art and holes in the ground was nobody's business – and, apparently, Alexander the Great was a great help when it came to digs. They were all in long-term relationships – either married or with long-standing partners. Gabby was the only singleton in the room, except, of course, Annabel, but nobody wanted to be the first to inquire what had become of Mr Fairbrother. Gabby said little about herself, preferring to keep a low profile, and when asked how she occupied her time had replied that she did a little freelance writing to keep the wolf from the door.

In need of finding the loo, Gabby sidled quietly out of the lounge and strolled slowly through the hall to the downstairs cloakroom, stopping to admire the many paintings that all but obscured the cream silk wallpaper that lay beneath. The walls of the cloakroom were no less impressive, hung with a myriad of carefully selected and beautifully framed small watercolours. Someone liked their art, she thought, but somehow she couldn't see that Annabel would have chosen them herself.

"I was just complimenting Annabel on her taste in art, Gabby, and Annabel was just telling me that my compliments are sadly misplaced. Apparently her ex-husband had delusions of grandeur and had copies made of the masterpieces. Makes sense, really. No one in their right mind would hang originals on their walls – Weybridge or not," Elizabeth said, her eye roving around the room.

So the art was down to the ex, Gabby thought to herself as she glanced absentmindedly over Annabel's shoulder. "Annabel, do you have a gardener?"

Annabel looked puzzled. "Yes, two actually but they're not here today."

Gabby said, "Well, there's a man tapping on your French windows and trying to get your attention if I am not mistaken. And he might just be getting wet. It's started to rain."

Annabel turned sharply. "Excuse me for a moment, girls. That's my ex, Charles. He should be picking the children up in an hour. Ethan has football practice this afternoon and Abby has ballet. He gets mixed up with it all – children are so busy these days. I'll have a quick word with him."

No one overheard the conversation between Annabel and her ex.

* * *

'Darlings', a word which had never had any place in their vocabulary at Burgess Comprehensive, were exchanged and the girls swore undying allegiances to one another as their husbands and partners arrived to ferry them home.

Gabby slipped on her coat and wrapped a scarf around her head, thanked Annabel for her hospitality and stepped out in the rain.

Six

"Would you like a lift?" the voice said.

Gabby struggled against the wind and rain to pull her raincoat hood over her scarf. All of her mother's warnings about taking lifts from strangers flew out of the window as the wind threatened to blow her off her feet and the rain stung her eyes.

"You probably don't remember me." The voice wound its window down. "I was the peeping Tom outside at the party – Annabel's ex. She just told me you were on foot to the station. Get in. I'm going that way. It's not fit for a dog out there. Promise I don't bite."

There was no elegant way to get into a Range Rover but right at the moment neither elegance nor appearance mattered one jot. For a fleeting moment, Gabby worried that the tan leather seats would get wet and her feet would mark the cream-coloured carpets but her conscience dealt with it in nanoseconds.

"I thought it was pretty mean that none of the others offered you a lift," he commented, slipping the car into gear. "By the way in case Annabel didn't mention it my name is Charles. Call me Charles."

"Thank you, Charles. You are very kind. I wouldn't go quite

so far as to say mean. I guess they just assumed that I had someone hiding around the corner waiting to sweep me up and whisk me away in a nice warm car. I don't want to take you out of your way." It was a lie: it didn't bother her one iota.

"No problem to me. I go right by the station. I think I've got my instructions right this time. It's Ethan to be picked up from football practice at four although God knows how they think they can kick a ball in this weather, and then Abby from ballet at four-twenty. Kids. All they want is a chauffeur these days." Charles looked right and indicated left out of The Hawthorns.

"And I'm Gabby. I was at school with Annabel but – how stupid of me. I do have a habit of stating the obvious."

"Were you close friends at school?" Charles glanced her way. She seemed a nice enough woman – well turned out, attractive, a bit shy, but she'd do nicely. Maybe he hadn't got the short straw after all.

"As it happens we weren't what you would call close friends. I didn't really fit in with Annabel's set. I was really surprised to receive the invitation from her. I have to confess that I nearly didn't come but curiosity got the better of me. I have really enjoyed myself. Everybody has been kind and who couldn't fall in love with your house?" Gabby said honestly.

"I must correct you on one thing, Gabby, it's not my house. Not anymore. It's Annabel's house – lock, stock, and barrel." Charles put slow emphasis on the lock, stock and barrel.

"I am so sorry. I hope you didn't think I was prying." Gabby shifted uncomfortably in her seat and decided to keep quiet rather than put her foot in it again.

Charles seemed happy to chatter away. "And this, Gabby,

is not my car either. I shouldn't be gossiping really, but it's no big secret. Annabel owns the car and lets me use it. She would die if she thought I was taking the kids to school or picking them up from their activities in an old wreck, which is about all I could afford if she didn't make this one available. It would do her reputation no good at all. Personally, as long as it has four wheels and an engine I wouldn't care one jot what I drove. Material things don't do it for me anymore. What time is your train?"

What an unusual man, Gabby thought. He was the first man she had ever met who didn't care about material things. "There's one at five to the hour and the next is at half past the hour." Gabby looked at her watch. Damn, she would just miss the five to the hour and have to wait.

"We won't make the five to train, too much traffic. It's all the yummy mummies picking their children up in their four-wheelers, parking both sides of the roads and then pushing their way into the traffic lanes. No consideration for others. Strange that – never thought of myself as a yummy mummy before but, as they say, if the cap fits wear it," Charles laughed.

"How about I buy you a cup of tea while you are waiting for the next train? I hear the Station café is quite posh. I'll still have plenty of time to get to Ethan. You would be doing me a favour."

Gabby hesitated. It would be a bit odd to be sitting drinking tea with Annabel's ex five minutes after she had met him, but what harm could it do? He was clearly neither a rapist nor a murderer. In fact, he seemed a thoroughly decent man. "Only if I buy the tea," she said.

"Deal," Charles replied, as he pulled into the station car park.

He was relaxed and easy to talk to and no sooner had they finished their second cup of tea than they heard the announcement on the tannoy: the 3.30 service calling at Surbiton, Wimbledon, Clapham Junction and Waterloo will shortly be arriving on Platform 2. Please stand clear behind the yellow line.

Gabby grabbed her raincoat and her bag. "You've been really kind. Thank you, Charles. I'll have to run."

"Can I see you again? I've really enjoyed our chat." Charles said, opening the door to the café.

"If you like. Here's my number. Call me." There was no time to think about it. The easiest thing to do was to hand him her card and run for the train, which was now sitting on the platform waiting to depart. "No harm done," she said to herself as she sat down in her seat. He probably wouldn't ring anyway and she could always say no if he did.

* * *

"I guess you're not always as honest as this, Charles?" Gabby put her hands under her head and stretched out on the picnic blanket. It was a beautiful summer's day – a clear blue sky and a gentle breeze.

"I didn't want to crowd you, Gabby. I wanted you to get to know, the real Charles, before I told you about the old Charles. I am not proud of the old Charles and I can't blame Annabel for divorcing me. I don't know what came over me. Misbehaving with the au pair. It was just the one occasion, but I think that I had been building up the courage to have a go for a long time. Maybe I thought she wouldn't be quite so willing, but I got that wrong," Charles laughed at himself with a tinge of regret in his voice.

"It was a bit harsh to divorce you for straying just the once, don't you think?" Gabby said.

"Hot-headed – that's Annabel. Once she makes up her mind about something there's no changing it. It all happened so quickly. Caught one day, and on camera, mind you, booted out the same day and divorced six months later. Likes to keep it quick and clean does Annabel."

"You don't seem to have too many regrets about it all." Gabby thought it was strange but touching in a way that he had lost so much but seemed not in the least bit angry about it.

"It's odd, isn't it? Even my best friends thought that I was losing the plot when I didn't contest the divorce or even the settlement she wanted. Money doesn't buy you happiness, Gabby. Those who think that it does are wrong. Of course, everyone needs enough to provide them with a reasonable standard of living but after that… It's people that matter more than money. I never thought I would hear myself saying that. I haven't exactly been the kindest or most generous person in my time. But to answer your question – a year down the line, no, I don't regret it. Somehow the arrangement works. We're not exactly bosom buddies, but we muck along pretty well.

"I don't miss the house or the swimming pool. I don't miss the fast cars and nor do I miss Annabel's unremitting social rounds or going to the races which we used to do regularly. I once owned a part-share in a horse – she was called Breeze. Annabel rides her now. If there is one thing I do miss, it's my paintings. You probably noticed them in the house. There are one or two paintings which are the real deal, but other than that nothing of great value. Mr Lowry and I are the best of friends. One of these days I'll tell you all about him and then I'll take you to see his works at the gallery in Manchester. There's one painting in there that I would give my eye teeth to own." Charles glanced at Gabby and smiled inwardly. She was soaking it all in. If only she knew. There was no way that Charles Fairbrother would ever walk away from a fortune.

Yes, she remembered the paintings and Elizabeth drooling over them until Annabel had put her right. "So now you live a simple life in your cottage?" Gabby said. It was cruel of Annabel to have left him with virtually nothing. She could at least have allowed him to take some of his paintings to put up in the cottage.

"I keep myself busy looking after a few small investments that Annabel kindly agreed to allow me to keep. Strangely enough, the separation and the divorce were the best things that ever happened to me. If you'd asked me a year ago if I could ever see myself living in a small rented cottage in Chertsey, cooking for myself, making picnics, going for long walks and enjoying the simple things of life, I would have laughed at you. But look at me now – in seventh heaven lying under an oak tree with the woman of my dreams."

Gabby laughed. "Flatterer. But it has been fun. I enjoy your company too." Annabel had made a big mistake in her opinion. She should never have let him go.

"So what you see Gabby is what you get – a pretty much penniless, but very contented forty-eight-year-old."

"Likewise, but still in my thirties. Same age as Annabel you'll be surprised to know," Gabby replied, "I'll never be rich but I enjoy what I do. I love my job – writing for me is a passion. I'm content with life as it is." It was an honest response, well almost. If she hadn't lost touch with Aunt Hetty and Uncle Max then she would have been truly content.

"I wish that we could spend more time together, but I have to consider the kids. Whatever Annabel may be, she's a good mother and she makes sure that the kids see plenty of me."

"I get that, Charles. Don't worry. If you don't mind me asking, does Annabel know about us? Does she mind?"

"I told her straight after our second meeting. She was fine with it. If I am not mistaken she's quite pleased about it. Better the devil you know than the devil you don't, she said. Not that she was comparing you to the devil." Charles laughed. "I think she's quite fond of you in her own way. And I also have an inkling that she too might have met someone. She did mention that she'd like to meet up for a coffee with you sometime."

"I don't think so. The only two things we have in common are that we went to the same school and that I am now dating her ex-husband, the latter of which is not a conversation that I would wish to have with her, however okay she is about us."

"Maybe you are right. Best left, hey?"

* * *

"You know what's wrong with Charles, don't you, Gabby?" Annabel said knowingly.

Coffee with Annabel was living up to expectations. Gabby had made excuses three times but the fourth time she had been cornered.

"I don't think that there is anything wrong with Charles, Annabel. He seemed fine yesterday," Gabby replied sharply.

"I don't mean yesterday. I mean generally, Gabby. He's

lonely – that's what it is and he won't admit it, not to himself, not to me and not to you. He's very fond of you, you know. In fact, if I read the signs correctly he's more than a little in love with you. Isn't it time you made an honest man of him?"

Gabby stared at Annabel in astonishment. What business was it of hers whether Charles was lonely or not? She was the one who had kicked him out. And what business of hers was the relationship she had with Charles?

"I appreciate your concern for Charles and myself but if you won't mind me saying, what plans Charles and I may or may not have are none of your business."

"I didn't mean to offend or pry, Gabby. You're quite right of course. It's none of my business except where the children are involved. And I know from what Charles has told me that you completely appreciate his responsibilities as a father. Let's not fall out. I want to be friends. Did you read the paper this morning? It seems we're in for a really hot September and an Indian summer after that. Won't that be great?"

Annabel deftly changed the subject. From now on she would stay on safe turf. She had the answer to her question. She could read it all over Gabby's face. Good.

* * *

Charles and Gabby were married four weeks later in Kingston Registry Office with no fuss and no guests – just the two witnesses that they needed: Sid, a pal from the golf club, and Susie, a friend of Gabby's from work. Their honeymoon comprised two nights in a modest hotel in London, a trip to see *Mamma Mia!*, followed by a trip to the National Gallery the following day. In between times they nestled between the sheets and made love.

Annabel sent them a painting from the house for their wedding present. Charles was delighted even though it was not one of the Lowrys.

Gabby sold her flat and moved into the cottage. Offering to use the money that she had made from the sale of her own flat to put down as a deposit on a small house for the two of them, Charles would have none of it. What was hers was hers and she was to keep it for a rainy day which might, he reflected hopefully, come sooner than she thought.

The Chertsey cottage suited her just fine. With an easy walk to the station, it took her only a little longer to get into town by train than it had from Surbiton.

Everything was perfect with the world – well nearly.

* * *

It was not by choice that she saw little of the children. Charles was under strict instructions that his time with the children was for him alone. According to Charles, however much Annabel liked and respected Gabby, she was unswerving in her view that the children must not be confused by the relationship. Charles explained that he had tried without success to persuade her that a stepmother was nothing unusual to children these days. Quietly, he would have been delighted to have Gabby's company on those days he had the children to himself, they ran him ragged. At times he wondered why he had ever agreed to have children at all.

The downside, of course, was that she saw that much less of her new husband than she would have liked and expected. Most Saturdays he was out with the children taking Ethan to a football match and taking Abby either to ballet, skating or to her riding lessons. Sundays had its routine as well – 'the family' had Sunday lunch together as they always had in the past. Gabby was not part of 'the family'.

The routine, which at first she had found hard to accept, soon became established and she gradually found herself begrudging his time with the children less and less.

The holiday periods were another matter altogether. It was almost nine months into their marriage when Charles broached the subject of holidays 'with the kids'. The summer holidays were almost upon them and Annabel and the children had been invited to stay for three weeks with some old friends of theirs. The invitation had been extended to Charles – a holiday without their father in Hawaii would not be fun for the children, Annabel had said.

Gabby listened open-mouthed. She could see where it was leading but didn't want to believe it. Was he seriously expecting her to give him her blessing to go off on a three-week holiday with his ex-wife and the children? The long and the short of it was that that was exactly what he was driving at.

Charles niggled away at it like a dog with a bone from morning until night, explaining until he was blue in the face that it was not his idea. He would far rather spend his time with Gabby, but maybe Annabel was right – the kids did need their father with them.

In the end, her defences collapsed and Charles had his own way. He promised that she could trust him implicitly and that he would ring her every day and would miss her more than she could ever imagine.

Gabby spent the three weeks putting in extra hours with

her writing and in between times working her way through a backlog of books while lying in the sunshine. The three weeks passed surprisingly quickly and everything returned to normal, until Christmas.

* * *

It was late on a cold December Sunday evening. Charles had excelled himself in the kitchen cooking lobster and a lemon syllabub, serving it with not one but two bottles of champagne. And then he had popped the question.

"Annabel received another of those bloody invitations yesterday from a friend of hers who has a chalet in Innsbruck. They are going out there on Boxing Day and staying over until the ninth of January. She is desperate to go and give the kids the chance to go skiing. She asked if you might let me off the leash to go with them."

The lobster suddenly tasted like cardboard. She knew Charles when he started down this track.

"The answer is no Charles. I will not let you off the leash. It's barely five months since you all came back from Hawaii."

"She has a way of making me feel guilty. If only I could be in two places at once."

"So what did you say Charles?" Gabby asked, looking him in the eye.

"I said I'd mention it. That's all."

"That's all, is it? I'm getting the distinct feeling that this is a done deal and that you're just going through the motions with me. Am I right or am I wrong?"

"Give me a break, Gabby. We'll have Christmas Day together."

Gabby shrugged her shoulders and scowled. What was the point of arguing? "Then I'll just have to make my own plans for Boxing Day and New Year. I shall go to Scotland. I probably forgot to mention that I have friends who live in Fife." It was true; she did know people who lived in Scotland but she had no intention of visiting them. Aunt Hetty had been constantly on her mind since she had received the note from Uncle Max. The news wasn't good. It was way past time that she made her peace with them.

Seven

"Gabby?" Uncle Max framed the door, a little stooped, a little more grey, a little less hair but still the same kindly blue eyes. "I knew you would come."

"Uncle Max," Gabby replied, tears in her eyes. "What happened? This whole place, it's falling down."

"One little mistake and a lot of years, my dear," Uncle Max replied despondently.

And then she was in his arms, her head resting on his old cardigan, his hand stroking her hair just as he had when she was a child. Nothing had changed. She was so thankful.

"How's Aunt Hetty? I got your card and I came as soon as I could."

"She's pulling through. It was not such a bad attack this time."

"This time?" Gabby said. "You mean that there have been others?"

"A few, yes. She didn't want me to worry you and she didn't want you to come running just because she was having a difficult time. I told her we should have told you long ago but you know your Aunt Hetty – stubborn as a mule. But this time I wasn't going to take no for an answer. The past is the past and I hated keeping it from you," Uncle Max said thoughtfully. "You look as though life is treating you well, Gabby. Come on in."

"I don't know what to say, Uncle Max. Sorry sounds so pathetic. When I walked out on you both I did intend to come back and put things right with you, but somehow it never happened." She knew that her words were totally inadequate. No matter how much Aunt Hetty had detested Dave it had been no good reason to walk away from the two people who had taken her under their wing and cared for her as they would their own daughter. Where had eighteen years gone?

"So how is Dave?" Uncle Max asked tentatively, not wishing to drag the past up.

"He's history, a long time ago. You were both right about him. I should have listened to you. When it fell apart I was just too proud to ring you and tell you that Aunt Hetty was right all along."

"Your Aunt Hetty is resting in bed, but she'll be so pleased to see you. She's such a worrier. There's been something on her mind for years and now she won't let it rest. She keeps saying that she can't go to her grave in peace without explaining things to you."

"Does that mean that she won't get better?"

"Oh no, not at all, Gabby. She's a tough old stick, but I think that she had almost given up hope of ever seeing you again. She'll be over the moon." Uncle Max pointed to a narrow staircase. "You go right up and see her and then we'll have that catch-up. Never a day has passed when we haven't spoken about you with love."

Gabby climbed the stairs and knocked quietly on the bedroom door.

"Come in," a loud voice called. "Don't stand on ceremony

whoever you are. I'm not made of china whatever you may think."

Gabby smiled and heaved a sigh of relief. Her aunt might have had a heart attack, but she was as vocal as ever.

"Gabby? Is that really you?" she asked, sitting bolt upright in bed. "Let me look at you. You're even more beautiful than I remember. Oh, I can't tell you how good it is to see you. You should have let us know. I told Max not to bother you but I have to confess that I am so glad he did."

"Let me prop the pillows up for you," Gabby said, trying to cover her embarrassment at the welcome that she so did not deserve.

"Don't smother me, my dear. Now, before you ask, Gabby, I'm doing fine. There is nothing to worry about. I'll be on my feet again in no time."

Gabby sat on the bed lost for words.

"And how is Dave?" Aunt Hetty asked.

"History. I just told Uncle Max – a long time ago. No love lost, Aunt Hetty. He was a mistake, just as you told me he would be. It took me a while but I walked away in the end. We don't need to mention his name ever again."

"I'm sorry about that, truly I am. Did Max tell you that there was something I wanted to talk to you about?"

Gabby nodded. "Yes, he mentioned that there was something worrying you."

"I'm sorry about Dave, but you not being with him makes what I have to tell you so much easier." Hetty squeezed her niece's fingers.

"Forget Dave, Aunt Hetty. He's the past. Concentrate on getting better."

"I can't forget him altogether, Gabby, at least not until I've told you the whole story. I need to explain to you why I was so opposed to your marriage to Dave all those years ago."

"It doesn't matter, Aunt Hetty. It's water under the bridge."

"That is as it may be, but I still need to explain a few things. You see, I was just trying to protect you. Your Uncle Max and I are the only ones who know the real story. It concerns your mother as well."

It was a long time since they had spoken together of her mother. Gabby remembered winter evenings in front of the fire with her Aunt and the many stories she told of their childhood, some of which were undoubtedly embellished and others of which were so incredible that they just had to be true. As sisters, they had been very close.

"You see, your mother knew Dave's father, Kirk, when she was a girl. I think she was sixteen at the time. There's no easy way to put this Gabby, but she had a baby with him and afterward, the baby was adopted. It was long before your father's time. She told Kirk that she was pregnant. He was young too and probably frightened about the consequences and denied that it was his. Anyway, our mother arranged for me to take your mother off on a little holiday until after the baby was born which we did. It was a girl. It was your mother's wish for the baby to be adopted. She simply wanted what was best for the child. It was never mentioned in the family again."

Gabby turned her face away and looked out of the window. As a child she had longed for a brother or a sister more than anything. She had loved her mother dearly, but had she ever known her?

"A girl?" she whispered, "So does this mean that I have a half-sister somewhere?"

"Yes, Gabby, but believe me I have no idea who adopted her or where she might be now. I do know that they called her Nancy. She would be in her early fifties now, probably with a family of her own."

"A sister. I have a half-sister?" Gabby could hardly believe her ears.

Hetty nodded. "When your mother met your father in her early twenties she told him nothing about it. He was a very Christian man and Victorian in his ways. Everything was black and white – there was no grey. He would never have married her if he had known. I always thought that they had a strange sort of marriage, but your mother was always very loyal to him and had great respect for your father. Even though Kirk lived just a few miles away their paths never crossed again until many years later. When you were ten years old, your mother received a letter from him. In it, he said that he wanted his daughter back."

Gabby sat back thoughtfully. "But he was my father-in-law. He never mentioned her after I married Dave."

"He wrote to your mother asking about the child. Your mother had long since closed that chapter and told him that she had no idea where the child was and had no intention of trying to find out. That sounds cruel, but it wasn't. She knew that the child had gone to a loving couple who could not have children themselves and the last thing she wanted was for the child's life to be disrupted. He kept writing and in his last letter he threatened that his next letter on the subject would be to your father. Your mother waited for the post to arrive every day so that she could intercept letters. She succeeded on several occasions but knew that her luck could not last. The past ate away at her – that she had had a baby and let her go and that she had never been honest with your father. Looking back over the years there have been occasions when I have wondered if your father had known about it all along. It would have accounted for the way he treated her. He was a cold fish, Gabby. She deserved better."

"So is that why she took her own life?" Gabby asked, forcing the words from her mouth. It was almost twenty-six years ago but the memory of losing her mother was as raw as the day it had happened.

"So you knew all along, Gabby?" Hetty shook her head. "I always hoped that you would think that she had died from natural causes. I couldn't tell you the truth – it was her dying wish was that no one, except Max and I, should ever know. I found her that day. She had left a letter for me explaining why she could not cope anymore but more particularly asking me to take special care of you."

"It wasn't difficult to work out," Gabby said.

"The doctor was very kind and mentioned her suicide to no one. I always held Kirk, Dave's father, responsible for her death. We didn't hear from Kirk again. And all those years later…you and Dave. I thought that Kirk had encouraged your marriage to Dave as a way of getting back at your mother. One way or another he was going to have one of her daughters. I couldn't tell you why I forbad you to marry him." Aunt Hetty took a deep breath, closed her eyes and slowly exhaled. "Can you ever forgive me?"

Gabby sat on the edge of the bed and gave her aunt a gentle hug. "But I shouldn't have walked out on you. Can we start all over again?"

Hetty smiled. "Let's put it all behind us Gabby and look to happier times. Now, tell me about you."

Ten minutes later Gabby drew breath. How had she managed to pack eighteen years into just ten minutes? Maybe that said something in itself.

"And then I met a very nice man last year and we got married soon afterward. We have our moments but you'll like him. I'll bring him to meet you both soon," Gabby said.

"And, what's his name?"

"Charles. And I'm now Gabby Fairbrother. That's the third surname I've had and I don't intend to have any more. Now, tell me when these attacks started, Aunt Hetty?"

"Oh, several years ago now, just after we moved here – a bit of age catching up with me combined with a lot of stress."

"I don't remember you ever getting stressed about anything. You always used to take everything in your stride and say that life was too short."

"It's another long story, Gabby. I'm getting just a little tired now so why don't you ask your Uncle Max about it over a cup of tea? Then come back and see us again very soon. I'm feeling so very much better now. Seeing you is the best tonic in the world. Don't be a stranger."

"Never again, Aunt Hetty. You're stuck with me now. I may even see you tomorrow. Love you."

* * *

By the time Uncle Max's story was finished they were both swimming in tea.

"So, Uncle Max you are telling me that this crook has just got away with it, that he walked off into the sunset leaving you all to live in this state? It's criminal. So, is that why that old lady is up a ladder pruning trees and Andy is mowing the

71

meadow trying to find a croquet lawn? It beggars belief. How can you possibly live in this mess?"

"We have no choice in the matter, Gabby. There are ten cottages occupied at Magnolia Court and thirteen of us living here. All the cottages are in the same state as ours and all the communal facilities are in an even more sorry state. We do our best to maintain it, but none of us is getting any younger. Would you like the guided tour? It's not a pretty sight."

Eight

Gabby climbed into the car and slammed the door shut. Andy, wiping the sweat from his forehead, looked up alarmed and waved as she yanked the car into gear and floored the accelerator. Out of the open window, she thought she heard Andy shout that she might leave a little gravel for another day.

Potholes. Bugger the potholes. They were the least of their worries.

In her mind she pictured the monster that had been responsible for leaving her aunt and uncle and all those other elderly folk in the state he had – an animal, uncaring, unfeeling and the scum of the earth. He had robbed them, robbed them blind.

And where had she been while all this was happening? In Surbiton, cocooned in her own cosy little world. She was as much to blame as anybody; there was no escaping it. If she had been there for them then maybe she could have helped them.

And how could they just accept it even after all this time, surrounded by constant reminders? The whole place was falling down around their ears. Their dreams had been shattered. What should have been the ultimate in retirement living was probably the worst place in the world to live out their retirement years. But to a man and dog, they had no option but to make the best of it. Nobody in their right minds would ever buy the properties from them. In their current state, they had little or no value.

When her anger subsided she put herself in Uncle Max's shoes. You can only fight for so long, especially a battle that cannot be won – the disappearing man. How could anybody disappear off the face of the earth in this day and age? But that apparently was precisely what he had done. Left them high and dry and vanished into thin air.

She had to admire Uncle Max's tenacity – three whole years he had stuck at building a court case and trying to trace the man so that he could be brought to justice. Nothing came cheap and it had almost bankrupted them all. Uncle Max had valiantly led the battle and long ago he had become battle weary.

It was more than criminal.

Now she knew why Dot and Dennis had been working on the trees and Andy was fighting to find the croquet pitch that might once have graced the lawns in front of the old mansion. They had no choice – do or die. There were no fairy godmothers to wave wands and no long-lost benefactors to pay people to do the work for them. They deserved a medal – every one of them.

Uncle Max had made the guided tour sound like a walk in the park but it was far from it. His words echoed in Gabby's ears – she was not going to forget them in a long time.

"In its time it must have been quite magnificent," Uncle Max had said. "It was originally built back in the early 1800s – that was the Regency Period – but in the Tudor Gothic Style.

A very odd thing to do but we have to assume that was what the owner wanted. It was built for Sir James Fotheringay. He was quite a leading light in the industrial revolution. I gather that he made his fortune in textiles. It must have many stories to tell. At one time it was a school and then a hospital and then a monastery. During the First World War, it was used as a convalescent home for injured officers. It reverted to being a school again after the war and closed its doors for the final time back in the mid-eighties. From what I have been able to find out it was in a pretty good state of repair then. Do you see those renovations on either side of the façade, Gabby? Done by a craftsman, I would guess. The bricks are such a rich red and so ornate in places. A lot of craftsmen worked on this house and many apprentices cut their teeth on it." Max gazed nostalgically up at the front of the mansion.

All Gabby could see was crumbling masonry, moss growing in gaps in the rendering and gargoyles around the top of the building, which were now almost unrecognisable: in short, a complete and utter wreck.

"Let's go in," Uncle Max had said. "This, Gabby, was to have been the heart and soul of the community where you would have found the residents' lounge, the cocktail bar, the main reception and the restaurant. The artist's impressions were truly magnificent – lovely deep sofas sitting on Persian and Indian carpets on top of oak flooring, not forgetting the grand piano in the corner of the room."

Uncle Max opened the huge oak front doors, rotting and creaking with age. Gabby had pictured what it would be like long before she stepped into the building and she had not been disappointed.

"It's quite safe to go in so long as we are careful. We don't lock the doors anymore. What would be the point? This was once the great hall. Can you imagine how magnificent it would have been in its day, Gabby? You can just hear the music and see all those elegant couples waltzing gracefully around the room."

However great it might have been once, it was little short of a bombsite. Shafts of light danced on the warped oak floor where roof tiles had been displaced, or had fallen away, making room for the elements to do their worst. A thick layer of dust covered the floor. Plaster had fallen away and congregated in great piles at the foot of the walls. Cobwebs drifted in the breeze from the thirty-foot-high ceiling.

"So did the restoration of the great hall ever get off the ground?" Gabby asked.

"Oh yes. It started when the first tranche of cottages was being built. There was scaffolding up everywhere. The stained-glass windows at the back were taken away, repaired and replaced. The roof was repaired or so we were told. We were so excited about it and quite happy to wait because we knew that it could not be done overnight. Besides we had the facilities in the old stable block at the back to use in the meantime. They were finished just before we moved into the cottages. We can walk through there now if you like."

Gabby remembered a fleeting moment of relief. At least they had had some communal facilities. It was not a total disaster.

The moment they walked in through the stable doors, her face dropped. A long corridor had been built the length of the stable block with several doors leading off to the right. It was damp and musky. A fading sign on the first door invited them to enter the Pool and Spa. The pool was empty, the lining cracked, and the once blue and yellow ceramic tiles that surrounded the pool were dangerously uneven and missing in places. Faded sunbeds, covered in cobwebs, were stacked against the walls and gave pleasure only to the spiders that had made them their home. Daylight streamed through gaps in the roof. Pathetically, buckets had been placed strategically around the pool to catch the worst of the rainfall. The adjoining changing rooms reeked of mould. There was no sign of a spa.

"But you said that you all used these facilities when you moved in," Gabby said.

"We did, but it was short-lived. For six months it was fine and then there was one problem after another. By that time he had disappeared. We closed the doors and left it. It's been like this since – beyond redemption."

The gymnasium had fared no better. Adjoining the pool-room, and sharing the same roof, it had suffered similar problems. Running machines, steppers, rowing machines and weight-training equipment had long since been abandoned. Rust coated the mechanical parts while the electrical cables and plugs had been pulled from the sockets for safety. An electrician, called in after a basic problem, had condemned every aspect of the installation work and declared the area to be a major safety hazard.

The library was sad beyond belief. Damp patches stained the walls and bookshelves hung precariously from walls. It explained why there were piles of books stacked up in the hallway of Uncle Max and Aunt Hetty's cottage.

After a few miles she eased off the accelerator – killing innocent motorists would do little to help matters unless of course one of them happened to be the monster who had built Magnolia Court and then left the residents to grapple with the consequences.

Their last port of call had been the golf course. Vimy Ridge, as Uncle Max referred to it, was set some fifty yards back from the mansion and the stable block and almost towered over both buildings. "That's the golf course, Gabby. It was to have been an eighteen-hole course originally, but then they had to reduce it to nine holes – something to do with making room for the clubhouse bar and freeing up space for the next phase of the development. Another twenty cottages should have been built there. We didn't mind. If we had wanted to do so we could do the eighteen holes by going round twice. It was no hardship.

"We may not have a golf course and we may not have a clubhouse, but we do have the nineteenth hole as we like to call it. Do you see that little timber box on stilts over there? Well, that is the only building on this site that has stood the test of time. It arrived on the back of a huge lorry. It was where the contractors sheltered when the weather was bad and made their mugs of tea. We've put a little generator in there now and a few electric fires and a kettle. That's our meeting place. It's not quite the great hall, but we like it. We try not to mention his name when we're together. It brings back too many unhappy memories. Life is a strange thing, Gabby. You really never know whom you can trust. His name was Harry Trumper, the man who first conceived all this and then robbed us of our dreams."

* * *

It was the third time that someone had sounded a horn at

her. Normally Gabby would have apologised for her careless driving with an appropriate gesture. The gestures that she returned that day were anything but appropriate, inviting more blasts from horns and several less than polite verbal responses. She couldn't have cared less. What did they know about anything? Gabby glanced at the sign ahead. In what seemed no time at all she was almost home – back to the safety of her cottage. There were no lights on; Charles was away in Innsbruck enjoying his après-ski while she was home with nothing to think about but the past eighteen years and Magnolia Court.

Gabby put her feet up in front of the television and flicked through the channels. It was all rubbish, but maybe that was what she needed to take her mind off Magnolia Court. No one was going to treat her aunt and uncle that way and get away with it. Easy words, but what the hell could she do where so many others had failed?

The weather forecaster predicted thunderstorms in the next day or two reminding Gabby that the residents would need to empty the buckets in the poolroom. All roads led back to Magnolia Court.

Gabby reached for the phone. She would ring Charles. He would know what to do. And then she hesitated. Wouldn't he think it a bit strange that she was only now telling him about the aunt and uncle whom she had not seen for eighteen years and that she was not in Scotland at all? Maybe she would tell him later.

Aunt Hetty, Uncle Max and Magnolia Court were now her number one priority. In the next two weeks, she would help them out with any job they pointed her way, and while she was there she would start to dig the dirt on Harry Trumper.

Uncle Max had told her to leave well alone, that it was all history and best forgotten. But it wasn't history to her; it was today's news.

Nine

It was the third day in a row that Gabby had spent at Magnolia Court. The first day back, she had helped Uncle Max put up some new bookshelves in the small hallway before taking Duncan down into the town in Andy's van. On the second day, she had donned her wellington boots and set off to help Andy uncover the croquet lawn. There had been whoops of delight when they uncovered four of the old croquet hoops, which were now 'in restoration' in Andy's sitting room.

"I told Jennifer that you would give her a hand today, Gabby," her aunt said. "She's up at the nineteenth hole giving it a makeover, whatever that may mean. I'm sure you'll soon find out."

"No problem. I'm on my way." Gabby slipped her coat back on and walked up to the nineteenth hole. Peering around the door she saw that Jennifer was up on the top rung of the stepladder seemingly hanging a curtain to the tune of Bali Hai.

"Hello Gabby, just in time," she called, without looking down. "Hetty mentioned that she'd send you up to give me a hand today. I've nearly finished hanging this one. You can give a hand with the others if you like." Jennifer slotted the last hook onto the ring on the curtain rail and let the curtain cascade to the ground. Wearing a Hawaiian shirt over a thick jumper, Jennifer descended the ladder chattering all the while. "Did I mention that I was a costume designer for a West End theatrical productions company and that I even did a bit of set design? This velvet came from one of the theatres. They were going to throw it away, but I couldn't bear to see it go so I've kept it all this time. This room is going to be transformed into one of the stage settings from *South Pacific* – always one of my favourite musicals. What beautiful sea-green this velvet is. When the sun shines it looks deep blue and on a grey day like this, it looks deep green – just like the sea. I'm going to introduce warm, sunny colours into the room with the cushions and I've got some lovely fabric smothered in seashells, which we can use to make table covers. Duncan found me a set of six huge posters of *South Pacific* on eBay and those will be pinned up on the two big walls. How about a cup of tea first?"

"Uncle Max told me about what happened with Magnolia Court," Gabby began cautiously. "It makes me mad. I wish I could do something to help."

"Nothing much you can do, dear," Jennifer replied, vaguely eyeing the curtains.

"There must be something. I thought maybe getting a picture of him might be a start. Do you mind me asking what you remember of him?"

"No, I'm quite happy to tell you anything I can remember." Jennifer frowned. "It was a long time ago, Gabby. We only met him once and when I say met him, well, that's not very accurate. You see it was in a very big conference room and he made the presentation about Magnolia Court from a stage. I was almost at the back of the room. There were probably

82

about a hundred people in the audience. He seemed to be such a nice genuine man, entirely selfless. He started off by telling us about his vision for a retirement complex – that was the word he used – and how much he wanted to be a trailblazer for luxury retirement living. He was a good-looking man but without any outstanding features – a good head of dark wavy hair, medium height, well-built but not overweight. He had the most annoying habit of keeping his hands in his pockets and jingling his change. You could hear it even from where I was sitting."

"I know someone who does just the same thing," Gabby laughed. "It's a man thing I think. We should sew up their pockets."

"He was quite articulate. I'd guess that he'd lived in the East End at some time. He was a smooth talker, that's for sure. Smiled a lot. Seemed very confident and comfortable in himself. When he announced that the first ten to sign up for a cottage would be taken on a trip to California to see a retirement complex similar to the one that he was going to build, you could have heard a pin drop."

"So, was that why you signed up?" Gabby asked, surprised that someone like Jennifer should have been taken in so easily.

"Oh no, it wasn't that, although it did sound attractive. It was the people I met when we went to look at the detailed plans. One of the architects was charming; the other one I wasn't quite so keen on. We all hit it off straightaway and we all decided that there was nothing to be lost by enjoying a bit of Californian sunshine. They promised to refund our deposit if we didn't like what we saw. Nothing to lose, was there? We were only there for three days but by the time we got back, it was as though we'd known each other all our lives. We really wanted to live together and that's why we all bought our cottages at Magnolia Court. Sorry that I can't be of more help. If you really want to find out more about him you should pop down and see Amy, and don't be fooled by what you find. She's as sharp as a needle when it comes to remembering things in the past."

"I'll do that. Thanks."

"Time to get on, my dear," Jennifer said, clearing the tray away. "Let's tackle that next curtain. How's your sewing?"

"Fair. I can sew in a straight line, but that's about the sum total of it. My mother was the one for that. She was an amazing seamstress." Gabby smiled to herself, remembering the mornings she had spent sitting beside her mother watching her work.

"A straight line will do to start. You'll soon get the hang of going round corners. There's a lot to be done. But this afternoon we're just hanging the curtains."

"I can help you with the sewing tomorrow if you like."

"No, not tomorrow. Tomorrow is my chemo day. We can pick it up again the day after," Jennifer announced matter-of-factly.

"I'm so sorry. I didn't know," Gabby said, taken aback by Jennifer's statement.

"No reason why you should. The others all know that I don't like to make a fuss about it. They understand. Breast cancer, you know. Happens to over forty thousand women each year – a bit like getting flu but needs a bit more careful treatment."

"Do you have a family to take care of you?"

"I have a daughter and a son. Janine lives in Carlisle. She's got three children to look after and another on the way. Jamie moves around a lot. I don't see much of either of them. I like to let the children get on with their lives. I've got all the help and support I need right here at Magnolia Court and at the hospital. My friends here keep their distance but are always here when I need them, and the Macmillan nurses are saints.

It had been just a bit tougher than Jennifer was prepared to admit to anybody. She'd gone to the hospital after receiving a recall following the biennial mammogram that she never missed. There was a one in twenty chance that anything was wrong, so the letter said. It was far more likely to be a little shadow that had shown up on the X-ray. She had been on her own when the radiologist told her that she had breast cancer. Thankfully, they had said, they had caught it early but would she like a cup of tea before she left? She remembered laughing and thinking that she couldn't quite share their view that there was anything to be thankful for and what was more it wasn't tea she needed – it was a bloody good gin and tonic.

During her next visit to the hospital, the oncologist and his nurse described the treatment that they would be giving her – surgery followed by chemotherapy followed by a course of combined chemo and Herceptin and nicely rounded up with a twenty-day course of radiotherapy. If all ran to plan, they said, she would almost certainly suffer from nausea, severe tiredness, other aches and pains and her brain would probably turn to jelly for a few days after each session. Laughing, they called it chemo brain. She remembered playing the game and returning the laugh – very funny.

A few friends in her old social circle outside of Magnolia couldn't cope with it. She had the big 'C' emblazoned across her forehead. To them she was no longer Jennifer but a friend who had cancer. They were soon conspicuous by their absence. The cards of sympathy had found their way straight into the bin – anyone would think she had died and she had absolutely no intention of giving them that satisfaction.

With every message of sympathy that came, she had become more and more determined to show them all that not only could she get through the process without making a fuss, but she would also continue to do all the things that normal people do, and if that included a few gin and tonics now and again then that was the way it would be.

Jennifer stroked her long strawberry blond hair thoughtfully and smiled at Gabby. "I suppose you're wondering whether this is all mine. Well, it's not. This is my best wig. My hair wasn't dissimilar to this before it all fell out. Quite amusing really – I spent a fortune on getting it cut and styled so that when it did eventually fall out, it wouldn't be quite so much of a blow. Sod's law, Gabby, it fell out the very following morning when I had a shower. But it will grow again – just a matter of time and in the meantime, I have to put up with my theatrical wigs, which I just love. And the best thing about it is that I can change the colour of my hair and my hairstyle any time I want to. I've got quite a collection of wigs."

"It doesn't seem to have stopped you getting on with things," Gabby said admiringly.

"It may not work for everyone Gabby, but to my mind, the way of getting through it is to keep busy – focus on other things. That's why I'm doing this project and then when I've finished this one I'll find another. And by the time I've finished that it'll all be over. I've always been a busy person, Gabby, and I am not about to change just because Mr C came for an uninvited visit."

"It sounds like the theatre has always been in your blood.

This room is going to look so colourful when it's finished."
Gabby thought it best to change the subject.

"I've always loved colour and fashion, Gabby. When I was
no more than a child, I begged my mother to teach me to sew
and after that, I made all my own clothes. You could buy the
fabric for half a crown in those days. What could you buy for
half a crown today? I spent every last penny of my pocket
money buying swathes of brightly coloured fabric down on
the market. My mother was horrified when I started to dye
strands of my hair to match my outfits. In the fifties it simply
wasn't done.

"Mary Quant was my heroine and all I wanted for my
birthday was to go up to London to Bazaar, Mary's boutique.
There was no question that we would buy anything. It was
more than enough to stand outside and gaze in the window.
I was a naughty girl – I copied her designs and made them
for myself. I was the envy of all my friends. And then I told
my parents that I wanted to make a career in fashion and that
I was going to start by going to the local art college. That
didn't go down well at all. Beatniks, druggies, long-haired
layabouts – that's what my mother called them. But she knew
she was on a hiding to nothing and so I did a one-year pre-
dip course and much to my amazement I got a place at the
London College of Fashion.

"My student days were the best days of my life and I didn't
waste one minute of them. I had a dream – my heart was
set on becoming a theatrical costume designer. I needed to
get work experience so I joined several amateur dramatic
societies as their wardrobe mistress. I studied during the day
and worked at the theatres in the evenings. It paid dividends.
I was 'spotted' as they say. A West End director came to

one of our little amateur productions and so admired the costumes that he asked to meet me after the performance and said that he had a job with my name on it just as soon as I graduated. I had delusions of grandeur, of course, imagining myself designing the costumes for the stars from day one. It wasn't quite like that – I had to start from the bottom. It was almost ten years before I had my own studio and responsibility for the design and production of costumes for one of his productions. It was *Showboat.* Can you imagine how thrilling that was? Where did the years go?"

"When did you give it up?" Gabby asked.

"It was in March 2002. So stupid. I fell off a ladder and broke my hip. I was sixty at the time and I knew that it wouldn't be long before I had to hang up my shoes and retire. That made the decision for me. I was looking for a new start. That's when the brochure for Magnolia Court dropped through my letterbox. It changed my life," she said. "For the poorer, but for the better. Now, less of me. Let's hang the rest of those curtains and I shall send you on your way. And if you want an excuse to pop in and see Amy, you can take this scarf with you. She left it at my cottage and I've been meaning to return it to her." Jennifer said nostalgically, as she opened the door for Gabby to leave, "I still dream about the theatre, Gabby. And I have a recurrent dream that I will be involved in one more production. I don't know what it will be but I am quite sure it will happen."

Little did she know that her dream would soon come true.

Ten

Gabby knocked on the door and waited patiently.

"Who is it?" she heard someone call from inside.

"Gabby. Jennifer asked me to stop by to return your scarf."

"Gabby? Oh, Gabby. How lovely of you to call. It's ages since I last saw you. Where have you been hiding? Come in, my dear. Don't stand there in the cold." A beaming Amy opened the door, delighted to see her afternoon visitor. "I've heard all about you from your aunt – all good I hasten to add. There's nothing like a happy reunion after so many years. I'm pleased for all of you. I was talking to Hetty long before Christmas and she mentioned that you might be coming to visit. Let's sit down and we'll have some tea and a nice chat. It must be going on for three, Gabby. I fell asleep when *The Archers* were on so that must have been just after two."

"Actually, Amy, it's almost four-thirty and you are right, it's definitely time for a cup of tea."

"Don't tell me I have been asleep for over two and half hours. I don't believe it. Well, that must be why I'm absolutely parched. You'll excuse me for one minute won't you, my dear, while I put the kettle on."

"Can I help?" Gabby asked politely, as Amy scuttled off towards the kitchen. For all the renovations that needed doing, it was a comfortable home with two chintz armchairs placed facing a gas-effect log fire separated by a pretty bow-legged table covered in a pristine white lace cloth.

"Here I am, Gabby. I've found my handbag now. It really worries me when I can't find anything." Amy sat down. Gabby didn't mention the tea.

Amy snuggled down in her chair and pulled her wrap over her shoulders. "These little cottages are terribly draughty, you know, Gabby. The wind whistles in under the doors and the windows might just as well be left wide open for all the good they do at keeping the warmth in. Now, what were we going to chat about?"

Gabby laughed and proceeded cautiously. "Could we talk about the man who left you all in this state?"

"You mean Harry Trumper, do you?" Amy said quizzically.

"Yes. Aunt Hetty and Uncle Max filled me in on the background. I still cannot get my head around the fact that such a thing could happen, and then for the man to disappear in a puff of smoke – it's just beyond belief."

"You're right about that, Gabby. I am parched, dear. Would you like a cup of tea?"

"That would be lovely, Amy. Let me give you a hand." Gabby got up and followed Amy into the kitchen; at least this time they might get a cup of tea. "I don't want to rake up the past, but I'm curious to understand what happened all those years ago. Would it upset you to talk about it?"

"I've got just the thing to start with," Amy said, pointing towards the bedroom. "I've got a copy of the original brochure and all the original artist's impressions of how Magnolia Court was going to look and all the wonderful facilities we were going to be able to enjoy. It's in the bedroom.

I saw it the other day. I must have had a premonition that you were coming. I know I put it somewhere safe. You finish making the tea and I'll go and find it."

Gabby sat back, poured a cup of tea for herself and listened as drawers were opened and slammed closed while Amy listed all her 'safe places' out loud.

"I'm just going to check my handbag, Gabby. I've got one of those big ones that you can put everything in and never find anything. Quite why I might have put it in there I don't know, but it's worth a look." Amy tipped the bag's contents out on the carpet. "Well, what do you know? What do we have here? I knew it was here somewhere."

The photograph on the cover of the glossy brochure was of a grand house, unmistakably the mansion at the centre of Magnolia Court.

"This is where it all started, Gabby. This was the brochure we were given when we were first introduced to the development." Amy opened the brochure to the first page. "This is the great hall. Isn't it beautiful? I can still see myself sitting on that purple velvet stool sipping my gin and it before dinner in the restaurant. Do you know that they planned to open the restaurant to non-residents for lunch and dinner? It was a clever idea – people could pop up to Magnolia, have a round of golf and then relax over a delicious lunch or dinner in the restaurant. It was a way of keeping the costs down for the residents. We were all for it and it's always nice to meet new people."

Amy turned the page. "And this is the swimming pool. And look at the lights in the pool and the handrails down the steps – just what we all needed. And it was only four feet deep from end to end. And those lovely comfortable chairs to relax in after a swim. You couldn't ask for more, could you? The hairdressers and the spa would have been right next door to the pool. We were so looking forward to our library as well – somewhere quiet where we could sit and read the papers. Duncan was going to teach us all how to use a computer properly. But the library was short-lived as well. It was so cold and damp in there and then the mould started to grow on the walls. We had to pack up and move everything out.

"And then there was the weekly schedule of events – trips to theatres, shops and gardens, craft lessons, the book club and all the entertainers who were going to come and visit us. But most important to us all, of course, was the promise of on-site care as and when we needed it. We would have been able to choose the right level of care to suit our needs and our pockets. There was going to be a small self-contained flat for a nurse to live in and a little surgery so that we could go and see him or her if we had any problems. And there was going to be somebody who would do a bit of cleaning around the cottages if we needed that little bit of extra help. That, Gabby, is really why I chose to buy my cottage at Magnolia Court. You see I knew a long time ago that I was beginning to forget things and that one day I would need to have friends close around me, some help with the housework and probably a little nursing care. We paid three hundred and fifty thousand pounds for each of the cottages – a fortune to all of us. Then we paid two hundred and fifty thousand up front for twenty years' subscription to all of the services within the community – including the care help. It sounds such a lot of money but at twelve thousand a year it wasn't so much. You can't get a room in a care home for much less than a thousand pounds a week. It would have seen me out, Gabby. I pride myself that I am not a fool and the whole thing made so much sense to me at the time. Of course, I wasn't alone in being taken in by it."

"A fool is something I would never, ever call you, Amy. Is there anything you remember about him? About Harry Trumper?"

"Well, not exactly about him, Gabby. We never really met him in person. Medium height, dark hair, broad shouldered, bushy eyebrows – something peculiar about them, probably in his mid-thirties, and he most definitely had an East End accent. He seemed a lovely man, kind, and the sort you'd like to have as a son and he was left handed. It's funny how some things stick in your mind."

Gabby sighed. A medium height, dark-haired man in his mid-thirties who was left-handed and jangled his change in his pocket – not much to go on.

"But I learned quite a bit about him. You see, I spent quite a lot of time down at the site soon after the mansion and stables refurbishment started. Mugs of tea – lots of mugs of tea – that's the way to a man's heart. I got on well with two of the fellows – one was called Stan and the other Dirk. I think they thought of me as their dotty old gran, a harmless little old lady, which of course is what I wanted them to think. But I had my suspicions about a few things. The progress seemed to be very erratic. It seemed from what I could gather that they were all employed directly by this Harry Trumper and had done work for him for many, many years, mostly in small-property development. Stan, who called himself the foreman, seemed to be in charge. There didn't seem to be a project manager. I sensed that none of them liked our Mr Trumper very much. He never once came to the site. I am sure that on one occasion I heard Stan refer to him as an utter bastard, excuse my language, and he then used words which began with C and F neither of which I care to repeat. He was angry about something. I gathered later that it was because some of the supplies hadn't arrived.

"And then there was that last fateful occasion. I went down with my tray of teas and there they all were huddled together. Well, I've never been one to stand back so I went over and joined them. 'Is this a private party or can anybody join in?' I asked Stan. He put his arm around me and – these were his very words – 'It seems Mrs A (that's what he called me) that Mr Wonderful has done what is commonly known as a bunk. We've not been paid and there is a notice up to say that the office is closed until further notice. I've rung round me mates and nobody has seen hide or hair of him for over a week. It's not just us that have been left high and dry, and then me mate told me about a rumour he had heard that the police were looking for him – something to do with a fire.' They packed up all their tools, got in their vans and waved to me as they set off down the track. Rough, but a nice bunch of men all the same. I could see that they didn't really want to walk out on us. And that was that Gabby. Last we saw of any of them."

Gabby sat back thoughtfully. What a mess, but at least now she knew that something had probably triggered Mr Trumper's sudden disappearance. "And how are you coping, Amy?" If she had needed some help all those years ago then surely she needed more now.

"Much better than I had expected, dear. It's a question of when needs must, the devil drives. But I've noticed just the last few months that I'm not as sharp as I was," Amy said sadly.

"Do you want to tell me about it, Amy? Why don't I put the kettle on again?" Gabby said.

Eleven

It was the easiest article she had ever written for the magazine and it would be published with the blessing of both Amy and Duncan.

The Reality Of Ageing

Getting older is not a disease, says Penelope Sarthe. She hears from an amazing 89 year old about how to age naturally and get the best out of later life.

Yesterday I met a very special lady and we talked at length about age and her memories.

On my way home, I thought back over our two-hour conversation that seemed more like minutes and started to question my own preconceptions of the more mature members of our society. I am ashamed to say that I found myself sadly lacking in understanding and sympathy and, as a result, I have resolved to do something about it. Starting now.

Let me tell you something about this lady first. She is in her late eighties and, you may find it strange that I say so, wise beyond her years. She describes herself as eighty-nine years young. She asked me to define the word 'old' which I struggled to do. She then went on to tell me that 'old' is a word that has little meaning: we are one day old when we are born, we are one year old on our first birthday, we are eighteen years old on our eighteenth, and if we are lucky we are quite old when we die.

We progressed to talking about her fears of which there were few. My special lady survived the war, lost her fiancé, her parents and a brother to the war. Working for the Foreign Office, she played a very significant role safeguarding the lives of many of her fellow citizens. In those days people knew the meaning of fear, but it was not something that any of them discussed or would admit.

Her fear now stems mainly from the media – people such as me who, through their work, have influence over the views of others. Needless to say, her comment made me sit up and take even more note of what she was about to tell me. She tells me quite calmly that she is probably suffering from dementia or Alzheimer's, or so she is led to believe from coverage in newspapers and on TV and radio. She recognises the symptoms in herself: loss of short-term memory, repeating herself and finding the organisation of simple tasks more difficult than they had once been. These she accepts as part of the natural ageing process. She reminds me that suffering from a deteriorating memory is nothing new in those of more mature years and only to be expected.

Awareness, she says, is the key to coping.

Her fear stems from the fact that the natural ageing process has now been labeled as a disease – dementia and Alzheimer's. She does not consider herself to be diseased. She explains that she perceives a marked change in the way that elderly people are treated by a society since the word 'disease' was introduced to describe their ageing. Diseases are frightening, diseases are communicable, and diseases are incurable, she tells me. The perception is that those with 'diseases' should be put away somewhere where they can do themselves and others no harm.

She tells me quite firmly that it is not in her imagination and cites, as one example, a recent trip she made to a supermarket when, because she was a little slow at organising her shopping and paying for her purchases, the customer behind her was heard to remark, "She's got dementia, you know. It's a disease. I read about it." My special lady explains to me that supermarket shopping is, for her, a trial, especially at the checkout when the list of questions is endless. Does she have her loyalty card? Would she like cash back? Would she like to pay for shopping bags? Would she like help with her packing? Would she like to use contact-free? Would she insert her card, enter the number and take it out now?

I sympathise with her. I find the whole process a trial myself and I like to think I am a co-ordinated, well-organised person.

She goes on to tell me that the brain is a funny thing, as she puts it. She is able to recall every moment of her younger days: dates, times, places, people – their names, faces, and families. Her recall of events of the past is quite astounding and, I would not hesitate to admit, far better than my own. She explains that she has simply reached the stage in life where her brain has absorbed so much information that it is now very selective about what it retains and what it regards as unimportant. Thus the day-to-day trivia is filtered out, but the important information remains. I am left wondering if it is not I who has the problem – my brain is terminally awash with day-to-day matters regularly clouding out more important issues in life.

She finds the words that 'disappear' a continual frustration. She tells me that she sees them in her mind's eye, but they hide away and on the bad days she has to rely on other people to fill the gaps in the conversation. On the good days, she finds and uses words that she probably last used in a spelling test at school. Where, she asks me, have these been hiding all her life?

I listen to my special lady telling me that things are not what they used to be. I find myself silently agreeing with her while the words that came out of my mouth were, "Times change, we have to move on with the times." As I drove home I tried to count the number of times in the past few weeks that I too have said that things are not as they used to be. I lost count when I left the motorway.

It is so often the case that we hear how crooks target the elderly and more vulnerable members of society. I was shocked to hear my special lady tell me about how she and her friends had invested most of their savings in their dream retirement homes: cottages within a complex served by a communal lounge, bar and dining room, library, pool and spa, golf course and onsite care facilities. The cottages were the first to be built and the residents moved in to them. Those of the community facilities that were built soon deteriorated and were condemned. Other facilities were never built. The developer disappeared leaving them high and dry. My special lady and her friends have come to terms with their situation, have learned from their mistakes and have been highly resourceful in turning a disaster into a positive outcome.

Following my meeting with this special lady I have rid myself of many preconceptions I had concerning our more elderly friends and replaced them with an image of a generation that is spirited, knowledgeable, philosophical and resourceful – one that has true grit.

If any of my readers feel a twinge of conscience about their own preconceptions, my message to you is that it is never too late to make amends.

Twelve

"It's just great to be home, Gabby. The snow was great and the kids had a wonderful time. I left them to get on with it for most of the time." Charles put his arm around her. "There's nothing like a good log fire in your own home and a lovely woman in your arms. I missed you. Tell me about your trip to Scotland. Did you enjoy it?"

"I enjoyed it as much as anybody could without their other half. New Year as you know is the big celebration in Scotland so we went to a local hotel for Hogmanay. Michael wore the full works – kilt, Prince Charles jacket, sporran and not forgetting the *skean-dhu* in his sock. I wore my black dress with the diamantes over the shoulders. It was fine. They send their love and want to meet up sometime," Gabby replied, ready to change the subject. "I had intended to stay up there until yesterday but I got called back to the office. Several of the writers are off sick so I came back early."

"They're lucky to have you at that magazine. What are you going to be working on this year?" Charles asked, sipping at a glass of whisky.

Gabby raised her eyebrows – since when had Charles shown any interest in her work let alone asked what she was working on? To her knowledge he had never read any of the articles she had written. "Actually I've got three assignments that are going to keep me pretty busy for the next few months. I don't think you would find them very sexy but they interest me: Alzheimer's and dementia, the injustices heaped on disabled people and then I am going to run a few articles on the plight of the Jews in Germany during and after the war."

"Crusader now, hey?" Charles laughed.

"You could say that. It's all going to take a lot of research and work so I might have to put more time in at the office than

I normally would."

"That's fine. There's a new restaurant opened up in Kingston down by the river. It sounds wonderful. I thought I might take you there for lunch next week to make up for leaving you on your own for so long. How about we go on Wednesday next week?" he asked.

"Sorry Charles – I've got an appointment that day. Thursday or Friday would be better for me." It was no word of a lie – she had already arranged to spend the day at Magnolia; Emanuel had invited her, Aunt Hetty and Uncle Max to take afternoon tea with him and Dinah in their cottage.

Gabby put her feet up and let her mind wander back to Emanuel's story; it was fascinating.

* * *

He was the son that they had not expected to be blessed with. Born six years later than his twin brothers and when his mother was in her late forties, they named him Emanuel, meaning 'God is with us'.

"Why can't Hyram and Aaron come with me?"

"We wish they could, Emanuel, but you have to go first. They'll be leaving a few weeks after you. They'll soon catch up with you and when they do, you'll have to show them the ropes. Now, won't that make a change?" his father replied gently.

Emanuel eyed his brothers standing quietly either side of his father. With normally boundless energy and unceasing banter, Hyram and Aaron were unusually quiet and distracted. It had been the same for the past three days. For a while, he had assumed that it was something that he had done that had upset them until his father had called him into his study. To get a summons into his father's inner sanctum was a very rare occasion and it usually meant a dressing down followed by passing a few hours in his bedroom when he would otherwise have been playing in the garden.

He straightened his tie, knocked gently and peered cautiously around the door. It would be the last real conversation he had with his father and one which he would never forget.

"Emanuel, my son," his father had said, beckoning him to sit opposite in one of the two large armchairs beside the fireplace. "You haven't done anything wrong. Today we need to talk man to man. Is that okay?"

He nodded vigorously, feeling very grown up.

"The day after tomorrow, Emanuel, you will be going away on an extended holiday. You must look on it as an adventure and an opportunity to learn about the world outside of this house and your school. You will meet a lot of other children the same age as you and I am sure that you will soon make some good friends. It will be a much longer journey than you have ever taken before. I will drive you to Vienna's

Westbahnhof and then you will take a train to a port in Belgium and from there you will sail to Harwich in England. You will have to be very brave."

His eyes prickled, but he would not cry. He was being sent away on a holiday, so his father was telling him, but holidays were always discussed and planned by the whole family and they all went together. This was not a normal holiday that his father was referring to and besides no one went on holiday in wartime.

He bit his lip. He had never answered his father back nor questioned his father's decision; such behaviour was most definitely not acceptable in his father's house. But, he reminded himself, they were having a man to man discussion, his father's own words, and surely that gave him the right to ask questions.

"You mean that you are sending me away so that I will be safe from the Nazis?" he stated, his lips trembling. He understood that his father was trying to protect him from the hard truth but not even a six-year-old could fail to miss what was going on around them.

His father smiled and held out his arms to him. "Come here, Emanuel. You are wise beyond your years, my son, and I was wrong to try and wrap it up as a holiday. You are right of course. It is not safe for you to stay in Austria any longer. That is why you and your brothers will be going to stay in England until this is all over. You will go to school in England, which will not be possible before long if you stay here. Your education is important. The Nazis will be defeated but it may take a very long time and in the meantime you have to stay safe so that when it is all over you can come back and help everybody rebuild our beautiful country. Do you understand?"

What he did not know at the time was that his father had worked tirelessly to secure a place for him and his brothers on the Kindertransport scheme that had been organised by the British. Priority was being given to those whose parents were already in concentration camps or no longer able to support them. Neither case applied to him or his brothers but his father knew that it would be months, if not days, before they too would be arrested and taken away.

"What about you and Mama?" he asked. His father had not mentioned how they would keep themselves safe.

"When Hyram and Aaron leave, we will close up the house and go and live with your Uncle Pierre and Aunt Rosanne in the countryside for a while." His father spoke reassuringly.

"Why can't we all go there together?" Emanuel asked. If it was safe for Papa and Mama then they too would be safe.

"The British have agreed to allow six hundred children to leave Austria and go to England, and you and your brothers are three of those lucky children. If we could come with you then we would, but it is not possible. You will all be much safer in England and your Mama and I will sleep soundly knowing that you are all safe. Do you understand, Emanuel?"

"Yes, sir," he replied and he had understood. He had overheard his mother and father talking anxiously about something they called Kristallnacht and recounting the terrible things that had happened that night. Emanuel knew that it was getting closer by the day and although he would not admit it to a living soul, he was afraid for himself and his family.

Time passed all too quickly; it seemed that he hardly had time to say goodbye to his pet rabbit who was soon to be rehomed with a neighbour, or to his teddy bear, bare of fur, minus one eye, but much loved all the same. He gave both of them the same message – that they must behave themselves while he was away and that he would be back to collect them both in the wink of an eye. He knew in his heart that it would not happen, but it was comforting to say it out loud to two of his friends who could not contradict him.

He was allowed to take one small brown suitcase with him. Judging from its weight, his mother had managed to pack all his worldly goods inside it, including a small brown package that contained photographs of the family and their home. He would have to wear a tag as well with a number on it, his mother had said. It was no different to going on a school trip when the teacher had to make sure that she did not lose anyone.

Standing hand in hand with his mother he squeezed his eyes tight shut: the shutter of his imagined box brownie opened and closed on every room in the house, on the grand facade of their beautiful home, on the garden with its endless hiding places and trees that he would climb when he was feeling in need of a little solitude and finally on his family, one by one. There had been no long goodbyes or hugs or kisses; they all knew what the consequences of that would have been.

"Take care, Emanuel. We love you," his mother said, dropping a kiss on his forehead.

"See you soon little brother," his brothers chorused.

"We have to leave now, Emanuel. It will take us an hour to drive to Vienna," his father had said, picking up his son's case.

The date was the tenth of December 1938, nine months before the outbreak of the Second World War. He often reminded himself that he had been one of the lucky children who had been selected to go 'on holiday'. His father had been correct in saying that there would be others of his own age on the trip, but there were also babies and boys and girls who were much older than him.

They all had two things in common – they were Jewish and they were all going on a very long holiday. He was soon aware that he was one of the Kindertransport children born out of Kristallnacht, the night of broken glass as he was later able to translate it – the night when there were mass attacks on synagogues, on homes, businesses, shops and department stores; the night when German Jews knew that the world had changed forever.

His father had not been allowed on the platform so they had said their last goodbyes in the main concourse of the station. "Be brave, little man. I will always be proud of you," he said, shaking his son's hand.

It was the longest few days of his life made bearable only by a young girl he met on the train who held his hand throughout the train journey and the boat crossing. She was his age, as brave as any boy he had ever met.

Both he and his new friend had been told by their parents that they had the same sponsor and should expect to be taken in by the same foster family on their arrival in England, but something had either gone wrong with the paperwork or it had been lost along the way. All too soon he lost touch with her – he was taken to a hostel in a sleepy seaside town in Devon called Dawlish while she, he found out much later, had been taken to a similar seaside town called Exmouth no more than five miles away as the crow flies but to a six-year-old, a thousand miles away. But his imaginary box brownie served him well – he would never forget her.

He had been lucky. He had been fostered out to a childless couple who lived in Oxford who sheltered him, fed him, nurtured him, encouraged him and most importantly loved him. In the long and lonely nights, he turned to the images on his box brownie, which never faded.

He studied everything English by day and, in the privacy of his mind and small room, studied everything that belonged to his beloved Austria by night. Rachel and Zach understood his need to stay in touch with his native language. Never discouraging him, they quietly warned him that he should take special care not to slip back into German outside of the confines of the house, and never when they had guests present. On the very first day he arrived at their house he had told them how grateful he was and that one day he would go back to his country and his family.

Daily he waited for news of the arrival of his brothers. Months after he had arrived in England, Rachel and Zach broke the news to him that Hyram and Aaron had made it safely as far as the coast of Belgium but not so far as the English coast. It had been a devastating blow but it had come as no surprise. Frequently he sat with them in the lounge listening anxiously to the news reports; the news was never good.

Over the following years he threw himself into his studies, winning a much-coveted scholarship to Oxford University. An exceptional student, by the age of twenty-six, he had a first-class degree and a doctorate in Classical Languages and Literature and an offer of a teaching post at Oxford.

Years later he was to learn that his mother and father had 'holidayed' with Uncle Pierre and Aunt Rosanne in the Austrian countryside for several years before taking their last 'holiday' together. They said their final goodbyes at Auschwitz in December 1943.

Dinah, the angelic little girl whom he had met on the boat, was never far from his thoughts, and it was with joy that he often remembered her. They had been drawn together like magnets, both drawing courage and hope from one another, and the magnetism had never faded.

* * *

He was in his late twenties when Dinah re-entered his life. It had never been a question of if, but when. The trail from Exmouth had taken him to Scotland and then to Yorkshire and then all the way back to London. She, like him, had excelled academically and joined the civil service from school.

After a short engagement, they were married in a small synagogue in Golders Green on a Sunday in June 1966. The traditional breaking of a plate at their engagement was followed, by the breaking of the glass at the wedding ceremony.

Their sons Hyram and Aaron were born in 1967 and 1970. Both boys followed in their parents' footsteps, achieving excellent results at school and first-class degrees at university.

Throughout their marriage Emanuel spoke little of the family or the home that he had loved and lost. After all these years, Dinah had still not persuaded him to visit their native Austria, but they both remained proud of their ancestry and German was their preferred language in the privacy of their own home.

For many years following their retirement they lived close by Oxford. Then destiny had led them to Magnolia Court to visit a fellow scholar who had but weeks to live. Emanuel had first met Ralph in Dawlish in 1938 and they had kept in touch ever since. Before he passed away, Ralph told them that they would find no better friends anywhere in the world than at Magnolia Court.

In 2009 Emanuel and Dinah bought Ralph's cottage. It had been both a trial and a blessing.

Thirteen

Greg waited anxiously in the waiting room. There was nothing in the world that he hated more than going to the dentist. If he had designed this room it would have been as soundproof as a padded cell. Instead, he had to sit there alongside others awaiting their destiny, listening to the never-ending whirr of the drill. There was an audible sigh of relief when it stopped only to be replaced with a loud groan when it resumed.

Greg ran his tongue around his teeth. He had cleaned them with his electric toothbrush twice before he had left the house and convinced himself that there could be nothing wrong with them. Reminding himself that this was only a check-up was a complete waste of time. The last two occasions had been only check-ups as well, but on both occasions he had left the surgery numb in one side of his face or the other and with considerably less money in his bank account.

Greg was early for his appointment. He hadn't intended to be but just when you didn't expect it, the train ran spot on time and the underground train even waited for him before closing the doors. Had he walked backward from the tube station to the dental surgery, he would still have been early.

He had read the *Telegraph* on the train, at least as much of it that was of any interest to him. He completed the cryptic crossword in record time much to the chagrin of the man who had sat next to him and was still struggling with the first clue when the train pulled into the final station.

Greg glanced down at the magazines on the coffee table and grimaced: *Women and Home, Slimming World, Cosmopolitan, Best, Country Life* and the obligatory Oral Health magazines. Out of the corner of his eye, one magazine hidden from sight at the bottom of the pile caught his attention. It was provocatively titled *Get a Life*. Judging from the photograph on the cover and the list of key features covered by the edition it majored in social injustices while claiming at the same time to have no political associations.

Greg reached for the magazine and thumbed through it. The majority of articles were lengthy and looked thoroughly indigestible, but one article stood out from the rest – it was in two parts and written by a journalist called Penelope Sarthe.

The headline on the first part was "The Reality of Ageing." It began: *Yesterday I met a very special lady...*

Greg read the first part of the article once and then again and then a third time, before moving on to the second part of the article entitled "What is disability?"

In the same week that I met that very special lady, I was privileged to spend the day with an exceptional man. I gave him a lift to the doctor's surgery for his monthly appointment and to pick up a few things that he needed from the shopping centre. He is elderly, aged 79, and wheelchair-bound. He lost the use of his legs some ten years ago as a result of a motorbike accident and at the same time suffered severe scarring to his face. He tells

me he was once a serious biker at weekends and evenings and had quite a few Hells Angels friends. He was quick to tell me that not all books should be judged by their cover and that he and his Hells Angels friends did more good work for society than wreak havoc.

My friend is remarkably independent. My role throughout the day was simply to load and unload the wheelchair into the boot of the car. He did the rest, including getting himself in and out of the car and propelling himself at a vast rate of knots to our destinations. I was amazed at how expertly he manoeuvred the wheelchair across roads, between lamp posts, prams and dogs and entering shops through doors with no more than an inch to spare on either side. I could hardly keep up with him.

I was surprised by his agility. I was shocked by the way he was perceived and treated by his fellow human beings.

Our first port of call was the doctor's surgery. The waiting room was full as always, with appointments running ten to fifteen minutes late. Nothing unusual there – indeed we considered ourselves lucky that we would not be there for coffee, lunch and tea. I found a seat and my friend positioned his wheelchair beside me, well out of the way of passing traffic. I noticed that several people glanced up from their magazines as we came in but quickly averted their eyes. We sat there in silence – no hellos, no chit-chat about the weather and no discussion about the delays. From time to time patients glanced at us but only when they thought we were occupied elsewhere. For a short moment I panicked.

Did I have jam around my mouth from breakfast or had I put two odd shoes on?

My friend was called in to see the doctor precisely fifteen minutes after we had arrived. At that precise moment, conversation resumed throughout the waiting room. My friend was not in the least disturbed by the episode and seemed hardly to have noticed the atmosphere within the room.

We progressed to the shopping centre where he wanted to buy some new socks. He was quite content with his holey socks that dated back to the fifties, but it had been pointed out to him that they did not look very becoming when worn with sandals. Reluctantly he had agreed to buy some new ones.

The socks he decided would have to last him for the rest of his life and thus he would only buy the best quality. While I drove, his head was buried in his iPad. He came up for air only when he had identified precisely what he wanted, where to buy it, how much it would cost and how he would navigate me to the store. I was happy to get on with the driving but could not help glancing sideways from time to time to see what he was doing. He was no different to every child, teenager or adult – he was engrossed in the pages that swam before his eyes. His fingers tapped away at the keyboard at a remarkable rate of knots.

My instructions received, I found the correct road and parked in a disabled bay outside the department store, the car displaying the blue badge on the window the correct way round. I unloaded the wheelchair and went with him simply to stretch my legs. My friend propelled himself through the aisles on a direct course to the shoe and sock department. I stood beside him people-watching – men's socks did not interest me greatly – until a store assistant arrived.

"What sort of socks does he need? Wool, nylon, long or short, winter or summer?" she asked, smiling at me. It was a while before I found my tongue. "Ask the gentleman. He is the one who will choose what he wants and he is your customer who will be paying the bill." I could feel my anger rising until I felt a gentle touch on my arm. He shook his head and said, "Not worth it."

My friend picked out three pairs of excellent quality socks, wheeled himself to the cash desk and wafted his credit card at the machine. "Thank you", he said and made a beeline for the door.

We had another two and a half hours remaining in the disabled bay and were in no hurry to get back. I asked him if there was anything else he would like to do at which he drew his smartphone out of his pocket and said with a grin, "Follow me." We then covered at least two miles up and down narrow streets crossing and re-crossing roads and dodging the traffic – I had my first lesson in Pokémon.

You may already have read the first part of this article about the special lady I met that very same week. I described her as spirited, knowledgeable, philosophical and resourceful. The description equally fits my friend in the wheelchair. A highly intelligent man with a very sharp brain, he too bought into the same dream retirement complex as the lady.

Today I have recounted just two incidents during the

day I spent with this gentleman: there were several other similar events. I plead guilty that in the past I have failed to see past the wheelchair to the person within. It is not a mistake I shall make again. My elderly gentleman could knock spots off any teenager in the technology game.

'Does he take sugar?' simply doesn't cut it anymore.

Greg sat back in the chair. In his head he recalled a violent argument – one that had never been settled.

For once, the check-up was just that and he left the surgery with both cheeks intact and only a little poorer. Picking up a takeaway, he drove home to his apartment, took a fork from the kitchen drawer, poured the food onto a plate and put a CD in the Bose. He chose Vivaldi, The Four Seasons, Opus 8, 'Spring'. It was always his first choice when he had something to celebrate and getting out of the dentist almost scot-free had to be cause for celebration. Most times he felt his spirits surge with the music but that night it fell on deaf ears.

Greg turned up the volume on the Bose. The Four Seasons bounced off the walls and went some way towards blotting out his thoughts.

Fourteen

Greg loved working on conservation projects. They were far more satisfying than the glass-faced multi-story office blocks that were squeezed into the minutest of spaces in the cities.

The design work for his latest project had been completed months ago and the contractors were on site. They had a good reputation for running to time and budget, but more importantly, they did not cut corners. If Greg specified a particular type of material then nothing could be substituted. In the office, this was known as 'The Greg Rule' and was often the subject of arguments when a project risked going into delay because the materials he had specified were not readily available. It was one thing that Greg was dogmatic about – it was not negotiable. He had learned that lesson the hard way.

Greg left the office and sauntered along to the underground station to take the tube to the site at Wapping to check progress with the site manager.

It was after the rush hour so there were plenty of seats available. He opened the *Telegraph* and started thumbing through the pages, but the words did not register. It was the first time he had ever done such a thing, but he had actually stolen a magazine from the dentist's waiting room. *Get a Life* was in his briefcase. Opening it up to the centre pages, he re-read the articles and overshot his stop.

"Hell and damnation!" Greg exclaimed out loud. Looking up, he saw a lady in a wheelchair opposite who lowered her paper and eyed him with amusement. "My apologies, madam. That just slipped out. I can't remember the last time I missed my stop. Have you ever heard of this magazine? I think it's fairly new. It makes you think. I'd recommend it to anyone." He returned her smile.

"I don't think so. What is it called?" the lady replied, looking up over her steel-rimmed glasses.

"It's called *Get a Life*."

He just couldn't get Penelope Sarthe out of his head. It was her fault that he had missed his stop. What did she look like? How old was she? Was she actually a 'she' at all?

* * *

The office was on the forty-third floor of the Shard with magnificent views across the River Thames to the City of London and far beyond. Greg stood by the floor-to-ceiling windows looking out across London. It was a bitterly cold January day. The snow was swirling around the building and settling on the rooftops far below. It was quite a magnificent sight but he was not in the frame of mind to appreciate it. He had something quite different on his mind. If the truth were known he had been completely at sea since he had first read her article the previous Thursday in the dentist's waiting room.

Greg opened his browser, typed *Get a Life* and then clicked on People and Profiles. "Penelope Sarthe, writer and re-searcher, has been a journalist for the past twelve years. She has written for many different magazines on the subjects of cooking, health and beauty. She has now turned her attention to addressing a wide range of social injustices."

The magazine was registered at 211, Fetter Lane, off Fleet Street.

Greg keyed in Penelope's email address and then clicked on 'subject'. What precisely was the subject? Damn it, he said out loud, he couldn't even define that. All he knew was that he had an irrational desire to meet up with her and unload his conscience on her. It was insane and potentially suicidal. He simply couldn't find the right words.

There were things he needed to do. He was paid to work not daydream. Greg opened his inbox and got on with the job in hand. It took three hours to respond to all of his emails and a further hour to complete a cost estimate that was way overdue. Normally the whole caboodle would have taken him no more than an hour. His mood had not improved. Greg shut down his computer and put his jacket on. He was already late for his afternoon appointment.

Dammit, he said to himself and started pacing the floor. By modern standards, it was a spacious office but it took Greg no more than six long paces to walk from wall to wall. He was a tall man – six foot four inches, slim build with broad shoulders. At forty-six he had a full head of hair, thick and brown with just a very few flecks of grey. He was blissfully unaware of how attractive he was. In his opinion mirrors had been invented solely to prevent men from cutting themselves when shaving. He had no love affair with a mirror.

Dawn had been his secretary for over five years. Well into her sixties and very efficient at her job, she knew Greg and his moods like the back of her hand. When he paced the

119

office something was definitely not right. "Is everything okay, Greg? I couldn't help but hear you pacing the room," she asked cautiously, poking her head around the door.

"Do you have a couple of sheets of paper and an envelope, please Dawn?"

"I've got plenty of time, Greg. I could always brush up my dictation skills and type a letter for you," she replied, surprised that he was even considering writing a letter. Wasn't that what email was for?

"That's very thoughtful of you, Dawn, but, no, I need to write a proper letter. And could you put a first-class stamp on the envelope, please."

Greg threw his jacket over the chair, pulled the sheets of paper towards him, picked up his pen and started writing.

Dear Penelope,

May I start this note by reassuring you that I am not some crank who regularly writes letters to journalists? You will no doubt wish to check my credentials before you choose whether or not to read the rest of this letter. I know that I would if I were you.

My name is Greg Olsen and I am an architect. I work for a company called ITF Developments. You can look us up online and you will find several articles that I have written on the subject of architecture and more particularly on the sympathetic refurbishment of buildings of architectural importance.

I read your two recent articles about an elderly lady and an elderly gentleman both of which I found thought-provoking.

I was unlucky enough to lose my parents a few years ago and, since reading your article, I have searched my conscience to check that I did not treat them as so many people seem to have treated your friends. I am pleased to be able to say that I found myself not guilty.

However, there was an incident in my career – many years ago now – that may have resulted in considerable stress for a number of elderly people. I am not proud of it and have always hoped that one day I could in some small way make amends for it. Your article brought it all back to me.

I would simply like to talk to you and ask your advice.

I will completely understand if I do not hear from you but just in case you feel able to reply my email address is golsen10@ITFDevelopments.com. I took the liberty of checking the registered address of *Get A Life* and noticed that your offices are in Fetter Lane. It is a twenty-minute walk from my own office. I used to frequent a coffee shop called Mantovani's, which is close to Fetter Lane, and I wondered if you would allow me to buy you a coffee.

Yours very sincerely,

Greg Olsen

Greg addressed the envelope, stuck the stamp on and put the letter in his pocket. He would post it on the way home. Smiling to himself, he felt strangely relieved and vowed that the next time he wanted to contact somebody he had not met before, he would either write a letter or pick up the phone. Email most definitely had its limitations and there was nothing less inspiring than sitting and staring at a computer screen.

* * *

Gabby sighed as she looked at her pile of post. It never ceased to amaze her how many people still preferred to write and send letters rather than use email. She always read the letters she received – she felt it only courteous to do so. People spent a long time writing them and the least she could do was treat them with respect and reply to those that sought a response.

Over the past week, the number of letters and emails she had received had grown exponentially – ever since she had written those articles about Amy and Duncan. By far the majority of letters in the pile were those from people thanking her for her understanding, for sticking up for them, and recounting their own experiences. Some correspondents suggested related subjects that she might like to explore in future articles – the standard of care homes for the elderly featured time and time again. It was another subject close to her heart that she would address later in the year.

One envelope postmarked Reading looked different. The letter had been written on headed notepaper and the envelope addressed to Get A Life – FAO Penelope Sarthe. She read it once and then again. It was an odd letter from a man calling himself Greg Olsen. Gabby reached for her iPad and Googled ITF Developments. Sure enough, there was a photograph of Greg Olsen together with a number of articles that he had written about architecture. He didn't appear to be anything other than that which he described in his letter.

To say she was not curious would be untrue but she was not in the habit of meeting strange men in coffee shops. Gabby tore the letter in half and put it in the waste bin.

* * *

Unusually the following morning the waste bin had not been emptied. Gabby picked up the bin and started towards the door: a tidy bin is a tidy mind, she told herself. Out of the corner of her eye she spotted the email address on the torn up letter and frowned: *golsen10@ITFDevelopments.com*. Several times during the previous evening she had wondered who he was and what it was that he had wanted to talk to her about. Now here she was staring at the same email address and wondering once again just what it was all about.

Gabby picked the pieces of the letter out of the bin and later that day wrote an email in reply:

Dear Mr Olsen
I am mystified why you should want to tell me about this incident in your career, but I have decided that I will give you the benefit of the doubt and accept your invitation to meet for coffee. I know Mantovani's and I will be there at 11am on Monday next week.
Penelope Sarthe.

Gabby pressed the send button before she changed her mind again. She had done some stupid things in her life and this was probably right up there with them. She could still change her mind and not turn up.

* * *

Greg spent a sleepless night, tossing and turning. The following day he had arranged to meet up with Penelope Sarthe whom he knew nothing about, to share with her his part in what could only be described as a scandal, even a criminal act. Had he completely lost his senses? What in heaven's name was he doing? She was a journalist after all. What if she published his story? It could be the end of his career. Was it a risk he was prepared to take? When he awoke the following morning, his doubts of the previous night had dispelled. He had lived with his conscience far too long. He was going to face the consequences whatever they might turn out to be.

* * *

Greg arrived early at the coffee shop and ordered an Americano with an extra shot for Dutch courage. The only customer in the coffee shop, he sat by the window watching the passers-by and wondered if any of them might be Penelope Sarthe. Would she be in her twenties? He doubted it – there were not many twenty-somethings sympathetic to the elderly. Would she be in her sixties or seventies? He doubted that as well. She had clearly been writing about people in an older age bracket than herself. So she was probably aged between thirty and fifty.

As he sat lost in a world of his own, thinking about what she might look like, a woman pulled out the chair opposite him and sat down.

"Penelope Sarthe, I presume?" Greg stood up and held out

his hand. "I'm Greg Olsen. Let me buy you that coffee I promised you. What will it be?"

"Cappuccino, please."

Greg stirred sugar into his coffee while Gabby averted her eyes and sipped her own coffee.

"I think the ball is in your court," Gabby began.

"Yes, it is. But now you are here I really don't know where to start," Greg replied. "Thank you for coming. Maybe that's a good place to start and to tell you that I admire your writing and your empathy for older people. I feel quite ridiculous now we are sitting here but having asked you to meet me the least I can do it to tell you why. Will you hear me out?"

"That's why I am here." Gabby sat back and waited.

"I am not unaware that you're a journalist but can I hope that you will keep what I say in confidence?" Greg asked.

"I can't promise that. Ask me again when you have finished telling me this story."

"I specified the materials that were to be used in a major build project, but someone changed my specifications to save money – a lot of it – and I didn't notice until it was too late. I should have been on the ball and spotted it straight away. I knew then that everything we had built wouldn't last five minutes. Looking back I reckon the developer saved himself a million, maybe more. I made my next mistake then. I threatened to expose him for what he was. His reply to me was 'Get a life' and you're fired – I'm not kidding. Ironic, isn't it? Here I am sitting opposite a woman who writes for a magazine by the same name. Maybe subconsciously, it was remembering those words that made me pick up that magazine and read your article."

Gabby listened, her eyes growing wider by the second.

"Instead of threatening to expose him to the press I should have gone straight to the authorities. Even then I thought that he was a decent sort at heart and would put matters right. How wrong can you be about someone? He laughed at me and told me that he knew some very unsavoury characters who owed him and that I was a dead man walking – his words, not mine – if ever I opened my mouth to anybody. He didn't need to fire me from the job. I had already told him to stuff it. And then a deposit of one hundred thousand pounds turned up in my bank account without my knowledge."

"Did you ask your bank to reverse the transaction?"

"It simply didn't occur to me that transactions could be reversed so, no, I didn't do anything about it. I was sure that I was being followed for several weeks and I was scared, I freely admit it and I was a coward. Laughable isn't it – six-feet-four and fit, I was scared. I wanted to stay alive and I needed the whole sorry saga buried to keep my career intact. How pathetic is that? So I walked away just as he wanted me to but I have never since stopped looking over my shoulder. I was fortunate to pick up a job with ITF. Now I am chief architect but I wouldn't be if they knew the half of it."

"What sort of project was it?"

"A retirement complex. I often think about all those elderly people whose dreams he shattered."

"How were their dreams shattered exactly?"

"They had all been promised that they would live in the retirement complex of their dreams."

"What was so special about it?"

"The complex was built around a beautiful mansion house. It was intended to be the social hub of the community. It should have been magnificent when it was finished."

Gabby's coffee had long since gone cold. She was speechless. Could he be talking about what she thought he was talking about? It was too much of a coincidence.

"Where was this retirement complex?" Gabby asked fighting to remain calm while feeling the fire in her cheeks.

"It was not far from Stroud. I still have the one hundred thousand – every penny of it. I vowed that it would stay safe and earn interest until such time as I could find a way to give it back to those people whose dreams he destroyed. Where did thirteen years go? It's past time that I put matters right, irrespective of the consequences. Thanks for listening, Penelope."

Gabby drained the cold coffee, hiding her eyes behind the oversized cup. He must not see her eyes, not until she had composed herself. Thirteen years. It had happened thirteen years ago.

"If you let me, I'd like to help you put matters right, Greg. Do you have half a day free later in the week?" she asked calmly.

"I have Thursday in mind. You trusted me with your story and now I am going to ask you to trust me without asking questions." Gabby looked him squarely in the eyes and saw an honest man. "Your secret is quite safe with me. I will not divulge it to anyone without your permission."

"Does that include your readers and your husband? My apologies for asking, but I noticed you are wearing a wedding ring. I'll need to check my appointments for Thursday."

"It does. You have my word. Email me if you can make Thursday and we'll take it from there," Gabby said as she picked up her handbag and prepared to leave, hoping that he had not noticed that her hands were shaking. "Thanks for

127

the coffee."

* * *

That night Greg checked his schedule for the following Thursday. It took longer than it should have done. He kept a note of his appointments on his iPad, on his computer at work, which didn't talk to his iPad, on his phone, which didn't talk to either of them and in a pocket diary that he carried with him.

His trusted pocket diary indicated that the Thursday would be okay. There were no appointments scheduled, so he could that take the day off. Just to make sure that things would stay that way he dropped an email to his secretary telling her to keep his diary free for Thursday.

It was all very disturbing. She was disturbing – and not knowing what she had asked him to trust her about was even more disturbing. But he had given his word so there was no alternative but to wait and see. Whatever else, he would see Penelope again and he was quite irrationally driven to do so. It was all totally out of his comfort zone. He liked to know what he was doing, when and where and with whom, but somehow he had to put it out of his mind for the next two days. There was no point in speculating he told himself, but he knew that he would spend most of the days and half of the nights going through every possible scenario.

The short email to his secretary followed by one to Penelope confirming Thursday disappeared into the ether.

All he could do then was wait and wonder.

Fifteen

"Aunt Hetty? Would there be any problem if I bought a friend this afternoon to my birthday tea?" Gabby asked.

"Isn't Charles coming with you?"

"No, he can't make it. He sends his apologies."

"Who is this friend, Gabby?"

"He's called Greg. He's just a friend, no more than that," Gabby said. "And we plan to get to Magnolia about one-thirty. I know it's early, but I want to show Greg around the grounds. Trust me, there is a good reason. So we'll be at the nineteenth hole by two. Nothing to worry about, Aunt Hetty, I promise you. Thanks." Gabby finished the call, heaved a sigh of relief and tried not to second-guess the conversation that would ensue between her aunt and uncle.

"She's bringing a man with her this afternoon, Max. He's called Greg. I have no idea what that girl is up to, but she wants to show him around Magnolia before the tea dance. I do wish she'd let the past stay in the past. None of us want to go through all that again. I know she's been asking everybody questions about what happened all those years ago. Have you noticed that camera is never out of her hands when she's up here?" Hetty said.

"I agree with you there, Hetty. Don't worry, it will run

its course and then it can all be buried again," Max replied soothingly. "Curious about this Greg though. We'll just have to wait and see, my dear."

* * *

"Did you write that card, Amy?"

"And what card would that be dear?" Amy replied absent-mindedly. She had other things on her mind. She was so looking forward to the tea dance and had always loved the cha-cha-cha, but she just couldn't quite get the rhythm right in her mind. It was so annoying – her feet were tapping away but not in time to the music she remembered.

"The birthday card you asked me to buy yesterday when I was in town yesterday," Jennifer replied patiently.

"Why did I ask you to buy a birthday card?" Amy asked uncertainly.

"It's Gabby's birthday today. We're going to her party in a few minutes."

"Yes, of course, I know that. How silly of me. I simply can't think of more than one thing at a time these days. I remember now. I think I wrote it yesterday evening and put it somewhere safe. I won't have lost it. It will either be in my desk or the bedside drawer – that's where I always keep things for safety." Amy rocked forward in her chair and heaved herself to her feet. "I shan't be a moment. Don't go away, Jennifer."

Jennifer glanced at the handbag beside Amy's chair. It was almost as big as a suitcase – anything could get lost in it. "Have you tried looking in your handbag?"

"It won't be there. I don't keep birthday cards in my

handbag. It's a stupid place to keep them," Amy shouted while rifling through the drawers again.

Jennifer smiled to herself. They went through this every time. It would be in her handbag. Amy put everything in her handbag and always insisted that she had not.

Amy came back in the room, sat down and put her handbag on her lap. "Maybe you are right. I'll take another look. Did I tell you that Henry and I go back a long way? I shall make sure that I am sitting next to him this afternoon. I met him during the war, you know. It's funny that we should end up buying properties in the same place after all that time."

Jennifer sat back and listened. If she had heard this story once, she had heard it a thousand times, but it was a small price to pay for the pleasure it gave Amy in recounting it.

"He was a handsome man in those days. I remember the very day we met. It was at a dance. We used to dance properly in those days, not like they do now, gyrating all over the place. It was a Friday night. Yes, Friday the thirteenth of June 1940 and the dance was at the Apollo Halls in High Wycombe. There were lots of girls there. He asked me to dance several times. Our best dance was the cha-cha-cha. I just don't understand why I can't get the rhythm today. Unfortunately, I had to leave the dance early. It was then that he met Charmaine. I didn't know her, but I heard about the wedding later. Those were the days. You were right, Jennifer. Here it is." Amy pulled the card out of her handbag, together with her precious Mont Blanc fountain pen. It had been a parting gift from a very senior officer at the end of the war. It was the most precious thing that she possessed. "Oh dear, I didn't write it after all."

'To Gabby,' she wrote slowly and deliberately. 'Many happy

returns. With love from Amy.'

Jennifer watched on as Amy positioned and meticulously formed every letter on the card and the envelope. It was a work of art; her hands were veined, lined and arthritic but steady as a rock.

* * *

Gabby waved goodbye to Charles and set the satnav to take her to St Francis Court, Water Lane, Twyford, the address that Greg had emailed to her – one hour and fifteen minutes provided there were no major traffic holdups.

Precisely one hour and ten minutes later she slowed down, changed gear, and following Mavis's instructions, "You have reached your destination", turned left off the main road.

"Thank you," she said to Mavis. Mavis was alive by the skin of her teeth after several recent incidents in which she had taken Gabby up high-hedged narrow lanes, some of which had been clearly marked 'Not suitable for motor vehicles'. At least today she had stuck to main roads and Gabby had not spent half the journey reversing to allow oncoming tractors, combine harvesters and grain lorries to pass.

Parking the car in a bay for visitors, Gabby looked up at the house. It was a beautiful house set in impressive gardens.

Greg already had his coat on. The front room of his apartment overlooked the main entrance and he had seen a car draw up in the visitors' bay and Penelope step out of it. He really did not know what to make of her. She was driving an old yellow Fiat which had probably been around the clock several times; it was not quite what he had expected, but what had he expected?

"On my way down," he called into the intercom as he opened the door and started down the broad mahogany staircase.

"Good morning, Penelope. I'm pleased you found me. Did you want to come up, by the way? I can offer you some coffee but I rather assumed from your email that we were going somewhere." Greg stumbled over the words. "It's good to see you."

"Thanks for the offer of coffee but maybe some other time."

Gabby climbed back into the driver's seat and fastened her seat belt. Greg followed suit. For a few moments, they sat in silence.

As the miles sped by Greg was none the wiser about the destination or what they might be doing when they got there.

"I guess that you are not going to tell me where we are going or why."

"You guess right, Greg. But I will tell you that it will take us a couple of hours so sit back and make yourself comfortable."

Comfortable was about the last thing Greg felt – the seats were small and lumpy and the suspension had seen better days. But it was not his physical comfort that troubled him. It was the unknown. Here he was letting this woman take him to some unknown destination for an unknown reason.

"Are we allowed to talk on this mystery tour?" Greg ventured.

"Sure," Gabby replied. "Tell me about St Francis. It's a beautiful house."

"It is," Greg replied. "I'm rather proud of it actually."

Gabby raised her eyebrows.

"The company won the contract to convert the house into apartments three years ago. It was once the family seat of a grand family back in the late 1800s. History has it that the family lived there until the fifties but had to let it go when they could no longer afford its upkeep. The house then became a boarding school for privileged boys. The school closed five years ago and stood empty for two years. There had been little money spent on it for decades and it was in need of a lot of work."

"Sounds familiar," Gabby remarked.

"The trust that managed it decided to let it go and one of our clients bought it. I pride myself that in bringing it into the twenty-first century I did so sympathetically and managed to retain the main features of the house both inside and outside."

"Impressive."

"I hope so. You'll have to take a look some time. The doors inside are all original, as are the fireplaces. The ceilings are twenty foot high and the rooms are all light and spacious. I loved the apartments we created so much that I simply decided I had to buy one. It made a big hole in my finances, but I have never regretted one single penny."

"It sounds wonderful."

"Maybe you'd like to see the house when we get back? For a single bloke, I make a mean cup of tea."

"Maybe," Gabby said, and returned to concentrating on the road.

"Do people call you Pen or are you always a Penelope?" Greg asked cautiously.

He would find out about that soon enough but for the moment Penelope would save any further explanations. "Penelope," she replied.

"So, Penelope, am I allowed to ask you anything about yourself?"

"Fire away, but I don't promise to answer your questions."

"You are married, I know that. Whoever he is, he's a lucky man. Do you have children?"

"No, no children, but my husband has two by his first marriage. It's just never happened to me. I've let nature take its course and nature has seen fit so far to exclude me from being a mum. That doesn't make me sad by the way. I'm quite content with the hand I have been dealt."

"But I guess you're a second mum to your stepchildren. That must be nice."

"Actually, no, I am not. I don't get involved with them. Charles sees them regularly and takes them out everywhere – often with his ex-wife in tow. And just in case you are wondering, that is all right with me as well. It was part of the deal when he got divorced and then something we discussed as grown-ups before we married. It works well and suits us both fine." Gabby's tone was just a little too sharp. She had said too much already.

Greg sat back and took in the scenery. It didn't sound like it was really okay with her, but maybe he was hearing what he wanted to hear.

"Your turn," Gabby started. "You said you were single in your letter to me. Has there ever been a Mrs Olsen?"

"No," Greg replied. "There have been a few near misses but that's about all, although one was a very, very near miss." Greg laughed. "She left me standing at the altar. No, don't laugh. I know that this is something that only happens to women, not men, but it did happen. I am not sure if I was more embarrassed or relieved at the time. We're still friends and we both agreed not long after, that we were getting married for all the wrong reasons. We were a couple and we had a circle of friends who all tied the knot at about the same time so we decided that we ought to do the same. You should have seen the look on her father's face when Annie refused point-blank to walk down the aisle with him. He had spent an absolute fortune on the wedding. Fortunately, he's got over it now. Annie met a very wealthy banker and they cleared off to St Lucia and got married on the beach. It didn't cost her father a penny. I haven't met anyone special since."

Greg glanced at his watch. They had been on the road for an hour and a half.

"It's just another five miles now. Does any of this appear familiar to you?" Gabby asked pointedly.

Greg glanced out of the side window. To be honest he hadn't been paying much attention to the scenery. He had been more intent on trying to work out the purpose of the day and find out more about Penelope.

There were fields as far as the eye could see and in the distance he could just make out a red windsock fluttering in the breeze at the end of what looked like a disused runway. There were neither planes on the ground nor any sign of any having taken off or landed. There was something familiar about it. He was certain that he had seen it before.

Gabby slowed the car down as they crawled through a small village, which unusually had a small shop with a post office and a pub. The village was quaintly called Home, and the pub was aptly called The Coming Home.

Greg did a double take – he had drunk in that pub before. He remembered the log fire, the real ale and the landlord who seemed to know everybody within a hundred miles. He tried to picture the last time he had been in there and with whom. And then it came to him. He had been there with a man called Stan and his team. The last time he had drunk there was when he was working on Magnolia Court.

Was she a mind reader? There was no way she could possibly know about his association with Magnolia. She was a writer – a journalist by any other name – maybe she was an investigative journalist as well and she had got his number. Greg's heart sank while his brain worked overtime.

"I don't understand, Penelope. Would you care to explain?" he asked, trying to keep his voice steady.

"All will become clear in a few minutes, Greg," she said. "Don't worry. I haven't got a hanging party planned for you. The balloons at the entrance, by the way, are because it's my birthday and we're invited to a birthday tea dance. But before that, I want to take you on a walking tour. After that, I'll introduce you to my aunt and uncle and some other friends of mine. Do you remember Amy and Duncan?"

Greg covered his face with his hands and hoped that the ground might swallow him up. "I remember them only too well, Penelope. So they live at Magnolia and that was what you were referring to in your article."

Gabby nodded. "Do you fancy a walk?"

* * *

"This is the mansion house. I am sure you would agree that St Francis puts it to shame. We won't go in there. There is nothing to see except broken windows, warped and broken floorboards and rubble. Let's go round the side of the house and take a look at the old stables."

Gabby led, Greg followed; neither spoke.

* * *

"And this is the swimming pool complex." Gabby opened the door to show him. It had been bad enough seeing what had happened to the library. The swimming complex made him shudder and grimace. It was no less than he had predicted but seeing it after all this time was an entirely different matter. He had never felt so ashamed in his life. There were no words that could repair the damage or express his feelings.

Greg followed Gabby silently as she walked him around the complex. "And this is what the residents call Vimy Ridge. Have you ever been there? It's where the Canadians fought a battle during the First World War. They left the battlefield exactly as it was after the battle – the ridge, the craters and the trenches. Looks pretty similar, doesn't it? I believe this area was going to be a golf course. Presumably, the trenches are where someone planned to put in some drainage ditches, and the rest of it is part and parcel of the design."

"Actually this was where another twenty cottages were planned to be built and behind them the golf course," Greg replied soberly. "I guessed that things weren't going so well. The first ten cottages were sold off-plan not long after the launch and then nothing, or so I heard. The sales dried up so the remaining twenty were never built. With just ten sold and a mega financial commitment on the mansion and the grounds, he would probably have been looking at a loss, and a substantial one at that. It explains why he had been cutting costs. I should have seen it and put a stop to it."

"You haven't seen the cottages yet, Greg. They are a disaster. He wasn't just cutting corners on the community facilities. Those cottages are damp and draughty. There are cracks in the walls, the windows don't fit and the roofs leak. Those elderly friends of mine live in them – they have no choice.

The cottages have no resale value." Gabby turned to face Greg. "Would you like to live here?"

Greg shook his head.

"You wanted to hand that money back to those people whose dreams were shattered, didn't you? Well, today is your lucky day."

"How?"

"That's where my birthday tea is going to be," Gabby said pointing to a small timber building. "They call it the nineteenth hole. They'll all be there. I needed you to see all this, Greg, but I do believe what you have told me. We all make mistakes and I am not blaming you and neither will my friends. Come and meet them."

* * *

"Aunt Hetty, Uncle Max, I'd like you to meet a friend of mine. This is Greg." Gabby waved Greg in through the little door.

"Gabby, my dear, how lovely to see you and happy birthday and any friend of yours is a friend of ours, of course. Welcome to our little community hall, Greg. You'll see that it's quite cosy," Aunt Hetty said, beckoning them in as the residents struck up a chorus of 'Happy Birthday'.

"What precisely should I call you?" Greg whispered into her ear.

"Gabby – like everyone else. Penelope Sarthe is my pseudonym at the magazine."

"Let the party begin," Jennifer shouted. "I'll pour the drinks. Henry – music, maestro please."

"If you'll excuse me, young man, I would like to ask this young lady for the first dance," Uncle Max beamed and held out his hand. "Hetty will introduce Greg to everybody else. Don't worry, Greg, you are in good hands."

"Is that okay with you, Greg? We'll deal with that other matter later – birthday party first," Gabby said, taking Uncle Max's hand.

Greg nodded, unsure what else to say or do.

"And this is Greg, a friend of Gabby's. Isn't it nice that he could come today?" Hetty said to the group sitting around the nearest table.

"Young man, your face looks strangely familiar. I never forget a face but then I can never place a face either. Have we met before?" Amy asked.

"You know, Amy, I was thinking just the same thing a few minutes ago, but I didn't want to be rude to the gentleman," Henry added.

"It's just so lovely to have a younger man in our midst for an afternoon," Jennifer said, flicking her hair over her shoulder. "Don't you just love our little community hall? It's modelled on one of the settings for the musical, *South Pacific.*"

"I think it's brilliant," Greg replied enthusiastically. Thank God she had changed the subject. "I loved that musical. I saw it in the West End many years ago. The theatre was packed, but I gather it was packed every night."

"Let me show you around, Greg, and I can explain how I have tried to bring that South Pacific beach right into our little community hall." Jennifer took Greg's arm. "I designed the costumes for a West End production of South Pacific and worked a little on the scene design as well. Wouldn't it be a coincidence if that was the same production that you saw?"

It would indeed, he thought. It probably was the same production. He had never believed in coincidence before today; he would never doubt that they happened again.

* * *

They were a wonderful crowd of people and it was not long before he found himself chatting away with them like old friends, the reason for his being there unasked and temporarily forgotten. They all worshipped the ground Gabby walked on. She clearly had a very special place in their hearts.

Time flew by. Penelope – he still hadn't got his head around the fact that her real name was Gabby – had said that they would have to leave by four-thirty. It was coming up to three-thirty and there was still the small matter of dealing with the reason that she had brought him to Magnolia. Greg caught her eye and looked at his watch. Gabby nodded.

"Thank you, everybody. Thank you for a wonderful birthday party. Thank you, everybody, for making me so welcome. Thank you for that fabulous tea. Thank you, Emanuel, for all those lovely words, which I am quite sure I do not deserve. Thank you for my wonderful fountain pen – I shall treasure it forever. And a very special thank you to my dear aunt and uncle for everything they have done for me during my life. And I hope you know that anything that I can do for all of you, I will," Gabby said. "Unfortunately I shall have to take my leave before long and take my friend Greg with me. Charles, my husband, is taking me out for a special dinner tonight. I promise I will bring him to meet you just as soon as possible."

"You have all been very kind to my friend, Greg, and you are probably wondering why he came here today with me.

I know some of you thought that you might have met him before in the past. And you are right. We, or should I say he, has some news for you. Let's all sit down."

The mood changed; the room fell silent. What was this news that Greg might have and were they going to like it? Where had they seen him before? Hetty glanced at Max with a knowing look. "I didn't like the sound of all this right from the moment that Gabby said she wanted to bring a friend, and then when she said she wanted to show him around I liked it even less," Hetty whispered to Max.

"By some amazing coincidence," Gabby started to explain, "Greg made contact with me over something that had been troubling him for years – something that he was not proud of and something that he wanted to put right, as far as he could. We have talked about it at length and I truly believe that he was the innocent party in what happened. You have met Greg before, but it was a long time ago. He was one of the architects who worked on this very site when it was built. I suspect that you might have met him in London when Magnolia was first launched. I am assuming that you were there, Greg?"

"Yes. I spent time with several of you showing you the plans and the artist's impressions of Magnolia. I do remember meeting some of you," Greg said, unable to look any of them in the eye.

Everyone listened in silence as Gabby recounted the story that he had told her in the coffee shop.

Uncle Max spoke first. "I don't suppose you know where the villain is now, do you? We tried to find him years ago, but we ran out of funds. You can't sue someone you can't find – that's what the lawyers told us."

"No. He closed the company down and disappeared, presumably with all its assets in his pocket. I have never heard of him or from him since. I tried to find him too but for a different reason. Shall I, Gabby, or do you want to?" he asked.

"You tell them, Greg."

"When I threatened to expose him for the crook that he was, he delivered some serious threats to me. He then disappeared as you know but not before he deposited money in my bank account, which, I am sure he had intended, would make me complicit in the crime. It has remained untouched in an account for the last thirteen years. There is now one hundred and fifty thousand pounds in that account and not a penny of it belongs to me. It belongs to you. I am so sorry. I should have returned it to you long ago. There are no words that can express how dreadful I feel about all this."

The room was silent, the residents wide-eyed.

"Why? Why did he leave us in this mess?" Peter broke the silence.

"He was a crook. I didn't see it when I first went to work for him. I was just so pleased that he chose me out of so many young architects to work on that magnificent house and the stables at the back. I believe now that right from the outset he planned to cut corners and cut costs and bring the project in at half the cost, at most. When sales dried up he cut his losses and walked away with your money. I was a fool for not spotting what was going on sooner. When I did, I confronted him with it."

Uncle Max looked around the room at his friends. Greg's words had opened a lot of old wounds and he could see the old hurt and confusion written on their faces. "I don't know quite what to say but thank you for being so honest. I hope I can say on behalf of us all that if Gabby trusts you, then so do we."

"Hear, hear," Duncan added. "She's a good lass and I agree she's a good judge of character. Now how much did you say, young man?"

"One hundred and fifty thousand pounds, sir," Greg replied. "I can give you a copy of the account statement if you like."

"That won't be necessary." Peter cut to the chase. "We have ten cottages occupied so what say you all that we split it ten ways – fifteen thousand to each household?"

Max glanced around the room. Everyone was nodding; there were no dissenters.

"That's settled then. I don't really like to ask you, Greg, but how did you intend to pay us this money?" Uncle Max asked.

Greg pulled his chequebook out of his pocket. "Right now and take my word on it these cheques will not bounce."

* * *

"Now that wasn't so bad after all, was it?" Gabby asked, smiling at Greg.

"I think they let me off remarkably lightly in the circumstances," Greg replied with relief. "I can see why you care for them so much and why you wrote those articles. Nobody in their right mind could think that they were stupid, far from it."

"I am glad you agree with me. Sorry about the Penelope bit but I wasn't sure at first that I wanted you to know my real name. It's Gabby Fairbrother by the way."

"Okay, Gabby Fairbrother – Penelope, whichever it is – may

I offer you that cup of tea when we get back to St Francis? I guess you have quite a drive after that."

"Good idea, but it will have to be a quick one. It'll take me another hour if I am lucky to get home. I would rather like to see this apartment of yours."

Most of the journey was spent in an amiable silence, both lost in their own thoughts: Greg wishing that he had met Gabby sooner when she was single; Gabby all too conscious of the man sitting beside her and reflecting on her own marriage; and both of them quietly pleased that they had made a group of elderly people very happy that afternoon. It was no consolation for all that they had been through but it had been a most welcome and unexpected surprise.

The apartment was just as Greg had described it – rooms of huge proportion and floor-to-ceiling windows through which the evening sunlight filtered. It was tastefully furnished and decorated – antiques mixed with modern pieces, neither of which looked out of place one with the other.

"Tea or coffee, or can I offer you something stronger?" Greg asked.

"Just tea, thanks," Gabby replied, watching Greg stride across to the kitchen to put the kettle on. It was the first time that she had noticed that he was a very good-looking man.

"Do you mind if I pour myself something a little stronger? It's been quite a day," Greg said, as he picked up a bottle of scotch, poured whisky and finally added the ice cubes.

"I know someone else who pours whisky that way," Gabby said.

"I picked up the habit from someone I knew. For the life of me, I can't remember who it was. Done it ever since," Greg replied, sitting down and taking small sips of his drink.

"Thanks for today. I really appreciate it. Anyone who says that they don't believe in coincidences should have been in my shoes for the past week and then they'd change their tune. When we first met I asked you if you would keep my story in confidence. May I ask the same question again?" Greg stretched out in the chair opposite Gabby.

"I will." Gabby said.

"Would you like to see the rest of the apartment? There are two bedrooms, a dining room, and a kitchen of course, and the most amazing bathroom with a big old-fashioned bath right in the middle. I hasten to add that wasn't my idea. We employed interior designers to select the wall coverings, the drapes, the kitchen units and do the bathroom layouts and designs. I remember the first time I used that bath I felt as though I was in the middle of a shop window and everybody was looking at me – not a pretty sight."

"I'd love to and then I had better be on my way. Charles will be wondering where I am," Gabby replied.

"So you didn't tell him where you were going today?" Greg enquired curiously.

"I made a promise to you if you remember – our secret. And probably best that it stays that way. Imagine what he would say if he knew I was here in your apartment and about to get a tour of the bedrooms. And besides, he's a busy man." Gabby put her mug on the table and got up. "Show me the way."

The master bedroom was stunning. She had never seen such an ornate four-poster bed. Draped in red velvet and covered with a snowy white duvet and sheets, it dominated the room. Silver photograph frames were lined up on a dressing table. "Are they your parents?" Gabby asked pointing to a picture of a man and a woman standing side by side in a garden.

"Yes. They were wonderful. That was taken about ten years before my father died. Amy and Duncan remind me of them. My mother had dementia in her later years and my father was in a wheelchair for years and fiercely independent." Greg picked up the frame and handled it fondly.

"And this one?" Gabby asked; it was a faded brown and white photograph of a couple sitting in deckchairs on the beach.

"That's my grandparents. Perhaps when you have more time I'll give you the full guided tour and introduce you to all these people in the photographs. They have some stories to tell."

"I'd like that," Gabby replied, glancing fleetingly at the rest of the framed photographs on the dressing table. One photograph caught her eye. It had to be Greg; he was standing on a wooden veranda in front of a weatherboard house, painted white. An endless white sandy beach stretched out behind the house. It was familiar. She had seen it somewhere before but where?

* * *

Greg waved goodbye. "I'll email you, Gabby, if I may?" he called. "Thanks for today." What he really wanted to say was that he would ring her every day, twice a day or maybe ten times a day and he couldn't wait until their next meeting.

Gabby drove home carefully. She liked Greg, very much, and maybe they would meet again.

It was niggling away at her. She knew that house in the photograph but it wouldn't come back. She also had a sixth sense that it was important.

Sixteen

For reasons that she preferred not to admit even to herself, Gabby had never told Charles about Greg or taken him to Magnolia Court to meet her only family and their friends. Fleetingly it occurred to her that it might have been out of spite; Charles lived two lives – one with Annabel and the children and the other with her – so what was good for the goose was good for the gander. She dismissed the thought as quickly as it entered her head. She hadn't told Charles for the simple reason that she had never told him about Aunt Hetty or Uncle Max. She had left him to believe that she had been brought up by her father until she had left home and married Dave. It was now too late to tell him the truth and besides it would mean admitting how ashamed she was of her behaviour towards them.

The days and the weeks had flown by. Gabby was consumed with following up on her articles about Alzheimer's and dementia and was inundated with correspondence from sufferers, doctors, nurses and carers alike. They all had strong views and entirely different takes on managing the problem. In between days of interviewing and of writing up her findings, she had managed to keep up her regular visits to Magnolia Court. Most weeks she managed a one-day visit, sometimes two. And the rest of the time she spent with Charles, enjoying walks in the countryside by day and curled up in front of the log fire by night.

She had not seen Greg since her birthday party. She had purposefully decided not to give him her personal email address. He already had Penelope's office email address – it was sensible to keep her business and personal lives separate. So far, Greg was strictly 'business' but it did not stop her thinking about him or looking forward to going into the office, switching her PC on and checking her email each day. Never a day had passed when she didn't find one from him.

He was careful never to overstep the mark, keeping his posts to one-liners about the weather and the occasional few sentences about his plans for the day. He never sought a reply from her and never asked anything of her, until that day when he wrote:

It's sunny outside today but can't say I feel sunny myself. I was thinking about your friends last night – not the first time I hasten to add. I'm so sorry for what happened and just grateful that you gave me the chance to repay a debt, at least as far as I was able. I often wish I could do more for them. I read your article in the February edition about the flight of the Jews from Germany during the Second World War – like everything else you write it was very thought-provoking. The next edition can't come too soon – I wonder what you will be writing about next? I might even buy an annual subscription to the magazine.
I have been psyching myself up to ask if you would like to drop over to my apartment so that I can show you all

those other family photographs that I mentioned when
you were last there. To be honest the photographs are
just an excuse. I would very much like to see you again
but I promise that I will show you the photographs as
well.

I do appreciate that you are a respectable married
woman. Such a pity.

Best wishes
Greg

Gabby grinned and felt a warm glow come over her. Had she
been waiting for him to ask? It was half-term the following
week and Annabel, as usual, had booked a holiday for the
children; Charles would tag along. The following Saturday
they would be going to Dubai for seven days. She would be
at a loose end – again.

She didn't want to give Greg the wrong impression. There
was no way that she would cheat on Charles and neither
would he on her, although in her quiet moments and when
she was at home on her own, she had fleeting visions of
Charles and Annabel together as a couple, but her concerns
were always dispelled the moment he came home. Greg was
just a friend whom she had met through her work and who,
coincidently, had been able to help her friends.

I have a couple of hours free next Saturday afternoon.
Photographs sound good. Would 3pm suit?

Gabby reread the message. It was about right. Send.

* * *

151

Greg spent the morning pacing the apartment. Mrs Ledder, his cleaning lady, had cleaned the apartment from top to bottom the previous day. He had insisted that she did four hours instead of the normal two. She had laughed; he was such a tidy man that she rarely found enough to do to fill two hours let alone four, but if that was what he wanted, far be it for her to argue. The silver shone, the windows sparkled, the carpet had tramlines from wall to wall and there wasn't a single speck of dust to be found. The one and only Royal Doulton tea set had been unpacked from an old tea chest, washed, and set out on a tray. There had to be a woman involved, Mrs Ledder surmised.

Satisfied that everything was shipshape, Greg wiped the dust off the covers to the photo albums with a soft cloth. It was a very long time since they had been out and even longer since anyone had been remotely interested in his past. There were so many photographs; it would take them hours and hours to look through them all. He would much prefer to sit back with her and talk about Gabby and Penelope but a promise was a promise. Or was it an excuse?

Greg peeked through the blinds as her small car pulled into the visitors' parking bay opposite the entrance.

"The choice is yours, Gabby. There's the family album which goes back through generations but I have to tell you that even I can't remember who some of them are, or there are Greg's own holiday snaps going back to when I was about twelve years old. Choose your poison." Greg held the two albums up for her to see.

Gabby glanced at the family album; it was the thickest, by far. If they started on that they'd still be sitting there at midnight and the following day as well. "Holidays sound

152

more fun and family next time."

He couldn't have asked for a better answer. There was going to be a next time. Bring it on.

Greg sat down beside Gabby on the sofa and opened the album to the first page. "That's me in Marbella when I was nearly twelve years old. Some friends of my parents owned a villa there with its own swimming pool. I remember that year because that was the year I learned to swim. My father crept up behind me and pushed me into the deep end, watched me go under and come up and then paddle like mad to get back to the side. I lost my swimming trunks in the process. My father roared with laughter and my mother took a photograph. Before you ask, that particular photograph is definitely not in the album.

"This one was taken when I was sixteen. My parents took me on a tour of India. It was my first visit to a Third World country and it was quite an eye-opener. We stayed at the most magnificent palaces and from the bedroom windows you could see the slums, which came right up to the palace walls. Armed guards made sure that the 'have-nots' never got through the gates. We traveled from place to place on a small coach. My parents found the whole episode terrifying and closed their eyes most of the time, but I thought it was a great game – no driving tests over there, no Give Way signs, and no lines on the road to warn about overtaking. Our driver was a lovely Indian gentleman with a permanent grin from ear to ear, hell-bent on getting us to our daily destination as fast as possible, no matter what the consequences. We survived."

Gabby felt completely at ease listening to him chat away about his holidays. He had obviously had a very happy and privileged childhood. He had wanted for little but there was no evidence that he had been spoilt. He was kind and thoughtful, considerate of others and mindful of those who were not as fortunate as he.

"I do envy your travels, just a little."

"Have you travelled much, Gabby?"

"No. Would you believe that I have never been abroad? I do have a passport though. I got it in case Charles decided to take me abroad for our honeymoon but in the event, we went to London, and when I married Dave – that was a long time ago – we went to South Wales. Charles travels a lot – he is always off to some exotic place or another." Gabby stopped herself. It was not right to be discussing Charles with Greg.

"Is that on business? Don't you go with him?" Greg looked puzzled. What husband wouldn't take a wife like this with him at every opportunity?

"No, he doesn't go abroad on business. I think I mentioned something about this to you when we last met. Now and again Charles goes with Annabel and the children on family holidays. Annabel pays for the holidays – she has very expensive tastes. Right now they are in Dubai, coming back next Saturday." Gabby listened to her own words and thought how ridiculous it sounded.

Greg took a deep breath and chose his words carefully. "If it works for you both, then that's all that matters, Gabby. You are a very understanding and considerate woman. What say we skip my younger days and jump to some of the later holiday snaps?" Greg asked.

"Sure," Gabby replied, relieved that he had been prepared to drop the subject.

"This one was taken a long time ago. It was the one and only time that I visited the Caribbean. Someone I knew had a house in Bermuda right on the waterfront. He invited me out there for a couple of weeks." Greg coloured and hesitated. "I can't even remember his name now, but I do remember the house." How could he ever forget? How had he managed to forget that those photographs were in the album?

Gabby reached out to stop him from turning the page. "Hold it there, Greg. Let me have another look at that photograph. It's the same one as on your dressing table, isn't it? You'll think this is odd but I'm sure I know that house. I've seen it somewhere else. I know I haven't been there. It's the white weatherboard and the blue around the window frames and the blue and white porcelain pots outside the front door and the red geraniums and the beach behind the house." Gabby squinted at the photograph. "It's so familiar."

Greg let her look at the photograph. "As you say, it's the same one as on my dressing table. That's where you have seen it before." How would it look if she knew that he had spent time in Bermuda with the very man who had left her aunt and uncle and her friends in such a mess? "I wish I'd destroyed that photograph now, Gabby, and a few others and put the lot in the bin. To be honest with you, which I should have been a minute ago, that house was owned by my boss at the time, Harry Trumper – the same man who ripped off your friends at Magnolia Court. It was right at the beginning of the project and I had no idea how it would all end. I can't change the past, Gabby, but I can get rid of those photographs right now." Greg reached for the album and tore the first photograph out.

"The disappearing man," Gabby said thoughtfully. "Uncle Max told me that word had it that he disappeared on a one-way ticket to South America. No trace thereafter. Just to satisfy my curiosity, what did he look like?"

"Over the page – there's a photograph of him if I remember rightly. The cleaner took one of the two of us together." Greg turned the page. "We were much younger then."

Gabby stared wide-eyed at the photograph and turned pale. Were her eyes deceiving her?

"Is there something wrong, Gabby? Are you ill? Let me get you a glass of water. I should never have mentioned his name." Greg jumped up and watched Gabby closely as she stared at the photograph, her face a complete blank.

She felt claustrophobic; she had to get out. Aware of Greg's eyes on her, she averted her own from his and pointedly looked at her watch. "I forgot, Greg. I forgot that I have to be somewhere else by five. If I leave now I might just make it. I'll email you."

"Let me help you on with your coat if you must. Was it something I said? Was it something I did?"

She was gone. The door slammed closed behind her.

* * *

Gabby raced down to the car looking over her shoulder to make sure that she was not being followed. Setting Mavis to 'take me home', she turned left when told to do so, turned right when told to do so, took the left lane, took the right lane, continued straight on – did everything she was told without question. Mavis could have been taking her to Timbuctoo for all she knew or cared.

She felt numb. Thinking about it would not help – the whole thing was crazy, unthinkable and unimaginable. She was losing her senses – her eyes had deceived her. Nothing made sense. Five minutes ago everything had been okay, but suddenly the world had been turned on its head.

Gabby looked in her mirror as the sound of an air horn assaulted her ears. There was a long queue of traffic behind her and a lorry sat within a couple of feet of her bumper flashing his lights. She glanced at the speedo and saw that she was doing twenty in a fifty zone and driving close to the centre lines of the road so that nobody could safely overtake her.

"Hell," she shouted to herself. "Hell, hell, hell." Ahead a blue sign told her that there was a parking layby within half a mile. She had to stop and get her head together before she killed both herself and everybody else on the road.

Gabby stopped the car, switched the engine off, slumped over the steering wheel and sobbed until her head pounded and her handkerchief was soaked.

She could not get the photograph out of her mind. It was the eyes, the bushy eyebrows that turned upwards towards the hairline, the square jaw, the full head of hair, the nose, the cheekbones, and the lips. Neither could the Bermuda shorts or the T-shirt disguise the body that she knew so well. Other than the greying of his hair and a few more facial lines he had changed little.

"Why? How?" Gabby banged the steering wheel with her hands. "Somebody please, please help me to understand. Am I going completely crazy?"

No one answered her pleas but then she had not really expected them to; she was not going crazy. She had to pull herself together. She was no more than five miles from St Francis but a good forty miles from Chertsey. She knew she would not be able to concentrate on the road. The safest course of action was to go back to St Francis, back to somebody who would understand and help her.

Gabby blew her nose, checked her mirrors three times and pulled out onto the road heading back in the direction of St Francis.

* * *

Greg sat by the window, a large scotch in hand. He needed it. She was one strange woman; one minute they had been sitting chatting about holiday destinations and paging through his photographs, the next she had bolted and he would probably never see her again. Goodbye Penelope, goodbye Gabby. Shit. Shit. Shit.

The photograph albums could go back in the cupboard and stay there forever, as far as he was concerned. No more going through albums if ever he invited another woman round to his apartment. But before he put them away he would remove every trace of Harry Trumper. He was not going to let that man ruin his life again.

What was it with her and the house in Bermuda? It was just one of several along the waterfront. They were all built of the same white weatherboard and, if he remembered correctly, they all had pale blue window frames and quaint little pots arranged on the verandas. So what was the deal with her? It was when she had seen the photograph of Harry that she had really flipped. Perhaps it was understandable; he had been the cause of a great deal of angst to her aunt and uncle and their friends. Maybe he shouldn't blame her for her reaction after seeing him in 'real life'. But surely she had overreacted? They could have talked about it and he would happily have answered any questions that she may have had. He had explained that he was out there with Harry long before Magnolia Court became a problem. Maybe he should simply have kept his mouth shut and told her that Harry was an old school friend.

Greg slammed the cupboard door shut at the same moment the doorbell rang, not once but continually – someone was leaning on it. "Yes? What do you want?" Greg snapped at the intercom.

"Can I come up please, Greg?"

"Is that you, Gabby? Of course." Greg opened the door to the apartment to see Gabby dragging her feet up the stairs, her head hung low, her face blotched where her mascara had run down her cheeks. She looked as though her whole world had fallen apart.

"I was driving dangerously. I could have killed someone. It was too far to go home so I came back here," she sobbed.

Greg opened his arms to her and she rested her head against his shoulders. "I knew there was something wrong when you left like that," Greg said gently. "What's upset you so much? Was it my photographs?"

Gabby nodded and looked up at him, tears forming in her eyes. "It's the man you stayed with in Bermuda, Harry Trumper, the same man that everybody thought had disappeared to South America on a one-way ticket."

"What about him? He's in the past – for me, for your friends at Magnolia, for everybody. Please don't let the past come back and haunt you. There was nothing you could have done to change things," Greg pleaded.

"That's just it, Greg. He's not the past – he's the present. I know him. I know him only too well."

Seventeen

"I always fancied going on a cruise, Dennis," Dot said, generously buttering her slice of bread; she liked bread on her butter, not butter on her bread.

Dennis looked up above his half-rimmed steel glasses. "Where did that come from, Dot? You never mentioned it before."

"Well, I could climb the mast if I wanted to. You know how much I always used to love climbing."

"They don't have masts on cruise ships, Dot."

"Ah, but they do have rock faces that you can climb. I've seen it on the television. There are holes for your feet in the wall and bits of rock to catch hold of, and you wear a harness – safe as houses. And can you imagine the view from the top of the rock face? My idea of heaven."

"A whole lot of sea is all you'll see from up there. I've got a better idea, Dot, and it's a lot cheaper. We still haven't finished trimming the branches of those trees, so how about after breakfast we get the ladder out and you admire the view from the top of the tree. It will be another job well done."

"You old romantic, Dennis. The only thing I'll see from the top of that tree is your lovely bald pate, a row of ageing old cottages and a derelict mansion. But seriously, why don't we think about a cruise? It would be one off my bucket list." Dot looked hopeful.

"Bucket list. Since when have you had a bucket list, my dear? The only use for buckets around here is to catch the water when we have a good old-fashioned English downpour," Dennis said with a laugh.

"We've got fifteen thousand in the bank now and it isn't earning that much interest. We deserve a bit of fun." If the truth were told it was burning a hole in her pocket; she was so excited about being rich again.

"Fifteen thousand doesn't go very far these days, Dot. It wouldn't start to cover the repairs that really ought to be done to this cottage. When some of those holes in the roof get a bit bigger we'll be going to bed with our raincoats on. No, Dot, I think we need to keep that money for a rainy day – literally. You never know what's around the corner as we found out when we bought this place."

"The voice of reason as always, Dennis," Dot sighed thought-fully. "If I am honest, that money has been giving me a few sleepless nights. You do remember that some of our friends contributed a lot more to the fighting fund than we were able to at the time. I did wonder if it was fair that we should get the same sum as everybody else. What do you think?"

"I think you should sleep soundly, my dear. Everybody put their last penny into that fund and I am sure the others would be very offended if we suggested that this windfall was divided up in any other way." Dennis couldn't deny that it had crossed his mind as well and that he had had a quiet word with Peter about it – Peter understood money. Peter had put his mind at rest in a few short words: "Ridiculous, old chap, we're all in this together" and that had been the end of the conversation.

"Ladder," said Dennis with a grin.

* * *

Henry poured himself a gin and tonic – light on the gin and heavy on the tonic. Not the way he liked it, but a bottle of gin had to last a long time these days.

The sleeve to *Mantovani's Greatest Hits* lay on the arm of the chair while 'Charmaine' drifted around the room from the old record player. It was his favourite vinyl and nearly worn out with playing. Charmaine was sounding decidedly scratchy these days, but the words were what mattered to him. He never felt alone when he played her song; she was there in the room just as she always had been.

For a moment he let his mind wander away from the words. My, it was a long time since he had seen fifteen thousand pounds and it had somehow renewed his faith in humanity that a man like Greg should, after all these years, think of them all. It was a drop in the ocean compared to the amount of money that many of them had put in the fighting fund. He alone had contributed forty thousand to the search and legal fees. It had made sense at the time.

Henry smiled at the photograph of his very own Charmaine, which took pride of place on the coffee table beside him. It was a relief that she had not lived long enough to see their home deteriorate. He remembered how excited she had been about their move to Magnolia Court – the new swimming costume and swim cap she had bought and the new set of golf clubs that had never seen the light of day. All of her things were still in their wardrobe, her dresses intermingled with his suits, her shoes mixed with his, her scarves mixed with his ties; her perfume on them was as strong and sweet as ever it had been. There were those who thought it was unhealthy to keep so much, but what they did not understand was that she was still there. Her spirit was everywhere and a great comfort to him.

"I'm waiting my Charmaine for you," Henry quietly sang the lyrics. He had met his wife at the Apollo Halls in High Wycombe. She was the most glamorous woman he had ever set eyes on and with the sweetest voice. They had walked out together for quite a while before they decided to get married.

The first of their children had been born just two years after they had married, the second after three years and the third after five years. They were all parents themselves now and before much longer they too would be grandparents. They had been very proud of them all. The little that Henry could leave them in his will would hardly be noticed in their ample bank accounts but hopefully, the grandchildren would appreciate the small trust that he had set up for each of them when finally it was time for him to meet up again with his Charmaine.

Henry turned back to the photograph of his wife. "Do you think, my dear, that it would be too extravagant of me if I bought myself a Bose music centre?"

Charmaine smiled back at him. "Thank you, my dear," Henry said.

* * *

Andy, Magnolia Court's very own handyman, curled up in his old leather armchair, a mug of builder's tea in one hand and a well-thumbed old copy of the *Daily Mirror* in the other. It was his 'lunch break' as he called it. There was always something to keep him occupied at Magnolia. That morning he had fixed two leaking taps, replaced one door handle, mended a door lock, replaced the hinges on a kitchen cupboard and replaced a piece of floorboard at the nineteenth hole. Not much beat him, except that infernal lawn mower, which hadn't worked properly since young Gabby had kicked it into action.

Post-Its were a vital accessory for everybody at Magnolia: a yellow Post-It signified urgent, a green Post-It signified important and a pink Post-It signified annoying but not urgent. Andy posted them all up on his kitchen cabinet in the order in which they arrived and set himself the target of dealing with yellow the same day, green within one week and pink when there was any spare time available.

He had been a handyman all his life and was very successful. Andy prided himself on his honesty and versatility and it had paid dividends. He was ever popular with a huge network of reliable friends who shared his values. If anyone ever needed a job done, which he, Andy, could not tackle, then he knew a man who could.

If anybody had ever told Andy that one day he might be able to retire he would have laughed at them. And then out of the blue, he scooped a jackpot on a lottery card – a quarter of a million pounds. His friends were delighted; if anybody deserved it, it was him, they said. The very same day the postman popped a brochure for Magnolia through his door – champagne and canapés at a posh London hotel, afternoon tea and all travel expenses paid. Andy persuaded himself that he deserved a day off and he hadn't been to London for years. No such thing as a free lunch, he told himself sternly before he set off, quite determined that he was not going to be persuaded to part with his new-found wealth.

It wasn't the high-pressure salesmanship or the promise of a trip to California that had tipped the balance – it was the people he met there. They were mostly retired professionals but right from the first moment he met them he felt totally at home in their company and nothing had changed in all the years he had lived here.

The lottery win together with the proceeds from the sale of his terrace house were just enough to buy his own cottage at Magnolia and pay the twenty-year service charge. There hadn't been much left in his pocket and there was even less after he had made his contribution towards the fighting fund. At the time he was embarrassed that his contribution to the fund had been far less than the sums that some of the others had contributed but no one seemed to care.

Now he had his fifteen thousand back in the bank and it felt like winning the jackpot all over again. An old copy of *Vintage Motorcycles* lay on the small kitchen table, three pages of which were dedicated to sales. Several months ago he had ringed one advertisement in particular. It was for a vintage Norton 50 that was badly in need of restoration. How he would love to be able to buy her and make her look as she once had.

He'd think about it and maybe give them a call in a few days' time, but in the meantime, there were Post-Its to be dealt with.

* * *

"Now where did I put that cheque?" Amy asked herself. "I

know I put it somewhere safe so that I could ask Peter to pay it into my bank next week."

Amy rifled through her desk; it was definitely way past time for a clearance sale. If she cleared the desk out completely then she might just find the cheque. If it wasn't there then it must be somewhere else. Amy emptied the contents of her desk on to her bed and sat down beside the pile of letters, cards, photographs, and boxes. It was a long time since she had been through them – every one of them a memory of times past, mostly good but some sad.

There were birthday cards, Christmas cards, letters and postcards from her sister in Australia. In a small silver box, she found her precious photographs of the man she had married; George was such a handsome and clever man and so brave.

One by one she replaced all her memories back in the desk. A small pile of used envelopes and old receipts that were no longer needed lay on the floor.

Amy smiled at her own forgetfulness: the cheque was sitting on the top of the desk under a paperweight just where she had put it. Fifteen thousand – such a lot of money. She would buy herself a brand new set of calligraphy pens and new inks and, just maybe, visit her sister in Australia one more time.

* * *

Peter banked the cheque the following day and thought nothing more about it. It was neither here nor there to him. He didn't need much money at Magnolia and he certainly didn't need the money where he was going. He would probably donate it together with his other assets to Macmillan Cancer which had been wonderful to him over the years and at the end of the phone 24/7 whenever he had needed someone to talk to. Or he might simply split it between all the other residents of Magnolia to whom he felt indebted for their friendship and companionship over the past thirteen years.

Unlike the other residents, he was less than impressed with Greg's grand gesture, as he called it in private. In Peter's eyes, Greg was equally as culpable as Harry Trumper. It would take a lot to persuade him that this architect could not have stepped in sooner and put paid to his boss's tricks.

* * *

Gerald held the cheque up to the light: it was a totally automatic reaction. How could you possibly differentiate between a forgery and the real thing under the low-energy bulbs that everyone was forced to buy these days?

It was genuine, not that he had any real doubt about it anyway. For a split second he screwed up his eyes. Was it possible to add an extra nought to the fifteen thousand and make it one hundred and fifty thousand? Unfortunately, the comma could not be removed and there was no room for the extra nought. A pity, he thought, but those days were best left in the past.

In the good old days, fifteen thousand would have been mere pocket money, but now it represented half of his savings and it was highly unlikely that another windfall would come his way for a very long time. He'd had a few of those in his time, mostly legitimate, some bordering on legitimate but a few most definitely not legitimate. The art world, he reflected, had been a strange world. There were those who adored beautiful things and would pay any price for them and those who simply needed to possess them to reflect their status in life.

The business and the thriving gallery that he had once owned had kept both him and his partner, Thomas, in a grand lifestyle for many years. He would always regret the day he had broken the eleventh commandment and been found out. In one fell swoop he had all but been wiped out. The grand lifestyle disappeared overnight, along with Thomas, his partner of ten years. But Gerald had few regrets; it had been fun while it lasted and he had been lucky enough to have sufficient money secreted away to buy his property at Magnolia with a tidy sum left over. From the moment he had met the other prospective buyers for Magnolia, he knew that he had fallen on his feet. He was gay and made no secret of it. The residents of Magnolia had never been judgemental and had always treated him with respect and as an equal. When the fighting fund needed fuelling, he had dug deep to help the cause.

So, what was he going to do with this flimsy piece of paper that represented the grand sum of fifteen thousand pounds? He had no idea, other than bank it.

* * *

Jennifer drew the curtains and switched on the Tiffany table lamp that was her pride and joy. Tonight she was going to put her feet up and simply luxuriate in watching one of the musicals from the new box set that had dropped on the doorstep that very day. It had been an extravagance to buy them but a fitting way to celebrate her new windfall.

Whatever would she do with the remaining fourteen thousand nine hundred and seventy pounds, she wondered? There was nothing she wanted for herself. She had a wardrobe full of clothes albeit bought from charity shops, but those were the places where she found all the things that she liked best. It was no good going shopping in the High Street even if she had wanted to spend money in them. All the clothes were for younger people and in her opinion dull, shapeless, cheap and disposable.

Definitely getting old. Jennifer laughed at her own thoughts. If she were sixty or even fifty years younger she would probably have loved the latest fashions.

Unconsciously she ran her fingers through her hair and it reminded her of how she had once looked. Now that would be a treat, she thought – a new wig but one made with one hundred per cent silky smooth human hair. In another year her hair might have the length but it was extremely unlikely that it would ever be silky smooth again.

Satisfied with her decision, Jennifer turned her attention back to *South Pacific*.

All the money in the world couldn't buy her the one thing that she so desperately wanted – her final performance.

* * *

Duncan had been looking at the screen for far too long. His eyes were getting tired and dry and he was blinking every few seconds. His desktop computer was his lifeline, his main contact with the outside world and most importantly his way of keeping his brain active. It consumed and fascinated him at the same time. Keeping up with technology was a 24/7 marathon. There was no time for complacency. He had to keep his finger on the pulse.

He remembered when he had first started working in IT or 'computers' as it was then called when computers filled rooms the size of warehouses and delivered far less power and functionality than the little box that now sat on his desk. The world had changed almost overnight with the advent of the desktop and the network and now almost every bit of information he needed was at his fingertips.

Duncan had been in right at the beginning of the IT revolution and had promised himself that no matter what he would follow its progress and keep up with it. He had done far more than that – there was almost nothing that foxed him. He thanked his lucky stars that God had blessed him with such an enquiring mind and the ability to solve the most complicated problems: the body was old and scarred but his mind was as alert and agile as a fourteen-year-old's.

His first saviour was his mind and the second, Magnolia Court. In return for a higher deposit and a marginally higher price, the cottage had been built around his mobility needs. Open-plan throughout, he had no need to negotiate doorways except the widened doorway that led into the small downstairs toilet and bathroom. It had enabled him to keep his independence – at least within his own four walls.

He passed the day shopping and banking online for his friends, managing his meagre investments, comparing and contrasting the latest desktops, laptops and notebooks and reading articles about the latest scams and hackers. He longed for a more powerful PC, which would enable him to do so much more, and a new screen that would save his eyes.

Five thousand pounds would make a very small hole in the fifteen thousand that he now had in the bank. He could afford that computer.

* * *

"I really don't think we can accept this cheque," Emanuel said. "It was Ralph who paid into the fighting fund, not us."

"And what did they all say to you?" Dinah reminded him. "That Ralph would have wanted us to have it?"

"But we don't need it, Dinah. Our pensions are probably worth more than most of theirs put together," Emanuel argued.

"That's not the point, Emanuel. It's their way of saying that we are as much a part of the community as they are. They'd be really offended if we argued or handed it back."

Number six Magnolia Court looked no different to the cottages either side; it was in the same state of disrepair. Years ago Emanuel had wanted to pay contractors to effect the repairs but Dinah had had the last word. It would set them apart from everybody else and that was not something that she wished to do.

"Let's just put it away safely for the moment, Emanuel. This is a gift from God to all of us," Dinah said.

* * *

Neither Hetty nor Max had voiced their views on the windfall in private or in public. The whole sorry mess was still raw for Max who had led the fight for justice. Greg turning up

171

and returning the money, however well-intentioned, had not helped – it had reopened old wounds. Gabby was not helping either; she still showed no signs of letting the matter go.

The cheque remained on the mantelpiece where they had put it after Gabby's birthday. By rights, they should have banked it weeks ago, but neither of them had touched it or mentioned it.

There had always been an unspoken agreement between them formed in the knowledge that one day Gabby would come back to them. She would be their sole heir and the proceeds from Magnolia, if any existed, and any other sums in the bank would be her inheritance.

Eighteen

"You just relax and tell me all about it when you feel up to it." Greg sat down beside her and put his arm around her shoulders reassuringly. He was in no hurry. He could see that she needed to compose herself before she was ready to talk. He was curious, more than curious. How could Gabby possibly know Harry Trumper?

Gabby wiped her eyes and blew her nose. "I know Harry Trumper – the man in the photograph with you in Bermuda, Greg, because I am married to him."

For a moment he was speechless. Greg took a deep breath, narrowed his eyes and gathered his thoughts. "That's simply not possible. They say that everyone has a double and I guess you've just seen Charles's double. It happens, Gabby." He lifted her chin and looked deep into her eyes. She looked deadly serious.

"I wish it was that simple, Greg," she replied quietly. "Harry Trumper is Charles Fairbrother, my husband. I'd recognise him anywhere. The years haven't changed him that much."

Gabby had never struck Greg as being neurotic or fanciful but right at that moment he found himself questioning her sanity. One moment they had been laughing at his holiday snaps, the next she had bolted and now she was back telling him that she was married to Harry Trumper.

"I couldn't go home. My head was all over the place. It still is. And what is home? Home is where I live with Charles, but I don't, do I?" she rambled.

"I'll make us a stiff drink," Greg said. He poured scotch into two glasses and added ice.

"I know someone else who always pours scotch in the glass first and adds ice afterward, but I've already told you that, haven't I?" Gabby said, watching Greg carefully.

He frowned and laughed. "Yes, you did mention it. As I told you before, I picked up the habit from someone along the way. Don't ask me when or why."

"Would that have been from Harry Trumper, Greg?" Gabby asked.

It had not crossed his mind before. An image of sitting in the sun, a bottle of scotch, an ice bucket and two glasses on a table beside him floated back into his mind. He was in Bermuda – Harry was pouring the drinks and he heard his words as clear as a bell: "Scotch and then ice in that order, Greg. Always that way around."

"Gabby, it may well be that I did pick up the habit from Harry Trumper but so what? Just because your Charles does the same thing, it doesn't mean he's Harry Trumper."

"Jennifer said that when he did his presentation on Magnolia he walked around the stage with his hands in his pockets jingling his change. Charles does that all the time. I am forever mending his pockets." Gabby drained her glass and shuddered. The scotch tasted bitter and burnt all the way down.

"Most men do that, Gabby," Greg said patiently.

"Amy said she noticed he was left-handed," Gabby continued. "Charles is left-handed."

"Half the population is left-handed, Gabby. So Charles is left-handed, jingles his change in his pocket and prefers scotch poured in the glass before the ice is added. That doesn't make your Charles a criminal. And that photograph is over thirteen years old, Gabby. I hardly recognise myself in it, let alone Harry. I do not doubt you, believe me, but think about it, Gabby. The odds are a million to one."

"Then it sounds like I won the lottery, Greg," Gabby replied flatly. "I haven't told you the best yet. You remember I said that the house on the beach in your photograph was familiar? Well, I have remembered where I saw it. There's no mistaking it. There's a photograph of it framed and hanging in the downstairs cloakroom in Annabel's house – the house that she and Charles shared before their divorce. Now tell me that I am wrong."

Greg shook his head, got up and paced backwards and forwards. Was he wrong to doubt her?

"I can see that you still don't believe me, Greg," Gabby said accusingly. "Can you get that photograph album out and do you have a magnifying glass?"

Greg sighed; nothing she had said was positive proof of her assertion that Charles and Harry were one and the same man, but he would humour her. "I threw the photographs of Bermuda in the bin, but I can retrieve them if it makes you happy." Maybe in looking at the photographs again, she would see that it was no more than a case of mistaken identity.

At arm's length, Gabby picked a photograph up and held it out to him. "Look closely at that photograph, Greg. Use a magnifying glass and see if you can see a scar on his left leg, just below the knee. It's three parts of a circle, if I am not mistaken."

Greg rummaged in a drawer, found a small magnifying glass and positioned the glass over the photograph. Jesus Christ, she was right. No one would have seen it with the naked eye.

"Charles told me that he fell off his bike when he was a boy and cut it on some glass. It never healed properly."

"Another drink?" Greg asked.

"Please."

Greg put his arm back around her shoulders. Gabby rested her head on his shoulder. This was the woman who spent her days protesting against injustice, selfishness and thoughtlessness and now here she sat like a discarded rag doll. Was there no justice in the world?

They sat together in silence, each engulfed in their own thoughts. They both needed time to absorb the enormity of what had happened and its implications for Gabby's life in particular, and maybe for Greg's life as well.

"Will you help me?" she whispered. "I can't do this on my own."

"You don't need to ask," he replied as he kissed the top of her head and stroked her hair; it was the most natural thing in the world. "Where the hell do we start? This is going to take some unraveling."

Gabby nodded. "I know. I've been thinking about it. If Charles Fairbrother is Harry Trumper then I am not married to him," she stated coolly. "It says Charles Fairbrother on our marriage certificate, but if that is not his real name then I can't be Gabby Fairbrother and I can't be his wife either."

"And neither can Annabel be the ex-Mrs Annabel Fairbrother nor the children Fairbrothers," Greg added thoughtfully. "Do you think she knows?"

"If she does then she's a better actress than he is an actor. I doubt it, but we can't rule it out." Gabby shook her head. Somehow she couldn't see Annabel living under a false persona or letting the children grow up with a false surname.

"We'll have to be methodical, Gabby – work our way through everything we know and sort the facts from the fiction and the assumptions. Are you ready to do that or would you like to leave it until tomorrow? I insist that you stay here this evening. I have a spare bedroom. You can't drive after those two drinks and I won't have you going back to that house for the moment," Greg said forcefully.

Gabby nodded. "Yes, let's try to make some sense of it all."

"So what do we know? We know that Harry Trumper disappeared and closed down his company in December '04 and that he disappeared with money that should have been spent on Magnolia – maybe a million, maybe two." Greg wrote the first fact on a list.

"And I know that he pocketed another two and a half million. Amy told me that they each paid two hundred and fifty thousand up front for a twenty-year subscription to all the community facilities including the care facilities that were promised to them. Ten times two-fifty. I know it sounds crazy to you and me, but, as Amy confided to me, twelve thousand a year wasn't so much to pay for twenty years of peace of mind and security."

"I didn't know that, Gabby. It's even worse than I thought then." Greg took a deep breath, slowly exhaled it from his lungs and made more notes. "So let's put ourselves in his shoes and bear in mind that he doesn't give a toss about people. He saves himself millions on the build and pockets two and a half million earmarked for future maintenance and care – possibly over four million pounds. What would you do in his shoes? I'll tell you – cut and run. Stick the four million in my pocket and disappear into the blue yonder."

"I think there's even more to it than that, Greg. Amy told me something interesting. Apparently, she used to chat with the builders and was pretty friendly with the foreman. On the day they downed tools and left the site he told her that there were rumours that the police were after him – something to do with his past and a fire."

"So maybe two good reasons to do a bunk, Gabby," Greg said. "Let's think about dates. When did Charles and Annabel get married?"

"October '05, I think. Ethan was born nine months later and he is now ten."

"So he disappeared in December '04 and reinvented himself as Charles Fairbrother by the latest in October '05 – roughly nine months." Greg thought about it. He had always assumed that Harry Trumper had left the country, but maybe he had never left England at all.

"Do you know exactly when he and Annabel first met?"

"I remember Charles telling me that it was at the races. I think it was the Epsom Derby. He had a share in a horse that was running there."

"That takes place in June. That narrows it down even further. If he met Annabel in June '05 and presented himself to her as Charles Fairbrother, which we have to assume he did, then sometime in the six months between December '04 and June '05 he changed his identity," Greg summarised. "Can I ask you some rather personal questions, Gabby?" Greg was about to get into deep water, but it had to be done.

178

Gabby nodded. He had never pried into her personal affairs before and she knew that whatever he asked her, it would be for a good reason.

"I remember you telling me earlier that you've never been abroad on holiday with Charles. Is that because you couldn't afford it?"

"That was part of it, yes. We live in a rented cottage and Annabel pays the rent. Charles has a modest income. I've seen the bank statements – he has never kept his financial situation a secret from me. He has enough coming in each month to pay the bills on the house, for his golf, and a little left over for us to go out and enjoy a meal occasionally or go off on day trips. Annabel even pays for his car so that the children don't turn up at parties in a heap of old junk."

"So if Charles is Harry then where is all the money? You can't hide that sort of money under the bed."

"He did have a lot of money once – he told me. He bought the house in Weybridge and he used to have a share in a racehorse. He told me that he had handed almost everything over to Annabel as part of the divorce settlement. The house must cost a fortune to run and there are exorbitant fees for the children's private schools. I knew all this before I married him. He was a generous man in his own way."

"Gabby, I don't mean to be unkind but just listen to yourself. I don't know another man alive who wouldn't fight for every penny that he could keep after a divorce. Nobody hands over that sort of money without a bye your leave or a damned good reason." Greg laughed nervously.

"You don't know him. He isn't like other men. He is different." Gabby stopped short and thought about what she was saying. Why was she standing up for this man who had unmercifully duped her family and friends and her as well? She loved him – that was why. No, correct that, she thought to herself. She had loved the man she thought he was.

"Gabby, you have to remember that we are not talking about the man you know as Charles Fairbrother. We are talking about a ruthless criminal called Harry Trumper. Nothing in this world is going to persuade me that in the space of six months, or even ten years, he changed from a greedy, mean crook into a loving family man with no interest in money. I am sorry that you love a man who doesn't exist. It must be heartbreaking for you," Greg said impatiently, shaking his head. "And this same man goes away on extended holidays with his ex-wife and his kids? Unbelievable."

Gabby nodded; as the minutes passed she felt more and more foolish but she couldn't stop herself. "Annabel puts the kids first every time. I knew before we got married that she might ask him to accompany them on the odd jaunt, but I have to confess I didn't expect it to be every school holiday for weeks on end. But in fairness to him, he always asks me if I mind. And in fairness to her, Annabel does ring to check it out with me."

"Oh, Gabby, sweet Gabby, you are just too nice for your own good. Doesn't it seem odd to you that they spend so much time together? Have they ever asked you to go with them as well? If he's a loving family man then I'm Charlie's aunt. Harry Trumper never wanted baggage, as he called it. The only reason I can think of that he got married in the first place and had a family was to cover up his past. How did you meet him? You don't have to answer that if it is too personal."

"It's okay. I received an invitation out of the blue to a school reunion from Annabel when I was living in Surbiton. At the time I couldn't work out for the life of me why she had invited me. I was never part of her circle of friends. Curiosity kills the cat, as they say, and in this case, it couldn't be truer. Weybridge was easy to get to and I was curious to see what she had made of her life. I hadn't expected to, but I actually enjoyed the party – there were several other girls there that I got on with reasonably well at school."

"It was raining when I left the party. I remember that – pouring with rain. I'd just left the house and I was walking to the station when a car drew up beside me. It was Charles and he offered to give me a lift. He had just dropped by the house to check something out with Annabel before taking off to pick the kids up from some event or other. I missed my train. We had tea together while I waited for the next one. One thing led to another. We fell in love. We married six months later. I'm sure he loved me," Gabby said.

"Maybe he did, Gabby. Let's not dismiss it entirely, but there's another possibility and it's a wild guess, I admit. Let's suppose that he needed to put some distance between his fortune and himself, for reasons that I can't begin to fathom, and he saw that getting a divorce and handing it over to Annabel would achieve that end. I am no expert in the law, but based on the little knowledge I have, he may have succeeded," Greg said.

"But why would he need to do that and why marry me, Greg? Do you think he always meant to go back to her?"

"Not one, but two sixty-four-thousand-dollar questions, Gabby. Maybe he really did fall in love with you or maybe he, or should I say they, were using you in some way. If my guess is anywhere near the mark, then yes, Gabby, at some point he would have gone back to her and his money," Greg said soberly. "Nothing we have talked about changes the fact that Charles Fairbrother is Harry Trumper and we both know what he is capable of."

"Do you think that Annabel is in on it as well?"

"It explains the invitation out of the blue. It explains the holidays, and it explains her not allowing you to be part of the children's lives." Whichever way he looked at it, it seemed to be the only rational explanation.

"So Annabel and Charles win. Aunt Hetty, Uncle Max, Amy, Duncan, Jennifer, me and all the rest lose," Gabby said defiantly. It was high time she stopped thinking of herself and thought more about all those wonderful people who had lost so much – at his hands. "Maybe we could appeal to her better nature – especially if Annabel doesn't know anything about Harry or Magnolia?"

Greg laughed. "Now you are being naïve, Gabby. Put yourself in her shoes. She, just like you, finds that she is married to a man who is not who he said he was, and, what's more, is an out-and-out crook who's been lying to her for years. What would you do? I know what I would do, and that is to make damn sure that neither he nor anybody else could touch a penny of my money. She'll look after herself."

"I just can't get my head around why he would get divorced and hand his fortune over to Annabel? Something cataclysmic must have happened."

"I can only surmise that someone else was after his money and he had to find a neat way to safeguard it, if only on a temporary basis," Greg said. "You wouldn't believe some of the stories he told me. I reckon our friends at Magnolia weren't the only ones to be ripped off by him. Maybe someone found out about his change of identity and was after him for money. God, how did I ever let myself get involved with that man?"

"I can ask myself the same question. And there's something else," Gabby said thoughtfully. "If Charles Fairbrother is Harry Trumper, then who is Charles Fairbrother? He has a passport, driving licence, bank account, investments, even a bus pass."

"The third sixty-four-thousand-dollar question. The very same thought just passed through my mind."

"The hardest thing of all is accepting that he never loved me." Gabby tilted her head and looked into Greg's eyes.

"How could anyone not love you, Gabby?" Greg whispered kindly. I do, he said to himself.

* * *

Gabby lay in Greg's arms under the snowy white duvet.

"You do know that I would never have done that if you had been a married woman." Greg propped himself up on his elbows and looked down into Gabby's face. She had a kind of innocence that was completely irresistible. He did not feel guilty; he felt elated. He had not taken advantage of her. It was she who, after the simple supper that he'd cooked, had led him to the master bedroom, and he who had not resisted.

He made love to her with more tender care than he had ever made love to another woman. More than anything he wanted to look after her and safeguard her from being hurt further, but he knew that it would be a long road.

Gabby felt warm and cared for. In Greg's arms she was safe.

They lay curled up together in one another's arms. They had done enough talking for the moment. Gabby's mind drifted back to Magnolia Court and the day that Greg had met Aunt Hetty and Uncle Max and all their friends and was thankful that they had all taken to him so well. Greg's mind wandered towards the future – was it possible that he and Gabby had a real future together?

"Will you take me to Magnolia again, Gabby?"

"It'll be your second home before long," Gabby said with a laugh. "Get used to it."

Greg lay back on the pillows watching Gabby as her breathing slowed and she fell asleep, exhausted. It was many hours before he slept.

Nineteen

Gabby sat at the table playing with her breakfast; she had no appetite for it.

"Regretting last night?" Greg asked lightly.

Gabby shook her head, looked up, smiled, and took his hand. "No way. You are the tops. I am just trying to get my head around where we go from here. It's as if I've found myself in the middle of a cryptic crossword and whichever way I look at it I can't see the answer."

Greg squeezed her hand. He wanted to protect her, but right at that moment he didn't know how he could do so. "I know exactly what you mean. I spent half of the night going round the houses and getting nowhere. The one thing I do know is that you need to get away from him. I meant it when I said he is a dangerous man. I know what he is capable of and it scares the pants off me to think what he might do if ever he found out that you knew anything about his past."

"That makes me feel so much better." Gabby laughed.

"I meant what I said last night. This is your home any time you want it to be. You could go back right now, pack your bags and move in with me – a fresh start, forget the past."

"Don't tempt me, Satan."

"Only it wouldn't be that simple. If I know Harry Trumper

he would be on your trail in no time. I can't see him just shrugging his shoulders when he finds you've just upped and left while he has been sunning himself in Dubai. He'd want to know why, and through his network, he'd track you down. And what would he find? You shacked up with his old mate, Greg, who threatened to spill the beans on Magnolia. And then he'd know for sure that he'd been rumbled. Neither of us would be safe then," Greg said soberly.

"So what do you suggest, Sherlock?" Gabby asked hopefully.

"The only sensible thing to do would be to go straight to the police and tell them everything we know. It may be our only option and they may still be looking for him. We've probably got enough on him to get him locked up for a few years –identity theft, fraud, maybe even bigamy. The only problem then is that with good behaviour he'd be out in a few years with a clean slate and hell-bent on revenge. I would not like to be around then."

"And if we did go the police what would be the chances of the residents getting back the money that he owes them?" Gabby asked, half knowing the answer.

"There are no guarantees when it comes to the law, Gabby. This is one glorified mess, and by the time the police and courts manage to untangle it, if ever they do, it could be years. Sod's law is that the residents will all be dead by then. And then, of course, there's the added complication of Annabel having all of the money – whether lawful or not."

Their coffee grew cold as the two of them sat opposite each other, mulling over the options, all of which seemed pretty dismal.

"So it's as I said to you last night – Annabel and Charles-slash-Harry win. Uncle Max, Aunt Hetty, and all the others lose," Gabby said dejectedly. "And we could end up dead. Is that how it is going to be? He owes them millions of pounds plus interest plus compensation, and I need my life back. There has to be a way, Greg."

Gabby sat back with a defiant expression on her face. "Just over three months ago, after I first visited Magnolia Court, I swore to myself that if ever I was in a position to do so I would make whoever was responsible pay for leaving them in that state. So how, now that I know who and where he is, can I just walk away? He owes them, Greg. He owes them however many millions it would need to restore every single part of Magnolia Court and keep them in the style they were promised for the rest of their lives. I don't think I could live with myself if I didn't do something."

"I couldn't agree more, Gabby. And unless you're prepared to pretend that none of this ever happened and continue to live your life as Mrs Charles Fairbrother, we have no option but to do something."

"The bottom line is that we need to get that money out of his pocket for Magnolia and then, and only then, can we afford to hand him over to the police and let them hang him out to dry."

"So, what magic shall we weave, Gabby? He isn't going to have that sort of money hanging around and for sure he isn't going to hand it over to you, me, or the residents," Greg said despondently.

"We've got five clear days, Greg. Charles doesn't come back until next Saturday. There's got to be something that we've missed – something that might at least explain why he divorced Annabel and married me. I think I have a right to know that if nothing else. Maybe that will point us in the right direction. At this moment we're up a creek without a paddle as they say, and, if we don't find that paddle in the next five days then I really don't know what we are going to do.

"I'm going back to the cottage right now to turn the whole place upside down. I've no idea what I am looking for, or what I will find, but there is nothing to lose." Gabby took a deep breath, got up from the table, and put her arms around Greg's neck. "I'll be back later if that is okay with you?"

"Tell me, before you go, does he do all his paperwork at home? I just wondered if he might have an office somewhere," Greg asked on the off chance.

"I'd forgotten that. Yes, he does. He doesn't go there often, only when he's checking up on his investments, so he used to tell me. An odd thing to do now I come to think about it. He could have done that from home."

"When you're back at the cottage see if you can find an address for the office and leave that side of it to me. Make sure you leave everything as you find it. The last thing we want is to raise suspicions," Greg said. "And if you're not back by five, I'll send a search party out. Keep in touch." Kissing her on the lips, he held her close and prayed that she would come back.

Twenty

The sky was grey, the clouds dark. There was rain in the air and a downpour not far off. With sadness Gabby remembered the many times she had come home from work on a dark evening to find the cottage lit up from within, the old coach lamp outside the front door glowing, and wisps of smoke swirling up into the sky from the chimney. She had always looked forward to those evenings with Charles.

But it was staring her in the face – it had all been a lie. One big fat lie. Gabby parked the car, fished her keys out of her handbag, strode purposefully up the garden path and opened the door.

A pile of post lay on the doormat – mostly circulars but hidden among them a postcard from Dubai. Gabby picked it up and turned it over.

My dearest Gabby, I wish I could say that I was enjoying myself but it is far too hot here and I miss you. I can't wait to get back. Arriving Heathrow Saturday 5pm. All my love, Charles.

Gabby's blood boiled as she reread the postcard. The lying cheating bastard, she said to herself. Switching on the light in the lounge, Gabby felt her mood change again. It was as if he was drawing her back to him again. Photographs of the two of them adorned one of the sideboards while another was reserved for the 'family' photographs. Now it was all too clear. Why would he want the children to get to know her if he had no intentions whatsoever of staying with her?

The hours flew by as she painstakingly pulled out one drawer after another. Normally she would have tipped everything on the floor, sorted through it and put it back but this time she had to be careful – everything had to go back in exactly the same order as she found it. By nature, she was not a tidy person and it was always Charles who tidied the drawers and kept them in order.

Gabby finished her search of the downstairs rooms, their bedroom and the small spare bedroom and sat down despondently. It was time to report in – to let Greg know that she had so far failed to find anything useful, but that she was safe.

* * *

"Not good news, Greg. Did I really think that he would have left anything incriminating in our cottage for me to find?" Gabby sighed. "Just utility bills addressed to Charles Fairbrother, bank statements which I had seen before, and correspondence from the golf club. Oh, and there's a file with his – or should I say Charles Fairbrother's – birth certificate, his divorce certificate, and our marriage certificate. That's it so far. One thing I can tell you – he hasn't lied about his birthday. It seems like he was born on the very day that we celebrate his birthday each year."

"Have you got that birth certificate to hand?" Greg asked. "At least we will know a bit more about Charles Fairbrother."

"Seems that he was born in Minchinhampton, to parents

Norman and Maria Fairbrother. Does that help?"

"We may be able to trace the family. It's a long shot. I'll get on to it," Greg said positively. "Did you find that office address?"

"Yes, I found a rental agreement. Would you believe that it's in Slough of all places? Have you got a pen? Why on earth would he choose to have an office in Slough? It's miles away. This is the address..."

"Good question. I'll check that out as well," Greg said. "When you've finished, pack a few clothes and come back here."

"Okay. There are just one or two places I haven't looked yet. Leave it to me. See you soon."

* * *

Gabby boiled the kettle. She needed a good boost of caffeine and then she would rack her brains. There was no safe in the house; she knew that for a fact. There was a small shed in the garden but that was where she kept all her gardening tools and she was quite sure that there were no boxes or drawers in there – which left the attic.

Shuddering at the prospect of the flies and spiders that were likely to drop on her head the moment she opened the loft hatch, Gabby slid aside the small lock that secured it in place and let it hang down on its hinges. Predictably dust and dead flies cascaded from the opened hatch into her hair. Fortunately, she had not spotted any spiders accompanying them. Taking the torch from her pocket, she climbed up to the third rung of the ladder and cautiously poked her head into the open space. Her heart almost stopped as her eyes alighted on two small cardboard boxes that had been placed within arm's reach of the loft entrance. Was this what she had been looking for? It was too much to hope for. Reaching in and pulling one after another towards the opening, she picked them up in turn and carefully set each of them down on the carpet beside the ladder.

There was nothing about the boxes that might indicate they contained anything special. Both bore labels from Amazon and both were addressed to Charles Fairbrother, The Poplars, The Hawthorns. Gabby cradled them in her arms and carried them downstairs. Sitting down on the floor beside them she eyed them with suspicion and anticipation – Pandora's box or another dead end? Gabby pulled her phone out her pocket and took photographs of both boxes so that she would be able to reassemble them exactly as she had found them.

Inside the first box, wrapped up in a polythene bag, she found a pile of photographs. Gabby snapped another picture. Her fingers trembling as she pulled the photographs out of the bag and slowly thumbed through them. They were photographs of paintings – his paintings – the ones that she had seen hanging on the walls at The Poplars. For a split second her heart went out to him – Charles must have taken the photographs as a keepsake when he had lost them to Annabel. Carefully replacing the photographs in the correct order in the polythene bag, Gabby slipped them back into the box. She was no closer to finding anything that might help them.

She opened the second box; more of the same. Gabby recognised photographs of more paintings she had seen at The Poplars and at the bottom of the box she spotted a small brown envelope inside which were two sheets of carefully folded paper. Gabby's eyes grew wide as she scanned the papers. It was a detailed list of paintings, each with an individual insurance valuation. The bottom line valuation figure was staggering. With hands shaking she picked up the phone.

"Greg? Are you sitting down?"

"What is it, Gabby, are you okay?"

"I'm okay, Greg, but in shock." Gabby paused and savoured the moment. "I've found Charles's fortune, or should I say, Harry's dirty money."

"What?"

"Are you ready for this?" Gabby asked excitedly. "There were two boxes just within arm's reach in the loft. They are both full of photographs and these are no holiday snaps. They are photographs of paintings and right at the bottom of the second box, there was an envelope that contained – wait for it – an insurance valuation for each of them." Gabby paused. "They are valued at millions and they're all hanging on the walls in Annabel's house. It explains so much, Greg, and what's more I'm not sure that Annabel has a clue what she is sitting on. I remember her telling us at the party that, other than a couple, they were all copies, but they most certainly are not," Gabby sat back and waited.

"Bloody amazing." Greg whistled. "No one but Harry would have the affront to hang his fortune on the walls for all to see. And Annabel has the lot, you think?"

"Or my name is not Gabrielle Fairbrother," Gabby said, laughing at her own joke.

"We must be thinking on the right lines, Gabby. He would never have signed all that lot over to her without a reason. He must think that someone is on to him. It's too easy. They get a divorce and he simply says that she can have the house and its contents. Nobody asks any questions. There's no money involved and nothing is being contested."

"So what do you propose, Miss Marple – rob the house?"

"And end up in prison ourselves? No, I don't think so. I don't think there are too many prison cells for mixed occupation. But we need to find a way of taking a few of those millions off him and redirecting them back to where they belong."

"I suspect there's a long queue to do that. Are you on your way back?"

"It's late, Greg. I think I'll stay here tonight. I need to think. I'm safe here for the moment. I promise I'll be back tomorrow morning. Can you wait?"

"I'll be here, Gabby. Goodnight, sleep tight and don't forget to lock the door and push all the bolts across."

"Goodnight, Greg. I'll see you in the morning."

It was past three in the morning when a plan took seed in her head.

"Crazy," she said to herself. "Crazy." Gabby grabbed a pen and started scribbling notes. It was probably the craziest idea in the world but what did they have to lose?

Twenty-One

Offices to Let. Apply within. The sign looked as though it had been there for years. Greg just hoped that what it stated was correct, otherwise it would have been a wasted journey.

He straightened his tie and walked confidently across to a small shabby, timber-framed building. Portacabins with small metal windows surrounded the car park reminding him of the containers that lined a dockside. He did a quick count: ten portacabins, seven of which had lights on inside; three were in darkness. One of them had to be Harry's office.

A middle-aged woman lounged behind a desk, feet up, with a mug of tea in one hand and a well-thumbed copy of *Riders* by Jilly Cooper in the other. Immersed in her book, she did not bother to look up when the bell tinged, announcing that a customer or a tenant might have come in to see her for a purpose.

"Sorry, ducks. I heard you, but I couldn't stop for a minute. Racy bit, you see. Why are they always black, I ask you? Quite had me going, or coming more like. What can I do for you?" she said. "I'm just holding the fort for an hour. The boss has stepped out – down to the bookies if I know anything about it."

"Actually, I'm looking for a small space to rent. A portacabin hadn't crossed my mind but seeing them, it might just work. The sign says Offices to Let. Am I in luck?" Greg leaned across the counter. It was impossible not to look at the woman's cleavage – a look that she did not miss.

"You might be. You just might be. One of the tenants moved out last week. Could do with a lick of paint inside and a good clean up but other than that there is a phone point – mobile signal is good. There's Wi-Fi included in the rent, one desk and one chair. If you have visitors you'll have to buy another one. One month's rent in advance. Access to the offices is six days a week, seven to seven each day," she reeled off, smiling up at him; a bit posh but nice, very nice. "And we don't have any illegal or funny business allowed in any of our offices. One whiff of it and they're out – only as you would expect in a respectable establishment."

"There would be absolutely no funny business. I'm a writer. I just need a hidey-hole away from home where I can get a few hours' peace. I've got three kids at home and two dogs, quite apart from the wife. No matter how often I tell her that I need peace and quiet to write she still finds something that needs doing."

A small shadow crossed her face but she soon recovered. "I'd keep you well occupied as well if you were mine, ducks."

"Is that an invitation?" Greg teased her, smiling broadly.

"Take it which way you like, but now you come to mention it…"

Greg laughed with her. "I'd be very grateful if I could see the empty unit please."

"Certainly, ducks. Follow me. It would be nice to have a real gentleman around the place." She winked at him and, bottom swaying from side to side in skin-tight leopard print pants, led him out of reception towards the portacabin at the far end of the car park.

"That your car?" she asked, pointing to the bright red Audi convertible. Greg nodded. "Smart. I like smart cars. One of our other gentlemen has a smart car – top spec Range Rover but he's away at the moment. We don't use keys. Everyone loses them anyway. There's a number you use to get in. If you sign up we'll give you the code but you're not to peep as I tap it in this time. Can't have you coming back and breaking in, now can we? At least not until you're a fully paid-up member of the club. Close your eyes now."

"Your wish is my command, madam," Greg said, making a show of covering his eyes. This was going to be easier than he dreamed possible.

After a moment of listening to some choice language, Greg peeped through his fingers. "Can I help you?" he asked, transfixed by her nails which were two inches long and painted every shade of the rainbow.

"It's these nails. Have the devil of a job typing with them but everyone knows me for my nails. They shouldn't make keypads this small. They just don't stop and think, do they?" she said, leaning towards him. "Maybe you could tap the code in. I'll whisper it in your ear and then you're to promise me that you'll forget it." He could feel her breathe in his ear and smell it tainted with the smell of tobacco smoke and garlic leftover from what might have been yesterday's Indian.

"Promise," he said.

The 'office' smelt worse than she did – of damp and dogs and probably a lot worse. The walls that had once been painted cream were scuffed and stuck with bits of Sellotape where notes had once been stuck.

"Mm, I should have brought the air freshener with me, but a good spray of lavender will soon get rid of the smell. I did say that it needed a lick of paint," she said, kicking a couple of boxes toward the corner of the room. The floor was covered with bin bags full of old empty files, screwed up paper, paper cups and unwashed takeaway containers. "We can clear all this lot in a jiffy and with a coat of paint, it'll look like new. Suit you down to the ground, it will."

"I'm not sure that it will be big enough," Greg replied, looking disappointed. "It's difficult to get a feel for the space with all this rubbish in here. Could I take a peep at one of the others?" he asked, brushing gently against her shoulder.

She shuddered pleasurably.

"If you were anyone else, ducks, then the answer would be no, but I like the look of you. You look like someone I can trust," she replied, resting her hand on his arm.

"I would be very, very grateful," Greg said.

"There are a couple of others I could show you. I shouldn't really, but the tenants are away this week so they'll never know, will they? What the eye doesn't see, the heart doesn't grieve over. That's what they say, isn't it? Better take a look before the boss comes back, though. He'd skin me alive, he would."

Greg nodded. "I quite understand and I would owe you a big favour."

"You would indeed. The office closes at five," she said with a gleam in her eye. "You can pick me up right outside the gates. There's a nice cosy pub just down the road. Mine's a gin and tonic – large that is."

"It's a date," he replied and made a mental note to be long gone by five o'clock.

"You'll have to help me with the keypads again and the same rules apply. You forget the number just the moment the door opens. Deal?"

"You have the word of a gentleman, my dear."

The second portacabin was neat and tidy in comparison to the first and there was plenty of space. Nothing looked familiar. Greg searched for a reason to view the third portacabin. "You said that the mobile signal was good but I've only got one bar up. Is it better in any of the others?" he asked.

"Don't see that it should be any different, ducks," she said. "But it's no skin off my nose. There's just the one more and then that's it." She pointed her finger at him as if he was a naughty schoolboy.

Greg tapped in the code at the third portacabin and opened the door. He waved his mobile in the air while glancing around: neat and tidy and clean. No clutter visible on the work surfaces, a comfortable easy chair, not cheap, and a bottle of whisky and a crystal whisky glass on the windowsill. "Better signal here," he said, wandering around the room, eyes darting left and right. This was it. It had to be.

"He keeps himself to himself this one and always seems to be away but we don't ask questions. This is the one with the posh Range Rover," she said, glancing out of the window. Greg understood – the boss might be back at any time. She didn't want to be seen in this portacabin and neither did he.

"I think I'll take the first one after you've cleaned it up. You've convinced me. You're good at your job. I hope the boss appreciates you," he said.

"You'll need to sign a contract and put down the deposit. Then we'll be seeing a lot of each other, won't we?" She was chuffed to have made a sale and a tasty new friend in the bargain.

"I'll come in tomorrow to do the paperwork but only if you will be here," he grinned.

"I wouldn't miss it for the world. See you later. Remember – five o'clock outside the gate."

"I'll be here." Greg blew her a kiss and waved to her as he reversed out of the parking space and drove away from the offices.

The traffic crawled all the way from Slough to Twyford, but he was in no hurry. He would have plenty of time to fix some supper, get changed and drive back into Slough after dark.

* * *

Greg dressed in a black sweatshirt, black jeans and black trainers – appropriate gear, he thought for what he had planned. Fortunately, there had been no signs indicating that the premises were patrolled at night either by a security guard or a dog – he hoped he was right. There had been no visible cameras and no indication that the premises were alarmed; Harry was slipping. Greg checked his bag – bolt cutters that would easily cut through the rusty chain that secured the two metal gates together, torch, gloves and mobile phone.

The offices were in a quiet industrial side street with little or no passing traffic but he decided that it would be wise to wait until well after pub closing time rather than take the risk of meeting up with anybody – especially 'ducks' from the office.

He could hear his heart beating as he walked towards the

premises. The street was dark and deserted. There were no street lamps to give his presence away. Greg put on his gloves. The bolt cutters bit through the chain like butter; the chain clanged as it broke. He started at the noise and looked around. Nothing stirred as he carefully eased one of the gates far enough apart to squeeze through. Closing the gate behind him, and holding his breath, he headed for portacabin number three.

Seven, nine, one, six, he said quietly to himself, repeating the numbers that he had memorised that afternoon. The lock clicked open. The small torch was enough to help him find his way around without being seen from outside.

He tried the desk drawers – unlocked. More bank statements, magazines advertising properties, receipts of no interest, a bunch of guarantees, travel brochures and a few odd keys – nothing useful. In the corner of the room, he spotted a small grey filing cabinet with two drawers. It was locked. Greg returned to the desk and picked up the keys. It would be nothing short of a miracle if any one of them fitted the grey cabinet; Harry would not be so careless. The third key he tried worked.

Greg carefully drew an old metal biscuit tin from the top drawer and opened the lid. It resembled little more than a collection of bric-a-brac from a junk shop – an odd collection for Harry Trumper to have kept.

One by one he examined the contents. A series of newspaper cuttings were held together by a rusty old paperclip and had clearly not been handled for a very long time. Greg carefully removed the paper clip, laid the cuttings out on the desk and photographed each of them. An old blue leather ring box nestled at the bottom of the box among old coins, watches, keys, a Swiss pocketknife, nail clippers and other assorted items. Greg lifted it out and opened the box. In it lay a pair of silver cufflinks with the monogram CF. It was hardly a surprise, but strange that he should keep them in this box in a filing cabinet in his office. Greg took a photograph and replaced the box carefully where he had found it.

A postmarked date on an envelope addressed to Charles Fairbrother, Waverley Court, caught his eye; it was dated twenty-third April 2001 – almost three years before Harry Trumper disappeared and four years before he reinvented himself as Charles Fairbrother. The letter had to be the property of the real Charles Fairbrother. Greg photographed the letter and the envelope.

In the bottom drawer, there was one solitary A4 ring file, not that old. Greg opened it to the first page and saw that somebody had written F U C K across the top of the first letter in the file. There were ten letters in the file. Whatever those letters contained it had not pleased Harry. Was this the key to the mystery? Resisting the temptation to sit down and read every page, Greg removed each page one by one, photographed them and replaced them in the right order.

Replacing everything in the cabinet as he had found it, Greg turned the key in the lock and put the keys back exactly where he had found them in the desk. Quite what he had found he would not know until he got home and had time to examine the photographs in detail.

He had been there too long; his nerves were on edge. It was past time to leave. Seven, nine, one, six. Greg locked the door to the portacabin and looked around. There was no one in sight as he left the premises. There had been no break-ins, nothing had been stolen. The only evidence that anybody had been there was the broken chain across the gates.

Twenty-Two

"So the chapter is finally closed," Hetty said with a sigh, slipping the last stitch off the needle. She put her knitting down on her lap.

"I hope so, Hetty," Max replied thoughtfully. "I had thought it was closed a long time ago until Gabby came back and brought Greg here with her. I know he gave us all that money and God only knows everyone is grateful, but it's been a bit like opening up an old wound again, at least for me."

"You did all you could, Max. It wasn't your fault that Harry Trumper disappeared off the face of the earth," Hetty replied supportively.

"Maybe I didn't know when to stop, Hetty. It would have cost us all a lot less if I had seen the writing on the wall. I simply wouldn't believe that somebody could disappear into thin air. It didn't seem possible. I'm relieved that most of them have got back some of the money that they put into the fighting fund although one or two of them are still well out of pocket. I've been wondering if we shouldn't give our share to them. I feel so responsible for all of it," Max said.

Hetty knew that there had been something on his mind. It was a very long time since she had heard him up in the night making tea and listening to the radio.

"If that's what you feel you should do, then you have my full support Max, but I can tell you now that they won't take the money." Hetty counted the stitches on her needle.

"How could we have been such fools, Hetty, to be taken in by a glitzy sales pitch and a free trip to California?" It was a rhetorical question, but Hetty was not going to let it pass.

"We were all taken in. The development was genuine, the plans were genuine and the complex was modelled just as they said it would be on that development we saw in California – except, of course, there was no old mansion. We had no reason to believe that our homes would fall apart in no time and the mansion would never be finished. We couldn't foresee what would happen any more than the rest of them."

"Did you remember Greg from back then, Hetty?" Max asked.

"I didn't at first, but then I did. I remember thinking what a nice young man he was when we met him. I remember that he walked me around and pointed out all the details on the plans to me. I also remember his enthusiasm and I could see that he was very proud of the design. I am quite sure that he is as upset as we are at the way things turned out. At least we have our trip to California to look back on."

"We do that, Hetty. And the best thing about it was the people we went with. We couldn't have wished for better friends and now neighbours. It seems as though we have known each other all our lives. It reminds me of the wartime. I was very young at the time, but I remember my mother telling me about the camaraderie and how everybody supported one another irrespective of their walks of life. It's always been like that here."

"It has and I for one don't ever regret coming here," Hetty

said positively. "Changing the subject Max, I'm just a little bit concerned about Gabby. She hasn't brought her husband to meet us – Charles, that's his name. It seems very odd to me. And she doesn't say much about him either. The only thing she has ever said is that he is away a lot of the time but that she is happy. I may be an old cynic, but somehow I don't think she is as happy as she makes out. Just a woman's intuition."

"I am sure she'll bring him to meet us when she is ready. You worry too much," Max replied without a great deal of conviction. The same thought had crossed his mind on more than one occasion.

"And I'm not at all sure that I liked the way that Greg was looking at her. I watched him and he couldn't take his eyes off her. That's not healthy. She's a married woman but the last thing that I am going to do is interfere. Look where it got me last time with her and Dave. I shall keep my counsel, as they say." Hetty counted the stitches again. "Damn. Can you get the phone, Max? It's a bit early for anybody to be ringing us. I'm sure that I have dropped a stitch. Seventy, eighty, ninety, one hundred. Good."

"Hello, Gabby. We didn't expect to hear from you so soon but always nice to hear your voice. How are you this morning?" Max was pleased, but surprised that she should ring so early in the morning. "You're coming down with Greg tomorrow morning? To what do we owe this pleasure?" Max asked suspiciously. He could understand Gabby visiting the following day but to bring Greg with her again?

Max shrugged his shoulders and for Hetty's benefit repeated Gabby's words. "You can't tell me why on the phone. I see, or maybe I don't see at all. And you want me to get all the residents together at eleven at the nineteenth hole."

Max's mind raced ahead. "And what am I supposed to tell them, Gabby? Just that it is very important. Hmm – is it about those cheques? Are they about to bounce? No? I'm not sure that I like suspense and drama any more, Gabby. It gives me sleepless nights… We're to trust you, I see. You know we trust you, but can't you just give us a clue? You're not ready to talk about it… I suppose so. We'll see you both at eleven tomorrow." Max sighed, resigned to the fact that he was going to get no more out of her.

Replacing the phone on the receiver, Max shook his head in confusion, turned and shrugged at Hetty who had once again started to count the stitches on her needle.

"Did you get all that, Hetty? She and Greg are coming tomorrow. We're to get everybody together at the nineteenth hole at eleven, and she won't tell us why. I am not sure that she is being fair to us. You don't think that she's going to announce her engagement to Greg or anything like that do you?" Max slumped down in his armchair. There were times when he worried about that niece of his.

"She's a married woman so I doubt it. We'll have to wait and see. Drink your coffee. There's no point in worrying about it. I'll wander around and tell everybody in a minute. It'll be something to do with this Harry Trumper business, mark my words. There'll be lights on in every cottage tonight wondering what's going on – no one is going to get much sleep." Hetty nodded knowingly.

"I wish she would let it drop, Hetty."

"So do I, Max, but you know Gabby."

207

Twenty-Three

Gabby put down the phone. She didn't like leaving Uncle Max and Aunt Hetty up in the air, but she had to talk it through with Greg and win him over before she shared her plan with the residents. He was expecting her at noon. Gabby packed a small bag with everything she would need for a four-night stay with him in the knowledge that she would have to be back at the cottage by Saturday.

As she drove to Twyford she turned it over and over in her mind. It was all still a bit sketchy, but the more she thought about it, the more she convinced herself that it could just work. She knew he would say that it was ridiculous – that it could never work, but he didn't know Charles as well as she did. He may have known Harry Trumper and worked for him, but he hadn't lived with him for eighteen months. She had.

* * *

"Coffee?" Greg suggested.

"What are you looking so pleased about?" Gabby eyed him suspiciously. The frown that he had worn the day before had been replaced with a broad grin. He had a glint in his eye and a spring in his step. "Make it a big pot of coffee. I've lots to tell you."

"And I you," he replied, heading off in the direction of the kitchen. He hadn't caught much sleep the night before. It had turned two in the morning by the time he arrived home and five by the time he had printed off all the photographs and worked his way through some of the contents, but it had been worth every minute. Greg yawned.

"Late night?"

"You could say that. I was practicing my breaking and entering skills until the early hours of the morning. And I have to say that looking back I quite enjoyed the adventure. Don't worry – I'm not planning to do it again." Greg was going to spin it out a bit – this was his victory.

"You did what?"

"That office you mentioned, I thought I'd pay it a visit. So I did, yesterday – twice actually – once during the afternoon when I met a charming young lady who called me 'ducks' and propositioned me. Then again after dark last night." Greg said, looking mightily pleased with himself.

"And?" This was leading somewhere, but Gabby could see that Greg was in no hurry.

"I found a few interesting things in your Charles's office, not least of all the key to the mystery. Why he kept important papers in that dump of an office – which is no more than an old portacabin – I'll never know. I can only think that he assumed that no one would expect to find the great Harry Trumper renting such a dump and he certainly hadn't considered that his wife would ever visit him there."

"Are you going to tell me or are you going to hold me in suspense for the rest of the day?" For an instant Gabby forgot about the plan she had in mind. She wanted to know what Greg had found.

"Letters in an A4 ring binder – from the Inland Revenue. I almost laughed out loud when I read them in the early hours.

I just couldn't believe that Harry Trumper could have made such an incredible mistake. It's unbelievable."

"I am not following you, Greg. What mistake? Can you just spell it out in words of one syllable, please?" Gabby felt herself becoming irritated. He was spinning it out too much and her patience was waning.

"Okay, Gabby. Sit back and listen carefully. Like everything else in this story, it's complicated. The letters are from the Inland Revenue addressed to Charles Fairbrother, The Poplars, The Hawthorns. The first letter came in July 2013 just over two years before you married him. It was about unpaid tax," Greg began.

"But Charles always paid his taxes on time. Annabel's accountant looked after his tax affairs, he told me. He wasn't sloppy about it," Gabby interrupted.

"Wait, Gabby. Wait for the punchline. The very first letter referred to unpaid tax dating back many years. It seems that Mr Charles Fairbrother had evaded paying tax for ten years from 1990-91 right through until 2000-01." Greg paused to see if she would make the right connection.

Gabby digested what Greg had said and slowly worked it through. "But he didn't assume Charles Fairbrother's identity until, at the earliest, late '04 or early '05. So, are you telling me that the *real* Charles Fairbrother owed the Inland Revenue?"

"Precisely, and what's more, the real Charles Fairbrother must have been a very rich man to ever owe the Inland Revenue that sort of money. The demand is for millions,

Gabby. Reading between the lines, it's taken them all that time to catch up with him. The irony is that Harry Trumper stole the identity of a man who was in a great deal of debt. He couldn't have known at the time. How beautiful is that?"

"But that letter you said was dated July 2013. I can't imagine that he's been paying it, so how has he managed to fend them off?" The penny slowly dropped. "This has got something to do with his divorce, passing his assets to Annabel and marrying me, hasn't it?"

"I'd put money on it, Gabby. It gives me no pleasure whatsoever to confirm my theory. I wish it had never happened, except, of course, I might never have met you. There are copies of letters he sent back to the Inland Revenue straight away claiming that he did not have that sort of money and it was all a mistake. The one thing that might have closed the matter down altogether, he couldn't admit – he is not Charles Fairbrother. So he played for time for a while and then put the next part of his plan into action. He let Annabel divorce him and take all his assets as part of the divorce settlement. No doubt he thinks that the Inland Revenue can't touch the money now. He *personally* has nothing of value for them to come after. I am not sure that he hasn't made a mistake on that one but that's beside the point right now. I can only guess that he married you to make the divorce look genuine and show that he had no intention of going back to Annabel even when the dust settled."

"Wow! So do you think the dust has settled, Greg?"

"I don't know, but the last letter in the file was dated just three months ago and it stated that the matter was under review and that he could expect to hear from them in due course. To me it sounds like they may be thinking about shelving the matter," Greg said. "I don't think it will be long before the dust does settle."

"And then he goes back to Annabel?" Gabby said, completing the story. "Happy ever after."

Greg nodded; she was taking it remarkably well. "Yes, that's about the sum total of it. Let's have that coffee now and you can tell me your news." The rest of his findings would wait for another day. There was more research to be done before he was ready to share it with her.

"I didn't sleep much last night either, Greg, but I think that I've come up with a plan to take a whole shedload of money off him and hand it back to the residents at Magnolia."

Greg opened his eyes wide and sat back to listen. This he had to hear. "Legal or not legal?"

"Depends which way you look at it. Does it matter so long as he never finds out the truth?"

"I am all ears. You have my undivided attention," Greg said.

"Charles has a passion for Lowry..." Gabby began. "And there is one Lowry that he wants more than anything in the world. He's even got a photograph of it framed and hung in our bedroom. He often stands and stares at it. There's been more than one occasion when he has said that he would give everything he had to own that one painting," Gabby said, finishing her outline of the plan.

"I hope you won't mind me saying, but you and Harry would have made a good couple. That plan is almost as Machiavellian as anything he would ever have dreamt up. I can see where you are coming from but I can't let you do it. How on earth do you think you can keep up the pretence that nothing has happened for the next three months or possibly more? I won't let you do it, Gabby. You can't go back and live with him," Greg said sternly. "If he so much as got a whiff of anything going on you'd be in serious danger. Forget it."

"I want one chance to talk to the residents at Magnolia and then let them make the final decision as to whether or not we have a go. If they say no, then I'll drop it. We'll find another way. If they're game then we go for it," Gabby said.

"You're mad. It's their money you're gambling with, Gabby. They haven't even had time to get used to having money back in their bank accounts. You saw how pleased they were to have something behind them. Are you prepared to gamble that away?" The more Greg thought about it, the more the dire consequences of failure played on his mind. "How would we feel if the plan fails? Let's face it, it is one hell of a risk."

"Give me this one chance, Greg. I need your support." Gabby looked him in the eye. She was deadly serious.

"Okay," he replied. "You can run it past them, but I don't like it."

"I'm glad you said that because I've organised a meeting with them all for tomorrow morning at the nineteenth hole. Believe me, if you hadn't agreed, I would have cancelled it."

Greg raised his eyebrows – another sleepless night.

Twenty-Four

After an easy trip, Greg parked the Audi in the car park and together Gabby and he walked slowly up to the nineteenth hole. It was five to eleven. The residents would all be waiting for them.

"Want to change your mind?" Greg asked.

Gabby shook her head. "No, there's no going back now, Greg," she said determinedly and knocked on the door.

Aunt Hetty gave her a hug and shook Greg's hand. "You two seem to be quite inseparable," she commented pointedly.

For a split second, Greg was lost for words – Aunt Hetty was a wily old bird. "I'm the driver," he replied courteously. She wasn't fooled.

"Shall we all have a cup of coffee? I gather from your uncle that there is something that you want to talk to us all about? Coffee first and then we'll all settle down comfortably and we promise to give you our full attention," Aunt Hetty said, turning to help Dot put the cups out and the biscuits on a plate.

Gabby drank her coffee, conscious that all eyes were on her. Her head swam – in a moment she had to find the words to explain everything in simple terms but in such a way that they understood that the decision was theirs and theirs alone.

The clock on the wall chimed the half hour. The cups, saucers, and plates were replaced in the cupboards where they belonged. The kettle was filled ready for the next brew. The residents settled themselves down in their chairs.

Gabby stood up, waited to get their attention and started nervously. "I am sure you are all wondering why I asked you to meet us here today – I would be if I were you. You must have thought it a strange request." She was gabbling, rambling, rather than getting to the point and increasingly aware of the worried looks on their faces.

"I think you may need to hang on to your seats. What I have to say will come as a shock to you all," Gabby continued. Bums shuffled on seats, legs were crossed and uncrossed, hearing aids adjusted and glasses repositioned carefully on the noses of those who wore them.

"I have found Harry Trumper."

The room fell silent. The residents gasped audibly. Gabby could see the wheels turning. Had they heard correctly? Was this some kind of joke? Whatever news they had thought she might bring, it had not been this.

Uncle Max covered his eyes and rubbed his forehead. "Oh Gabby," he muttered despairingly. "I asked you to leave it alone, didn't I?"

"I wish I could have Uncle Max but I couldn't," Gabby replied sympathetically. She hated herself for being the one to upset him.

"Where?" Dennis was the first on his feet. "Just let me get my hands on him."

"Not if I get there first, you won't. I'll sort him out," Peter shouted, waving his fists in the air.

"Does this mean that we have to start all over again and

take him to court?" Henry asked softly. After all this time, all he wanted was peace of mind and his music.

"Please, Gabby. I beg you. Leave it," Uncle Max implored.

Gabby raised her arm. The room quietened.

"You will understand why I can't leave it when I tell you, Uncle Max." For a fleeting moment she wished that she had never come back into their lives. At least she could have saved them this heartache.

Gabby looked at Greg who nodded back at her. They both knew that there was no going back – it had to be said. Gabby waited for the residents to settle down again and drew courage from Greg's silent support.

"I recently, and by recently, I mean in the last few days, saw a photograph of him. Greg was showing me his holiday photograph album and there was one of the two of them together. It was taken long before the trouble. Greg told me that the man standing beside him was Harry Trumper. I recognised him immediately. He was about fourteen years younger in the photograph, but I would have recognised him anywhere."

"But, Gabby, you never met him. Come to that neither did the rest of us. We only saw him from a distance when he opened the presentation about Magnolia Court at the London seminar," Aunt Hetty whispered, confused. How could the girl have recognised him?

"The man in the photograph," Gabby hesitated, "doesn't call himself by the name of Harry Trumper any longer. My guess is that he changed his name not long after he disappeared, and that was why you were never able to find him."

She closed her eyes and took a deep breath. "His name, God help me, is Charles Fairbrother."

Hetty and Max turned and looked at one another. Neither of them spoke. Had their ears deceived them? Had their memories deceived them? They were neither of them getting any younger, and from time to time it was all too easy to get the wrong end of the stick, but had they?

"Gabby," Max started slowly and deliberately, "not everybody in this room knows that your surname is Fairbrother and that your husband's name is Charles. Would your aunt and I be right in thinking that you are talking about the same man?"

"You are, Uncle Max. Charles Fairbrother, the man I married, is Harry Trumper."

Hetty wept.

A cloud of silence descended on the room as the residents stared at her with incredulity and then at each other.

"Jennifer," Amy whispered to her friend, "I know that I have early-onset dementia – the TV keeps telling me I have – but tell me that I didn't hear what I think I may have heard?"

Jennifer leaned towards Amy and put her arm around her. "I think, my dear, that you just heard exactly the same as the rest of us."

Greg sat quietly at the back of the room. He knew that he had no choice but to let Gabby have her head. Aunt Hetty pulled out her hanky, mopped her eyes, blew her nose and shook her head. She couldn't look at Gabby and neither would she be able to face any of her friends again.

"That this day should ever have come," Hetty whimpered in her husband's ear.

"You have to believe me that I had no idea." Gabby tried desperately to remember the words she had rehearsed to herself in the car. "He was Charles Fairbrother when I met him. I have never known him as anything else. I married Charles Fairbrother in good faith and I have a marriage certificate to prove it. And Charles had been married before to a woman called Annabel, an old school colleague of mine. They have two children. Annabel is Annabel Fairbrother and the children are Ethan and Abby Fairbrother. How could I possibly have known that he was anybody other than Charles Fairbrother?"

Max had known Gabby long enough to know when she was spinning a yarn. There were tears in his eyes as he got up from his chair and drew her into his arms just as he had done so many times when she was a child. Wiping away her tears, he whispered, "Oh, Gabby, life has not been kind to you, has it? We believe you. It's cruel and a tragedy but it's going to be okay. Aunt Hetty and I will always be here for you – you know that don't you?"

Dot broke the silence. "I'll put the kettle on. Strong tea – that's what we all need."

"Well done, Dot – saving the day as usual," Max said, braving a smile. "This has come as a shock to us all and not least of all to our Gabby. By the sound of it, she's the innocent party in this and she has lost a damned sight more than bricks and mortar. Come on, Hetty. It's wartime spirit we need now. Dot needs another pair of hands."

Dot and Hetty poured the tea and handed it round. Dennis took the small silver flask from his pocket, took the stopper out, emptied a good slug into his teacup and passed the flask on.

"I assume there's more to tell, Gabby. Are you ready to go on?" Uncle Max asked. "I think that whisky has done us all the world of good. We're ready if you are."

"Yes, there is more. I need to tell you everything." Gabby spoke slowly and clearly. She had had but a day to get her head around what had happened, but it was still complicated, incredible and almost unbelievable in places. "I met him almost two years ago after a school reunion party that had been organised by Annabel, his ex-wife. It was pouring with rain after the party and Charles gave me a lift to the station and we talked, and he asked to see me again. We saw a great deal of each other over the following six months. He was kind and considerate. We fell in love and were married soon after. We live modestly in a small rented cottage in Surrey," Gabby explained as calmly as she could. It ripped at her heartstrings to see the distress in their faces.

"And do you still love him?" Aunt Hetty enquired gently.

"No. I love the Charles I thought I knew, but I hate the man he is. I am just beginning to realise what a fool I have been. I don't think he ever loved me. He has always spent more time with his ex-wife and his children than with me. I think I was a pawn in their game – nothing more and nothing less," Gabby admitted, embarrassed at her own stupidity.

"What do you mean by a pawn, my dear?" Amy asked kindly. "I feel sure no one would be so unkind as to use you in that way."

Greg stood up at the back of the room. "Do you mind, Gabby?" Gabby nodded.

"I hope you won't mind me helping Gabby out, but as you have probably realised, I am very fond of her, and I know how difficult it has been for her to come here today to give you this news. Before we came here, we spent hour upon hour trying to make sense of it all. We believe that Harry did a disappearing act in order to avoid a big loss on Magnolia

219

and because it is possible that the police were after him for some other reason. He still walked away with a great deal of your money."

"I can confirm that the police were after him," Amy interrupted, "Something or other to do with a fire. At least that's what the foreman, Stan, told me. I remember it clearly. It was the day that all the workmen packed up their tools and left."

"There were rumours that he had taken a one-way ticket to South America, but it was only a rumour. Whether he went abroad or not we don't know. It doesn't matter. What we do know is that Harry Trumper disappeared and Charles Fairbrother reappeared six months later complete with identification, passport and a great deal of money in the bank. Not long after he married his first wife, Annabel," Greg explained as simply as he could.

"Our best guess is that some two or three years ago, somebody to whom he owed a lot of money found out about his new identity," Greg said. He glanced across at Gabby. She understood – he was going to simplify the story as much as possible. It was all the two of them could do to get their heads around it, let alone expect the residents to do so.

"What better way to make sure that nobody gets their hands on your money than to divorce your wife, and through the divorce transfer your assets into her name?" Greg stated and waited for the implications of his words to sink in.

Uncle Max scratched his head and rested his elbows on the table. "But I still don't see where our Gabby fits into all this."

"It's brutal, Max, but I think simple. Gabby is no more than part of the cover story. Charles married Gabby after a divorce in which his wife took everything he owned away from him, and with his blessing. And in case anyone was in doubt about the legitimacy of his divorce, he married Gabby. He maintains the façade by living with Gabby in a rented cottage and on a limited income. And as Gabby has already mentioned, he spends more of his time with his ex-wife and his children than he does with her." Greg glanced once more at Gabby, pleased to see her expression serious but strong.

"Then he's not only a thief. He's a liar and a cad as well," Henry shouted angrily. "What a dreadful trick to play on an innocent young woman. We should call the police right now and get him locked up where he belongs. She'll have to stay here with us until he's behind bars."

"Have you confronted him, my dear?" Jennifer asked Gabby curiously.

"May I answer that, Jennifer?" Greg asked. "We decided to take no action until we had spoken to all of you. Fortunately, Fairbrother is away in Dubai with his ex-wife and their children until Saturday. It gives Gabby some much-needed breathing space and time for us all to think," Greg said firmly.

"But this sort of thing only happens in story books," Dinah whispered to her husband. "Not in real life and not to people we know, Emanuel."

"I wish that were the case, Dinah," Emanuel replied quietly.

"Gabby," said Aunt Hetty, "I think I have followed this so far but tell me, if he is not who you thought he was, are you actually married to him? I probably haven't expressed that very well, but you know what I mean."

"As far as I know, Charles Fairbrother does not exist, so I cannot be married to him whatever my marriage certificate might say."

"Well, that is one blessing anyway," Aunt Hetty said with a sigh. "Thank heaven for small mercies."

"So that's it then," Peter said gruffly, picking up his jacket and starting to put it on. "There's no time to waste. Henry is quite right – someone's got to ring the police. One way or another we can wave goodbye once and for all to any infinitesimal hopes that we might have had to nail him to repair this shambles. Good riddance is what I say."

"Peter, hang on a moment, please," Greg said. "I will be honest with you all. If I had my way it would be the end of the matter – let the police deal with it. But Gabby has ideas of her own. At times she can be quite unreasonably stubborn especially when she has her heart set on something. Will you hear her out?"

Maybe some good would come out of it all, Hetty thought to herself. Greg clearly cared deeply for her niece and if she were not mistaken, she cared deeply for him.

"In my opinion, we're wasting our time. Just tell the police what flight he is due back on and get them to pick him up there and then," Peter said.

"I'd like to hear what she has to say," Uncle Max said, looking around the room. Heads were nodding in agreement.

"And me," Aunt Hetty added.

Peter took his jacket off and sat down.

Gabby stood up. It surprised her that she felt so calm and collected about sharing her plan. Anything was possible with Greg at her side and Uncle Max and Aunt Hetty batting for her.

"I think you all know that I was never more shocked and horrified when I first came to Magnolia Court and saw the state of the place, notwithstanding all your hard work. I promised myself then and there that if ever I was in a position to do anything about it then I would not hesitate to do so.

Needless to say, I did not for one minute think that the opportunity would present itself, but it has. My aim is to take three million pounds off Harry Trumper to use to restore Magnolia Court and then – and only then – let the police deal with him. If we go to the police now, I don't believe that you'll see a penny of your money again. Don't forget that Annabel, his ex-wife, holds the purse strings now", Gabby said.

"If I had a pound for every hare-brained scheme and badly worked business plan that crossed my desk when I was in banking and finance I would be a millionaire by now," Peter whispered loudly to Henry.

Henry raised his eyebrows. Gabby had aroused his curiosity. "We lose nothing by hearing her out," he whispered quietly.

Gabby put her hands together and concentrated hard on her words. "For the plan to work we have to play to his weaknesses... my plan is premised on his passion for paintings by Lowry." Gabby explained what she had in mind. The more she listened to herself, the more it sounded like sheer madness – doomed to failure – a non-starter.

"...And it is my firm belief that working as a team, we can pull it off." Gabby sat down and congratulated herself that she had explained her idea as clearly as possible. There had been no interruptions and no questions asked. Wide-eyed the residents had listened and hung on her every word, and she could see from their faces that they had understood the gist of it. It was now up to them.

"Gabby," Uncle Max stood up and took a deep breath, "I know you want to help but I'd be much happier if you let the whole thing drop and we went to the police. He's dangerous.

What you are suggesting is, how can I put it, totally beyond our capabilities. And, as you quite rightly point out, there are a few rather major snags. You have to remember that we are not so young anymore, and neither are we that adventurous. I am sorry, my dear."

"Hold on, Max. Speak for yourself," Duncan interrupted abruptly, wheeling himself to the front of the room. "Less of this 'we're not so young anymore' and 'not so adventurous'. There's life in this old dog yet. None of us are in our graves yet, and as for our brains, they're as sharp as they ever were, especially if we put them all together. I say we explore Gabby's plan a bit more before we dismiss it out of hand. When have we ever been negative about anything?"

"Forgive me if I am being a little slow, Gabby," Peter interrupted, "but didn't you say that the two of you live on a meagre income in a rented cottage? Where's this three million or so coming from, I'd like to know?"

"It's hanging on the walls of his ex-wife's house. His one passion in life has been art. He has bought well. I've seen the valuation of his collection and it's worth a lot more than three million. He has got the money," Gabby replied calmly.

"Really?" Peter raised his eyebrows. Maybe she wasn't quite so stupid after all.

Greg kept his counsel and said nothing. This was between Gabby and the residents of Magnolia Court. If she succeeded in persuading them, then he would be with her all the way. If they didn't agree he would take her home – to his apartment.

Gerald counted the tea leaves in his cup and turned it all over in his mind. Yes, the plan was pure Le Carré but was it so impossible? It irked him that this man had not only taken them all for a ride but had now done the same to Gabby.

And now they knew who and where he was. They would gain nothing by going to the police – he would plead poverty. They might get a few thousand pounds out of him but it was a drop in the ocean compared to what he owed them.

Dennis watched with a thoroughly puzzled expression on his face as Gerald took a coin out of his pocket and tossed it in the air. "Heads, I do. Tails I don't." he said out loud. "It's heads."

"My friends." Gerald stood up. "If I could have your attention for one minute?"

All heads turned towards Gerald. "Now you all know what I did all my life before I bought my lovely cottage at Magnolia Court. If not, let me remind you that I was an art dealer and Lowry was one of my favourite artists too." Gerald waited to give them time to recall some of the stories that he had told them. "Well, I am ashamed to admit that not everything I did was entirely legal or above board. I hasten to add that I was only caught out the once and I learned my lesson the hard way. Nothing too serious, but it cost me a pretty penny to buy my way out of it. To this day all of my clients remain happy with the work I did for them." Gerald smiled – he was not in the least bit ashamed of anything he had done in the past. He viewed the services he had provided with pride.

"I know precisely how to deal with acquiring the painting to make this plan stand a very good chance of succeeding." Already he had a list of names in his head, some could be discounted straight away, and others might have passed on by now, but there were still others who he thought would be ready to do business with him again. "I can acquire the painting, Gabby, so that's the main 'snag' out of the way. Isn't the rest of it just a case of stage managing and delivering our own little production? Let me explain what I have in mind…" Gerald sat down with a self-satisfied grin on his face – this was going to be fun.

"And just how much do you think this little lot might cost Gerald?" Peter asked, flabbergasted at what he had just heard.

"To acquire the painting you'll get little change from fifty 'k'," Gerald said nonchalantly. "And then there's the cost of luring the fish to the bait. The key to success is meticulous planning and authenticity in everything we do – none of which comes cheap. My guess would be around the hundred 'k' mark. And, mark my words, it won't happen overnight. We will have to be patient if we are to pull it off."

"And how do you think we're going to come up with that sort of money?" Peter demanded, rapidly losing patience with what still appeared to him a hare-brained scheme.

A deadly silence descended on the nineteenth hole. The answer was obvious but who was going to be the first to say it?

"I've already spent thirty pounds but there's still fourteen thousand nine hundred and seventy pounds in my bank account and I really don't know how I am going to spend it, so I say let's do it and here's my cheque." Jennifer fished her chequebook out of her handbag, tore a cheque out of it and waved it around the room for everybody to see.

"Come on, everybody," she continued. "This is probably the last chance we will ever have to do something entirely reckless and, you never know, it might just work. I haven't felt so excited for a long time. In fact, I feel like a twenty-one-year-old all over again." It was the answer to her prayers – her last production, her last performance.

"I didn't really want to go on a cruise anyway, Dennis,"

whispered Dot. "And besides, we've got loads of buckets. We don't need to buy any more."

"Well, Charmaine, what do you think, my dear?" Henry said to himself. "Are we in? I guess I could manage without the Bose for another year or so."

"There will always be vintage bikes waiting to be restored," Andy reflected.

Duncan put his hand up. "I say we go for it. Let's show them what a bunch of old codgers can do. You might need to shell out a few bob for a new computer for me. I'd have my work cut out with the old girl I've got now. My fifteen thousand is still intact and needs to work for me."

"I think that I might be able to do my bit to help make it work too," Amy said quietly. "Did I ever tell any of you what I used to do during the war in my spare time? My hands may be a little arthritic and stiff but I haven't lost the art of it, believe me. I can do all the counterfeiting of documents that we may require. Count me and my fifteen thousand in. My sister will just have to come over from Australia to see me if it all goes wrong. But if it works then I shall buy myself a first-class ticket there and back."

"Dinah and I would be happy to volunteer to take the lead roles," Emanuel called. "He wouldn't recognise us from Adam. It's a bit of luck that we were second-time buyers of our cottage."

"Consider your auditions to have been successful, Emanuel. You and Dinah will take the leading roles." Gerald laughed. He was already enjoying himself immensely.

Peter looked around the room at his friends. They all had far more to lose than he and so far none of them had opted out of the plan. Hare-brained it might be but he couldn't help smiling at the prospect, however remote, of taking Harry Trumper to the cleaners. It was no more than he deserved. "I'd be happy to manage the finances," he announced. "So you'd better count me in as well."

Henry held out his hand to Peter. "Well done, old chap. I knew we could count on you."

"You've even persuaded me, Gabby." Uncle Max stood up. "Might it be time for a show of hands? The proposal is that we go with the idea outlined by Gabby and that one hundred thousand pounds of the money that Greg returned to us last week goes back in the pot to finance the venture. All those in favour?"

Gabby caught the faintest glimmer of a smile on Greg's face as every hand in the room shot up in favour of the proposal.

"Thank you, everybody." There were tears in her eyes, but they were tears of joy. She would not let them down. "May I suggest to you all that we vote Uncle Max in as project chairman?" Gabby asked.

"And if I may, Mr Chairman and Gabby, may I suggest a name for our little venture?" Gerald asked. "I suggest The Silver Sting. We 'Silveries' are going to sting that man until he doesn't know what hit him."

Hetty looked at her husband with a smile – the old Max was back again. "It's a little early, but I think it's drinks all round," Uncle Max said. "Hetty, Dot…"

Twenty-Five

Greg slept fitfully, waking every hour on the hour to check that Gabby was still there after two blissful days and three blissful nights. The following day, Saturday, she would be returning to the cottage. For two whole days they had put Harry Trumper out of their minds and concentrated on themselves. Luxurious late mornings and sensual early evenings had left just sufficient time for a leisurely breakfast, a walk along the Thames towpath, a light lunch at a local pub followed by an afternoon of reading the papers from cover to cover and an early supper. It had been idyllic. If only it could last, but in the next few hours Gabby would be packing her small bag, going back to the cottage and not returning to St Francis for several months. It was the first time Greg had ever lived with a woman and it felt as though they had known each other forever.

From time to time Harry's name had crept into the conversation. Greg could not stop worrying about Gabby and the plan still bothered him. And then he let his mind wander back a couple of days to the meeting at Magnolia. If he had not seen it for himself, he would never have believed it. By the time they had left the nineteenth hole, every last one of the residents had volunteered for one or more tasks that would need to be done to see the plan through. They seemed to have a new lease of life and had hardly noticed as he and Gabby left, so engrossed were they in it. The capability of the residents did not worry him; Gabby's ability to maintain the pretence with Harry did. Repeatedly she had reassured him that she was up to it, but now and again he noticed a dark shadow creep across her face. He knew that she was thinking about Saturday and all the days thereafter which she would have to spend with Harry Trumper without giving anything away.

It stuck in his throat to even think about it – the two of them spending hours together, sitting together over supper and, worst still, going to bed together. He was frightened for her and jealous at the same time. He had told her that she was to ring at any time, day or night, and that he would be there for her even if he had to break every speed limit on the road. She just had to get herself to safety until he could get there.

"It will be okay," she said looking at Greg knowingly as she gave him one final hug and left for 'home'.

* * *

His text arrived in the afternoon. The plane would be landing at five, he would be out of the airport and on his way home by five-thirty. He would drop Annabel and the children off first and be back in Chertsey by about six-fifteen. He had missed her dreadfully.

Gabby's fingers shook as she texted him back, "Missed you too."

He was late. Gabby glanced at the bottle of wine open and breathing on the table. She needed a drink badly but common sense told her that the less she drank this evening the better

230

her chances of carrying through the pretence – one glass of wine and no more. She had told herself that tonight was going to be the toughest of them all; every day after that would get easier. It was wishful thinking, she knew, but she prayed that he would be jet-lagged and after a few glasses of wine would simply fall asleep.

"I'm home." She heard the garden gate open and close and the key in the door.

Gabby felt a lump in her throat "Act one, scene one," she said to herself with a great deal more confidence than she felt.

"Have I missed you," Charles said, dumping his case on the floor and throwing his arms around her. "You missed me too? These are for you – nothing but red roses for my Gabby."

It was always the same – red roses when he came back from one of his trips. "Of course I have. I always do when you are away, you know that." Gabby kissed him on the cheek. "And I've got your favourite dinner in the oven, just waiting for you. It's good to have you home Charles."

"You're my favourite dinner when I get home. You know that. The inner man can wait for satisfaction until later. Right now the outer man wants to show his wife just how much he has missed her. What do you say?" Charles held her by the shoulders and looked into her eyes. "You look sad, Gabby. You really have missed me, haven't you?"

Gabby averted her eyes. "Yes, of course, I have – in every way. But dinner will spoil if we don't have it in the next few minutes."

"You always say that when I come home and we always just turn the oven down and eat later. We are not going to change the habits of a lifetime, are we?" he said firmly.

He was right. Whenever he returned from a trip the very first thing they did was spend an hour together in bed before putting on their dressing gowns and going downstairs for dinner. She could not fall at the first hurdle. Suddenly she realised the enormity of the commitment she had made to the residents, but she could not let them down. Her thoughts drifted back to Greg and instantly she dismissed them.

She felt Charles's hand in hers and, weak-kneed, followed him up the stairs to their bedroom.

He took his time undoing the buttons of her blouse; he liked to savour the moment. Carefully he cupped his hands under her breasts and lifted them out of her bra. "Beautiful," he said. "I haven't seen anything so perfectly formed since I went away."

She closed her eyes and felt his tongue playing with her nipples, first the left and then the right. She felt them enlarge and looked down to see them deepen in colour. She did not want her body to respond to his advances but she could not stop it from doing so.

He slipped her panties to the ground, stood back and looked at her. She could see the bulge in his trousers. "Magnificent. I could look at you for hours," he said. "Lie down."

Slowly and carefully he entered her until her whole body seemed to be full of him. He was a skilful lover and never failed to bring her to orgasm at the same time as he came. Gabby hated her body more than ever she could remember.

* * *

She had passed the first test. Charles lay back, exhausted, satisfied and pleased with himself that Gabby had fully shared the moment with him.

"Let's eat. Sex always makes me hungry." Charles laughed. "Dressing gowns on and let's go."

It occurred to her at that moment that she had never been more than his mistress. He showered her with flowers, complimented her on every possible occasion, bought her little presents, kissed her in public and made love to her whenever the opportunity arose.

It crossed her mind that Annabel might be jealous of her, not that she had ever given any indication of such in their conversations. Maybe to Annabel, it was a price worth paying. Better to share her husband for a short while than to lose everything.

* * *

Gabby smiled her way through dinner. Charles talked endlessly about Dubai and the places they had visited: the Dubai Mall, the largest mall in the world, where Annabel had bought designer outfits for the children; the Dubai Aquarium and Underwater Zoo; the Wild Wadi Water Park where Charles had been forced to accompany the children on every one of the thirty rides. The hotel had been magnificent as usual.

Gabby listened, laughed at his jokes, and asked questions about the places they had visited while at the same time dreaming that one day she and Greg might go there together. Silently she added a few thousand pounds to Harry's bill – it would be his treat when that day came.

Gabby poured the last of the wine into his glass. She had kept to the one glass as she had promised herself. Charles had drunk the rest of the bottle.

"It's early I know, Gabby, but I am bushed so I'm going to unpack my suitcase and hit the sack." Charles got up from the table.

"No problem," she replied, thankful for this one small respite. "I'll clear up first and then follow you up."

"Tomorrow I'm due at the golf club. We're teeing off at eight. I might be back by six or I might be back late – it depends on who I meet in the bar," he said, picking up his suitcase and climbing the stairs. "Maybe we can do something on Monday?"

"Maybe," she replied. "But there's a lot on at work. I may even have to be away for the odd night."

Charles fought to keep his eyes open. If he weren't so tired then he might talk her out of all this extra work but there again, it would give him even more time to do what he wanted to do. It was an ill wind.

Gabby took off her dressing gown and, careful not to wake him, crept into bed beside him praying that he would sleep through the night.

* * *

She had not expected to sleep but unbelievably she had slept for eleven hours. It was ten o'clock already. She couldn't remember the last time she had slept for so long but maybe she hadn't had a great deal of sleep for the previous three nights. Gabby smiled to herself remembering the early nights and the late mornings and everything that had happened in between.

The other side of the bed was blissfully empty. Charles had

long since left for his golf match. Gabby heaved a sigh of relief, slipped on her dressing gown and slippers and went downstairs to make herself a cup of tea. If she dressed quickly she could be with Greg in an hour. But how was she going to look him in the eyes after the previous evening? Finally, deciding that a phone call would be easier than a face-to-face meeting with him, she picked up the phone.

"Gabby, is that you? I've been worried sick. Where are you? Can we talk?" Greg asked, relieved to hear her voice. "How did it go?"

"I am at the cottage and Charles has gone out to a golf match. The coast is clear for the moment. In answer to your last question – as well as can be expected, you know," she replied vaguely.

"No, I don't know, Gabby, that's why I'm asking." She sounded different, distant and evasive. It was not like Gabby.

"I'm coping, but it hasn't been easy. He doesn't suspect anything, that's what matters," she replied.

"Did he –?" Greg asked, before he could stop himself.

"Yes." Gabby knew what he was referring to.

"Maybe we should rethink this whole thing, Gabby. You can't keep putting yourself through this." He understood why she was doing it, but he so desperately wanted her to stop – stop right then.

"No, Greg. We've committed ourselves. I got through last night unscathed and I will get through however many days it takes to nail the bastard." She had to sound determined and confident even though the tears were sliding silently down her cheeks.

"When will I see you?" Greg asked anxiously.

"Wednesday. I've told Charles that I might have to be away

on business one day this week. Let's make it Wednesday."

"If you need me, Gabby, just remember I'm here for you."

"I know and I love you for it, Greg. Bye for now." Gabby hit the red off button and let her pent-up emotions flow.

Twenty-Six

He had one address book for friends and another for business, the latter a small, well-thumbed, leather-bound book which had not seen the light of day for many years.

Gerald picked up his business book. The entries were indecipherable to anyone but himself. The information was far too sensitive to risk it getting into the wrong hands. Letters were transposed with punctuation signs and numbers. No doubt the Bletchley gang would have been able to unpick it in a matter of hours, but to most, it would be gobbledygook.

In his mind Gerald discarded several of his old associates, none of whom specialised in the style of painting he needed. There were three he remembered who had the right experience and skills. It was a long time since he had spoken to any of them and none of them had been youngsters at the time. He simply hoped that one or more of them would still be alive and kicking and not riddled with any debilitating disease affecting their eyes or their hands.

The sort of thing he was looking for would not come cheap. He had warned Peter that it could eat up over half of their budget. In this business you paid the price. Cutting corners always led to disaster and even a long stretch at her majesty's pleasure.

It would take time, he knew that, and he had warned the others that this part of the project could not be rushed. Getting hold of the materials alone might take weeks; the wrong canvas, the wrong paint, a frame made from the wrong wood and the game would be up before it even started.

His first choice was a man known within the trade by the nickname of Fingers. No one who did business with him knew his real name. Neither did they know where he lived or carried out his work and they did not ask. To do so would sound the death knell and the end of a partnership before it began.

His second choice was a 'master' known by the inner circle as Chameleon. Aptly named, by day he was a high court judge, so some said; a highly respected individual unrecognisable under his wig and his cloak, and by night one of the 'masters'. Chameleon was probably the fastest of the 'masters' and by far the most expensive. While time was important the budget was still limited.

His third choice, equally skilled in the style of the artist, was a man who answered to the name of Red. Nothing and nobody could ever persuade Red to rush an assignment. The word 'deadline' was not in his dictionary and neither were tomorrow, next week or next month. Red did not negotiate on time. He was driven solely by quality and payment at the end of the job. It was unlikely that Red would even consider taking on the assignment and he hoped that he would not have to ring him.

The 'masters' had their own networks for acquiring materials and their own network of specialists who would test the finished product. Many were legitimately employed by famous galleries – even specialists needed the occasional windfall, especially when they were nearing retirement. And these were the people who had access to the latest technology. If the final product sailed through their tests then it would sail through any.

In the same way that Gerald was fanatically careful about who he dealt with, they likewise picked and chose their clients; relationships and trust were built over many years. Gerald had been off the scene for a long time but he had no doubt that they would welcome him back. He had never failed to pay a bill on time and discretion was his middle name.

Each of the masters carried a phone, which was used solely for business purposes, the numbers of which were known to only a select few.

Gerald tapped the first number into his business mobile. The phone rang out six times before a voice answered. "Hello."

"Hello Fingers. I hope that life is treating you well and it is bounteous?" Gerald said. It was the only salutation that Fingers would respond to. There was silence on the other end of the line. Gerald could hear the wheels turning.

"Is that you, Gayman? Long time no hear."

Gerald smiled to himself. Fingers never forgot a friend, but he had not expected him to recognise his voice so quickly.

"Correct. It's Gayman, you clever old dog. Retired from the business more than ten years ago. I am looking for a favour. It's for a good cause," Gerald replied.

"You mean your pocket?" Fingers joked.

"No, someone swindled me and some good friends of mine out of a couple of million. You don't want to know. It's payback time."

"Before you ask, I haven't done anything for several years," Fingers said, remembering that Gayman had always been good to do business with – always clear on what he wanted, no changes, reasonable on the timescale and never haggled over the price.

"I am sure you haven't lost your touch or I wouldn't be ringing you," Gerald said. "I've never asked you for anything fast in the past, have I?"

"No, you haven't. You know my policy, Gayman. It's never changed."

"Hear me out. It's a Lowry. The original is in the Lowry Gallery. You know it. The buyer's desperate and will soon be convinced that the one in the Lowry is a copy and he can acquire the real deal," Gerald said. The first one to speak loses, Gerald thought, as he waited patiently for a reply.

"More bloody stick men, I presume? Which one?"

Gerald named the painting. It was well known and had changed hands for three million not so many years ago. It was on loan to the Lowry in perpetuity. The owner could not afford the insurance to keep it on his own property.

"How soon?" Fingers asked cautiously.

"Four weeks from detailed instructions."

"Five. Not a day less – only for you, Gayman. Two weeks to get the materials, two weeks to do the job, one week tests. I assume you want me to deal with the marks?"

Gerald heaved a sigh of relief. Six weeks had been his tops – five was a bonus.

"It won't come cheap. Twelve hours a day, fourteen days. Probably the last one I'll do. Certainly the last Lowry. Tricky buggers they are. Fifty. Take it or leave it, Gayman."

Gerald hesitated. Should he knock Fingers down? Chameleon would be a lot more expensive and Red would never do it on time. He knew from experience that it was not

240

an unfair price for the job.

"Take it," Gerald replied. There would be no more calls between them. Any other contact that was necessary would be via runners, and he had never seen the same runner more than once. They had done business together going back forty years. Although Fingers would be in his late sixties or seventies now, he was the best in the business.

"Deal," Fingers said. A man of few words. "And you, Gayman, make sure you screw the bastard."

The phone went dead. All that had to be said had been said.

Gerald sat back feeling very pleased with himself. He had no doubt that Fingers would come up with the goods and on time. Gerald picked up the phone to Peter.

"The article has been ordered," he said. "It's fifty and it has to be cash, used ones. Seven days credit and then the full sum. It covers everything including the materials and testing."

"Isn't that a bit risky, Gerald?" Peter replied, putting on his banker's hat. "I would have thought that twenty per cent up front and full payment on delivery was more like it. Easier to get hold of ten thousand cash than fifty."

"Not in this game, Peter. My source has never let me down and won't this time either. I'll stand guarantor if it makes you feel happier — my cottage in the event of non-delivery."

"I am not questioning your integrity or his, whoever he might be, but what if he gets run down by a bus?" Peter asked, agitated.

"He won't. He never goes out." Gerald did not know for sure, but reliable sources had told him that Fingers was a recluse and never ventured outside of his own front door.

Peter wrote the cash figure on his spreadsheet. In all the years that he had been in banking he had never had to come up with fifty big ones in cash and in used notes. It would be an interesting challenge but one that he was more than capable of sorting out.

"How do we get the cash to your man?" Peter asked.

"You leave all that to me. There's a system and it's as safe as houses. The fewer people who know about it the better," Gerald replied.

"Consider it done." Peter put the phone down and smiled.

Twenty-Seven

Duncan printed off the last of the photographs just before the printer sent out its usual warnings about low ink. There were ten photographs – interior and exterior shots. Hopefully, they covered most things. The property he had found ticked almost all the boxes which was nothing short of a miracle. The list of must-haves that Max had given him had been eye-watering and he had sincerely doubted that he would be able to find anything that would remotely fit the bill. Unfortunately, it exceeded the budget that Peter had set.

* * *

It was the first Monday morning Silver Sting project meeting, and everybody was reporting back on progress. The meeting was set to start at ten-thirty prompt. Only Emanuel and Dinah had messaged that they would be late since Emanuel had a doctor's appointment, which he could not change. Gabby had had to start back at work that day so would not be present, so Max had told them.

Duncan's task had been to search the Internet and find a fitting residence for a baron somewhere in Germany or Austria. Emanuel and Dinah were the only residents whose name they could guarantee would not be recognised by Harry Trumper. Since both spoke fluent German, Germany or Austria were the obvious choices to stage the finale.

Three hours later, Viertel popped up on the screen. It was located in the Mostviertel region of lower Austria, one hour from Vienna, one hour from Linz and just forty minutes from Linz airport – not that the budget would run to airfares. According to its history, it had been commissioned in 1760 by an industrialist who had his own unique ideas about the style of architecture he wanted. It had changed hands just after the 1860s. Three of the original towers of the house had been restored while the fourth had yet to be restored. It was an imposing building on three levels with a large basement in which the kitchen was housed. With ten bedrooms described as fully refurbished, five bathrooms, two magnificent salons, an impressive wood panelled dining room, it looked perfect. Access to the house from the main road was via a long undulating driveway separated by pristine lawns and lined with bushes, shrubs and trees. And best of all it was available for short term letting.

There would be little point in getting everybody excited if it were neither available nor within their budget. Duncan girded his loins and emailed the owner of the house whose name was Franz Neumann. The cover story he was to use was that the house was to be used as a film set for several scenes in a low-budget movie.

Dear Herr Neumann,

On behalf of my client, who is an independent filmmaker, I am looking for a house such as yours

that a film company might be able to hire for a period of one week for the purpose of filming scenes for a low-budget film. There are just two scenes that will be filmed in the house itself. I do assure you that the film is in good taste and will contain nothing remotely controversial. The subject, however, is under wraps and as such I am not at liberty to tell you more about it. The team would propose to bring its own house staff to take care of the crew and the cast.

My clients are looking to commence filming in mid-April. I would be grateful if you would respond by email with an indication of availability and price.

Yours very sincerely,
Duncan Gillespie
Consultant, Location Services

He had sent the email at five on the Saturday afternoon. It was unlikely that he would get a reply before Monday's project meeting. Minutes later his computer pinged.

Dear Mr Gillespie,
Fortunately, I do speak English having attended school in England when I was young. My written English may not be so well.
Your enquiry is intriguing and it would be good to me if the house were to feature in a film. I assume that you will include location details in the credits and that you may let me reference it in my own publicity of the house.
It so happens that the house is free to rent from Monday 6th through until late on Sunday 12th April.

We have guests booked at the beginning of the month and further guests arriving here on Monday 13th. April is a most lovely time of year when the pear trees blossom on the meadows.

Your client will like it.

The cost for using my house will be £2,500 sterling per day. A refundable deposit of £5000 is what you will have to pay when you make your reservation.

If you wish to make a firm booking then please arrange to transfer £5,000 within 48 hours. I can email you with bank transfer numbers.

Yours very sincerely,
Franz Neumann.

"Attention everybody. Let's bring this meeting to order," Max said, handing out sheets of paper to all of the residents. "This is the agenda for today. There are two issues that are both fundamental to the project and which are also our largest items of expenditure – the painting and the location. And then there are a few less urgent but, nonetheless, important matters that we need to discuss. Duncan, the floor is yours." Max sat down.

Duncan wheeled himself to the front of the room. "Right, everyone. My task was to find the venue for the main action in Austria or Germany. I should say right now that there were not many options, but I have found one that I believe fits the bill and I have some photographs of it here with me if you would care to gather around. The house is located in southern Austria."

Duncan studied their reaction; it was just as he had expected. There were gasps of surprise and whoops of delight. Any moment now they would be arguing about which of them would be lucky enough to have a role in the cast.

"One small problem, however," he added, with a serious note in his voice. "It will cost seventeen thousand five hundred pounds for seven days rental, exceeding our budget by seven thousand five hundred."

"Then it's a non-starter," Peter said, without hesitation. He had set the budget and they all knew what it was – this sort of expenditure would blow the budget sky high.

"But we could afford four days," Jennifer said, thinking out loud. "We would be hard pressed, but it could be done."

"Might be possible," Andy interrupted. In charge of logistics, he had already purchased maps of Europe, Germany, and Austria and studied route options. "We won't be able to get to the house until the third day after we leave here and when we do arrive most of us will too tired to do much more than unloading. Then following day we need to get ourselves organised and ready to receive our visitor. On the third day the action can take place and on the fourth day, we can bid goodbye to our guest. If we're smart we can be out of there on the fourth day."

"That works for me. Four days at two thousand five hundred a day fits in with our budget," Peter said. "Maybe you can get it for less? There will be all sorts of unforeseen expenditure crawling out of the woodwork before we're finished."

"What about I try nine thousand five hundred for four days?" Duncan offered. "I might be able to swing it. He seems like an amiable chap, and besides it's by far the best option we have. You've seen the photographs. It's perfect."

Peter nodded reluctantly. "Give it your best shot, Duncan."

"Thanks, Duncan. Good job," Max added. "Gerald?"

"The painting is due to be delivered here on the first of April." Gerald paused. "I suggest that we give ourselves a contingency of four clear days for delivery here. That's April fifth. If it is going to take us three days to get there, then we book the house from Thursday April ninth through until Sunday the twelfth. Duncan, I need sight of any significant paintings in the house – there must be some. If our baron is supposed to have an interesting collection of art then we can't afford for the walls to be plastered with also-rans. We might have to hire some."

"More money?" Peter interrupted.

"If necessary," Gerald said.

"The ninth to the twelfth has my vote," Max confirmed.

"I'll ask Franz to send me some more photographs when we've agreed on the price and I'll check out those precise dates with him," Duncan said.

"Okay, everybody. Good work one and all. Let's get on with it." Max said.

* * *

Two hours later Duncan left the meeting with a list as long as his arm. What would they do without him? It was a joy to know that his technical skills were in high demand and he was a key player in the project.

The first task was to email Franz to try and agree on the price. And then he needed to set up a website for the film company so that should Franz decide to do so, he would be able to check them out. And then there was another website to be set up: the baron at home at Viertel. Duncan was in his element.

Duncan sent the email to Franz and started on Emanuel's website. Freiherr (Baron) Emanuel Levi von Mostviertel – it had a nice ring to it. His plan was to set up a simple but impressive website that told the story of the family history and the restoration of the house. There were plenty of excellent website templates he could use for the build.

At eight that evening his email pinged.

Dear Duncan,

My wife and I have discussed your offer and have agreed that we can rent the house to you for four days for the sum of £9,500.

I am curious to your request to see photographs of what you call significant paintings in my house. Are you planning to rob me? I am happy to take a risk on you and attach to this email some photographs, which I hope will meet your request.

The dates 9–12 April are fine with both of us. And yes, we do have room for you to park your coach out of sight at the back of the house. I presume that you asked that question because you do not want it to feature in your film?

On arrival, my wife and I will greet you and then show you around our house and how things do work – especially in the kitchen – your cook will need to understand that. Since you are arriving late in the day we will make you a cold meal.

I will prepare eight bedrooms for you as requested. I look forward to receiving the deposit by 10 March. My

bank details follow.

Yours sincerely,
Franz Neumann

Duncan banged the desk in delight and replied.

Perfect. A few loose ends remained but he had achieved all three of his objectives for the day. Now he could close the computer down for the night and retire for a well-earned rest.

Twenty-Eight

Gerald sank down in one of the two chairs by the fireplace. He was one of the few people to whom Amy had ever confided her real past. He assumed she had trusted him with the knowledge because of their shared love of art – very different types of art but art all the same.

"*An Owner's Inventory of Paintings*?" Amy carefully opened the book that Gerald handed to her, which he said he had borrowed from a friend of his. The brown leather cover was faded, marked and worn from years of being handled by one generation of the family after another. The first entry dated back to 1789. The entries were mostly in black inks, although some later entries had been made in blue and purple. Interestingly, while the paper had faded with age, the inks remained as vibrant as the day they had first touched the paper. Each entry was scripted, although the handwriting, of course, changed with the style popular at that point in time. Fancifully, Amy saw each of the writers in her mind's eye: this one had been written by a young vital woman; the next by an older, frailer gentleman, and the next by a scholar. The book was indeed a work of art.

Amy had been drawn to calligraphy as a child, and her parents encouraged her to work at it. The bookshelves in her childhood bedroom were filled with the works of Edward Johnston, the father of modern calligraphy, and his pupil Graily Hewitt – her heroes of the moment. They were books way beyond her years. On her seventh birthday, Amy's parents had given her a set of broad-nibbed pens and brushes and a set of inks. They had been her proudest possession for many years. By the time she had reached her fourteenth birthday, she had joined the Society of Scribes and Illuminators – the youngest ever member. It never crossed her mind to make a career out of her talent. In those days young girls did not have careers. They married, had families and looked after their husbands or, if their parents had more open minds, were allowed to study at a secretarial college. Fortunately for Amy, her parents had been made in a more enlightened mould and she had been allowed to attend a secretarial college.

Her fingers caressed the edge of the pages as she turned one after another, and imagined the grand rooms in which the paintings had been hung, and the bureau or desk in which the book had been carefully stored.

Amy smiled inwardly and felt a warm glow creep through her body. It had been a very long time since she had done anything like this. Her work had been top secret then. She had signed the official secrets act and had never spoken about it to a soul. Not even her parents or her sister had known what she had contributed towards the war effort. Gerald, and more latterly Gabby, were the two exceptions.

She had attended Pitman's Secretarial College where she had learned shorthand and typing. With an outstanding speed of one hundred words of shorthand per minute, she had soon been singled out as exceptional and had almost immediately been offered a post with the Foreign Office. It was not only her shorthand speed that had been noticed, as she was soon to find out.

Unbeknown to her at the time, the Foreign Office had been looking for a small number of women whom they could train for a very special and demanding job. They needed right-handed young women with excellent eyesight and agile hands that were steady as a rock, and a good brain.

* * *

Of the ten girls with whom Amy had trained, only two made the grade – herself and a lifelong friend called Pauline. The three-week course had been gruelling, and each day they returned home with eyes smarting and fingers sore to the bone. The responsibility that they would carry on their shoulders when they started operational work had been drummed into them from morning till night. Mistakes were not tolerated. At first, she had nightmares about it, but they soon faded as she grew in confidence and her work became faultless.

Amy often wondered what happened to the documents she crafted. Did they save lives, or were they one-way tickets to heaven? Forever hungry for news, and searching the answer to the same perpetual question, Amy read everything that she could find about the war and scanned the obituaries daily, always wondering whether any of the dead had been those secret agents who carried her documents in their pockets. Of course, she would never know – nobody knew.

On one occasion she had been asked to deliver a set of papers by hand. It was a last-minute assignment and she had worked well into the night to complete it. There was no one else available to do the handover. Picked up by a black saloon and driven through the pitch-black streets to a small hotel in Highgate, her instructions were short and simple. She was to go to room six, knock six times on the door and wait for a reply. Her contact would then tell her that 'He would be sleeping in late the following day', with which she would hand over the papers and leave.

Even in the dim light of the room, she could see that he was a handsome man and probably in his early thirties. She had handed over the papers and wished him good luck. She knew from the documents she had prepared for him that he was heading deep into enemy territory and that his life would be in danger the moment he parachuted from the plane to the moment he made his way home, if ever. She was not to know at the time that they would meet again many years later and be married. They had enjoyed twenty-five blissful years together, and then he had died. He had been captured during the war, tortured, and left with terrible injuries that later took their toll.

"Yes, I can craft an *Owner's Inventory of Paintings*. It will be a first, but I have had far more difficult assignments in the past, Gerald. I have my pens and inks and everything I need in a box in my desk," Amy said. She stood up, walked across to her desk, pulled open a drawer and extracted a large black tin box.

Gerald couldn't help but glance at the slightly crooked, arthritic fingers, but he, like others, also noticed that her hands were steady as a rock. She carried teacups that were filled to the brim from one room to another without ever spilling a drop. Her eyes were as clear as a bell, and she was probably the only resident in Magnolia Court who had no use for spectacles.

"I know what you are thinking Gerald." Amy had noticed the direction of his eyes. "You're wondering if I can do it with hands like these." She didn't mind; if she had been in his shoes, she too would have her doubts.

"Let me show you some recent examples of my work. I've just started writing my Christmas cards. I always start at this time of the year. It takes me almost a full year to do them to my exacting standards." Amy handed a pile of written cards to Gerald. "Open them," she said.

Each card was addressed to the recipient together with a Christmas wish. The script was far superior to any he had ever seen, including other scripts that he had commissioned at great expense from his underground network.

"Outstanding, Amy." Gerald grinned and handed the cards back to Amy. "You are a true artist."

"I have a large magnifier that fixes to this table and a day light which I use to supplement the natural light. Find me the right leather-bound book with aged pages, and give me a written list of the entries and the crossings out we need and I'll fill it for you. It will take a couple of weeks at least but you won't be disappointed." Amy smiled.

"And there are two other things, Amy. We need a family album for Emanuel. He has a few photographs from his childhood he tells me. I'll find a suitable album and some additional photographs, which will fill in the gaps in his past. I will need you to script names, places and dates alongside the photographs. I'll give you the details. And finally, I need a bill of sale. I have found some copies that were written at about the same time." Gerald finished.

"Of course," Amy replied, miles away. She was already thinking about the style of the entries that she would use in the *Owner's Inventory of Paintings*. It was a blessing that she had kept all her reference books. "It will be my pleasure."

She might forget what she had been doing the day before, or even an hour earlier, but she had never forgotten all she had learned as a young woman.

Twenty-Nine

Emanuel had happily agreed to school them all in basic German, although he didn't hold out much hope that they would be able to manage more than a few simple greetings and questions, but that was all Jennifer wanted. It was fortunate, as Gabby had confirmed, that Charles knew no German whatsoever and would be highly unlikely to spot that the accents in the house were far from authentic.

Jennifer wanted more in-depth tuition. Having studied German to higher certificate level at school, there was no doubt in her mind that with a couple of weeks of tuition she could be word-perfect again. It was her fail-safe, so she said. If anything untoward happened while they were in the presence of their visitor, it was vital that she should be able to communicate with both Emanuel and Dinah in a language that their guest would not understand. He was happy to humour her.

Emanuel spent a leisurely afternoon designing a few simple exercises for the first German class later that day.

It was annoying that he and Dinah had missed the Monday morning planning meeting but Max had soon put his mind at rest – half an hour spent working his way around the walls at the nineteenth hall would bring him up to speed.

Half an hour before the lesson was due to begin, Emanuel strolled up to the nineteenth hole and, as suggested, started on the walls. It was impressive – each area of activity had been allocated its own space on the wall. They had adopted the system that Andy insisted on for maintenance work – yellow Post-Its signified urgent, green Post-Its were important and pink Post-Its were to do but not urgent. Each Post-It had a name and a date by which the activity had to be achieved. It was a relief to find that other than German lessons, learning his script and digging out his old family photographs, there were no other activities against his name.

The fourth and last wall was plastered with photographs of a house. Emanuel screwed up his eyes. Even without his glasses there was something vaguely familiar about the photographs. He reached for his glasses from his top pocket, put them on and moved closer to the wall.

Eighty years melted away before his eyes. It had changed, but it was all too familiar. He was standing on the front steps, his father holding the car door open and his mother and brothers were waving good-bye to him. He was climbing the old oak tree in the meadow and his brothers were teasing him for wearing odd socks. His mother sat working on her tapestry beside one of the huge inglenook fireplaces while his father was in his study working. He was in his father's study listening to his father telling him that he was going away on holiday, and then he was saying goodbye to his one teddy bear, bare of fur, minus one eye.

The box brownie was once more working overtime.

Emanuel steadied himself on the back of a chair. Long, long ago he had been told that the house had been burned to the ground after the war, but here it was, looking just as he remembered it. Never had he thought he would see it again. The pain of the memories that he had long since buried stabbed at his heart.

A Post-It with Duncan's name stated that the house had been booked and that the deposit had been paid.

When he had agreed to play the role of baron, never in his wildest dreams had he imagined that the location for the action would be Viertel. Austria was such a big country with so many grand houses – it was beyond belief that they should select that one house out of all the others.

Emanuel looked more closely at the photographs. Had he known that the house had remained intact then maybe he would have gone back to claim what was rightfully his. Whoever owned it now and was restoring it, clearly cared for it as much as his father and all the generations preceding him had done. But could he bear to go back there? Could he play the role in which he had been cast in his own ancestral home?

Dinah had never seen it in person. He had described it to her in vague terms but she would not recognise it from the photographs.

Emanuel drew up a chair, sat down and stared at the photographs. The house had been booked and paid for. It was a key part of the plan. He was a key player in the plan. He could not let them down and what they did not know would not harm them.

Thirty

"We're just back from Manchester," Gabby said. "A whirlwind trip but worth it."

"And we've both learned quite a lot about Lowry." Greg raised his eyebrows. The last place that he had thought they would be going that day was Manchester, but when Gabby had a bee in her bonnet, there was no point in arguing with her.

"So, you think the plan is sound, Gabby?" Uncle Max asked.

"As safe as houses. We timed the whole thing from the moment we walked in through the door of the gallery. And we checked out the hotels as well. Emanuel must stay at the Lowry Hotel. Where else would a man of substance with a love of Lowry stay if he were visiting Manchester?"

"There's just one date when I can be sure to get Charles there and that's the twelfth of this month – his birthday. I won't tell him where we are going but he'll probably guess as soon as we get on the Manchester train and then it will be too late for him to do anything about it. But, trust me – he'll be delighted. Charles would never turn down the opportunity to spend the day with his beloved Lowry."

"A week tomorrow? We'll be ready at this end, my dear," Aunt Hetty cut in. "Jennifer has completed the script for scene one and rehearsed Emanuel and Gerald until they are blue in the face. She'll settle for nothing less than word-perfect."

"I'll get Duncan to book the hotel and put Andy on standby to drive them up to Manchester," Max added, scribbling in his notebook. "Jennifer will be going with them just in case she is needed."

"If there's nothing else, Gabby, I need to get on. Dot and I are about to be introduced to Jennifer's designs for the costumes for Austria. The weeks will fly by now. Did we tell you that the house for scene two is booked from the ninth to the twelfth of April?" Hetty said, putting on her coat. "Max will show you the photographs. It's quite splendid. The Baron von Mostviertel can't be seen to be living in a caravan." Hetty giggled.

"The Baron Mostwhat?" Greg exclaimed.

"Believe it or not it did belong to a baron at one time. Drop by the cottage for supper later if you have time. We'll be there after seven this evening – at six we have a German lesson to attend. Must go."

* * *

"Jennifer, scene one is going to be on the twelfth of March. We've just discussed it with Gabby. It's the man's birthday and she's taking him up to Manchester for a birthday treat. I do hope that the script is complete. I've just told Gabby that it is. And have you sorted out what Gerald and Emanuel will be wearing?" Hetty gushed as she walked in the door.

"All sorted, Hetty. Hello Dot. We're working on Austria today," Jennifer replied, picking up her sketchpad and opening it up to the first page, "We've got quite a bit of work to do but

I've tried to keep it to a minimum. She was in her element: producer, set designer, costume designer, scriptwriter and last but not least, actress.

"Don't you think some of these designs are a little theatrical, dear?" Hetty was looking at Jennifer's sketches.

"Not at all, my dear," Jennifer replied more sharply than she had intended. "We can't have the baron and his wife looking like something the cat dragged in from the street, now can we?"

"Let's start with Emanuel." Jennifer pointed proudly to the first sketch. "This is his daytime outfit, old upper class made of fine cloth. People dress very well in Austria, you know, in high quality clothes. The style is sophisticated, tailored, and worn with beautiful accessories. I've already found just the jacket in the charity shop. It's hardly been worn. It may need a few nips and tucks but it shouldn't take long. Dot, can I assign that task to you, please?"

Dot nodded warily.

"Let's move on to Emanuel's outfit for the evening." Hetty and Dot looked at the sketch of a distinguished gentleman dressed in a smart navy blazer with tailored trousers. An arrow in the margin pointed to the shoes. 'Handmade', it read. "Dinah tells me that he has all three in his wardrobe. We just need a Rolex watch. Has anybody we know got one of those?"

"If anyone round here had a Rolex, they'd have sold it by now," Dot said.

"Well, maybe we'll have to do without it. Hopefully our guest will be more interested in paintings than Emanuel's watch. And Emanuel will have to wear exactly the same outfit at the Lowry."

"Now, Hetty, can you work on Dinah's outfits, please?

There won't be too much to do, I promise. She's about the same height as me but just a little bit broader in the beam, if you know what I mean. She can wear my grey silk dress for daywear and for the evening I am going to lend her my Chanel, and that is a dress that I did not buy in a charity shop. She's expecting you, Hetty, in about fifteen minute's time. It breaks my heart, but there are some good seams on it. If you have to let it out then do it."

Hetty nodded – so far she was getting away lightly.

"Dinah tells me that she has some pretty black shoes that will complement the grey and some sparkling dancing shoes that will work with the Chanel for the evening. Can you check both out, Hetty? We really could do with a sparkly necklace – not diamonds, because Emanuel obviously can't afford those. Possibly opals with the grey and turquoise with the Chanel. Now I'm half sure that I've seen Amy wearing just the thing. Perhaps you'd pop in and have a word with her, Hetty?" Jennifer crossed shoes and jewellery off her list. "And now we need to turn our attention to the below-stairs staff starting with Henry. He will play the role of the butler. He'll make a good butler. Dark jacket, white shirt, grey and black striped trousers, black tie – that's all he needs. His dinner suit may have to suffice if we can't find the striped trousers at the charity," Jennifer said.

"I've got a couple of white cloths he can wear over his arm," Dot said, relieved that Henry's would be one less outfit to be stitched.

"Nice touch, Dot," Jennifer complimented. "Perfect. Andy is going to run me around the charity shops in Stroud this afternoon. I've got a list as long as my arms."

"Have you thought about how Henry is going to carry trays

up from the basement to the dining room? He's a bit wobbly on his pins these days you know," Hetty said.

"All covered, Hetty. There's a dumbwaiter. I'm not suggesting that Henry's dumb of course. It's one of those contraptions where you put the food on a tray, pull some ropes and hey presto the dishes rise up to the floor above. He was in the navy. It will be a piece of cake to him. And now, Hetty, your outfit. As cook, all you need is a chef's jacket and a skull cap. And then black stockings and black shoes. Just like this…" Jennifer turned the page.

"I don't see that I need any outfit. I'll be sweating away preparing a meal for that dreadful man. I'll not get time to come above stairs." Hetty frowned. "Personally, I'd like to lace each course with arsenic. It's no more than he deserves."

"Arsenic after we have our money, Hetty. Not before. And what if he decides to come down to the kitchen to compliment you on your cooking? You must have a chef's jacket and hat just like this one." Jennifer thrust a drawing under Hetty's nose.

"And, Dot, as kitchen maid you'll wear the same as Hetty. Hire them if you must." Jennifer said.

"And then we've got Max and Andy to think about. Andy's no problem – as the odd-job man he can wear anything as long as it is clean. Max had better wear his black dinner suit. If waiters can wear black dinner suits in Indian restaurants then they can wear them in Austria."

"Gerald and I have already discussed his attire – all good so we don't need to worry about him. That just leaves me." Jennifer's eyes sparkled as she turned the page again. "I've sketched it out just so that you can see how it will all look on the night. I'm taking the part of the elderly eccentric sister which is why my outfit is just that bit more unusual than the rest. You'll be pleased to know that there is nothing for either of you to do on my account. I bought the dress and accessories some fifty years ago and it still all fits like a glove. I just have to rid the boa of the smell of mothballs. Did I tell you about the ball I went to when I first wore this ensemble?" Jennifer asked dreamily.

"I think, Jennifer, that you have mentioned it on occasion," Hetty replied, raising her eyebrows towards Dot.

"Why does Emanuel need a dotty sister anyway?" Dot asked, never one for using two words when one word would do.

"As producer and director, I have to be there on the spot. I'm scripting the action right now and my role when we are there will be that of prompt. If anyone loses their lines, I'll be right there to help. And if my German is good enough by then, which of course it will be, I shall be able to converse with Emanuel and Dinah in German and our guest won't have the faintest idea what we are talking about. How clever is that?"

"I've been thinking," Hetty interrupted. "Don't you think that our guest will think it a bit odd that all of Emanuel's house staff will soon be in need of Zimmer frames?"

"Speak for yourself, Hetty. I can still climb a tree as well as I could when I was a nipper. But you've got a point," Dot agreed.

"You may be surprised to know that I have anticipated that question and it is covered in the script. When Emanuel is describing the house to our guest, he will also tell him that when he returned to Austria he sought out as many of his father's old house staff as he could find. He felt he owed it to them to give them a roof over their heads and a job of work for the rest of their lives. How neat is that?" Jennifer added, pleased that so far she had not missed anything.

Jennifer gathered up the designs and passed them to Dot. "I will leave all this in both of your capable hands. Don't forget the German lesson – eighteen hundred hours at the nineteenth hole."

"She's given herself the right part – dotty sister," Hetty commented as she and Dot closed the door behind them.

"She has indeed," Dot laughed.

Thirty-One

"You look just the part, Gerald."

Gerald rarely blushed but he wasn't sure that Jennifer hadn't gone just a little over the top with her costume design. At first he had been told to wear whatever came out of his wardrobe, but then she had changed her mind. The bright green scarf tied in a knot to the side of his neck wasn't entirely his style, neither was the cream double-breasted blazer with the matching green handkerchief carefully folded and hanging out of his pocket.

"Jennifer, I really don't have to dress like this for people to see that I am gay. I only have to open my mouth. And don't forget that my whole life has been spent on art, so I do know what I am talking about." Gerald felt just a little exasperated.

"I know all that, Gerald, but we mustn't make even one tiny slip-up. No room for complacency today. I can take it for granted, I hope, that you went through your lines before we left today." Jennifer was in her element. It was a convincing script, the actors were well rehearsed and today they looked splendid, just as she had hoped. Any moment now the curtain would go up on the first act. The one thing that worried her was that Charles might recognise Gerald, but it was a million to one chance against. The last time they had been in the same location Charles had been on stage presenting his plans for Magnolia Court, while over a hundred people had sat in rows way back in the audience listening to him. He had not joined them after the presentation nor had he accompanied them on the California trip.

"Yes, Jennifer, I have been through all my lines like a good boy. Calm down, darling. It is all going to be fine." Gerald loosened the neck scarf so that he could breathe a little more easily.

"Time check." Jennifer looked at her fake Chanel watch encrusted with diamantes. "It's time. Action. Stroll casually through that door, chatting as you go and stand in front of the Lowry," she said, giving them both a gentle nudge in the right direction. It was so, so exciting. It would have been even better if they had allowed her to use a clapperboard.

"Don't forget. Wait until they are standing right next to you before you say the opening line. And say it loud and clear."

Gerald nodded to Emanuel. "Let's go."

At almost the same instant Gabby walked through the door opposite arm in arm with Charles. Those who did not know better would say that they were the perfect couple, totally at ease with one another and thoroughly enjoying their stroll around the gallery.

* * *

It was his very favourite gallery but it was the first time Charles had been back to visit for many years. Charles delighted in surprising Gabby with his knowledge and she, in turn, delighted him with her interest.

Gabby gave herself a pat on the back. Lunch had been a

great success. He had been quite effusive in his praise for the chef at the exclusive restaurant and touched by the small birthday cake that the chef had delivered in person to the table with their coffee. Politely the waiter had reminded them that the table had been rebooked from two o'clock. The unbudgeted expense of tipping the waiter heavily had been worth every penny. They left the restaurant bang on time.

Gabby checked her watch. The list of questions that she would ask if they were running early was indelibly printed in her mind. The tactics for persuading him to move on faster were less well defined. The research she had done proved invaluable. When she judged they were making insufficient progress she asked fewer questions and moved on to the next painting.

At three-thirty Charles held the door open for her as they stepped into the 'right' room. With immense relief, Gabby saw Emanuel and Gerald approaching from the opposite direction, deep in conversation with one another.

There was just the one 'masterpiece' in the room, such was the importance of this one particular work of art.

Gerald waited.

"Do they know that this one is the copy?" he whispered loudly to Emanuel.

"They do now," replied Emanuel, never once letting his eyes stray from the painting. "Once the tests were all completed to their satisfaction, they put the two paintings side by side and called in the world's leading authority on Lowry's work. He had no doubts whatsoever. One hundred per cent sure, was what he said. The real one is now back where it belongs – at my home in Austria. In a few weeks' time that brass plate will be changed to read 'Copy of *The Industrial Heartland*' and mine will, at last, be officially recognised as the original."

"Did the gallery make you an offer for the original?" Gerald enquired discreetly.

"Of course. Three million to take it off my hands. They were very anxious to obtain it. For a while, I was tempted, but then I thought about it. To my mind, they have a quite exquisite copy here and I don't think that they really need the original as well. Had I not bought the original for them to see, then they would never have known that theirs was a copy. Hundreds of thousands of people pass through this gallery each year and stand exactly where we are now. Would any of them know the difference?" Emanuel let his eyes wander over the painting. "I think that this copy has earned pride of place in the Lowry."

"Then you'll keep the original?" Gerald took the lead from Emanuel and slowly took in every detail of the picture. "It isn't easy to find him in this painting, but there he is – that tiny little speck right in that corner walking away with his suitcase."

"Unfortunately, I cannot keep it. Three million will be just about enough to finish the restoration of my family home. My father's dying wish was that the house should remain in the family so that every future generation could be born and live there. I am sure that my grandfather never understood the responsibility that he placed on my father's shoulders nor he on mine." Emanuel looked sadly at the painting and shook his head.

"I have decided to find a collector who loves art as much as my father did and who will look at it every day and never part with it, but it is easier said than done, my dear Gerald."

"How right you are, Emanuel. It so happens that my gallery

is closed for our annual holidays for the whole of April. If it would be of any assistance to you I could come over and help you find and vet prospective buyers," Gerald suggested, casting his glance sideways. Charles's feet were glued to the spot, his eyes glued to the painting, his ears glued to the conversation between the elderly Jew and the 'dandy' with whom he was speaking.

"I would really appreciate that, Gerald. Thank you. Right now it's time for an old man to return to the Lowry – such a wonderful hotel. I couldn't resist staying there. I shall have a nice pot of tea in their wonderful airy lounge in the company of the one and only Lowry, followed by a siesta and a good read this evening." Emanuel removed his glasses and rubbed his eyes. "It has been a long day. You have my number, Gerald. It is kind of you to offer to come out and help me, and I would appreciate it very much. Let's stay in touch."

Gerald followed Emanuel as they left the room.

* * *

"That's pretty special, isn't it, Gabby?" Charles stared at the picture and shook his head. "It's priceless, quite priceless. What I would give to own that."

"If you say so, Charles," Gabby replied. "It looks much the same as the other ones to me."

Charles glared at her.

"Did I say something wrong?" Gabby asked.

"This, Gabby, was his finest hour," Charles replied as if in a daydream. "I was just thinking," he said, changing the subject, "You've given me a particularly wonderful birthday and we've still got two hours to spare before the train. You're a girl in a

271

million, you know that? So I want to do something for you."
Charles reached into his pocket and drew out his wallet. "I
want to spoil you. Here's two hundred pounds and I want
you to take yourself off to Harvey Nichols and buy yourself
something special. If it costs any more just let me know."

"I couldn't possibly," Gabby protested. "It's far too much.
You really can't afford it."

"You are worth every penny, Gabby. Off you go. I shall
start at the beginning of the gallery and work my way around
it all over again, and I'll see you by the departures board at
Piccadilly ten minutes before the train goes."

"Thank you, Charles. Thank you so much. I can't remember
the last time I went shopping and bought something special,"
Gabby said, giving him a hug and a peck on the cheek.

Gabby raced out of the gallery and grabbed the phone out
of her bag. "Unless I'm mistaken, the fish is biting and he'll
be on his way in a matter of minutes," she said.

* * *

Fifteen minutes later Emanuel was back at the Lowry Hotel.
Taking a seat in the lounge where he could easily be seen,
he ordered a pot of tea and picked up a copy of *The Times*.
Emanuel felt his eyes closing. *The Times* was far more effective
than any sleeping pill.

"Excuse me," Emanuel heard from afar, "didn't I just see you
at the Lowry? I can't get enough of them. I don't mean that I
have a collection. I just mean that if I could set up a bed in
that gallery and live there then I would be happy as a sandboy.
He's my hero. My name's Charles, Charles Fairbrother, by
the way."

Emanuel blinked several times and shook his head to wake up, folded the newspaper up and looked up at Charles. "Yes, I do vaguely remember seeing you there. Won't you join me? I was just about to ask for some more tea," he added, without dropping his Austrian accent.

"How kind of you. Do you live in England or are you just visiting?" Charles enquired as he pulled up a chair.

"I'm here for a few days only this time. One or two things I had to sort out, you know how it is," Emanuel said casually, signalling to the waiter. "Tea for two, please, Timothy."

"Certainly, Mr Levi. Give me two minutes, sir."

Charles made a mental note – Levi, a good old-fashioned Jewish name.

"And where would home be, Mr Levi?" Charles asked.

"Austria. It is a beautiful country. The scenery is stunning and the air so clean and pure. It's very different to your English cities. I never tire of the seasons in Austria, although my home, which is quite ancient, can be quite chilly in the winter," Emanuel replied thoughtfully, remembering Jennifer's words. Just answer his questions; don't offer your life story on a plate; let him work for it.

"I know what you mean but there's something very charming about older properties. No one builds houses with character these days. How old would your house be?" Charles sipped his tea, Earl Grey, no milk, and tried not to grimace.

Emanuel said, "It dates back to the mid-18th century, 1760 to be precise. It has been in the family since the 1860s. We lost it during the war when the Nazis commandeered it and turned it into a hospital for injured officers. It remained unoccupied for almost forty years after the war and, as you can imagine, fell into quite a state of disrepair. I was fortunate in business and returned there some years ago now. The restoration is still in progress but one day it will be finished and then it will be quite magnificent again."

"Sounds expensive," Charles sympathised.

"It is. Very."

"I would liken an ancient house with all its history to a great painting. They both tell such a rich story. Maybe we are kindred spirits. *The Industrial Heartland* – what a masterpiece. Can you imagine having that hanging on the wall in your house? Beyond anybody's wildest dreams."

"It is a particular favourite of mine, and yes I can..." Emanuel replied, and sighed. "Oh well..."

"Something troubling you?" Charles moved fractionally closer to Emanuel.

"Yes, there is something on my mind, and it would be good to share it with somebody who has no interest in it. I keep turning it over and over in my mind but never reaching a decision. That's what happens when you get a bit older." Emanuel paused, closed up his paper and laid it on the table. "I have a painting that my father acquired which I may have to sell in order to finance the final part of the restoration of my family home. I have just about exhausted all other avenues of finance and now I really do have to make a decision," Emanuel confided.

"It must be an important piece if it is going to finance a big restoration," Charles said. He felt his heart beat faster. Any minute now he would hear the story of the original Lowry.

"It is. You see..." Emanuel hesitated and looked hard at Charles. "I own the original *Industrial Heartland*. The one in the Lowry gallery is a copy, a very good copy, but nonetheless a copy."

Charles whistled and feigned disbelief. "Unbelievable. Unbelievable. That is quite astonishing."

"I was quite astonished too when I found it. My father hid all of his artworks before the Nazis arrived which was just before my sister and I were packed off to England. We were young. I would like to say that it was an exciting flight to safety, but I remember full well that we were scared from the moment we left to the moment we arrived in England. Many years later and not long after we started the restoration work we uncovered a bricked-up alcove in the old wine cellars. That was where I found the Lowry."

"And you have it in England with you now?" Charles asked, signalling to the waiter. "Would you care to join me in a cognac, Mr Levi? After that story, I think I need one."

Emanuel nodded. In other circumstances, he might even have liked the man sitting opposite him. "The painting is where it belongs at home in Austria. It's a little early for me. I don't often imbibe. But I feel rather sad today so maybe for medicinal purposes only."

Over cognac, Charles confided to Emanuel that his one ambition in life had been to own a Lowry, but not just any Lowry. There had only ever been one for him. It had nothing to do with status; he was simply consumed by the man's genius and had a passion for his work. If ever he owned the one of his dreams he would die a happy man.

Emanuel laughed. "If ever you have three million pounds to spare it could be yours. Even if you don't, you would be very welcome, Mr Fairbrother, to visit my home and share my painting. But I doubt that it will be there for long. As I said earlier, I will have to part with it soon. But now, if you'll excuse me, I have to retire. Good afternoon. It has been a pleasure. Maybe we will meet again."

"That, Mr Levi, is an offer that I can't refuse," Charles said quickly. "It's a while since I visited Austria and once the painting is sold I will probably never get the chance to see the original."

"You would be most welcome. If you give me your contact details I will be in touch with you when I get home. Don't worry, I am a man of my word. You'll see the painting before it leaves my home."

Charles took his card out of his pocket and handed it to Emanuel "Good day, Mr Levi. It has been a great pleasure," Charles said. "I look forward to meeting you again soon."

Emanuel picked up his copy of *The Times* and shuffled towards the lift, waving to Charles as he left. He could hardly wait to report back to headquarters.

Thirty-Two

Headquarters was located in Suite 24 of the Lowry Hotel.

Jennifer opened her second miniature bottle of gin. Act one of the show had gone like clockwork and they had been over the moon to have received Gabby's coded message: the fish is taking the bait. It was all like something out of a spy thriller. Now it was waiting time. It was unthinkable that Charles might not have come to the hotel after having been lured there so brilliantly.

Jennifer lay outstretched on the cream chesterfield sofa. Was Emanuel following his script or was he winging it? Her nerves were frazzled. Long years in the theatre had taught her that once rehearsals were complete and the show was live on stage, there was nothing more one could do – only sit back and put your complete trust in the cast.

Gerald attacked the decanter of sherry on the desk and paced backward and forward on the deep pile carpet.

* * *

"Ah, I hope you have left something in the drinks cabinet for me," Emanuel said, bursting through the door and throwing his jacket on the nearest chair. "You know, Jennifer, I have missed my vocation. I should have taken to the stage years ago."

"Would I be right in thinking that you have already had one or two?" Gerald asked, hanging on to his chair as he pulled himself to his feet to greet his fellow conspirator.

"My good friend Mr Fairbrother and I did have a couple of cognacs together and very good they were too. I hasten to add that he paid. I rather think Gerald that in your case it's the pot calling the kettle black." Emanuel pointed at the now almost empty sherry decanter.

"So," Jennifer said, pirouetting around the room and waving her purple scarf in the air, "did my maestro give the performance of his lifetime?"

"My dear," Emanuel bowed deeply in front of her, "you would have been proud of me. Not only was I word-perfect, but he led the conversation and not once did I have to prod him in the right direction. It was nothing short of a virtuoso performance if I say so myself."

"Then I think we should toast our success," Gerald said, raising his glass.

A short tap on the door startled them all. Emanuel looked around. "Did either of you call for room service?" he whispered. Jennifer and Gerald exchanged glances and shook their heads.

"Bedroom. Hide now. Take those glasses with you." Emanuel reached for the snowy white Lowry Hotel dressing gown that had been meticulously folded and draped across the armchair and checked that Gerald and Jennifer had left nothing in the room. "Just one moment and I will be with you," Emanuel called. "I was just about to have a little nap."

He opened the door. "Mr Fairbrother. To what do I owe

this pleasure?"

"Did I disturb you? I'm so sorry if I did. Reception gave me your room number. I thought I heard voices," Charles said apologetically.

"No, no, just the radio. I've just turned it off."

"I am so sorry to disturb you, Mr Levi, but I was thinking about what you said. I was in a taxi heading for the station and then two minutes later I told the driver to turn around and drive right back to this hotel. I just couldn't face the possibility that you might sell that masterpiece to someone who wouldn't appreciate it. It would be even worse to see it, fall in love with it all over again, and then lose it straightaway. I know this is very presumptuous of me, but if you would be so kind, Mr Levi, I would appreciate the opportunity to be the first to make you an offer."

Emanuel closed the door. "Come in, Charles. May I call you Charles? Do call me Emanuel. Mr Levi sounds so pompous and old-fashioned. You have caught me completely off guard." This was one act that had neither been expected nor rehearsed; he was on his own. "Do sit down. You know I really hoped that I would never hear those words. Silly of me, isn't it? Talking about parting with it is one thing but actually doing it is quite another." Emanuel mopped his brow with his handkerchief.

* * *

Jennifer held the crystal glass between her ear and the door. Gerald rolled his eyes in her direction.

"But would you consider it?" Charles persisted. "I would need to see the painting first, of course, and to go through the provenance with you."

"I am not sure. I am not at all sure," Emanuel dithered.

Jennifer listened anxiously. For God's sake don't dither too much, Emanuel.

"I'm just being a silly oversensitive old man. It was my father's, you know. I do know it has to be sold – there's no question about it – and you seem such a decent man." Emanuel wiped a tear from his eye and gradually recovered his composure. "You will have to forgive me. The answer to your question is…" Emanuel hesitated for effect. "Yes."

Charles held out his hand. "And the price is two and a half??"

Emanuel nodded. "No, my dear Charles, it is three million pounds. It's been valued at slightly more than that, but I am willing to let it go for three."

"When can I come and see it? Yesterday would be great for me," Charles asked eagerly.

"I won't be home for a few weeks, Charles. I have business to attend to in Europe first. Let me check my diary." Emanuel got up and reached for his jacket. Wherever he went, his diary went with him. "I will not be home until the ninth of April. Maybe you would like to come out for the day on the eleventh. That's a Saturday and of course you will do me the honour of staying overnight with me. My very good friend, Gerald, who is an art expert, will be staying with me then. I feel sure that the two of you will get on very well indeed."

Charles hesitated; he didn't need a diary to remember dates. "You couldn't have picked a worse date, Emanuel. That's the date I go on holiday. I'll be back the following week and I'm free at the beginning of April."

"That is a pity, Charles. Are you sure you couldn't change

your plans? After all, as you just said, it would be such a pity if I had to sell it to somebody else." Emanuel's face crumpled – the date was critical to the plan.

"I feel sure we can find a date that will suit both of us, Emanuel. You email me some other dates and we'll find one that works," Charles said confidently. The man needed three million pounds and he had just made him an offer. No one in their right mind would turn it down.

"Of course, Charles. I am sure we can. We'll pick you up from the airport when you come. We would be delighted if you wanted to bring your wife with you?" Emanuel couldn't resist the temptation. Would Charles tell more lies? "My wife, Dinah, would be delighted to spend time with her. We live in the Mostviertel region of Austria, in the south and it is very beautiful."

"I do have a wife, but she is no connoisseur of art. She prefers to spend her days in her health club or out riding," Charles replied.

Emanuel fixed a smile on his face. "I quite understand." He had proved his point. The man was making a direct reference to his ex-wife. Gabby hated health clubs and hated horses even more.

"Then that's settled. You shall come. I will get back to you with suitable dates." There was little else he could say. You'll have to forgive us when you arrive at my house, but as I mentioned we are still under restoration – I apologise in advance but it may be just a little noisy during the day. And I hope you won't expect the service to be quite like the Lowry. My house staff are mostly quite elderly, but they do their best. They were employed by my father and when I returned to the house I sought them all out to give them an income for life and a roof over their heads. I guess I'm just an old softie at heart."

Charles laughed. "I wouldn't want you to go to any trouble for me. Au revoir, Emanuel. Pleasure to do business with you." Charles held out his hand to shake on the deal and left.

* * *

"Heavens above." Jennifer slid down to the floor and nursed her head. "We didn't see that one coming."

"We paid the outstanding balance on the house yesterday. It's the weekend of eleventh and twelfth of April or our plans go, if you will excuse my language, completely tits up," Gerald replied glumly.

Thirty-Three

The health club was no more than fifteen minutes' drive from the house – expensive and exclusive and adults only. However much she loved her children, preferring them immeasurably to any others, Annabel drew the line at kids playing hide and seek around the club and jumping in and out of the swimming pool on top of her.

She went there twice a week for a quick workout, and then once a month she treated herself to the full works. The kids were at school and her parents were collecting them for a sleepover. Today was her pamper day.

"Good morning, Mrs Fairbrother," the receptionist called brightly. "I see that you're in for a facial, body massage, hair, and nails today?"

"That's right, Sally. Work out first, then a swim, then the sauna, followed by a good book in the solarium, and by that time I shall be ready to be pampered in the spa – massage and facial today and then the hairdressing salon and finally my nails."

Annabel flashed her membership card at the entry machine, pushed the gate, grabbed two snowy white towels out of the basket and headed for the changing rooms.

Taking a deep breath, she took the stairs to the gym two

at a time. There were always one or two of the personal trainers standing or sitting at the top of the stairs and she liked them to think that she was just as fit as they. Daniel and Sebastian, her personal trainers, were twenty-eight and twenty-two respectively, both handsome, muscular, fit and highly personable. She would have liked to take either one of them home with her.

Always the same routine, it took her fifty minutes precisely to work her way around the treadmill, the rowing machine, the stepper, the presses and the weights.

Removing the sweatband from her head, she shook out her hair and mopped her forehead with the towel. It felt good, although the muscles in her calves were complaining just a little more than usual.

The day had only just started and it was looking good. She had the sauna to herself and threw water on to the hot coals with gay abandon until the perspiration ran from every pore in her body – the perfect precursor to relaxing in the solarium and then cooling off in the swimming pool.

Her masseur, Sammy, was a huge brute of a man with black skin that shone like polished ebony, but he had the most gentle, sensuous touch. Long fingers probed her back, neck and shoulders, and found the tiny little knots that she did not even know existed – Annabel purred like a kitten and let her imagination run riot.

Frances, the young girl who did her facials, was quiet and unassuming but good at her job. Annabel lay on the comfortable bed, a fleece over her body, staring up at the ceiling with its blue sky and puffy white clouds. It was the one hour each month when she completely relaxed and let all other thoughts drift away. It had been a lifesaver for the past eighteen months. Her skin tingled as she lay back and thought about nothing. Time stood still until Frances quietly muttered that she was finished and removed the headband.

Sophie, the hair stylist, always looked forward to seeing Annabel, who went on such exotic holidays to places that she could only dream about. Fortunately, Annabel was never lost for words when it came to narrating stories about the latest holiday or the next one that she had planned. It saved Sophie from boring her with her recent visit to an all-inclusive in Majorca – a place that Annabel told her she had never visited. Dubai sounded amazing, and Annabel's plan for a short break in the Canaries in a few weeks' time and then the summer holiday to Mauritius and the Seychelles made her salivate. She had noticed that Annabel often spoke about her two children but had not mentioned her husband for a couple of years. Sophie assumed he was still on the scene – who else would pay for all these exotic breaks? Sometimes it was better not to ask too many questions.

It was three by the time that her nails had been filed, nourished and polished, and Annabel was ready to go home. The rest of the afternoon and the evening would be spent in the company of a good bottle of Chablis and six recorded episodes of *Loose Women*, her favourite TV programme.

Annabel opened the bottle and put it in a wine chiller. A good wine deserved to be served at the right temperature and out of a good glass, she said to herself. In the background, Denise Welch and Zoe Tyler had already started a heated argument about trans-dressers and whether or not they really needed both male and female names. Annabel slipped off her shoes, put her legs up and rested her head against a pile of cushions at the other end. Heaven, she thought to herself –

sheer heaven.

She giggled; by the end of the third episode, the wine had somehow evaporated. Picking up her glass to check that there was no hole in it, she decided that maybe she would have just one more glass. In passing it occurred to her that drinking wine on an empty stomach was not such a good idea, but one more really wouldn't make much difference, now would it?

The wine stayed untouched in the glass on the coffee table. Annabel slept as soundly as a baby. After an hour, the TV switched itself and the screen went dark.

* * *

Half-asleep, she thought that she might have heard something in the house. She opened her eyes. The room was in darkness, the TV switched off. It had been light when she had got home. Annabel glanced at her watch. The last time she had looked it had been five and now it was after midnight. She had been asleep for over seven hours – too much physical exercise and relaxation, she decided. The wine had nothing to do with it.

Annabel strained her ears to listen. She was sure that she could hear something. Ethan and Abby were away so it couldn't be them. "Charles, is that you? It's late even for you to drop round. What excuse did you give Gabby this time?"

There was no reply. Annabel felt the first waves of panic course through her and with her head pounding, got to her feet and looked back towards the hallway. A man stood in the doorway, clad from head to foot in black and wearing a balaclava. It was the last thing she remembered.

* * *

She was lying on the settee, her feet and head supported by cushions. She remembered drinking too much, but this was more than just a hangover. Reaching up to her hair, she screamed as she felt something wet and sticky on her fingers and fragments of something sharp in her hair. Beside her on the floor lay the shattered wine glass.

Staggering to her feet, Annabel switched the light on and looked around the room. It was the same room, but it looked like an empty shell. Where Charles's paintings had once hung there remained nothing but shadowy squares on the walls. The same emptiness pervaded the hallway and the dining room. And then she remembered the man in the balaclava. He must have hit her. She must have passed out. But why then did she find herself lying on her own settee with her head carefully propped up on cushions?

The phone rang a dozen times and went to voicemail. Annabel rang again with the same result. She was not going to give up. He had to answer sooner or later.

"Yes?" said a voice.

"It's me, Charles. We've been fucking burgled and I was attacked. My head is bleeding. How long ago? What the fuck does it matter how long ago, Charles? I am on my own and I'm scared. Just get around here now. Yes, I'll lock the front door."

Charles jumped out of bed and pulled on his trousers and a sweater as Gabby woke up to see what all the commotion was about. "It's Annabel. We – I should say – she, has been burgled and she's hurt. I'll ring you and let you know how things are."

Charles drove the distance between Chertsey and Weybridge at breakneck speed, slowing down only for the three cameras that he knew he would have to pass en route. He was both worried and angry. Annabel getting injured was not part of the plan.

* * *

Annabel held her head as she walked slowly through the hallway and locked the front door. Shit, she said to herself, knowing that she only had herself to blame. It had been mid-afternoon when she returned home and she had not bothered to lock the door and then – well, the rest was history. No sooner had she put her feet up again than she heard a key in the door.

"My God, Annabel. I was so worried. Let me look. Perhaps I should take you to A&E right now." His words tumbled one over another.

"Great idea Charles. If you think I am going to sit in A&E for five hours waiting for somebody to come and bathe my head, and then tell me that it will heal itself, then you have another thought coming," Annabel said, recovering quickly at the prospect of a trip to the local A&E, which according to statistics was one of the worst in the country. "I'll bathe it myself – and I only had my hair done this afternoon. What a waste of time and money."

"Let me do it for you. I'll get some cotton wool and some warm water. If it needs it then we are going down to the hospital whether you like it or not." Charles breathed a sigh of relief. If all she was concerned about was not sitting around in A&E, and her hair, then she would live.

"Look what they've done," Annabel said, pointing to the spaces where once paintings had hung. "Look, Charles, all your paintings and more besides – all gone. Why? Why, when they were copies anyway? What good are they to anyone?"

Charles looked around the hall, the lounge, and then the dining room. There was nothing there. Nice job.

"The bastards. My life's work. I never told anybody about them," he raged.

"What do you mean you never told anybody about them? They were all hanging on the wall for every Tom, Dick, and Harry to see. Everyone knew they were here – all our friends, all the tradesman who worked in the house, the cleaner, the window cleaner – you name it. Everyone knew they were here. They're pretty much worthless, so why?"

"There's something I never told you, Annabel – for your own good. None of them were copies. They were the real McCoy. I didn't tell you because I thought it might worry you being in the house on your own with money dripping from the walls," Charles said stonily. "And now they are gone."

"You mean that they were really valuable?" Annabel replied incredulously. "Those ugly stickmen and scary faces were worth a lot of money?"

Charles nodded. "Millions. Whoever did this knew what they were after."

"Are we insured?" Annabel asked hopefully.

"We are. I made sure of that. I am going to ring the police right now, not that it will do much good. He'll be miles away by now." Charles picked up his mobile and tapped 101, followed instructions and eventually spoke to a human being. Was anybody hurt, the voice asked? Yes, he replied, but not badly and, no, they didn't need an ambulance. We need you to catch the burglar and recover the stolen goods, he said. The voice calmly told him that they would send somebody around in the morning and reminded him to check the windows and lock the door.

Without an incident report number, there would be no insurance claim.

Thirty-Four

Greg didn't know whether to laugh or cry when Gabby told him that there had been a burglary at The Poplars and that Harry's collection of Lowrys and other artefacts had been stolen from under their noses. Neither of them had voiced their thoughts out loud – was it a coincidence that Harry needed three million pretty damn quick and that an insurance payout on his collection would probably raise that sort of money?

Anything was possible, but it didn't entirely add up. Insurance companies were notoriously tardy in making payouts especially when the sums of money were huge. They would take their time studying the police reports and taking more statements from the owners and then, no doubt, call in an insurance risk assessor just to make sure. It would be months if not years before he saw that money. There was nothing that he wouldn't put past Harry Trumper and it was more than likely that he had staged the burglary himself, planned to pawn the paintings and then recover them when the insurance paid out. It could double his money.

Gabby had said that Annabel had been knocked unconscious by the burglar, but that other than a small cut had sustained no serious damage. Would Harry go so far as to risk Annabel being hurt by staging a robbery? It was possible.

It had been an ill wind. He had had Gabby to himself for another whole three nights while Harry played chaperone to Annabel, until such time as she could once more sleep peacefully in her bed.

* * *

Another weekend loomed long and lonely. The apartment seemed empty without her. Greg got out the file and laid all the printed photographs from his office heist on the dining table. This weekend he intended to make some progress on tracking down the real Charles Fairbrother. He had intended to get on to it a lot sooner but ITF Developments had other ideas. Several of his projects at work needed his personal attention, and he had had to work long hours with his team.

So what do I know so far, he asked himself? The birth certificate stated that Charles Fairbrother was born on 12 March 1966. His parents were Norman and Maria Fairbrother and his place of birth was Minchinhampton, Gloucestershire. The real Charles Fairbrother had been a wealthy man – it was the only explanation for the tax demands from the Inland Revenue. The letter addressed to the real Charles Fairbrother that Greg had found in Harry's office had been sent to an address in Peckham: *Flat 3, Waverley Court, London Road, Peckham, SE15 6YF.* It appeared to have been sent to him from an aged aunt:

Dear Charles,

I was surprised to receive your change of address card

but it did prompt me to make one final effort to get in touch with you. I am not getting any younger and it would be my dying wish to see you again and talk to you before that day arrives. You know where I live. Please write.

I hope you know that whatever your eccentricities, I have always had the highest regard for you. As a boy, you were very different to your siblings, and I could see from the earliest age that you would make your own way in life, and that family was of little consequence to you. It was a tragic accident and I hoped sincerely that you would return for the funerals. To lose both your parents and your siblings in that way must have been quite devastating.

I feel sure that you will have been very successful in whatever your chosen career and that money will be of little consequence to you, but I would like you to know that you are the sole beneficiary of my will.

Aunt Margery

The letter was dated 7 April 2001. It was highly unlikely that Aunt Margery would still be alive – probably a dead-end, but it was interesting that Harry had kept the letter locked up in the drawer. Was it possible that sometime in the future, when he was totally confident about his identity change, that he might claim his inheritance? Unusually, there was no address on the top right of the letter. Maybe Aunt Margery had lived at the same address all of her life and found no reason to include it.

And then there were the silver cufflinks with the monogram

CF. Greg put them aside; they were not helping.

The newspaper cutting was another matter altogether. A report from the *Peckham Times* read:

On the night of Friday 3 May police, fire brigade and ambulance attended a fire at Waverley Court, London Road, Peckham. The fire brigade attended the scene within ten minutes of the call received, but by that time the fire was a raging inferno and there was nothing that could be done to prevent the building from burning to the ground. The fire resulted in the sad loss of three lives: Mr Alfred Trumper (87) and Mrs Ada Trumper (83), and a tenant recently moved into one of the flats. The lives of a young Asian couple, a family of four and a single female who 'worked nights' were, by the grace of God, spared, all of whom were away from the property when the fire broke out. Mr Harry Trumper, grandson to Mr and Mrs Trumper, and Landlord of the property said that he was devastated by the loss of his grandparents who had been a rock to him from childhood, and was sorry to hear about the death of the other man. Mr Trumper named the tenant to the police but next-of-kin have yet to be informed. Fire investigators have completed their report and have concluded that the fire was probably the result of an unattended lit candle in one of the flats. The authorities have confirmed that all fire safety certificates for Waverley Court were up-to-date and that an inspection of the property had been carried out just weeks before the fire. The coroner's verdict is accidental death.

The funeral of Mr and Mrs Trumper, much loved

members of the local community, will take place on Friday 10 May at St Mary's, Peckham, followed by a burial at Nunhead Cemetery, Peckham.

Scrawled in the margin was the name Sam Smith, followed by an exclamation mark and an arrow that pointed to the word, tenant.

Beside the report, there were three photographs: one of Waverley Court and two larger photographs of Mr and Mrs Trumper on their wedding day and, later in life, with their grandson, Harry, aged fifteen.

Had sentimentality been Harry Trumper's downfall? Why else would he have kept those newspaper cuttings about the fire at Waverley Court, other than that his grandparents had been precious to him, and the cutting was the last that he would ever see written of them?

Greg mentally checked his rationale. It was all beginning to fall into place.

The only evidence that linked Harry to Waverley Court and Charles Fairbrother was locked up in Harry's office.

By rights, he knew he should share his theory with both Gabby and the police, but it was no more than that – a theory. There was nothing to be gained by telling Gabby. It would serve only to frighten her even more. There was nothing to be gained by telling the police until such time as he had his hands on the evidence – and they had executed the plan.

In just a few weeks' time The Silver Sting would be done and dusted, whether with a successful outcome or not, and then it would be time to get Gabby out of there. It couldn't come soon enough.

If he was right about everything, then, armed with the

evidence from the office, he could get Harry Trumper locked up for life.

It was time for another visit to portacabin number five. He had to get his hands on the evidence, and there was not a moment to lose.

Thirty-Five

"Gabby, are you able to talk? We've hit a snag," Jennifer said.

"Yes. I've got fifteen minutes before I meet Charles. I'm at Piccadilly right now, waiting for him," Gabby glanced around to make sure that Charles was nowhere in sight. "Let's make it quick, Jennifer."

"He can't make the date," Jennifer said.

"Who? What date?"

"Charles. The weekend of 11th and 12th April. He says that he will be away on holiday and can't change it. Everything is up in the air now. It's all gone wrong. Emanuel tried his best to persuade him to change his plans but it didn't work. It's left that Emanuel will contact him with some alternative dates. We can't do that, Gabby. The house is booked and paid for. Quite apart from the money, we know for a fact that the house isn't available during the rest of April. It would mean putting the whole thing off until May or June. I just don't know what we are going to do. It's all falling apart. It's a disaster."

Gerald and Emanuel sat quietly in the background and listened to the conversation. She was right, Gerald thought, it was definitely heading for a disaster. On a positive note, the Lowry would look very nice in his sitting room.

Emanuel went through it over and over again in his head. He should have managed the conversation better. He should have stood up to the man and told him that it was that weekend or no weekend at all. He had got carried away on the euphoria of the moment.

"Charles will be away on holiday that weekend? It's the first I've heard of it." Gabby's heart sank. She could not keep up the pretence with Charles for one month longer let alone another two months. Had he mentioned going away? No, he had not.

"So he didn't tell you?" Jennifer asked.

"Of course not, Jennifer." Gabby heard the irritation in her voice. "I'm not cross with you. The damned man plays games. He always leaves telling me things like that until the last moment, the path of least resistance. Damn him and damn Annabel."

"Shall I ring Max?"

"Yes. Do that, Jennifer, but tell him not to change anything until he hears from me again. I've got to go, I can see Charles coming. It's not all over yet." Gabby finished the call and dropped the phone into her handbag. She had three hours on the return train journey to come up with a plan otherwise, The Silver Sting was dead in the water.

"I dropped in at the travel agents this morning, Charles and picked up some brochures. I was thinking how nice it would be if you and I could go away on a short holiday together. I've got time off just before Easter. We could go for a week," Gabby said.

Charles didn't look up. Where had all this come from? "I can't afford it right at this moment, Gabby. I've just paid the insurance on this cottage, the gas bill, and the water

298

bill. Why all bills have to come in the same month I'll never know. Annabel doesn't pay for everything you know. Maybe we'll have a simple break in the summer." Charles buried his nose back in the newspaper. He would have to have the conversation with her sometime or other. Maybe he was worrying over nothing. He'd been expecting a fight over the Dubai trip which hadn't materialised. Perhaps she would be equally understanding about the plans Annabel had made for the week before Easter, but it was looking unlikely to be the case.

"As it happens, and don't hit the roof, Gabby, Annabel has organised a short break for the kids. It's nothing exotic this time, just seven days in the Canary Islands leaving on sixth April. The kids break up the Friday before. If she wasn't paying, then I wouldn't even think about going, but she is, and I've already agreed that I'll tag along."

"Tell her you can't go. That we are going away. Put me first, Charles, just for once. There are times when I wonder who you are married to – me or Annabel. I will be quite happy to simply go out on day trips. At least we will have a break together. We haven't had one since our honeymoon, and what was that? Two days in London."

"I know. I know. I'll make it up to you. I'm a father, Gabby. It's what father's do."

"You are unbelievable and I'm getting mightily tired of it, Charles. In fact, I'm beginning to wonder why I married you in the first place. Maybe it would be a good idea to call it a day right now. What's one more divorce? If you go with Annabel this time then it's the end for us."

Gabby crossed her arms, pursed her lips and looked out of the window. He had to believe that she was serious. It was a risk but she had to take it.

"Hey, hey, Gabby. This doesn't sound like my girl talking." Charles stood up and held his arms out to her. Divorce from Gabby right at that moment in time was definitely not part of the plan. Hopefully, it wouldn't be long, but not yet. "I didn't know you felt that strongly about it. You should have said something sooner. The last thing I want is to lose you."

"I mean it, Charles. I've had enough." Gabby turned away.

Charles contemplated the options. At any other time, he would have dealt with it with a few choice words but it simply wasn't convenient to rock the boat right now. The look on her face told him that she was serious and would not easily be placated. Annabel would simply have to understand. "Okay. Day trips sound good to me. If it makes you happy, I'll tell Annabel that she's on her own this time."

"Promise me?" Gabby said.

"I promise."

* * *

"He's not going away Uncle Max. I put my foot down and for once he seems to have listened. He doesn't normally back off but he did this time. Annabel is off to the Canaries on her own. Theoretically, he is now free on April eleventh and twelfth. If he has a choice between losing that painting and taking me out on a couple of day trips then I know what it will be. Lowry wins.

"Now, Max you need to get Duncan to spring into action and fast. He's to get an email from Emanuel to Charles to tell him that there is another prospective buyer in the market who has offered the same price, and who will be going out to Austria on the 10th April. Duncan and Emanuel can dress it up however they like, but his intention needs to be clear – Emanuel is prepared to sell to the other buyer."

"What if he backs out, Gabby?" It was a possibility that Max hardly dared contemplate. It was all on the roll of a dice, but what other way was there?

"He won't. Trust me. He's got this far. He won't back out now. Unless both Greg and I are sadly mistaken he's got the money in the bank, waiting." The matter was not up for debate. "Get it done Uncle Max, please. And get it done now."

Gabby put the phone down and hoped against hope that she had done the right thing.

Thirty-Six

"Ladies and gentlemen, Silver Sting team members, if you have all got your tea then I would like to call this meeting to order." Max stood up and waited until he had the team's full attention. Hetty sat proudly beside him. How happy it made her to see the old Max, full of spirit and determination, back with her.

"I am pleased to be able to tell you all that we are finally back on course. It was a close run-thing, but thanks to Gabby we live to tell the tale. Today, as you know full well, is the sixth of April and tomorrow ten of us will be crossing the sea to Austria to implement the final and most important phase of our project. I only wish that everyone was going with us, but it is vital that we have a small team back at base to handle any issues that may arise, so I would like to thank Duncan, Peter and Amy for volunteering to form that team." Max cleared his throat and checked his notes. "As chairman may I say how proud I am of each and every one of you. You all deserve a medal for all your hard work over the last few weeks.

"This project is important to all of us. Not only are we going to redress a gross injustice, but we are also making a stand for the older generation. I believe that our little ruse could well

302

go down in history as an example of what can be achieved when people, irrespective of their age, pool their skills and work together as a team. Regrettably, we cannot write the story – none of us would like to spend the rest of our days at Her Majesty's pleasure – but maybe someday someone will write it for us." Max paused and looked up at his friends, hoping that the words he had written for the occasion did not sound too Churchillian.

"I wish he'd bloody well get on with it," Peter whispered in Henry's ear.

Henry nodded sagely. "I've got several more chapters of *Wines of Germany* to read yet. It's quite hard going, you know, and if our guest does ask me about the wines, I do want to sound reasonably knowledgeable."

Max waited until the side conversation had died down before continuing. "The minibus leaves at 0800 tomorrow, so this is our last chance to go through everything, to make sure we have everything we need with us and that we have not missed anything. I spoke to Gabby earlier today and she is fairly confident that Charles – Harry – call him what you will, is intending to catch that plane. Apparently, he has already informed her that he has to be away for the weekend – some cat-and-dog story about a golfing competition in the nether regions of Scotland. He's also had a suit cleaned ready for the occasion. So that is good news."

"Brilliant. Just brilliant. This is one competition that he isn't going to win. It gets better and better," Jennifer gushed, rubbing her hands together.

Max smiled. Her enthusiasm was catching and she had done more than her fair share to buoy everybody up over the past few weeks. "It is, Jennifer, quite brilliant, as you say, but right now can we all please turn to the agenda and I will receive your reports. Andy, would you like to go first?"

Andy stood up and shuffled his feet. "I'm just going to cover the key points right now. The minibus will be delivered here at 1600 hours this afternoon. It is a ten-seat minibus, and there will be ten of us, including me, on board. Keep your overnight bags to a minimum and place them on the floor in front of your seat.

"As Max has said we depart Magnolia at 0800 and we arrive in France at 1700 French time where we will all change our watches onto French time, which is one hour later than in the UK. We should arrive at our B&B near Brussels not long after 1900.

"On Wednesday we have another early start and our destination will be just west of Frankfurt.

"If we leave Frankfurt on time at 0800, we should arrive at Viertel by about 1200 hours on Thursday. We'll get the bus unloaded and I'll park it out of sight as instructed by Franz.

"Do we get the chance for cups of tea on the way? I will have to go to the little boy's room a few times." Henry put up his hand.

"All allowed for in the schedule, Henry." Andy smiled and continued. "I think that about covers it. Any questions?" Andy sat down with a sigh of relief.

"Jennifer, you next." Max checked his notes.

"My report is short and sweet. All the scripts are written and we've rehearsed them more times than I care to remember. I am happy that we have the best group of actors in the UK. All costumes are complete, thanks to Hetty and Dot, and everything is packed in the large suitcase," Jennifer said, and sat down again.

"Excellent. Make sure all your medicaments are packed and that you wear comfortable shoes. I have packed a first-aid kit just in case," Max said.

"Hetty, my dear, it's your turn now." Max smiled at his wife.

"Thank you, Max. The menu for the special dinner on Saturday night is all sorted, and Dot and I have bought all the ingredients on the assumption that there will be no time for shopping when we arrive. All fresh produce is being packed in iceboxes. Sandwiches for the outward journey have all been prepared.

"We will prepare sandwiches for the return journey before we leave Viertel. That's it, Max. Dot and I have everything under control."

"So that just leaves the cost of the B&Bs and dinners on the way, and umpteen cups of tea," Peter said, making a note to add the tea breaks into the budget.

"That's right," Hetty replied. "I think I've passed all the receipts for the food on to you."

"All accounted for, Hetty, and well within budget. Good work," Peter confirmed.

"Henry, would you like to give your report?" Max asked, noticing that Henry's head was beginning to nod.

"Well, yes. We have three bottles of wine for the dinner, all especially selected, a bottle of fino sherry for pre-dinner drinks and a bottle of cognac to accompany coffee. All within budget. Maybe I should have bought a few bottles for our celebration when we get back."

"Excellent, Henry. Let's not get ahead of ourselves, though. There'll be plenty of time to celebrate if – I mean when – we pull it off," Max said encouragingly. "Dot, Dennis, is there anything that you would like to add at this point in time?"

"I don't think so, Max," Dot replied for both of them. "Hetty's covered the kitchen elements. Dennis is going to be an angel, as always, and clean up after us."

Dennis nodded contentedly – that was about the sum of it.

"Emanuel, Dinah? Is there anything that you would like to report today?"

Emanuel looked at Dinah. "We've got all of my family photographs – not that there are too many of them – put into silver frames so that they can be displayed around the house. Gerald has given me a most interesting insight into all the paintings that he has hired for the occasion and, of course, our friend, Mr Lowry. We've been through the layout of the house that Duncan obtained from Franz and I think we could both walk around it blindfolded." What he didn't add was that he knew the layout of the house better than anybody, possibly even better than Franz.

"That sounds very professional, Emanuel. And you're happy that everyone has mastered basic German?" Max asked with a broad grin on his face. Having listened to himself and Hetty repeating phrases in German from Emanuel's lessons, he hoped that neither of them would be called upon to exercise their skills in public.

"Let's say that everyone has made a valiant effort. As it happens the plan is that we will speak English anyway as a courtesy to our guest – that being the case, we should have no trouble communicating with one another."

"Amy?" Max smiled at Amy who sat patiently, legs crossed and arms resting on her knees, waiting her turn.

"It took a long time, but all of the documents that Gerald asked me to do are complete," Amy stated slowly and clearly. "*The Owner's Inventory of Paintings* was a sheer delight to create.

The bill of sale is complete and in the envelope. Gerald has checked and double-checked the entries in the *Inventory* and on the bill of sale. And the family photograph album is an absolute work of art, and I have to say that most of the credit goes to Duncan. What he can't do with that computer of his is nobody's business. There are photographs of the family – a few of which are those that Emanuel had – but the rest are complete fabrications but so very authentic."

"Thank you for that, Amy." Duncan nodded, pleased that his work was appreciated.

"Gerald?" Max said.

Gerald stood up, shuffled a couple of papers and put them away in his top pocket. "Six most suitable paintings on loan, and the Lowry wrapped and ready to go. All documentation complete, so there should be no problem with customs. The story is that the artwork is being taken to Austria for an exhibition in aid of charity and all of it will be returned to the UK within eight days. There are signed letters of authority from the galleries that have loaned them to us. I shall carry all the relevant documentation myself. I have a first-cut plan of where the paintings will be hung in the house based on the photographs that Duncan managed to obtain from our dear friend, Franz."

Max laughed. "Thank you, Gerald. I'll ask Peter to report last, so maybe Duncan you could bring us up to speed, please?"

Duncan wheeled his chair to the front of the room. "I must say right at the start that Franz could not have been more helpful. He and his wife will be there to meet you when you arrive and will walk you through the house and show you how everything works before beating a hasty retreat to the gatehouse for the duration of your stay. Travel insurance policies and European health insurance cards are all in here," he said, handing a folder to Andy. "So you will be covered in the event of any medical emergencies. Andy also has the hotel booking forms, your passports, currency and the Eurotunnel ticket.

"Max has The Silver Sting mobile, the phone that has been used for all of our communications, except for Gerald's calls which he assures me are totally untraceable. We will dispose of it at the end of the project and *whoosh* every shred of evidence about our calls will disappear into the ether. It's a little trick I picked up from one my hacker friends. So far there have been no hits on our film company website. I can only assume that Franz trusts us. I noticed that there have been several hits on Emanuel's website that I set up several weeks ago. I assume that this is our man checking him out. It confirms everything that he has been told about Emanuel and his family without giving away too much. For authenticity I've included a few facts about Emanuel's distinguished career, none of which contradict his story. In small print it mentions that the family house is available to rent through his on-site manager for exceptional occasions, and links Emanuel's site to Franz's website. Again fortunately for us there is nothing on Franz's site that suggests that he is any other than the manager of the property. On Saturday afternoon soon after your visitor arrives the websites will disappear as if they never existed. That concludes my report, Max."

"Excellent, Duncan. Thank you. And finally, Peter?"

"Well, we're within budget. Emanuel's bank account has been set up, but what a palaver. I took a rather circuitous route to achieve it, but we got there in the end. Please don't ask questions. Thank God I retired from banking when I did.

It would test the patience of a saint now. I'll be monitoring the account every minute of the day and night if necessary. The moment the sum is paid into Emanuel's account it will be transferred to another account which neither our man nor the authorities will be able to find if ever they ask questions. And all that remains to be said is, good luck everybody," Peter concluded.

"Then, my dear friends, I think we all deserve a small sherry, don't you?" Max said.

The sherry poured, Max raised his glass "The toast is…The Silver Sting."

Thirty-Seven

Andy looked up through the windscreen. If he were not mistaken there was a shower on its way. As the first few drops of rain splattered on the windscreen, he closed his ears to the voices of The Silver Sting choir, led by Jennifer, as they struck up their own rendition of 'Singing in the Rain'. He really had to give it to her – always on the lookout. If she noticed the slightest lull in spirits, she led the chorus in either one of their wartime favourites or, and more often than not, one of the songs from *The Sound of Music*. The motorways were alive with the sound of music, if not the hills.

He had no complaints; they had all been very patient, had drunk their cups of tea in record time and not once had they failed to go to the little room before leaving a rest stop.

The first day had been the longest, during which they had travelled almost three hundred and fifty miles. Leaving Magnolia at nine, it was after seven by the time they arrived at the B&B just outside of Brussels. No one had objected to a quick supper followed by an early night.

The second day they reached the outskirts of Frankfurt by late afternoon.

On the third morning, the atmosphere was charged. They were almost there and about to put the plan into action. The

Silver Sting choir was silent.

"Just ten miles to go," Andy called out to the back of the bus.

Jennifer looked around the bus and saw, as Andy had seen through his rear-view mirror, a sea of anxious faces. It had been a long and gruelling journey with little sleep in the unfamiliar beds. "Come on now, everybody, we're nearly there. How about a chorus of 'Rule Britannia'?" she called as she sang the first line. "Join in." It was infectious, as she knew it would be, and the last few miles sped by.

Andy checked his speed, signalled right at the sign for Viertel and turned in through the stone archway. The bus fell quiet again as they cleared the arch, passed a small, but well-kept gatehouse and proceeded at five miles an hour up the drive.

The grass beneath the elms that lined the driveway was one mass of bright yellow daffodils nodding in the spring sunshine, while behind the trees, rhododendron bushes drooped with the weight of buds, waiting for the moment to burst. With the house in the near distance, the elms gave way to a sea of pink and white where cherry trees had shed their blossom.

All eyes turned to the magnificent gardens and the house beyond. "Are we sure this is the right place, Emanuel?" Henry whispered in his ear. Just look at that house and those magnificent turrets – I've never seen anything like it in my life. It's like something out of a fairy tale."

"Oh yes," Emanuel replied wistfully. "This is the place."

Andy turned the bus into the circular driveway in front of the house and waved to the man standing on the front steps. In late middle age and dressed in a green corduroy jacket with an open-necked shirt, the man smiled and walked towards the bus. A woman emerged from the house behind him dressed in a fawn polo-necked sweater, brown trousers and a fur gilet, and ran down the steps to join her husband.

Andy turned to the back of the bus. "Emanuel, I think it's time for you to meet Franz and Margarita."

Emanuel pulled on his jacket, straightened his tie and made his way to the front. It was the longest walk ever.

"Guten Morgen, Herr Neumann, Frau Neumann," he said, extending his hand first to Herr Neumann and then Frau Neumann.

"Herzlich willkommen. You must be Emanuel," Franz said, changing from German to English as a courtesy to his guests. "May I present my wife, Margarita. You must call us Franz and Margarita, if it pleases you. I am happy to speak English. It is good for my learning. My wife also speaks English."

Emanuel looked into Franz's narrowed eyes and wondered what the other man had seen in his own. If it were possible he would have described it as a spark of recognition, but that was fantasy. He had never, ever met Franz Neumann before that moment.

"The house looks perfect. We are honoured that you are allowing us to share it with you for a few days." Dinah slipped her arm through Emanuel's arm. "And this is my wife, Dinah, Dinah Levi," Emanuel said.

Franz cast a puzzled look at his own wife. Her eyes told all. She too had seen the similarity and made the connection.

Margarita broke the moment of awkwardness. "Bring your friends in. We have tea waiting for you and have sandwiches and pastries in the small salon. We have two strong men who will help you unload the suitcases and boxes but not until after we are all refreshed," she said, beckoning to the party.

The scent of lilies assailed their noses as they entered the house. A large round refectory table stood on the polished oak floor laden with a magnificent display of lilies, blue hydrangeas, and foliage. "Is this your own work, Margarita?" Jennifer asked, walking around the table and admiring the display from all angles. "It is quite exquisite. You have such an eye for colour."

"It is," Margarita replied, gratefully accepting the compliment. "And all the blooms come from our own garden and hothouse. The garden is my domain. Franz takes charge of the house and the restoration and I am in charge of interiors and garden."

Gerald lingered in the hall and discreetly examined each of the portraits. He had read about the *Lipizzan horses*, a breed made famous by the Spanish Riding School of Vienna but had never before seen quite so many portraits of them. None of them, he judged, were high-quality art, but all were extremely well executed. Over tea he must take Franz aside and question him about their history and the artists. It would not do for their guest when he arrived to ask questions that they could not answer.

Margarita poured tea, and handed the sandwiches to her grateful guests, all of whom were even older than Franz had led her to believe. It was intriguing that between them they planned to make a film, and equally puzzling that none of them were able to tell her what it was about.

Gerald chatted animatedly with Franz who clearly knew his art and explained to him that they had brought just a small number of paintings with them to feature in the film. They would, of course, treat Franz's own paintings with the utmost care and return them all to their rightful place at the end of the filming.

"Perhaps Gerald and Emanuel would like a guided tour of my collection," Franz suggested, turning to his wife "Would the rest of you excuse us for a moment, please?"

Emanuel and Gerald followed Franz out of the small salon, through the hall and into a large room in which burned a roaring log fire in an enormous inglenook fireplace. "Some of the finest works are in this room. We thought you might all like to relax in here this evening. It will turn cold later and this is the warmest room even though it is the largest of our salons," Franz said, warming his hands beside the fire. Gerald and Emanuel followed suit, content to watch the flames that licked through the logs.

Emanuel looked up and stared into the ormolu mirror that hung above the fireplace. His heart missed a beat as he looked at the picture on the wall behind him and into the eyes of his father. "Do you recognise him, Emanuel?" asked Franz.

A shiver ran down his spine. Emanuel shook his head. "My father in his study. It was painted when I was five years old," he replied guiltily. "I thought that portrait would be long since gone. I heard that the house had been destroyed in a fire."

Gerald looked from Emanuel to the painting open-mouthed. "My, oh my. What a turn-up for the books. This is another one that we didn't see coming. *He* is really your father?"

Emanuel nodded, lost for words.

Gerald put his arm around his friend's shoulder. "Now what precisely is it that I am missing here, Emanuel, and how come that portrait is hanging up there?"

"I am happy to answer that question for Emanuel," Franz

said. "It is a part of this house – it was painted in this house. The study that you see in the painting is through the other end of the house, as Emanuel knows only too well. The painting was hanging right here when I bought the house. The Nazis used the house as a rehabilitation home for injured officers during the war. The portrait was badly damaged. I suspect that they threw drinks and glasses at it and probably worse, but it was not beyond repair," Franz continued. "Did you come here to revisit your home, Emanuel? If so, why didn't one of you tell me? So you are now the baron?"

Gerald scratched his head, mopped the perspiration from his brow with his handkerchief and spoke. "Don't tell me, Emanuel. You really are a baron?"

"I suppose that I am." Emanuel nodded and turned to Franz.

"I owe you an apology," Emanuel said. "But it is not as you think. This was my childhood home. My father and mother sent me to England when I was just six years old. I was one of the Kindertransport children. My two older brothers left weeks after me but never made it to England. My parents closed up the house and went to stay with family in the country, but there was nowhere to hide. Years later I found out that they had been taken to Auschwitz. It was all too painful, too poignant, and then I was told that the house had burnt down, which is why I did not come back. Coming here was not my idea. My friends knew nothing of my association with this house."

"And what of this film? Is there any film at all?" Franz raised his eyebrows.

"It's a long story, Franz," Emanuel replied, resignedly. "Would you both mind if I had a couple of minutes with Max in private?"

"Not at all. I'll ask him to come through and then Gerald and I will wait with the others. Gerald, after you," Franz replied smiling benignly at the elderly gentleman in the picture hanging on the wall. "Whatever it is, you can trust me, Emanuel."

* * *

Emanuel looked up at his father and knew without a shadow of a doubt that he would never have condoned his son lying to a friend under their own roof, his own roof. And Franz was a friend; a man who had at vast expense, and with infinite care, restored their home. Emanuel wandered around the room stroking the pieces of furniture that he remembered so well, all now lovingly polished and adorned with photographs of the new family.

Turning, he heard the door behind him open. Max stood in the doorway, his eyes tuned in to the portrait that monopolised the room. "Good God, Emanuel, you are a chip off the old block if ever I saw one. No wonder Franz couldn't take his eyes off you when we arrived."

Max rested his hand on Emanuel's arm. "You should have told us before we left. We might have spared you this." Max was one of the few who knew Emanuel's story and he had quietly wondered about the wisdom of staging their production in Austria.

"I found myself in an impossible predicament, Max. I didn't see the photographs of the house until after Duncan had booked it, and then I couldn't ruin the project for everybody. You would never have known about it if it hadn't been for my father lording it up there on the wall. He was a great man. He and my mother filled this house with love." Emanuel spoke with a heavy heart.

"We don't even have to unpack Emanuel. We can just get back on the bus and go back home and everything will be just as it was," Max said decisively. "No one will blame you. We've always managed fine at Magnolia in the past. We'll do it again and forget all about Harry Trumper."

"I owe the others an explanation and I owe an explanation to Franz and Margarita and my wife, of course," Emanuel said solemnly, "I didn't even tell Dinah."

"As chairman, Emanuel, it's my responsibility to explain at least some of it to the team and our hosts. You can fill in the gaps, and let's see where we go from there, my friend," Max said kindly. "I'll go and ask Franz if we can all congregate in here while we explain."

Max turned and left Emanuel moving silently around the room from one memory to another.

* * *

"Would everybody like to take a seat, please? There is something that Emanuel and I would like to share with you all – that is, if you can't work it out for yourselves," Max said, turning his head towards the portrait on the wall. The first is that this beautiful house was once Emanuel's very own home and that," Max pointed to the portrait, "that gentleman is Emanuel's much-loved father. Emanuel quietly shared most of his story with me many years ago but not that Viertel had been home." Max turned to Emanuel. "Do you feel able to tell everybody?"

Emanuel nodded, and drifted off into the world of his

childhood, describing his family, the house, the gardens and then the end of the dynasty. No one spoke; there were no dry eyes in the house by the time he had finished and sat down. "Will you forgive me for not telling you, Dinah? It was wrong of me."

Dinah put her arms around her husband and held him fast.

Max picked up where he had left off. "And now my good friends of Magnolia, Emanuel and I have had a brief discussion and we feel that it is only right and proper that we share our true purpose in being here with our gracious hosts, Franz and Margarita. I have volunteered to do that."

Heads nodded in unison. Having now met Franz and Margarita none of them had felt comfortable with deceiving them. It was better this way.

With a heavy heart, Max started from the beginning and left nothing out. The Silver Sting team sat silently listening to Max while watching Franz and Margarita, whose expressions gave nothing away.

"And so, Franz, we will take our leave of you. The money that we have paid you for our stay will, of course, remain yours," Max concluded.

Franz took a deep breath, stood up and looked at them all. "I admire you. You have true spirits. That is what the English are known for. And, if my dear wife agrees, you are not going anywhere." A broad grin spread across Margarita's face. She could always rely on Franz to do the right thing.

"I don't understand, Franz. What else is there to do?" Gerald was the first to speak.

"It is at the ends of your nose, as the English say," Franz replied, laughing.

"It is?" Henry asked, mystified.

"Don't you see? My dear friend, Emanuel, was going to pretend that he was the owner of this great house and now he doesn't have to pretend at all. It is perfect. It was meant to be. He knows this house like the back of his hand. What could go wrong? I am more than happy for Emanuel to borrow his house for a few days. My friends, your project, The Silver Sting, lives, and if you would allow us, Margarita and I would dearly love to join in your conspiracy."

Jennifer whooped, jumped up and punched the air in her excitement. "Three cheers for Franz and Margarita."

"Hip, hip, hooray. Hip, hip, hooray. Hip, hip, hooray!"

"Thank you all. It is not needed. I am as excited as you must be. Now we have work to do. This evening we have a good supper and check out the plan."

* * *

An Austrian stew was simmering away on the Aga. Margarita seemed to have the ability to magic a feast out of nowhere. Hetty was never more glad in her life to know that Margarita would be by her side in the kitchen – the Aga would almost certainly have defeated her before she began. Like old friends, they talked through the planned menu, while Dot laid out all the ingredients that they had brought with them, checking them off against her own list. Margarita said that there was nothing on the menu that she would change. It was authentic and very achievable. Her only regret was that she would not be sitting at the dinner table enjoying it with their guest. If Max was agreeable then she would serve the dishes to the table, while Henry poured the wine for the party; the dumb waiter would not be necessary.

319

The bus unloaded and the suitcases placed in the guest rooms, Andy drove the bus round to the back of the stables, parking it carefully out of sight while Franz took Emanuel, Dinah and Jennifer on a tour of the house. Emanuel soaked it up, wondering if Franz had second sight – other than the colour schemes, of which he approved wholeheartedly, the house had hardly changed in more than eighty years. In severe contrast to the restored parts of the house, the last quartile awaiting restoration at the rear of the property was near to crumbling and supported by scaffolding. It was almost impossible to believe that when Franz had taken on the house it had all been in the same state of disrepair. "Now perhaps, Emanuel, you can see why I sympathise with your plight. I know what it takes to restore a beautiful house. When your mansion house at Magnolia is restored to its former glory then Margarita and I will be your first guests."

Gerald took personal responsibility for unloading the artwork from the bus and setting it carefully down in the hall, checking once more that each painting had been recorded in the *Owner's Inventory of Paintings* that Amy had so meticulously prepared. Even to the discerning eye, it was almost impossible to tell the fake from the real thing. It would not be unusual that some of the lesser paintings were unrecorded.

The Lowry, he decided, would be hung in the hall away from the harsh daylight and the ruinous effect of the smoke from the log fire.

Max occupied an hour checking in with Duncan, Peter and Amy back at base. After two abortive attempts at working out the right country calling code, he managed to get through. There was a stunned silence at the other end of the phone as Max explained the turn of events of the past few hours. In the background, he heard Duncan relaying the story, word for word, to Peter and Amy, before finally handing the phone over to Peter.

"It's an omen, Max. A good omen. Just don't forget that Emanuel must get that bill of sale signed so that I can deposit it with the bank the moment you folk get back."

"Noted," Max replied dramatically. "Expect my next communication on Sunday at approximately 1030 hours which is when our guest will be departing. Don't do anything back there that we wouldn't. Over and out, Sting."

Max chuckled to himself, hit the red and put the phone in his pocket.

* * *

They took supper in a kitchen warmed by the Aga and filled to bursting with the excitement of co-conspirators. Exhausting every possible angle of the plan and filled with renewed confidence, the Silver Sting retired for the night. Franz led Emanuel and Dinah to the master suite. "It is only right and proper that these are your quarters for all your stay. Margarita and I will be happy in one of the other rooms," Franz said, closing the door behind him.

Thirty-Eight

Gerald stood back and admired his work. The six paintings that he had shipped over looked as though they had been hanging there from time immemorial. He had made inspired choices. The painters, mostly German and French, were little known, but with time he was sure that they would join the ranks of the great. Most of them, so the story would be told, had been acquired from galleries in Paris, Rheims, Strasbourg and Berlin to replace paintings that Emanuel had already had to part with to fund the restoration. Emanuel, Gerald had ensured, was word-perfect about the galleries from which he had bought them. They were the last six entries in the *Owner's Inventory of Paintings*, which recorded acquisitions and sales dating back to 1860 and now sat gathering a suitable layer of dust on the oak sideboard in the grand salon. The Lowry, according to the inventory, was one of the last acquisitions that had been made by Herr Levi in 1936 when Emanuel was no more than four years old.

Gerald strolled back to the hall to peek one more time at the Lowry. "There you are, old son," he said "hiding in the corner as usual." Measuring thirty by forty inches, The Industrial Heartland was a poignant reminder of times past and a masterpiece. Emanuel would claim to know little about the history of the Lowry, or how his father had come by it, other than from the details recorded on the bill of sale which stated that the picture had been bought from a gallery in Salford, Manchester for the sum of two thousand pounds on 1 October 1936. He was, after all, only four years of age when his father had acquired it.

* * *

The kitchen was a hive of activity. Hetty was already a past master at managing the Aga and was threatening to have one installed in the cottage when their ship came in.

"Anybody would think he was bloody royalty," Hetty muttered, pushing her hair back from her face. "I bet the Queen doesn't eat as well as this."

Max looked up from his checklist. "If I had my way he'd be heading straight for the Tower – not being pampered like this. What I wouldn't give for five minutes in the same room with that man. I tell you, Hetty, he'd be lucky if he came out alive."

"Just remember, Max, that this next twenty-four hours is worth three million pounds to us, and then you can do what you like with him, but I think that Gabby and Greg have got their own plans on that score," Hetty replied.

* * *

Persuading Gabby that he had to go to Scotland for a golf match had, surprisingly enough, been a walk in the park. The flight left Heathrow on time. He had been up since three and on the road by a quarter to four. A little weary, Charles sank down into his seat, buckled his seat belt and accepted the glass of champagne offered to him. It was a little early in the day for champagne, but it was no more than he deserved. Everything was coming up roses, as they say. He was on his way to buy his lifetime dream. Annabel's bang on the head had soon healed and been forgotten, and Gabby seemed unconcerned that he was taking off for a night without her. To cap it all he had struck gold the previous day. It was finally over – the letter that he had been waiting for had arrived. The taxman had conceded defeat and he had it in writing. It was almost three long years since that first letter had arrived, and now he could sleep tight in his bed, and life could soon get back to normal. In a few days' time, he would be back where he belonged. Life could be a bitch at times, but right at the moment, it was all going his way.

Shielding his eyes as the plane broke through the clouds into brilliant sunshine, Charles allowed himself a few minutes to reflect. It had all happened in such a short space of time, but that was not a bad thing. Often the longer you had to think about something the less likely you were to do it. Life was a matter of chance, and the winners were those who grabbed the opportunities. That had always been his way and, touch wood, his instinct had never let him down, even if now and again he had had to make a few unplanned strategic withdrawals.

* * *

He had liked Emanuel from the first, but he would not underestimate him. Underneath that veneer of elderly indecisiveness, he sensed that he was a man of great determination.

324

He was still in two minds as to whether or not he would chance negotiating on price again. It went against the grain not to do so, but maybe on this one occasion he would very reluctantly bend his own rules.

The money was in the bank. He had personally visited the City to set it all up, at no small expense to himself, but there was always a price to be paid if you wanted to stay below the radar. Fortunately, he had contacts going back years who owed him a few favours. And it was at the bank that the Lowry would reside until such time as he decided it was safe to display it in the place of his choice.

There had been the small matter of shipping the painting back to England without attracting duties and inviting unwanted attention; the latter being the most critical. The last thing he needed was anybody snooping into his private business or his background. Once more one of his mates from his distant past had come up trumps. Smuggling goods into England was his stock in trade. One call to his contact and the wheels would start turning.

After sinking the second glass of champagne, Charles dozed and woke three hours later to the announcement that the plane was starting its descent into Linz. The temperature was four degrees, the high for the day eight degrees and neither rain nor snow were forecast.

* * *

Franz stood outside the arrivals door wielding a handwritten sign that read 'Herr Fairbrother'. Charles grinned as he spotted the late-middle-aged man dressed in a bright orange duck down jacket over a yellow polo neck sweater, sporting a blue pom-pom hat on his head.

"Willkommen, Herr Fairbrother. Guten Tag. My name is Franz and I am your driver. Sorry, my English is not so good," Franz said with a broad grin on his face. He was already enjoying the adventure enormously. "I can take the bag. You follow. Thank you."

Franz led Charles to an old BMW 5 series parked at the far end of the short-stay car park and opened the door for him. "Forty minutes to the house."

Charles sat back in the worn soft leather seat and buried his head in *The Times*. Franz weaved his way in and out of traffic, his hand never far from the horn while his right foot knew of only two positions on the accelerator – full on or off. Charles glanced briefly at the interior of the car. He hadn't expected a limousine, but it did cross his mind that a clean car was not an unreasonable expectation, but so long as it got him there he didn't care.

"We are near now," Franz shouted in his ear, eased off the accelerator and drove slowly under a huge stone arch. "This is home." Franz glanced sideways at his passenger.

Charles did a double take – this was not the humble house that Emanuel had led him to believe. "Impressive. You sure we're at the right place? You haven't picked up the wrong party from the airport? I'm here to see Emanuel Levi," Charles said uncertainly.

"It is the house, Herr Fairbrother. It is the home of the baron," Franz replied proudly. "My boss, as you English say."

"Did you say 'baron'?" Charles whispered quietly. Surely he had misheard the driver, or there was a very great deal that Emanuel had not told him.

"Ja. The Baron – Freiherr Levi – is a poor baron." Franz

laughed. "He spend all his money on the house so the car is not so good."

Charles gazed wide-eyed at the gardens as Franz drove at the prerequisite 5mph up the drive. Staring at the house beyond, Charles sat bolt upright, folded his paper neatly and straightened his jacket. Never before had he been a guest of a baron. Even from a distance, he could see that the front of the house had been restored, and that there was scaffolding to the rear of the house, presumably waiting for a shedload of money to materialise. Three million pounds and the rest, he thought to himself. It was unlikely that Emanuel would be in the negotiating game.

Franz leapt out of the car and ran around to open the passenger door at the exact same moment that the huge front door opened and Emanuel, dressed in a tweed jacket and corduroy trousers, stepped out hand outstretched to receive his guest.

"Charles, I hope you had a good flight and that Franz behaved himself. Welcome to my humble abode. I am so sorry about that other little matter. The buyer was really piling on the pressure, but I really didn't want to sell it to him," Emanuel said earnestly.

"Well, hello again, Emanuel. You didn't tell me that you have a title and I wouldn't call this house a humble abode. Should I address you as 'Baron'? I'm really not familiar with the correct way to address an aristocrat. I can see why your father wanted the house preserved for future generations, and if you don't mind me saying so you've done a not half bad job so far."

"Thank you, Charles, and remember, I am just Emanuel to you. Nobody uses their titles anymore," Emanuel replied graciously. "Yes, the house is beautiful, or it will be when it is finished. It has cost me a great many of my family's proudest possessions, but I do not resent one single brick. My wife, Dinah, has tea waiting for us in the small salon. And then perhaps you would like to freshen up. Do come in, my dear Charles."

Charles followed Emanuel into the hall. After the bright light of the spring day, his eyes took a while to adjust to the darkness. Emanuel lingered in the hall just long enough for Charles to notice the paintings and to catch his first sight of the Lowry.

Emanuel smiled secretly as Charles moved silently towards it and looked up reverently. He could see the longing in the man's eyes.

It was everything that Emanuel had promised. "Breath-taking and quite magnificent. I can't find the words to describe how I feel right at this moment," Charles said, unable to drag his eyes away from the painting.

"You may spend as much time as you like with it later, Charles, but right now tea awaits," Emanuel said earnestly. "This way please."

Emanuel led Charles into the small salon that ran the length of the front west wing of the house. "Allow me to introduce my wife. Charles, this is Dinah. Dinah, this is Charles Fairbrother."

"It is all my pleasure, madam. I feel quite humbled to be your guest," Charles said.

Dinah chatted animatedly about the house. The interior furnishings, she said, were her domain with a little help from her sister-in-law, Jennifer, whom she described laughingly as a little eccentric. Charles would have preferred to get right down to business and discuss the Lowry, but clearly that was not the way business was done at Viertel – the niceties had to be observed, and when in Rome, do as the Romans do, he reminded himself.

Charles listened as intently as he could while unable to prevent his eyes straying to the sideboards and the sea of photographs in their shiny silver frames neatly displayed upon them. Some were brown with age, while others, more recent, were recognisably Emanuel and Dinah's own sons and grandchildren. It did not escape Emanuel and silently he thanked Max for his eye for detail. Photographs of the family would not have been something that would have crossed his mind, but without them, the house would have seemed impersonal and a lot less credible. Emanuel picked up on Charles's curiosity and, feeling very much within his own comfort zone, spent the next half an hour talking about their sons and the grandchildren.

Dinah looked at her watch. "Emanuel, we are talking far too much. Charles will want to freshen up after such a long flight." Turning to Charles she said, "I hope we haven't bored you too much. Franz will have taken your suitcase to your room and I will show you the way. I do hope you will be comfortable with us. We will meet in the grand salon for drinks at six if that suits you. Our good friend, Gerald, is staying and will be joining us for drinks and dinner, and also my sister-in-law, Jennifer."

"Perfect," Charles replied, wondering briefly how he was expected to spend an hour and a half freshening up. It would take no more than ten minutes to get changed and ready for dinner. And Gerald – presumably that was the name of the man whom he had seen with Emanuel at the Lowry.

329

* * *

Charles changed into his suit and lounged on the sofa in the ornate, but distinctly masculine bedroom where his every need had been anticipated. The paintings that adorned the walls were largely of horses: portraits, hunting scenes and the racetrack. None of the painters were known to him and the subject was not one that he enjoyed. Fleetingly the racehorse Breeze flashed through his mind, but she had been a means to an end, and later a useful distraction for Annabel. He was sorely tempted to take himself off down to the hall and spend time with the Lowry but the implication had been that he should pass this time relaxing and preparing for the evening's festivities. There were times when he could well do without etiquette if that was what it was.

Charles lay back on the sofa and listened to the tick-tock of the grandmother clock. He pictured the Lowry hanging on the wall opposite the fireplace at The Poplars, where one day it would reside. It was worth waiting for, and worth every penny he was going to have to pay for it.

* * *

"You must be Charles. Oh hello, Charles," a high-pitched voice called from below. "I was just coming up to get you. Do come down and you can escort me in for drinks. It's such a treat to have an extra man in the house. I'd better make the best of it. I think Emanuel, Dinah and Gerald may have beaten us to it."

Jennifer lived up to expectations. She was an apparition dressed in a floor-length, low-cut, flowing gown of purple and silver with a feather boa draped around her neck. Her hair was piled high on her head and fixed in place with diamante combs. She stood at the foot of the stairs, her arms flung wide and for all the world looked as though she was ready to catch him if he fell. Charles hesitated and forced a smile – there was no other way down the staircase. "You must be Jennifer," he said brightly. "Your brother and his wife mentioned that we would meet at dinner. May I say how wonderful you look?"

Charles held his smile and kissed the back of her hand, making a mental note to lock his door later on – a drama queen if ever he had seen one, and one that could easily eat him for breakfast if he wasn't careful.

"And such a gentleman as well. My, we are going to have fun tonight," she gushed sliding her arm through his. "We so rarely have visitors. When Emanuel told me you were coming I just couldn't wait. We have quite a banquet planned for you and we've raided the wine cellar. You are honoured – Emanuel rarely opens it up. I'll show you the way, and how about I pick you up in the morning right after breakfast and give you a full guided tour? The bedrooms are quite divine and my bedroom, dear Charles, is to die for," she teased unmercifully.

Jennifer tottered alongside him on high-heeled shoes that click-clacked on the wooden floor, her arm firmly entwined with his. "We're in here tonight for drinks – the grand salon. There's a wonderful log fire. This house is such a warm welcoming place." Jennifer opened the door and winked unseen at her co-conspirators. "After you, dear Charles."

Instantaneously forgetting Jennifer, his attention was caught by the portrait on the wall opposite the fireplace. It was the spitting image of Emanuel and, judging by the clothes worn by the man, it could be none other than Emanuel's father.

"Good evening everybody," Charles said, and nodded towards the portrait. "There's no mistaking who that must be. Your father I presume, Emanuel?"

"Correct," Emanuel replied, "It is of value only to the family I am pleased to say, so I shall not have to part with it. It is as much a part of this house as my wife, my sister, our children and our grandchildren." Emanuel turned his head towards the other walls. "I am afraid that the rest of the paintings in here may disappoint you. The best are long since sold. There are a few that I purchased relatively recently to replace them. I could not leave the walls bare. Gerald helped me choose them and assures me that in many years' time they will be a good investment for future generations. Forgive me, you have not been properly introduced to Gerald – he is a very knowledgeable man. It was he who uncovered the greatest treasure of all."

"I'm pleased to meet you, Charles," Gerald said, eying the other man, while keeping his expression friendly and welcoming. The lying toad, he thought to himself.

Charles sipped his sherry. A whisky on the rocks would have been far more welcome, but it had not been offered. "Would it be indelicate to discuss your greatest treasure?" He did not want to appear too keen, but at the same time, they all knew that if business was to be done it had to be soon.

"Not at all, Charles. You will, no doubt, want to reassure yourself of its provenance. I would be disappointed if you didn't. If the ladies would excuse us?" Emanuel looked first at his wife, and then at Jennifer.

"Of course, Emanuel. Jennifer and I will check that everything is properly prepared in the dining room and we will meet you all in there. Shall I tell the cook to serve in half an hour's time?" Dinah asked.

Emanuel nodded as Dinah and Jennifer left the room and closed the door behind them. Jennifer crossed her fingers and winked at Dinah.

"Did I tell you how the Lowry survived the Nazis, Charles? Forgive me if I did, but it is an important part of its history. When I was a boy, just before I was sent to England, my father told me that one day when I returned I should never take anything at face value. I didn't know it at the time, but that was his way of telling me how to find his precious possessions. They remained hidden for a long while after I returned, until one day I was down in the wine cellar selecting wine for dinner. I was feeling thoroughly indecisive that day so I stood back and just looked at the rows of bottles sitting in the rack trying to make a decision. Quite out of the blue I heard his voice repeating those same words. Then I had the strangest sensation that part of the wine cellar was not as I remembered it as a child – not that he took me down there often. I remembered it as being deeper than it was. To cut a long story short, I brought in labour to remove the bricks behind the wine rack one by one and, lo and behold, behind the wall was a storage area no bigger than eight-foot square. And within it, I found many beautiful paintings including the Lowry, all carefully wrapped to safeguard them from damage and damp. The Nazis cleared the wine from the rack but never did discover the hidden storage area. I will happily take you down to the cellar, Charles, and show you just where they were stored. It is quite fascinating," Emanuel said, taking a gamble.

"Not necessary, Emanuel. You hear these stories. It's just good to know that not everything was destroyed during the war," Charles replied, impressed by what he had been told.

"And this is the family's *Owner's Inventory of Paintings*. Unfortunately, you will see that there are more crossings out, particularly of late, than there are entries. The Lowry, as you can see, was bought on the first of October 1936," Emanuel said, moving the book towards Charles. Gerald stood back – this would be Amy's finest hour. He knew for certain that every listing in it was of a genuine painting with the correct painter's name assigned to it and authentic dates. He had been through it time and time again. If the *Owner's Inventory of Paintings* passed the test then they were well on their way.

Charles took his glasses out of his pocket and turned the pages one by one studying the entries. "Lot of history here, Emanuel." If the truth were known he had never before set eyes on such a record, but he was determined not to let it show. He had to trust his own instincts. Charles looked first at Emanuel and then at Gerald; neither revealed the slightest concern at the time he was taking to study each of the entries. His gut feeling told him that it was genuine.

"And the bill of sale?" Charles asked.

"In the safe. I will get it for you." Emanuel walked towards a small oil of a child in repose and removed it from the wall, revealing a small safe. "I believe this is it."

Gerald immediately offered a pair of white cotton gloves to Charles. "It is very delicate, as you would expect."

Charles put the gloves on and carefully withdrew the fragile, browned bill of sale from the envelope, the ink faded with the years.

"My father hid this and others with the paintings," Emanuel said.

Charles nodded, replaced the piece of paper in the envelope

and handed it back to Emanuel. "I can't argue with that," he said.

"We should look at the painting next, but before that maybe I could just show you a few pages from one of my family photo albums." Emanuel took down an album from the bookshelf and opened it. "This, Charles, is a photograph of the Lowry taken back in 1936 in this very house. My father was so proud of it that he commissioned a photographer to take a picture of him standing beside the picture in the very same place that it now hangs."

There was no doubt that it was taken in the hall and there was no mistaking the likeness between the man standing beside it and the portrait in the grand salon. Charles raised his eyebrows – this was indeed an unexpected piece of provenance.

"Gerald, could I please ask you to take the Lowry down and explain the markings to our guest," Emanuel asked, and turned back to Charles. "I should probably apologise for my impudence. I very much doubt that a collector like yourself needs anything explained to him."

"By all means," Gerald replied, leading the party out into the hall. Charles watched, his heart in his mouth, as Gerald climbed up on the stepladder and lifted the picture clear of its fixings and handed it down to Emanuel.

It was now Gerald's turn for the finest act of his life. Leaving nothing out, Gerald described the frame construction, the type of wood, the canvas, the colouring, the markings and all of the characteristics of the painting that together proved, without a shadow of a doubt that this was indeed the real thing.

Emanuel looked at the painting. "I wonder what my father

would really say if he knew that I was letting it go?" he whispered softly. "Maybe..."

"I'll not insult you with negotiating on price. It's three, isn't it?" Charles said brusquely. He could sense that Emanuel was wavering.

"Well, yes, that is what we said," Emanuel replied uncertainly. "But now the moment has come, I am not so sure..."

"Let's shake hands on it." Charles held out his hand to Emanuel. "If you give me your bank details and excuse me briefly before dinner I can make a phone call, and the money will be in your account within two hours. The painting will be collected first thing tomorrow from which you may gather that I have planned in advance for this moment."

Emanuel scribbled down the details and handed the piece of paper to Charles.

* * *

Henry stood tall and straight as a board waiting to pour the wine that would accompany each course. He was under strict instructions to say nothing. He was to bow, pour a taster into Emanuel's glass and on instruction pour the wine for the guests, and never to allow their special guest's glass to be empty.

Charles drained every drop of wine poured for him and left nothing on his plate, insisting that the highest compliments should be paid to the cook.

Margarita nodded and curtsied. "Danke, Herr Fairbrother."

Imperceptibly, Jennifer moved her chair inch by inch closer to Charles until their knees were touching. "Maybe you might like that tour of the house this evening, dear Charles? I have some excellent dessert wine in my room."

Charles took one look at Jennifer and decided that the sooner he extricated himself from her clutches the happier he would be. Besides he had achieved everything that he had come for.

"If you will excuse me, ladies and gentlemen. I had a very early start this morning and it is time for me to retire. You have been most gracious hosts and I am just sorry that I will have to leave early in the morning to catch my flight." Charles turned to Emanuel. "It has been a pleasure doing business with you, sir. Goodnight."

"Goodnight, Charles. Breakfast will be brought to your room in the morning, and Franz will be waiting for you outside at ten-thirty." Emanuel pushed his chair out, stood up and held out his hand.

* * *

Reluctantly they had all agreed with Max's suggestion that there would be no discussion and no celebrating until such time as Charles was safely back on the plane and the money was tucked away in the bank.

Bursting with excitement The Silver Sting retired for the night and slept the sleep of the dead.

Thirty-Nine

"Gabby?"

"Greg? It's so good to hear your voice. It seems like an eternity. Did Max manage to get in touch with you? I just couldn't believe it when he told me about Emanuel and the house and Franz and Margarita. And Peter tells me that the money went into the bank and is now somewhere safe and sound, no questions asked, as I understand it. What an amazing bunch of people; I'm so proud of them all," Gabby said without catching her breath.

"Yes, Max got in touch this morning and I gather that they are on their way back. I have to say that I thought your plan was doomed to failure, but it worked. And you were right not to underestimate them. They were just brilliant by the sound of it. It's time to start closing the whole thing down, and it's good to hear you sounding so cheerful. Boy, have I missed you. What time is he due back?" Greg asked on a more serious note.

"I'm fine – hanging on in. He's due back at about six this evening – in two hours' time."

"Right, there's something you need to do for me before that. I need you to book a table for the two of you for lunch tomorrow at a restaurant that you use regularly and then let me know which one you have booked. Can you do that? I'll be joining you at some point. Can you also make sure that he sits with his back to the door? I don't want him bolting as soon as he sets eyes on me."

Gabby took a deep breath. "Is this showdown time? I'm not sure that I'm looking forward to it. He owes me for being away for the weekend so the lunch shouldn't be a problem. What if I can't get him there?"

"You can. Think positively. It's critical Gabby. And Gabby, when I come to the table do not acknowledge me or show any sign of recognition. I need you to sit there while Harry and I are talking, acting like you haven't got a clue who I am or what I am doing there. You're Charles's wife – act naturally. If it goes to plan – which it will – you and I will be walking out of there together, and he will be walking out in the opposite direction. Trust me, Gabby, this is the final scene. I know what I am doing. I've been doing a bit of sleuthing myself in the last couple of weeks and I've got enough on him to make him run a mile."

"Share it with me?" Gabby asked.

"No, not this time," Greg replied firmly. He wanted to tell her everything, but it would be easier for her to act out her part for one more day if she did not know the whole of it.

"Okay," Gabby replied.

"Give yourself something to look forward to, Gabby. To-morrow afternoon we'll be up at Magnolia waiting to welcome them all back and join in the celebrations. It's been a long haul, hasn't it?" Greg added.

"I'll remember that, Greg, and thanks. Now I have jobs to do. I'll text you with the restaurant details. Bye."

Charles had jumped at the idea of lunch.

* * *

The table was perfect. Gabby made a beeline for the seat by the wall. Charles sat with his back to the restaurant. That morning he had been sweetness and light and treated her like royalty. Fleetingly she had remembered the old Charles and the idyllic picnics by the river, the walks in the countryside and the intimate moments in front of the log fire. It was difficult to believe that it had all been a sham.

"There's something we need to discuss Gabby." Charles waved the waiter away and poured wine into their glasses.

"I do hope it's not going to spoil our lunch." Gabby's heart sank. The look on his face told her that whatever he was about to say it was serious. God, she thought, has he found out about Magnolia? Has he found out about Greg? Has he found out about the Lowry?

"You know, Gabby, you're a great girl and the last eighteen months have been the best time of my life. Meeting you was the best thing that could have happened to me. You caught me on the rebound, of course, but I don't regret one single moment of it." Charles rested his hand on hers and fiddled with her wedding ring.

"That's sweet, Charles. I am so pleased that I have made you happy, but why the serious face?" Gabby said.

"The thing is, Gabby, Annabel and I are soul mates, always have been. There's no easy way to put this. We've both decided that breaking up was the wrong move for us. We want to give it another go. I'm really sorry."

He had just confirmed all their suspicions, but to hear it put in words still shocked Gabby. "I don't know what to say, Charles. I'm speechless."

Charles picked up the menu and studied it. "Shall we choose?"

Gabby looked up and saw Greg striding in their direction. How could he have known that she needed him in that instant more than ever before?

"Long time, no see, Harry," he whispered as he pulled out the chair next to Charles.

"Who the fuck are you? Sod off." Charles looked up.

"You know precisely who I am? How long is it? Thirteen years. You haven't changed much Harry. Same old back street language."

"If you don't fuck off right now I'll have you physically removed from this restaurant. Maybe I'll do it myself."

"I'm not going anywhere Harry. We've got some business to sort out. I suggest you curb your language before it's you who gets thrown out." Greg said. Fortunately neither the table to the right or left of them was occupied but heads were beginning to turn elsewhere in the restaurant.

"My name is not Harry. It is Charles Fairbrother. Read my lips. Now get out."

"No can do, Harry. Sorry, and I must apologise to the lady for my rudeness in interrupting her lunch." Greg glanced at Gabby apologetically.

"What's going on Charles?" Gabby asked.

"He's leaving, Gabby." Charles glared stonily at Greg. "He's a crank."

"I wonder if Annabel would call me a crank if she knew the half of it." Greg threw the first punch.

"What's Annabel got to do with this? Who is this man, Charles?" Gabby kept a poker straight face.

"You miserable bastard. You leave Annabel out of this or

you'll live to regret it."

"That, Harry is up to you. You'll have to hear me out if you don't want me to talk to Annabel."

"Make yourself scarce, Gabby. We'll finish our conversation at home later." Charles pointed to Gabby's jacket on the back of her chair. "It's all a misunderstanding but I need to put this man right on a few points – in private."

"I am still your wife at the moment, Charles, so whatever he has to say he can say in front of me as well," Gabby snapped back angrily, "And especially after what you've just said to me."

"I've warned you once already. No one gets a second warning." Charles glared at Greg. "You remember what I told you last time? Nobody crosses me and lives to tell the story." The table shook as his fist slammed down on it.

Gabby interrupted. "So you do know this man?"

"A long time ago, in another life. He was a loser then and he's a loser now."

"Who's Harry?" Gabby looked from Charles to Greg. "It's a simple question."

"Perhaps I could answer that question for you, Harry?" Greg said.

"You've done enough talking. This stops now. We're leaving." Charles threw his napkin on the table and signalled to the waiter. "The bill."

Greg shook his head. "It wasn't an idle threat when I said I'd talk to Annabel. Is that what you want? Sit down, Harry and don't make a scene. You'll hear me out if you know what's good for you." Greg drew breath and looked at Gabby. "I know for a fact that the man you believe to be your husband has been living under a false identity for eleven years or more.

His name is Harry Trumper. It's my guess that this would be news to his so-called ex-wife, Annabel as well. No doubt she too thinks that she was married to Charles Fairbrother."

"I changed my name by deed poll. Satisfied?" Charles cut in.

"Won't wash, Harry. I guess I'd better tell this lady the whole story. Harry Trumper was born and bred in Peckham, South East London, a market trader and then a small-time property developer and landlord...the interesting part of the story begins in 2001. You owned a property called Waverley Court, a block of four flats, one of which was rented out to your grandparents. Is that correct so far, Harry?"

Charles ground his teeth and glared at Greg. "So what if I did?"

"That block of flats burnt down in May 2001, and your grandparents burnt to death in the fire...the date is important. Another man was killed in the fire. I think you told the police that his name was Sam Smith." Greg waited. Had he guessed right? Harry did not deny it.

"As I was saying, Harry, Waverley Court burnt down. The coroner concluded that it was an accident. So, Harry, here is the sixty-four-thousand-dollar question and only you can answer it. Think carefully before you do. This man, Sam Smith, whose family the police were never able to trace, was his real name Charles Fairbrother?"

Bulls-eye. It was written all over the man's face.

Greg pursed his lips and raised his eyebrows. "I stole a few things from your office, Harry. One was a letter addressed to a Mr Charles Fairbrother at Waverley Court dated *three* weeks before the fire. You wouldn't have that letter in your possession if you hadn't been in his flat before the fire. It would have gone up in smoke together with all of Charles Fairbrother's other documents. I think Charles Fairbrother was dead before the fire started. I think you set fire to that block of flats. And I think that you invented the name Sam Smith. I think you were responsible for the death of your own grandparents. The real Charles Fairbrother is cremated on the spot, leaving you with a new identity to use, as and when needed. You knew your luck would run out one day." Greg hesitated to let it sink in. "I think the police would be interested to hear about it."

Charles's eyes smouldered. "So you're a fucking thief as well as a bloody architect now, are you?"

"DNA, Harry. It'll take the police five minutes to work out that you are not Charles Fairbrother. He has an aunt who is alive and kicking, but, of course, you know that." Greg said, letting the DNA stroke hit home before playing his ace. "And a witness came forward, Harry – someone saw you going into Sam Smith's flat and leaving minutes before the fire broke out. That's why the police had reopened the case. You kept Charles Fairbrother's identity papers tucked away ready for a rainy day, didn't you? Harry Trumper disappeared off the face of the earth round about the end of 2004 if I am not wrong. You got wind of the fact that the police were asking questions about the fire, so what did you do? You abandoned the development of Magnolia Court and pocketed a great deal of money that did not belong to you," Greg said. "And Charles Fairbrother came back to life a few months later. You simply shed one skin and put on another."

"Your bill, sir. I take it that you won't be taking a meal?" The waiter dropped the bill on the table. "When you are ready."

Gabby sat back barely able to believe what she was hearing.

This was news to her. God, she had been living with a monster. What he had done to her friends at Magnolia was bad enough, but to kill his own grandparents and another man was inconceivable.

"But the real Charles Fairbrother wasn't quite what you thought he was." Greg continued. "He was a clever man. Made millions in his lifetime by the sound of it but had a real dislike for paying taxes. It must have come as quite a shock when you got that first letter in July 2013. How much were they after recovering – was it two million or was it more than that? I have been through all the correspondence. I guess you had no choice but to play for time."

"Later." Charles shouted, waving his arm in the air. The waiter shrugged his shoulders and walked away.

"And just six months later your wife divorces you and you hand all your worldly goods to her. Did you think that in transferring your assets to her that the Inland Revenue wouldn't be able to touch it?

"I'll tell you what I think. I think that you married this lady sitting opposite to make your divorce from Annabel that bit more credible and that you had every intention of going back to your first wife just as soon as the Inland Revenue backed off."

Gabby stared straight ahead at the man sitting opposite her. "He's right, isn't he? The two of you suddenly deciding to give your marriage another go was a lie. It all makes sense now. You've spent more time with her than ever you did with me in the last eighteen months."

It was time to deliver the final blow. "You received a letter from Inland Revenue last Friday, didn't you?" Greg said calmly. "I think you might have had some bad advice anyway. The Inland Revenue would have gone after that money whether it was in your name or your ex-wife's name. The letter was not from the Revenue. I sent it to you to smoke you out once and for all.

"In short, Harry, I think the police will be very interested in talking to you about three murders," Greg continued. "And then there's identity theft, and fraudulent use of another man's identity. And then there is the small matter of getting married, not once, but twice under an assumed name. And last but not least there's the small matter of walking away from Magnolia Court and pocketing all that money."

Charles sat up and squared his shoulders. He was not finished yet. "You can go to the devil. If I was you I would go down to the funeral parlour and book my funeral right now." There were plenty of heavies where Harry came from. There was nothing they wouldn't do for cash.

"My guess is thirty years. In the event that you or anybody lays a finger on me or anybody I know, or do anything that I don't like, the evidence goes straight to the police – I've made sure of that. I did learn a few tricks from you." Greg said calmly.

"Bastard."

"I may be, but it could be worse. I am going to offer you a get out of jail free card. I believe you once wanted to take a long holiday in South America, so now's your chance. There's a flight that leaves at nine tomorrow morning from Heathrow non-stop to Buenos Aires. There are seats available. I've checked. Be on it. I'll be there at the airport watching and if you are not on that flight then look forward to thirty years. Don't come back." Greg turned to Gabby. "Can I give you a lift somewhere?"

Forty

Charles sat at the table and stared unseeing at the bill in front of him. Ten minutes earlier everything had been falling into place. In a few hours' time he had planned to walk back into Annabel's life, a bottle of champagne in hand, waving the letter from the Inland Revenue at her. Suddenly Charles Fairbrother was in trouble, big trouble.

* * *

It was no more than twenty-four hours since he had rung her from the airport with the words: "It's time, Annabel. I'm on my way home for good."

She had hardly been able to believe her ears. "Where are you calling from? I can hear announcements in the background?" she had asked.

"That, Annabel, does not matter. Suffice to say that I had a bit of business that took me abroad for the weekend but I am on my way back now, right now. Did you hear what I said?" he had asked, grinning into his mobile.

"Yes, I think so. Does that mean what I think it means?" she had asked, hardly able to conceal her excitement.

"Just that Annabel," he had replied. "We're in the clear. I

heard on Friday. I didn't call you right away because I still had a few loose ends to tie up," he had said, adrenalin pumping through his body at the thought of the coup he had just pulled off in Austria.

"Does Gabby know you're leaving her?" she had asked breathlessly.

"She will on Monday, and I very much doubt that once I've told her she'll want me hanging around for long. I'll give notice on the rental contract for the cottage on Monday. If I know Gabby at all she'll be straight down to the solicitor's office filing for divorce, but if she isn't then it makes no difference to us, does it?" he had replied, hoping that Annabel would agree with his summary of the situation.

"Not one iota. Who cares about a piece of paper anyway?" she had replied.

"Expect me, complete with my suitcases, between two and three tomorrow. The flight is being called now so I have to go. Bye for now."

* * *

Annabel sang to herself in the mirror. Her hair shone and, if she was not imagining it, her eyes were whiter and brighter than they had been for years.

Throughout the morning she had ignored the continuous alerts from her PC. It was nothing out of the ordinary – emails from Selfridges, from Harrods, from holiday companies, from Amazon, from Sky, from Bose, from restaurants and hotels that they had regularly frequented, and those that went straight into the spam box.

There was one email, however, that she did not want to

miss when it came in. It would be from Voyages Jules Verne to confirm that they had been able to accommodate her flight upgrade request for their holiday to Mauritius and the Seychelles; the deposit had to be paid immediately.

A cup of coffee first, and then an hour to deal with emails. It would help pass the time while she waited for Charles. Annabel stroked her latest acquisition, the Delonghi Magnifica bean to cup coffee machine, and dropped the coffee beans into the grinder. Simple, she laughed to herself and pressed the start button. It had only arrived two days before, but she knew that Charles would love it, especially when he discovered that it could be programmed to remember exactly how each of them liked their coffee prepared.

Coffee in hand, Annabel pulled up a chair, sat down at her desk and opened her laptop.

Perfect, Jules Verne never let her down. She would pay the bill and tell Charles about it when he arrived. It would be their second honeymoon.

Annabel glanced down through her emails – rubbish, delete, rubbish, delete, rubbish, delete, rubbish, delete until her eye caught one that seemed to be addressed to her personally. The subject heading read "ANNABEL YOU NEED TO READ THIS." It had come in at 1.45pm – a matter of minutes ago. The address was golsen10@ITFDevelopments.com. She did not recognise it, but there were no attachments, indicating that it was not intended to deliver a virus into her computer. Curious to know what it was about and, who had sent it she clicked it open.

Annabel scanned the first few lines of the letter:

Dear Annabel,

You do not know me, but I used to be employed by your ex-husband long before he met you. I ask you very sincerely to read on. This email contains information that affects you and Ethan and Abby.

Startled, Annabel sat back in her chair and stared at the screen. Whoever this was, he, or she, knew her name, her email address and the names of both her children. It was scary. She read on.

It was a shame about the divorce from 'Charles' but I understand that you had good reasons for doing so. Divorce normally follows infidelity by one party or the other but there are those that happen simply as a result of financial problems...

Annabel reached to grab her phone and swore as she upended the mug and watched the dark liquid spread across the desk and run down on to the Chinese rug. Ignoring the trail of coffee, she reread the last two sentences. Was she reading too much into it? Was it her conscience that was reading between the lines? Was it blackmail? How could this person possibly know what went on behind closed doors? It was a magnet. She read on, oblivious to the stain on the rug.

I hope that you are sitting down, Annabel, because my next sentence will come as a shock to you. Your ex-husband's name is not Charles Fairbrother. It is Harry Trumper.

Nonsense, she thought – stuff and nonsense. This phantom

writer was out of his, or her, tiny mind. Someone was playing a sick joke on her. She'd never heard of Harry Trumper. Charles was Charles and always had been. She read on.

I believe that he changed his name from Harry Trumper to Charles Fairbrother in January 2005 although it might have been a little before that. It is not, of course, illegal to change one's name provided that all of the appropriate authorities are informed of one's wish to do so and that it is done legally. It is illegal, however, to assume the name of another without informing the authorities. This is called identity theft and it is fraudulent.

Annabel thought back to her first meeting with Charles. It had been in June 2005 at Epsom races.

The real Charles Fairbrother was burnt to death in a fire that occurred in May 2001 at a property owned by Harry Trumper. At the same time, Trumper's grandparents perished in the fire. Although the evidence at the time pointed to the fire being started accidentally, several years later new evidence came to light, and the police decided to reopen the case. It is my belief (and I think that of the police) that the fire was started deliberately by Harry Trumper, which makes him a murderer. Harry assumed the identity of Charles Fairbrother when he heard that the police were planning to reopen the case. I realise that all this may sound far-fetched, but believe me, I have evidence to back up the story, evidence that I discovered in your ex-husband's office in Slough.

Life has some unfortunate twists and Harry (Charles,

as you know him) failed to do his homework as well as he should have done. The real Charles Fairbrother must have been a millionaire many times over to owe so much money to the Inland Revenue. HMRC eventually traced Charles Fairbrother to The Poplars and wanted the money due to them. Does any of this ring a bell?"

Annabel felt her blood run cold. Charles had not told her to whom he had owed a large amount of money. He had simply said, "It was a deal that went wrong". Was it just possible that this person was telling the truth?

I was sorry to hear about the burglary. It must have been very frightening for you. I sincerely hope that you are fully recovered and that you were well insured. It may (or may not) surprise you to know that the stolen goods had a street value of just over £3million. I hope that the insurance company will see their way to recompense you.

How could he possibly know about the burglary? Annabel shivered and unconsciously looked around the room and through the door into the hall. The front door was locked, the windows were locked – she was safe. She was losing it – there was no reason that she should not be safe in her own house. She remembered being surprised when Charles had announced after the burglary that the paintings were not copies or fakes as he had originally told her. He had said that he would deal with the insurance company for her.

Quite apart from the demand for money from the

Revenue, I happen to know that your husband needed to get his hands on a very large sum of money at short notice, and it occurred to me that he might attempt to sell a few of his (or your) possessions in order to raise the money. I had not thought that he would go to such extremes.

Her head was swimming. It was ridiculous, utterly ridiculous, but it made sense of so many things, particularly how calmly he had taken the news that his beloved paintings had been stolen. If there was any truth in what this person was saying he had been completely uncaring about her safety.

Shocking as all this will be to you, I strongly suspect that by now I shall have cast some doubt about your husband's true identity and character in your mind. I believe that seconds before you opened this email you may have been preparing for his return home. I am informed that on Friday last he may have received some good news in the mail – wish it were true. Although I am ashamed to admit it, the letter he received informing him that the Inland Revenue was dropping their case against him for repayment of back tax was from me – a forgery. I knew that this was the only way that he would reveal his true colours and confirm the suspicions that I had had about him all the way along.

Annabel's hand shook and an icy shiver ran from the end of her fingers down to the ends of her toes. There was more.

This is complicated but perhaps I can be of assistance

in outlining your options. The way I see it is that you turn a blind eye to everything that I have told you, stand by Harry (or Charles to you) and take the good times with the bad times. Only you can define what the good times might be. I can help you understand the bad times. The Inland Revenue are intent on their pound of flesh irrespective of your divorce and the assets that he transferred to you as a means of avoiding payment. I have it on good legal authority that you were both mistaken in thinking that a divorce would resolve the matter. So you can kiss goodbye to worldly wealth. If you can find it in your heart to forgive him and are thinking that his debts can be repaid from the insurance company pay-out on your burglary then I regret to inform you that you are mistaken. An anonymous email has been delivered to the Insurance company suggesting that the burglary might not have been what it seemed to be. They will not pay out.

Broke? Destitute? No showcase house, no top of the range cars, no private school for the children, no holidays, no personal trainer, no lunch clubs? The list went on. Everything – she could lose everything. Tears of anger and frustration rolled down her cheeks as she read the last paragraph.

He has not treated either you or your children well, Annabel. Indeed he has done little other than cheat and lie to you since the day you met him. You owe him nothing. For your own safety and that of your children you need to get out. The only way that you will ever do that is to expose him for what, and who, he is. The *debts*

belong to Charles Fairbrother. It pains me to rub salt into the wound but you cannot legally be married to a man who has been dead these past fifteen years – and therefore neither can you be liable for his debts. You will need a good lawyer, and I feel that it would be in your interests to appoint one right now. Expose him now and minimise the risk to yourself and your family. One phone call to 999 is all it will take. Then collect the children from school immediately and take them to your father's house until such time as the police have done their job. If you choose to stand by him then I wish you well and will pray for your safety and that of your children."

Annabel stared at the screen. Just half an hour earlier she was looking forward to getting back to a normal life. Try as she might, she could not deny the truth staring her in the face. Charles had lied to her about who he was, about his debts, about everything. How could he have put her life in danger by staging a burglary? Had he ever loved her? Was he ever intending to tell her the truth about his past? For God's sake, she wasn't even married to him. For God's sake, the children had his name on their birth certificates. Fuck, she had been living with a murderer all these years. Fuck, the children had a murderer for a father.

Annabel picked up the empty coffee cup and threw it with all her strength at the antique mirror above the fireplace where once a Lowry had hung.

The phone was answered after two short rings. "Police, how can I help you?"

Forty-One

Harry slammed the car into reverse and backed out of the parking space scattering gravel high and wide as he spun the wheels, oblivious to the damage he was causing to other vehicles parked nearby.

He found himself driving like a maniac. He had to find the small blue pocketbook that was somewhere at The Poplars. In it were the numbers of associates that he had not contacted for years, but none of them would have forgotten Harry Trumper. A blast on a horn brought him back to reality as he narrowly missed a car entering a roundabout.

In his heart he knew it was a waste of time. For the first time in his life he knew that he was defeated. Finally, he admitted to himself that he simply didn't have the pull that he once had with his associates. Word was out for Harry Trumper; he'd broken the golden rule and killed not one, but two, of his own. The favours that he might once have pulled in were in the dim and distant past. It was game over.

Careless, he'd been too damned careless. First with the fire at Waverley and then with leaving the evidence in his office, and now he was going to have to pay for it – in spades. But there was one thing they had got wrong although nobody would ever believe him. Charles Fairbrother had been dead in the flat when he had found him – a sad suicide victim who would never in this life or the next have need of an identity. And they were wrong that he had been careless in not checking out Charles Fairbrother – he had – meticulously – and there had not been one damned scrap of information about him on the Internet or anywhere else. The little bastard had managed to remain anonymous until after his death.

Hate came nowhere near describing his feelings for Greg Olsen, the slimy little shit who'd threatened to report him all those years ago over Magnolia.

He needed money, and the safe at The Poplars never held less than twenty thousand. It would be a start. And then somehow he would organise for the Lowry to be shipped to South America and then they would never have to worry about money again. He needed Annabel at his side. Together they could make a new life in Buenos Aires. After all they had gone through she surely would not let him down now.

There was too much to do and not enough time to do it in. First stop, The Poplars to get cash out of the safe and pick Annabel up. His passport was at the cottage. Maybe he should make that his first stop? Then there were calls to be made to the bank and to the airline. The most important call of all would see the Lowry redirected to South America.

His mind was everywhere but on the road, as he turned left into The Hawthorns. He did not see the three unmarked police cars draw in behind him and block his exit.

Forty-Two

It was on the TV, in the dailies and the weekend papers – the Harry Trumper trial was big news. A witness had come forward to the police and had testified that he saw Harry Trumper leave the property just seconds before the flames engulfed Waverley Court all those years ago. The same witness further testified that he had seen the same man, in what was now known to be the flat that had been occupied by Charles Fairbrother.

His defence had argued that Harry Trumper had found the man, Charles Fairbrother, already dead in the flat but had not been able to convince the jury that the fire had been an accident. When combined with a long, long list of Harry's misdemeanors over the years, the jury decided that they did not believe a word he said and found him guilty on the count of all three murders.

Inland Revenue followed the trial carefully and watched glumly as all hopes of ever recovering their back tax faded into the dim and distant past. If the real Charles Fairbrother had disposed of his assets before his death as seemed to be the case, then they had no choice but to drop the pursuit of back taxes. Both Gabby and Greg were pleased for Annabel's sake. It was she who had made the brave decision to report him to the police.

Gabby and Annabel were both called as witnesses and told the story about how each of them had been duped into marrying the man known as Charles Fairbrother; neither of them had any idea of his real identity or past deeds. Annabel admitted that in a moment of serious misjudgment, she had agreed to stage the divorce and was complicit in him meeting and marrying Gabby. Receiving a serious reprimand for her part in the series of events, the judge decided that she had suffered enough and gave her a short suspended sentence. The judge also ruled that neither Annabel nor Gabby had ever been legally married to the man they knew as Charles Fairbrother.

Greg had been called to testify since it was he who had found the damning evidence in Harry's office. Reprimanded for breaking and entering into the office, the judge praised Greg for his foresight.

When giving evidence neither Gabby nor Greg made one single mention of their association with Magnolia or of the Lowry that Harry had recently purchased. It pleased them to think that when Harry was eventually released he would find that he had a worthless painting; it was poetic justice.

It suited Harry equally well to leave the story of the Lowry untold. It would be his pension if ever they let him see the light of day again.

Annabel knew nothing of the Lowry other than that Charles had staged a burglary in which she had been hurt in order to raise cash for some unknown reason and knowing what she did, had dropped the insurance claim.

The police visited Magnolia Court to talk to the residents. The file on the disappearance of Harry Trumper dating back to 2004 was dusty but not closed. It was entirely up to the residents, they said, if they wanted to take action against Harry Trumper now that he had finally been found. Hetty and Dot dosed both police officers with gallons of tea and cakes that they had made especially for the occasion and led them up the nineteenth hole to meet all their friends. Max was the spokesman and informed the two very nice police officers that, having discussed and considered the matter, they all felt that it was past history. They were very happy at Magnolia Court and had no desire for old wounds to be opened up again. The deeds for the property were, however, a different matter. They would sleep so much better in the knowledge that no one could take their homes away from them.

The deeds arrived four weeks later. Magnolia in its entirety was now formally owned by the residents of cottages one to ten in perpetuity.

Forty-Three

Beams of light cascaded from on high through the deep royal blue, crimson red, purple and white stained-glass windows and danced on the cream-coloured, deep-pile rug that ran almost the length and breadth of the great hall. Rich brown oak floors peeped between the edges of the carpet and the walls and finished at the entrance to the mansion. A sweeping oak staircase carpeted in deep purple led the eye from the great hall towards the mezzanine where the residents met and entertained their friends, for lunch or for dinner. The meals were selected from a menu, ordered by Hetty and Dot and delivered by a smart young man in a van and then simply popped into the microwave when required.

Deep sofas alternated with comfortable upright armchairs for those of the residents who needed a little help getting up and down. Cushions in reds, purples, blues, oranges and every combination of the same colours lay on the sofas and armchairs ready to support backs, heads or feet. It was neither regimented nor untidy. It simply looked like home. Packs of cards, boxes of dominoes, draughts, chess and mah-jong lay on the coffee tables together with the daily papers.

A baby grand piano had pride of place alongside the bar. The bar stools had been upholstered in purple velvet. Bottles lined the shelf behind the bar, their colour reflected back into the room by the mirrored wall behind. Cocktails and Henry's music hour started at six each evening.

Needless to say, Jennifer's hand could be seen in all the furniture and fittings. She had had the most glorious time selecting the fabrics from catalogues, and carpets from samples that had been delivered to her door. The walls were adorned with artwork carefully selected by Gerald to complement the panoply of colour – all legal, he had assured his friends.

What had once been the library in the stables was converted into a small bedsitting room with bathroom and kitchenette for the live-in carer, Mary, who was Irish through and through, and recently retired from nursing.

Two low-level bookshelves built of the same oak as the staircase occupied one whole wall of the great hall. Gradually the residents dusted off the precious books that had been stored in their cottages and brought them into the hall for everyone to share and enjoy.

The office – always referred to as 'Duncan's office' – was his pride and joy and occupied yet another corner of the great hall.

A huge corner table supported a state-of-the art computer with screens that would not have looked out of place in a cinema. It was here that he now did most of his work and here that he spent hours teaching his friends the basics of computing. In the evening the screen doubled as a TV. Duncan retained charge of the remote control – he did not trust them that much.

The swimming pool complex was now almost exactly as it had been depicted in the original brochure. The pool was four foot in depth throughout, had easy-rise steps leading into and out of the water and numerous handrails to ensure safety at all times. Heated summer and winter, the pool was used regularly by the residents and, for a small annual sum that paid the heating bills, made available for use by the townsfolk. Bright yellow and blue sunbeds and high backed, easy-rise deck chairs surrounded the pool and provided a warm, comfortable area for the residents to relax after their swim. A local hairdresser came up to Magnolia once a month and performed miracles on the men and women alike in the small hairdressing salon next door to the pool area.

The nineteenth hole was converted into a sewing and games room. At one end there were large tables for the ladies to sit and sew while at the other end a half-sized snooker table took up most of the space for the enjoyment of the men. After much debate the golf course was not built. Fifteen years ago, they decided, it might have been a different matter, but now they were quite content to potter and sit in the newly landscaped gardens. Dot and Dennis insisted that they were quite capable of maintaining the grounds and bought a new petrol mower and pruning shears.

The cottages were refurbished; windows, doors, and guttering replaced, kitchens and bathrooms stripped out and replaced and painted inside and out. They were soon unrecognisable from the sad little dwellings of just a few months before.

Jennifer took it upon herself to set up The Silver Sting Theatre Company with the plan that once a year they would stage a small production and invite the townsfolk to attend. They had such wonderful talent among them all, she explained expansively, that it would be nothing short of criminal to let it go to waste. And when she wasn't busy with The Silver Sting Theatre Company she organised outings for them all to the theatre, to garden centres, to National Trust properties and exhibitions of all kinds. Andy bought an old minibus and within a matter of months had it spick and span and ready to take them all wherever they wanted to go.

The most wonderful thing of all was that it had all only cost two million pounds. Greg had designed and specified everything and the contractors regularly used by ITF Developments had fallen over backwards to do the work once they had heard the story. The remaining one million pounds had been divided among the residents, and with one hundred thousand pounds in each of their bank accounts, they knew they had little to worry about for the rest of their days.

Each of the residents paid a modest annual sum into an account, which was kept solely for the purpose of maintaining the properties and paying for the live-in care service. Peter kept the books and presented them to the residents at each of their monthly meetings.

Magnolia Court had never looked so good or felt so much like home.

Forty-Four

Max and Hetty were more excited than they could ever remember. Gabby and Greg were planning to get married, and most exciting of all, they wanted to be married at Magnolia Court if it could be arranged. Hetty had missed Gabby's first wedding, but this was one that she was not going to miss. Hetty told Gabby in no uncertain terms that she and Max would pay the expenses. It was a day that she had dreamt of since Gabby had been a child, and she would not take no for an answer, however much either of them might want to argue with her.

Max lost no time. Pulling on his coat, he hot-footed down to the great hall, which was where Duncan could be found most days. "Duncan, we have work to do. How do we go about getting a licence to hold wedding ceremonies in the great hall? Gabby and Greg are getting married."

In a matter of seconds, Duncan pulled up the relevant websites and together they read the detail. It was more costly than they had thought, but it also sparked off another idea – if they got the license then there was nothing to stop them offering Magnolia Court as a wedding venue for other brides and grooms; another small, but useful, money-making venture that would help fund the community. Peter

365

called an emergency meeting of the resident's committee to put the proposal to them. There were whoops of delight when Max and Hetty announced that Gabby and Greg were getting married, and even more when they were told that the venue for the wedding would be Magnolia Court. Duncan submitted the application and Peter paid the fee on behalf of the residents.

The date was set for the eighteenth of June 2017. Max would give Gabby away, Jennifer would be her bridesmaid and Greg had chosen Duncan, who had never before been known to shed a tear, to be his best man. The only guests whom they had wanted at the wedding were family and friends from Magnolia, but they were more than happy for Hetty to invite Franz and Margarita, the couple who had lent them their wonderful home in Austria and made such a huge contribution to the success of their project.

With three months in hand, the *Silveries* sprang into action and it was all hands to the pump once more.

As the wedding date approached, Dot, Dennis, and Andy worked like beavers to ensure that the grounds were in tip-top condition and ready for the wedding photographs that would be taken both on the steps of the mansion and in the gardens. Jennifer drew sketch after sketch of how the great hall should be decorated for the occasion. Hetty, Dot, and Dinah poured over cookery books and slaved away over hot stoves preparing the wedding breakfast. Henry consulted with Gabby on the music she would like for the service and moved his new Bose down to the great hall in readiness for the occasion and carefully selected the wines. Amy, having already meticulously scribed the wedding invitations, busied herself with the order of service sheets, the place cards, and the menu cards. Gerald was tasked with commissioning a painting that they had all decided would be a very appropriate wedding present for the happy couple. Duncan studied best man speeches late into the night before he eventually decided to ignore them all and wrote one from the heart. Peter managed the finances and happily drove back and forth to the town for supplies. Max liaised with the registrar and dealt with the licence inspection visits and wrote checklists so that nothing was missed.

* * *

There were boxes of tissues scattered throughout the room and not a dry eye in the house as Gabby and Max entered the great hall. Walking slowly up the rose-bordered aisle that Jennifer had created, Gabby looked radiant. Her copper-coloured hair had been tamed into a soft French bun pinned with tiny sprigs of ivy. Small wisps of hair cascaded in front of her ears softening the style and partly hiding the pearl earrings that matched the string that she wore around her neck. She had chosen a sage-green chiffon for her dress, which draped elegantly from both shoulders and finished just below her knee. In her hand, she carried a posy of cream roses from which cascaded strings of more ivy. She looked adorable. Jennifer walked demurely behind her. In contrast, her outfit was eccentric and colourful in the extreme, but not out of place. Looking entirely the proud father, Max had chosen to wear a grey morning suit and top hat. It was a first and probably the last opportunity and one not to be missed.

Greg, tall and handsome in grey morning suit, waited patiently with the registrar and Duncan, his best man, whose wheelchair, much to his initial embarrassment, had been dressed with the same roses that lined the aisle.

Gabby looked at Greg, her eyes filled with love, and made her vows, all memories of her first marriage and her sham marriage to Charles forgotten in the moment. Greg's lips moved as he made his vows to her, but so lost in her own joy was she that she did not hear them. It was the applause of the wedding guests and Greg's lips on her own that awoke her to the realisation that they were now husband and wife.

The wedding breakfast was delicious, the speeches short and poignant and the portrait of the residents posed against the now restored mansion was a wedding present that they would treasure for the rest of their lives.

Franz had asked if might be permitted to say a few words. "You may remember the story that Emanuel told to your special guest of a secret room in the cellar where his father hid valuables to protect them from the Nazis. Later he confided to me that it was in his imagination only. He was wrong. Incredibly, there was a room just as he had described it and in it we found many paintings. Emanuel and I have spoken about it. His wish is that a few of them are returned here to hang in your great hall and the rest are to be sold to finance the completion of Viertel. Margarita and I are deeply indebted to every one of the Silver Sting and especially to our dear friends Dinah and Emanuel. Without you, it would have taken us many years to finish the restoration of our home. You are all welcome to come and share our home at any time."

Hetty stood up and took Gabby's hand. "May I borrow your wife for a few moments, Greg?" she asked, turning to Gabby. "There is just one final surprise for you today, my dear. I believe it might just have arrived. Max and I have been very busy in the past year and with a lot of help from Duncan, we managed to find what we were looking for. Do you remember when you came to see me when I was ill that I told you that you had a half-sister?"

Gabby nodded. "Yes, I do remember – the baby that my mother had adopted?"

"The same one Gabby," Hetty replied with a tear in her eye. "And I told you that no one other than your mother knew of her whereabouts?"

Gabby nodded.

"Well, my dear, we found her for you." Hetty looked towards the door and smiled, "I believe she has just arrived."

A tall redheaded woman, beaming with joy, walked towards her. "I'm Nancy, Gabby. Your sister."

About the Author

Angela Dandy, author of thrillers, *The Silver Sting*, *The Silver Dollar* and *The Gypsy Killer* also writes plays, one of which has been performed on stage in her home town of Stratford-upon-Avon.

From a corporate career to carer, from carer to being cared for - a survivor of breast cancer, Angela reinvented herself as an author and playwright in 2015. She has made it her mission through her writing to be the voice for those whose abilities are often underestimated or are excluded from society for reasons outside of their control.

Living in a warm and caring community, she is an active member of a writing group, a playwrights' group and a drama group. In her spare time, Angela enjoys theatre, spending time with her family, travelling, gardening and entertaining.

You can connect with me on:
- https://www.angeladandy.com
- https://www.facebook.com/angeladandyauthor

Lightning Source UK Ltd.
Milton Keynes UK
UKHW041958130922
408822UK00002B/379